NINE HOURS TO RAMA

NINE HOURS
TO RAMA

STANLEY WOLPERT

Random House   New York

To
the memory of
Nathan and Frances Wolpert
gentlest of souls

Natu, Apte and Gandhi are the actual names of the people involved, but all the other characters are fictional and are not intended to represent real individuals, either living or dead.

1

Natu woke with a chill. Instinctively his hand reached out for the cover he had kicked aside. His searching fingers touched the dank concrete of the floor beside him. Then came the piercing wail of a train from the tracks outside, and he remembered. He sat up swiftly, folded back the mattress pad, and probed blindly with both hands over the freshly exposed patch of concrete. Though he shivered, for an instant sweat covered his body. Then his hand locked over the gun, and he was calm.

The piercing wail had become a slow chugging throb. Now the clanging of the platform pipe by the station attendant announced that the train had arrived. As though the whole world could not hear and see it for themselves! But what else did those fellows in their fancy uniforms have to do all day except clang their stupid pipes, and wake up anyone who was trying to sleep?

Except Apte, Natu thought, turning in the direction of his friend's low steady wheeze. In the faint charcoal-gray light of the shuttered retiring room Apte looked like a sack of guavas or dirty laundry left toppled over on the pancake mat. He had tucked the cover securely around him in every direction, over his head as well as under his drawn-up feet and protruding rear. Natu picked up one of his chappals and aimed the slipper with perfect precision.

The discarded sack came to life, arms and legs appeared, finally a startled head, cursing. Natu grinned, but in the stupor of his half sleep Apte failed to respond, blinking sullenly as he reoriented himself in time and place.

"Well, you should be happy it was not a policeman who threw it at you," Natu said, by way of consolation.

"Yes, yes, that makes me very happy," Apte replied wearily, rubbing his knuckles into his eyes. He felt as though he had not slept half an hour the entire night. His head felt like stone. He tried to lie down again.

"Why don't you go get us some tea," Natu advised.

"What time is it?" Apte asked. "Can't we sleep another hour or two? Those damn trains kept me up all night."

"Oh, I saw how long you were up! Sure, sure. Get some tea, will you, before I freeze to death in this miserable climate." Natu hated the North, especially in January. It was their climate he felt which made the people here so cold and mean, so different from his own, though of course they were all of one Nation now. One happy Nation!

Apte began to mutter something about people who wanted tea going to get it themselves, but saw that Natu had withdrawn into one of those deep silent moods he could never penetrate, sitting yoga-like, legs crossed on the mat, staring back into himself rather than ahead it seemed, transfixed like an idol of stone. Then he too remembered what day it was, and sleep no longer mattered. Now the weariness left him as thoroughly as it had gripped him a moment before. He stood up, walked to the corner of the room where the clay water jug and the basin were kept, squatted to relieve himself, and rinsed his hands with some water. He rinsed his mouth too before setting the basin out onto the rear porch where the sweeper would come to empty it.

From the porch he could see concrete roofs hanging suspended over the long station platforms on their concrete pillars. Glistening black and silver between the platforms were sinewy rails, one of the tracks obscured by the steam-bathed monster engine which had just

[2]

pulled in. The incomprehensible din of a thousand voices rising and blending together from the platforms below held him there for an instant. Then he leaned over the rail, and was tempted to shout down in a voice like thunder which all of them would hear, and which as it rumbled would hush them to awesome silence—"Today we will liberate you!" Suddenly he saw the sweeper approaching and hurried back into the room, securely bolting the door.

They had not quite finished their tea when the peremptory knocking began. Instinctively Apte looked to Natu, who said nothing, but put down his cup, took the small pistol from under his mattress, and released the safety catch. There was a pause while whoever it was waited silently. Then the knocking began again, accompanied by a high-pitched voice ordering, "Please will you open up this door."

"What is it you want?" asked Natu, motioning to Apte that he should try to see who it was through a crack in one of the window shutters.

"We are the retiring-room manager," the voice replied. "You must open up this door please."

There were in fact two of them standing in the corridor, Apte could see, a slight young man of obvious insignificance who did the knocking and shouting, and several paces behind him a more formidable and rotund person who carried a clipboard with papers on it and wore a dirty pith helmet. Apte recognized the latter as the man who had taken the money for this room two days ago, and nodded to reassure Natu that it was just the retiring-room manager.

"All right," Natu shouted. "Give me a second to put on my shirt, will you!" He replaced the gun carefully, and walked over to unbolt the door. "Well, why do you come here disturbing people so early in the morning, eh?"

"This is the retiring-room manager," the young man said defensively, but the other merely waved his assistant aside, and ignoring Natu's indignant question informed him, "You will have to vacate this room by twelve hundred hours promptly. Be certain please that all of your possessions are removed out of here no later than eleven hundred fifty hours so that the room can be prepared for its next occupant."

"That is impossible," Natu said. "We cannot leave before three."

"No, that is out of the question, Mr. Narayanrao," the railroad official responded. Narayanrao was the pseudonym Natu had used here. His real name was Godse.

[3]

"Nonsense," Natu said. "I will pay you for another day. I was going to come to see you as soon as I finished my breakfast, but since you are in such a rush I will pay you right now."

The official shook his head negatively. "It is against our regulations, my good man. We are only permitted to rent our retiring rooms for forty-eight hours to a party. Your forty-eight hours expire at twelve hundred hours, and there is a long list, you see." He waved his precious clipboard with a flourish as though the mere sight of its grimy pages scribbled on in a half-legible hand would silence further discussion of the matter.

"Never mind," Natu said. "You will have to stretch your regulations a bit. Here is my money." He took a roll of notes from his shirt pocket and started counting off the proper amount.

"My good sir, I am a government official," the retiring-room manager intoned with such an air of solemnity that one might have thought he was the Prime Minister. "I am not empowered to change the regulations, but merely to see that they are carried out. You are obviously a gentleman or I would not waste my precious time arguing with you, but I beg you to appreciate my position, and to cooperate."

Natu winced. Control yourself, he thought, for he knew too well how long they had all planned, and struggled, and waited for this day, and how much was at stake. If he should lose his temper now with this bloated idiot, this petty cog in the miserable mess of a bureaucratic machine they had inherited from the hateful British bastards, if he should spit as he wanted to spit into that stupid cavernous mouth with its betel-red teeth of an Indian uttering words in the sickening Oxford accent it had acquired by aping its master's voice for so many years, if he should grab that soft jowled neck as his fingers itched to grab it and squeeze till the blood followed those unseeing eyes out of their sockets, there would be the momentary release he yearned for now, the satisfaction which lasts an instant, but all the rest would be thrown into jeopardy. He closed his eyes and waited for his blood pressure to subside. He needed this room until three. It would be too risky to leave before then. There would be too many hours to kill in aimless wandering around the city, too many hours in which someone might recognize him. How many of them are combing the city for a glimpse of my face right now, he wondered, not without pride, yet with some anxiety. There were few places as conducive to anonymity as a railroad terminal, and who

[4]

would ever think of finding him in a traveler's retiring room? So far it had proved the ideal nest—but now?

"Look here," Natu said, affecting as amiable a tone of voice as he could manage. "You are a government official, of course, but my partner and I are men of business. Do you suppose that we have no regulations in the business world? Let me assure you there is no end to them. Regulations as to what we can import and what we cannot import, what we can export and what we dare not export, how much we can spend and how much we can charge—enough regulations to fill up fifty of your clipboards!"

"Yes, quite so, then you understand," the other nodded.

"No, but wait! Do me the honor of hearing what I have to say. Despite all of our regulations we businessmen hold one thing most sacred, and do you know what that is? I will tell you: it is the principle that the customer is always right! Mind you, the *customer* is to us even more sacred than the regulations—"

"Ah, well, but I am sorry—"

"Let me finish please! I do not say that we break the law to satisfy a customer. That is out of the question as we both well know," Natu continued. "The law must *never* be broken, and yet! Where would we be today, tell mc, if we none of us had opposed the tyrannical law of the British? How many years did our own Prime Minister spend in jail, eh? Ten years, and three months, not a day less, as you, a government official, know much better than myself."

The retiring-room manager glanced uncomfortably at his assistant. He did not like the turn which this conversation had taken and tried to escape by muttering how busy he was this morning.

"Surely," Natu pressed on, "you as an official of our independent Nation also must have participated in our freedom struggle. Isn't it so?"

The corpulent clerk, grade twelve in the Railroad Service of India, extracted a filthy handkerchief from his pocket and mopped his brow, though it was much too cool for him to perspire. It was a question too often put nowadays, and one he never could answer, for he did not find it easy to lie, yet the truth made him seem so cowardly, almost a traitor to his motherland, which he loved with his heart and soul. He was simply not a man to court imprisonment by any infraction of the law, British or otherwise.

"I can see that you fought valiantly," Natu said, detecting his adversary's relief at not having to answer the embarrassing question. "Naturally, we all did. My partner here was one of our leaders in the

[5]

resistance movement—" He paused while they looked admiringly at Apte, the assistant staring with that naked reverence so typical of youth when confronted with heroism. "But all this is beside the point. I only mention it to indicate that law and regulations must be treated with flexibility. The customer, remember, comes first, and in this case as citizens of the government we are your customers, since you personally represent our government."

"In my humble capacity only," the other added, obviously flattered. "I try my best to be fair to everyone who comes to me in need of a place to stay for a night or two while waiting for his train or looking about for hotel accommodation. With a million refugees in our city from Pakistan I don't have to tell you how hard it is to find a bed in Delhi. . . ."

Natu let him talk on to his heart's content about the arduous character of his job, the great difficulties in his way, the all but insoluble decisions he was daily called upon to make, the temptations —and many of them most attractive monetary temptations—set before him, and he was after all a poorly paid clerk, a humble officer with seven children to support, etc., etc. Natu knew better than to interrupt.

"But look here, I tell you what," the retiring-room manager finally got around to saying, reaffecting his official tone and manner, "I can promise you nothing, you understand, but we shall wait and see. Perhaps by eleven hundred fifty hours some of the customers on my list will have found themselves accommodations elsewhere—"

"Yes, yes, fine," Natu said, holding out his five rupees for another day's rent.

"No, I cannot accept your money now," the other protested. "If I accepted your money then I would have to give you a receipt and if you had a receipt that would be my official pledge! Let us wait, and I will try my best. . . ."

Just then another assistant brought some newly arrived passengers down the corridor to ask the "Retiring-Room Manager Sahib" if he could possibly give them something, anything, for one night only, just till the morning Mail for Calcutta. Fussing officiously, he brandished his clipboard like a sword as he went off surrounded by suppliants.

Apte bolted the door. Natu stretched out on the pad, and stared at the motionless blades of the ceiling fan, hanging spider-like above him.

"Hey, Natu, that was great the way you talked to him! He is frightened of you. I think he will let us stay."

"Maybe."

"That was nice what you said about me," Apte added, squatting on the bare floor beside his friend, taking out cigarette paper and tobacco, pouring a line of tobacco down the middle of one of the tissue-thin slips of paper. "What would that idiot say if he knew who we were, eh, Natu? What do you think he would say?"

"They are worse than the English dogs," Natu said, ignoring Apte's banter, fixing his eyes now on the lizard who clung to the ceiling above the fan, defying the law of gravity with his suction-cup feet, walking the ceiling as easily as everything else walked the floor.

"Who is worse, Natu?" Apte asked, licking the paper's gummed edge and trying to close it around the tobacco so that the homemade cigarette would be as smooth and round as the more expensive manufactured ones. It never worked. His cigarettes always came out flat and lumpy.

"The black-faced white men," Natu said, "who run our country for us. They talk like the white men. They dress like them. They act like them. Only they can't change their skin. That is why they hate their skin color so much, because they can never change it. That is why they hate everyone else who is black."

The lizard waited patiently. For a long time it did not move, defying the first law of the universe, ignoring the great rule of physics every schoolboy was taught since the English Sahibs brought their gift of Western learning. The lizard waited like a painted design on the ceiling till he appeared to become part of the ceiling stucco, till all the other insects forgot he was there, till unwary of him they returned to his domain, overconfident in the power of their wings, ignorant of his speed, unsuspecting. Then he struck. Swift as a bullet he moved, silent as a bird, lashing out with his tongue curved like a spoon to swallow them up, locking them inside his jaws before they could die, consuming them whole and alive, devouring them in the airless prison vault of his gut. Natu felt a sudden warmth surge through his blood as he watched the lizard hunt. Only his jaw muscle flickered as he lay there outwardly calm, but he responded almost as though he had been touched by Rani's fingers, almost as though those ineffably subtle hands had caressed his naked torso and spine, sending currents of electric fire into his toes and half blinding his eyes till he wanted to consume her.

"Yes, you are right," Apte said, after pondering the matter of the

[7]

black white men awhile. "I had not thought of it that way, Natu, but I can see you are right. Should I make you a smoke?"

"No, you better get us some food."

"Of course, but let me finish my smoke first."

"And get some beer," Natu added.

"Katuk said we should not drink any beer today," Apte reminded him, hesitantly, because he too loved beer, though not so much as Natu.

"Never mind what Katuk said. Buy four bottles."

"Maybe four bottles is too much, Natu. We do not want to feel dizzy, and if we have to leave here early in the sun it could make us light-headed. I will get two bottles."

"That is all right if you do not want any for yourself, Apte. But I will need two bottles, so you get as many more for yourself as you like."

"Maybe I will get three bottles," Apte suggested, but Natu had already closed his eyes indicating that he would not discuss the matter of the beer any further. Apte continued to smoke in silence until his fingernails could no longer grip the nicotine-stained butt. He put on dark glasses before leaving the room. Natu accompanied him to the door.

"Remember," Natu warned, "talk to no one. Say just enough to indicate the foods you want. Get back as fast as you can."

"Yes, yes, I am very careful," Apte assured him, but there was an intensity in Natu's tone that had frightened him, reminding him what for some reason he had again momentarily forgotten, that it was not to be tomorrow or next week or next month, but today. "Natu, what time is it?" he asked.

"Don't worry, there is still plenty of time. Go."

Locking the door as soon as his friend was outside, Natu leaned his back against it and sighed a deep sigh. There is still all of nine hours, he thought. It was not really very much left to a lifetime. Yet he knew it would pass slowly. Though if he went to Rani . . . No, that would not do, thinking of Rani now. He decided to check his gun. He pulled out the cartridge and made sure it was filled, slipped it back carefully into the handle, stared at the trigger, then at the highly polished black luster of the barrel. It was the color of her hair, and as smooth, as shiny black. Not as soft though. Nothing was as soft. He bit into his lower lip till he could feel the pain. Then he put the gun down. He looked at his watch again. He paced off the room, first one way, then the other. Eight and fourteen. Together that made twenty-two. He could not remember if twenty-two was a lucky or an unlucky number. He no longer believed in numerology anyway. Once he had believed in it, when he was sixteen and his child-bride, who was twelve, lay dying of the hemorrhage he had started inside her. He had gone to the numerologist in their village then, and was told that since the number of his wife's age and of the day of the month coincided there was nothing to fear. He returned home relieved and happy to be able to bear such good news, but could hear the wailing lament of his mother long before reaching the house. The bride he had known for little more than one week was dead. There was of course no legal penalty since everyone understood such accidents did occur, and his father was the most highly respected Brahman of the village.

Natu stripped off his shirt, folded it neatly into a small square, set it down on the floor, bent over till the top of his head rested upon it, and using the leverage of his arms and outstretched fingers pressing against the floor, slowly raised his legs and body to an upright position in mid-air. The rush of blood to his head felt warm and soothing. He inhaled slowly through dilated nostrils, waiting till it seemed his lungs were ready to burst before exhaling and taking another breath. The longer he held the air the purer it would cleanse his blood. He knew that the Westerners thought it all nonsense, just as they thought that walking on coals and lying on a bed of ragged glass was somehow accomplished by fraud. Everyone scoffed at what they could not understand, or denied the possibility of what they themselves were too weak to accomplish. From this new perspective the lizard no longer seemed suspended upside down. Their roles were reversed now. Natu was the one hanging in mid-air. He wondered what the lizard thought about him. They were highly intelligent creatures, he knew, and in the Deccan, where he came from, they grew to enormous size. Before the British conquest his people had used these giant lizards in battle to help them climb the sheer cliffs which made some of their fortresses otherwise unassailable. The story Natu had loved best as a child was that of Tanaji, who stormed the Fortress of the Lion by tying a rope around the tail of a giant lizard and hurling him up against the one wall of that formidable hill which the Muslims never guarded since it was so vertical they thought no man could climb it. By hauling himself up on the rope hanging from the lizard's tail, Tanaji did the impossible, and then anchored the rope himself for his men to follow. Moving like the panthers who also lived in those hills, Tanaji and his warriors cut the throats of every

[9]

Muslim guard, and were inside the fort before an alarm could be sounded. Tanaji himself was killed, but the fortress was won, and from that fortress a Maratha Nation had been welded together, and from that Nation an Empire. Then the British came and all of it was stolen from his people. Now the British were gone but the grasping Gujeratis and Uttar Pradesh Imperialists had taken their place, and his people were still treated like dirt.

Soon Natu stopped thinking about anything but his breath. He concentrated all his attention on the air as it flowed through his nostrils, moving to his lungs, joining with the blood and racing through his arteries and veins. He followed the flow of a single air molecule from the inner reaches of his heart to his stomach and entrails, to his toes and fingertips, to the wheels of invisible life-force at the core of his spine, and the base of his brain, those wheels whose activation and union brought mystic powers and ecstasies of passion beyond the reach of ordinary sense perception. He was able to stop thinking about time, about Rani, about this evening, and about the tomorrow which he could not imagine. He lost the consciousness of himself as Naturam Vinayak Godse, aged thirty-seven, weighing one hundred and thirty pounds distributed over a muscular five and one-half feet of height, balanced on his head on the concrete floor of a retiring room in Delhi on the morning of January thirtieth in the one thousand nine hundred and forty-eighth year of the Christian Era. His true Self had become one with the substance of Himself in the air he inhaled, and with that air he moved through the unreality of his other self, which the outside world called Natu, but which in moments like this he knew to be illusory, transient, forever dying, and therefore really unworthy of clinging to in the first place. In reality he was neither more nor less than the air, which from the dim dawn of time had wafted over the universe, and which to the hour of its ultimate expiration would wash all the shores of life, cleanse all the bodies, and bring music to all the leaves and singing blades of grass. Being all things he was nothing. Losing his individual identity he had gained the world.

Then he heard the signal which was Apte's knock.

"I was followed," Apte whispered, out of breath as he put down his bundles and rushed to peer through the shutter at the vacant corridor.

"Are you sure?"

"Sure. But I think I lost him."

[10]

"You *think?*"

"Well, I am fairly certain, Natu, but you know how clever they are."

"Idiot, then why did you come back here?"

"Where else could I go?"

"Anyplace! Were you born with half a brain? Haven't we said a hundred times, a thousand times, every time we have met together with Katuk and the others, that if we are ever being followed the last place we will go is where another of us is hiding? Well? Where is your tongue?"

Apte stared at his bare feet. He could not answer, for it was true, they had planned it that way a thousand times. Yet all he could think of when he sensed that he was being followed was to return to the comforting presence of his dearest friend, the one person in this hostile city with whom he felt safe, whom he trusted entirely, whom he would not hesitate to follow into a wall of fire, or into a raging sea, for as long as Natu was there the worst hazards could be overcome, and even if they could not be, there was at least the overriding comfort of being able to show Natu that he, Vishnu Apte, was also unafraid. Now he could not raise his eyes to meet Natu's reproachful stare, and his tongue felt like lead.

"All right, never mind that now. Tell me what happened. I want to hear every detail of what happened since you left this room."

"Natu, I—I am—sorry if—if I have done wrong—"

"I say never mind! When did you sense you were being followed? What did he look like? Now pull yourself together and speak. We may have to leave here at once!"

"But suppose they are waiting downstairs?"

"Who? You have not told me one thing about them yet! How many were there?"

"No, no, I only saw one," Apte began, despite his shame so gratified to realize that Natu was waiting eagerly to catch every word he uttered that now he was anxious to tell of his adventure in all its detail. "An odd-looking fellow—"

"What do you mean *odd?* Did he have four ears?"

"No, what I mean to say is that he did not look like a police type, you see. He was so shabby, unshaved—in fact, I would not ordinarily have noticed him if I didn't practically stumble over him entering the liquor store."

"Idiot, were your eyes on some Sindhi lady's belly?"

"Natu, I tell you he was just lying there like a beggar."

[11]

"Of course, but isn't that how they always wait for us, the cobras? Coiled up as though they were dead, as innocent-looking as a cake of dung, just part of the landscape. My God, Apte, have you forgotten everything we learned in the last ten years? Who was it that caught Kakaji, tell me? A blind woman he helped cross the road! Who trapped Bhausahib? Never mind, this doesn't help us! Talk, I am listening."

Natu removed one of the quart bottles of beer from its newspaper wrapping. It was warm, but he rarely drank it any other way. He pried off the cap against the bolt which locked the door. The creamy foam gushed out before he could cover the bottle top with his lips. Apte swallowed vicariously as he watched.

"Well?" Natu asked, between gulps.

"Let me have one sip, Natu."

"After you finish telling."

"There is not really much more to tell. I bought the beer as you told me, being very careful not to engage in any conversation with the clerk, who was a snoopy fellow, and wanted to know how long I had been in Delhi, and said I did not look as though I came from these parts, and was I a refugee from Pakistan? You know how those shop people can snoop around! But he did not get anything out of me, I assure you. 'Look here, mister,' I said to him, 'I have come to buy your beer and not to answer your questions so you had better stop wasting your breath and my time!' I did not give him a chance to find out anything."

"Why did you have to sound so hostile? It makes people suspicious."

"What was I to say?"

"Nothing! Just let him talk and nod your head as though you are an idiot! That should not be too difficult for you!"

"But Natu—"

Though they had begun in whispers their voices got louder, and for the last few sentences they had practically been shouting. Then a soft tap upon the door rang through the room like an explosion, and they stood paralyzed, Natu with his bottle half raised, Apte his mouth wide open, as though they were one frame of a movie film suddenly frozen over the lens.

The soft tap came again, followed by a voice neither of them recognized, calling "Sa'ab?"

"Who is it?" Natu asked, still without moving.

"Dhobi, Sa'ab. Anything to wash?"

[12]

"No, nothing today," Natu said, going quickly to peer through the blind.

"Thank you, Sa'ab. Salaam," the voice said, and Natu kept watching till the bare legs of the laundryman had moved beyond the range of his vision.

"Natu, do you think—?" Apte whispered at his ear.

"Shhh!" The clatter of chappals slapped the corridor floor as a billowing wave of flaming orange sari silk flowed by, wafting behind it the strong scent of a heady perfume.

They retreated to the far side of the shadow-shrouded room, and squatting to the floor, Natu indicated that Apte should squat beside him.

"How far did he follow you?"

"Maybe two, maybe three blocks."

"Speak lower," Natu cautioned. "How did you shake him off?"

"I jumped onto the trolley."

"Where?"

"Outside the station, going toward the Kashmir gate."

"Good. What about him?"

"I don't know."

"Didn't you look back?"

"He was gone."

"Did he get on the trolley?"

"I couldn't see. You know how crowded they are, everyone hanging out both sides. I almost got killed. It was very difficult."

"Yes, yes, and where did you get down?"

"Maybe three, maybe four blocks, as soon as I saw a taxi."

"You took a taxi?"

"Of course. I wasn't going to walk back. He might still be there."

"Good. Where did you tell the taxi to take you?"

"Here."

"To the station?"

"Of course, where else? How do you think I am back here?"

"You could have told him to let you down a few blocks away, couldn't you? Then you could have walked here, eh?"

"Yes, but what is the point of that? It only would be more trouble and give more people a chance to see me." Apte felt pleased that he was able to muster such cogent arguments in justification for his actions, though at the time he could only think of returning as swiftly as possible to the comfort of Natu's immediate presence.

"Yes, very clever!"

[13]

"It is kind of you to say so, Natu."

"And suppose the taxi driver was a spy for them?"

The smile left Apte's lips. He stared at his filthy big toe, encrusted with the dirt and soot, the urine and dung of the market place and the station lobby.

"No, you did not think of that! All right, then we have to expect they know we are at the station."

"But how can we be sure?"

"Exactly, we cannot be sure! You lost your head because I was not there to explain to you what by now should have become so obvious—"

"But I did not say three words to the taxi driver, Natu! I got into the cab and said 'Station. Hurry.' That is all. I did not even wait for change of my rupee when he stopped!"

"Ah, that is even better, Apte! That was masterful. You jumped off a trolley going in one direction, raced across the street to a taxi, ordered him to rush off to the station in the other direction, and were in such a hurry that you gave him eight annas tip, and ran into the station as fast as you could. And you weren't even carrying a bed roll! What is suspicious about that, eh! Let me tell you in one word —everything!"

Apte trembled. He too now expected the worst. In fact he was convinced of it. He remembered the piercing stare which the bearded Sikh driver had fixed upon him when he turned to take the money. There was no servility in those eyes, no gratitude for the generous tip, only a cold, penetrating hardness, such as he had seen before in the faces of the English who had hounded them all through the war when he and Natu operated underground digging up railway tracks and planting homemade bombs in public buildings and theatres. Suddenly that face flashed before his eyes, and Apte was certain the driver had been more than a spy, that he was in fact a police magistrate, perhaps one of the superintendent's deputies. He did not inform Natu of this, since what he already said had been damning enough, and he did not want Natu to hate him more. Yet he could not keep his hands from trembling. He grabbed a bottle of beer, finishing almost half the quart before he felt steady again. He dried his lips with his sleeve, and squatted facing his friend.

"Do you think they sent up the dhobi, Natu?"

"It would not surprise me if they did."

"Then we must leave here at once."

"No, that would be too dangerous. Let us eat."

"But if they know we are here then every minute we stay—"

"Ah, then you have devised a plan," Natu said. "Tell me, where shall we run?"

"What do you mean? I have no plan. We shall leave and—and go —we could take a train someplace—anyplace."

"To Poona?" Natu asked him. It was their home, six hundred miles south. It might as well have been six thousand. "Shall we go to Poona, Vishnuji?" He did not often call Apte by his first name.

Then Apte realized the absurdity, the cowardice, of his suggestion, made in a moment of overpowering fear, compelling him to think of nothing but his own safety, provoking him to forget their mission and the plan so carefully formulated, seducing him with the alluring temptations of freedom, of escape from the net that was bound to draw closer about them every hour now, which they were pledged not to escape from, but to remain hidden inside of, till 5 P.M., when they would have to emerge into full view of all, after which there could be no escape. No escape, he told himself, yet secretly he could not help thinking that perhaps there would be some way out.

"No, no, of course, we must not go too far," Apte shamefacedly agreed. "But what good will it do if we wait here for them to take us?"

"It is safer to wait than to run. This station is a big place, and anyway"—Natu smiled his infectious, warm smile which sent beams of strength and confidence from his brilliant, usually sad-seeming eyes—"they may not know we are here after all. Remember, Vishnuji, we are needles in their haystack, eh? We have tricked them a few times before, my friend. Come, let us eat."

Apte's responsive smile, and the vigor with which he hurried to spread the tasty morsels he had purchased over the flattened-out newspapers in which they had been wrapped, satisfied Natu that his bravado bolstered the flagging spirits of his companion. Natu himself was not deluded, however, either by his own carefree tone of voice or the words which in themselves did nothing to fortify their position. Yes, they had eluded the police before, several times at close quarters, escaping once from the rear room of a house while its owners were being interrogated by C.I.D. men in the front room. And all through the war, while they labored every night to disrupt communications and harass the British as much as possible, they carried on every day with publication of the newspaper Natu edited and Apte owned. It had never been easy, but this was not the same. What they planned now was a venture different in kind from anything either they or any member of their organization had ever undertaken before. Prior to

[15]

this the most daring escapade had been Katuk's successful bombing of the theatre attended by half a company of British soldiers. Ten of those soldiers had died, almost a hundred of them had been wounded, but who had ever heard of any one of them? No, this was something in a class all its own, and because it was, Natu knew that no second-string force of a provincial constabulary had been assigned the job of stopping them. And no amount of money or effort would be spared. A hundred of the nation's best agents, possibly a thousand, were scouring the capital at this very moment, he expected, and they would leave no straw unturned till they found their needles. Inwardly he cursed the mishap of ten days ago. Who had ever suspected then? Who had ever dreamed they would try it? They had been free to meet as much as they liked, wherever they liked, to plan to their heart's content, for the police had slept soundly, and if only that idiot Katuk had thrown the bomb straight— Never mind, he thought, for it did not help to relive that golden opportunity now. Yet had they suc- ceeded on the twentieth! All of them but Pahwa had escaped. Pahwa. For ten days now the police had him, their youngest, their least hard- ened, their most vulnerable and talkative—ten hours would have been enough to make Pahwa reveal all he knew. Natu swallowed his rice without tasting it. They know, he thought, they must know we are here.

"Try the gulab jamin, Natu, it is first class," Apte said, licking the sugary syrup from his fingers.

"So you have found your appetite, eh?"

"Yes, yes, I have always treasured gulab babies." He popped an- other of the golden molasses balls into his mouth, and continued talking as he chewed. "Hey, Natu, remember when I ate fifty-five at one sitting? I bet you did not think I could do it? You must have thought I would vomit first—hah, that is what Baburao said, you know. It cost him ten rupees, that miser! Oh, that was a first-rate wedding I would say—"

The paper had been crumpled together and the food left yellow stains of grease that made it still harder to read, but it was the picture that caught Natu's eye, just a small picture, a one-column cut.

"—Yes, first rate! That is one thing you must say for Baburao, even though he is a miser," Apte continued, noisily sucking his fingers, too much absorbed with his eating to have noticed that Natu wasn't pay- ing the slightest attention to him, but was carefully smoothing out the crumpled portion of print under the partly greased news photo of the

[16]

smiling couple that appeared on this society page, which now served as their floor covering.

Tennis Champion Mehta, the caption said, and his lovely wife grace our city with a brief visit. They plan to stay at the Palmyra Palms.

"Was it last year, that wedding?" Apte asked, "or two years ago? Hey, Natu, when was it that I ate all those gulab jamin? Seems to me like only a few months ago."

"What?"

"That wedding for Baburao's youngest daughter. Can you remember when it was?"

"September 1946," Natu said, still staring at the photo while his fingers scattered rice over those faces, toying aimlessly with the mound of steaming rice, dropping grain by grain over the caption as well as the cut, covering it entirely with the rice the way a child might bury some small treasure under a handful of dribbling sand. "It started the night of the sixteenth."

"Yes, that is right, it was 1946," Apte agreed. "But how can you remember the date like that?" he asked in amazement.

"How can you remember the number of gulab jamin you ate?"

"But—what do you mean? I have never eaten so many before or since at one sitting. That is a big thing, after all."

"I see," Natu said, softly, without bothering to explain to Vishnu Apte that it just so happened he remembered that date because that was the night he met Rani for the first time. . . .

It was one of those wedding celebrations that started on Friday and continued through Monday, a big noisy affair which everyone had to attend at some point or other. How could you tell Baburao that you had previous appointments all day and night Friday, Saturday, and Sunday? Natu had thought of begging off by claiming he had a story to cover in Bombay, but that would have been too obvious an insult, and Baburao was after all one of his paper's leading advertisers. There was really no evading the man, but he had not gone to the palatial estate on Ganeshkhind Road until after he knew the ritual would be over, until well after eleven in fact, when at least the musicians would have begun, and Baburao would have unlocked his liquor closet.

"So, Godse, at last you have come to me!" Baburao bellowed, as he got off his motorcycle amid the glare of strings of colored light bulbs which obscured even Orion and the North Star that night. "Here I am beginning to think you have forgotten your Baburao! Well, well,

[17]

well, well, come along! Come along, and gaze upon the blessed couple, you bad boy! Where have you been all these hours? Slaving away at tomorrow's editorial, is it? Look here, Godse, I will tell you something to write about—"

The fleshy arm of his host was draped around his neck, all but choking him, as they went through the garden toward the garish silk pavilion specially erected like a huge carnival tent for the occasion. Though the interior of Barburao's home was vast enough to accommodate twice the crowd of several hundred gathered like moths about the brightness of his bounty, the silk and bamboo pavilion was a mandatory part of the sacred ritual, and Baburao liked to think of himself as a pillar of tradition, a patron of orthodoxy. He had indeed hired no less than seven Brahmans for the nuptials, one to do nothing at all but stand by in the improbable event that another of the six, who minutely divided the ritual labors, would either faint or forget his lines or die of a heart attack. Baburao covered every angle. It was the secret of his phenomenal success. He was nobody's enemy. He made his fortune by supplying the British Army camped in Poona with its brass buckles and water bowls. Yet he virtually supported the National Congress in the city singlehanded, by contributions known only to the Working Committee and a few other insiders. His gifts to Natu's organization equalled those from all other local merchants combined, and no issue of Natu's paper appeared without a full-page advertisement depicting an alluring beauty, standing beside a palm tree and gazing wistfully at the full moon, under which it said, "If You Need Brass—It's Baburao's." No one knew precisely how many other entrepreneurial plums his ring-covered fat fingers had penetrated, or to exactly how many acres of cotton and tobacco land he owned title. There were rumors that he had once purchased the Taj Mahal, and then sold it back to the government at a profit.

"Ah, here we are, here are the blessed babes! Feast your eyes on them, Godse! Have you ever seen a more beautiful bride, I ask you? Look at this necklace I bought her. Show him your bangles—don't be so shy!"

He lifted his daughter's arm as though it were a window fixture for displaying his brass, and prodded Natu's back to focus his attention on the jewel-encrusted bangles of gold. Natu tried to appear suitably impressed, then managed to escape Baburao's clutches as soon as one of the servants diverted the host with news of some crisis that had arisen when a woman's sari caught fire in the kitchen.

Natu managed to find the champagne without being stopped by

too many of his readers on the way. As he had passed the long cloth covered with platters of every variety of food, from mutton curries to mangoes, he noticed Apte bent over a huge bowl of gulab jamin. Their friends were cheering him on, and one of them called Natu over. Apte paused long enough to shout, "Natu, I have eaten forty-three!"

"Forty-two!" someone irately insisted.

"So! Call me a liar for one gulab jamin, do you?" Apte seemed ready to punch the fellow. "Just for that I will eat ten more!"

The champagne was cold, and Natu finished his first at the servant's tray, carrying a second glass out to the garden. The air was fragrant with jasmine, and the flower called "queen of the night," which opens only after darkness falls, but whose perfume was lovelier than all the blossoms of day. He had bent closer to the vine, cupping the petals of one bud in his hand, when he heard a voice say, "Do not destroy it," and at first he thought it was his imagination. Then she stepped from the shadow cast by a tall hedge.

He plucked the flower, and held it to his nose as he stared at her, then threw it aside.

"That was cruel of you," she said. "And after I asked you not to."

"Natu is my name," he told her, because he never could resist a pun.

"Well, I think you're very mean, whoever you are."

She was obviously married or she would not have spoken to him alone, yet he was not used to hearing even married women speak that way, or for that matter look at him as haughtily as this one did, as if she were not only his equal, but even his superior, the way the English women looked and spoke. Yet she was not English.

"Who are you?" he asked.

"I am named for the flower you destroyed," she said.

"Rat Rani? Is that your name?"

"Well, Rani is anyway," she explained, brushing aside the long strands of hair that fell luxuriously to her shoulder and had half hidden her haughty eye. "What are you drinking? Champagne? Let me have some."

"What will your husband say?"

"I'm sure I haven't the vaguest idea. Anyway, he should have brought me a glass himself. Are you afraid of him?"

"Should I be?" he asked, holding out the glass, not for her to take, but elevating it to her lips, stepping toward her as he did so till they almost touched. Bending ever so slightly to sip the drink she did not

[19]

avert her eyes from his naked stare, or modestly lower her heavily painted lids. He thought he detected just the faintest trace of a smile as her lips touched the glass.

"Should I be?" he asked her again, after she had finished drinking.

It seemed that their eyes held for a long time before she answered.

"Oh, I don't know," she said at last. "Lots of people are, I suppose." Then casually, but glancing aside first, as though to be sure no one was within earshot of them, she added, almost too casually, he thought, "But I'm not."

"Ah, that's most interesting," he said, and before tasting the champagne again he turned the glass so that he placed the portion of the rim, stained red by her lipstick, to his own mouth. He did it slowly, almost ritualistically, and all the while her eyes watched and then when he closed his lips over the trace that had been left by her own, she lowered her lids and smiled.

"Natu, I have eaten fifty-five!" Apte yelled triumphantly, holding his bloated stomach as he approached them.

Natu hoped that perhaps if he said nothing in response, Apte would take the hint and go away. He should have known his friend better.

"Do you hear what I say, Natu? Fifty-five gulab jamin, and I had already finished my meal! What do you think of that?"

He did not so much as acknowledge his friend's achievement with a nod of recognition, or a smile, or a word. For her eyes had not turned away in panic at the sound of Apte's voice, but continued to hold his stare as though testing his daring with her own, as though in unspoken challenge she were telling him, "You see, I am not afraid, if you are not." Her eyes were so remarkably expressive, haughty, yet luminous, warm, pain-streaked, he thought, that he sensed they said many things to him. Or was he simply reading into a bland expression of faint interest and possible mocking amusement at his arrogant self-confidence a monologue of his own passionate creation? For though she was not the most beautiful woman he had ever seen, there was something about her which magnetized him, quickening his pulse, intensifying his sense of self-awareness, awakening him to a pitch of consciousness he rarely felt any more—only at times when he wrote an editorial of which he was proud. None of the women he knew could do that to him. There was a servile simplicity about them, about their minds as well as their all too willing bodies, which left him feeling unused, unchallenged, untouched. Even the Sindhi girls of Bombay, those vivacious whores, who so fashionably cut their hair short in the Western style, and smoked cigarettes, and perfumed their long bellies, had begun to bore him. Their gyrations were always mechanical, their hysterical laughter always reserved for the same jokes and moments of intimacy, their songs all sung with a hollow ring. She is different, he thought, there is something about her.

"Oh, my, it is Mrs. Mehta, isn't it?" Apte suddenly shouted, as Natu's silence tempered his enthusiasm over the gulab jamin long enough for him to recognize the slender, elegantly clad woman facing his friend. "But I had heard you were in England!"

"Yes, and now I'm back," she said. "How nice to see you again, Mr. Apte."

"Then you know each other?" Natu asked stupidly, almost angrily, for he wondered why Apte had never introduced them before.

"Of course, but who doesn't know Mrs. Mehta? Where is the Champion tonight?" he asked her. "I haven't seen him." Natu realized from the genuine awe with which Apte said "Champion" that she must be the wife of Maginlal Mehta, the Parsi playboy who had just won the All-India tennis singles crown.

"To tell the truth, Mr. Apte," she said, "I haven't set eyes on him since a few minutes after we arrived this evening. I expect he's out back at the court showing his admirers the serve he used on Govind. Perhaps you could watch too, if you enjoy that sort of thing."

"Yes, what a good idea," Natu said. "Then you can tell me about it tomorrow, Apte!"

"Oh, no thanks," Apte said, massaging his stomach gently. "I am much too full for tennis right now."

"No one is telling you to play it," Natu persisted, wondering just how obtuse even Apte could remain.

"But I can never watch a game without getting all excited. You should have come with me last week to see her husband play, Natu! I told you it would be a terrific game, do you remember? What a service he has, eh, Mrs. Mehta?"

"I'm told it's—I think they call it super," she said.

"Yes, yes," Apte agreed. "Super!"

"I see you don't care much more about tennis than I do," Natu remarked to her.

"Oh, don't I? Perhaps not, though I should hardly venture a guess at that, especially since—well, we haven't even been introduced as yet, have we, Mr.—?"

There was too much of the English tone and manner in the way she said it for Natu to fill in the name for her. Remember your place, she had said in effect, and he hated her for it. She is no better than the rest of them, he decided, draining his glass, and watching her now not with the warm passion he had felt, but with a cold, penetrating contempt.

"But he is Naturam Godse," Apte eagerly explained. "I certainly thought you must know each other since you—well, since—"

"The fiery journalist, of course!" she said, saving Apte the embarrassment of having to explain that since they were talking alone in the garden he took it for granted that they had at least learned each other's names. "I admire your editorials very much, Mr. Godse."

"Oh? Can you read Marathi?" he asked, not without acerbity.

"Of course," she said. "How else would I read your newspaper?"

"I don't know. I thought perhaps one of your servants translated for you."

"Well, you're wrong," she said. "I assure you I do all my own reading—and thinking."

"Let me congratulate you, Mrs. Mehta," he said.

"If you aren't being sarcastic—" Then she hesitated as if she wanted to say a great deal to him in a less distant tone, but suddenly changing her mind or losing her courage, briskly added, "Thank you! Now if you'll excuse me, I must find my husband."

She walks like a queen all right, he thought, watching her proud stance as she moved so effortlessly away, the colored lights reflected like jewels in her sari's sequins. She walks like a Rani.

"I am afraid I will never understand women," Apte confessed.

"Let us get something to drink," Natu muttered. "Come, tell me how you manage to eat so much without getting as fat as Baburao."

"Ah-hah! Did I tell you how many gulab babies I ate tonight?"

She turned the path past the corner of the house and was no longer in sight.

"Natu, are you listening to me? Natu?"

"Natu? Do you hear me? I ask what are we to do if they come?"

What are we to do if they come? The question echoed in his mind, and looking from the patterns his fingers made of the rice to the fear-lined countenance of his companion, Baburao's garden quickly receded to the dark silence of half forgotten memory, and instead of the rat rani's fragrance his nostrils tasted the dry coal-soot filtering through the retiring room from the station tracks below.

"What do you mean, Mr. Vinayakrao?" Natu asked him, without smiling. "Do you expect any visitors?"

[22]

"That is no good, Natu! They know who we are! We cannot bluff them with our false names."

"Bluff? I do not understand you, and my name is not Natu, please remember that. It is very essential for you to remember, Mr. Vinayakrao, that my name is Dinesh Narayanrao. You do remember that, don't you?"

"No, no, it is useless," Apte said, getting another bottle of beer. "They are not fools, I tell you. They will recognize us at once. They will know as soon as we open our mouths—"

"Calm yourself, Mr. Vinayakrao. Perhaps you had better try to get some sleep."

"Sleep? How can I sleep? I have not been able to sleep the past two nights. Do you expect me to sleep now, when for all we know they are coming up the stairs this very instant, and you sit there as though we have nothing to fear! I know, you think I am an idiot. You think I am too stupid to understand! Well, maybe you are right. Maybe I have been an idiot to listen to you this long without saying a word—"

"You have had enough to drink, Mr. Vinayakrao, better give me the bottle."

"Stop calling me that name, Natu. I know what my name is supposed to be if anyone asks me, but you don't have to call me that all the time!"

"I said give me the bottle!"

"No. Leave me alone, will you!"

Natu did not close his hand, but struck Apte on the cheek with his open palm. It was a stinging blow, though he did not put all his power behind it, just enough to sober his friend. At the same time he took hold of the bottle and deftly wrenched it from the other's grip. He stood drinking the beer till Apte stopped his sobbing, and lapsed into a stupor of deep, noisy breathing, intermittently punctuated by low animal-like groans. He felt now that it had been a mistake to let Apte accompany him, but this time they had drawn matchsticks because no one had volunteered. After last week they knew that their chance of escaping would be practically nil.

"Are you all right now, Vishnuji?"

"Yes."

"Good. Do you want a drink?"

"Please." He returned the bottle after a long swallow.

"Now, listen to what I say. It is probable that they know we are somewhere in the station, that is granted. But it is more than probable that they have never seen us, and even if we assume they have sent to

Poona for our pictures, remember we have shaved our mustaches—
Are you listening?"

"Yes."

"They may notice some resemblance from our pictures, but they
will not be positive since we have no mustaches, and they will not
want to take the wrong people since they cannot afford to waste any
more time. Therefore, if they come here, they will have to question
us, and everything will depend on how we behave. In nine cases out
of ten, men hunted by the police betray themselves. If we act guilty,
then we are guilty, no question about it! At this point I tell you we
are our own worst enemies. Is that clear?"

"Yes. But . . ."

"But what?"

"Suppose they bring Pahwa?"

He had not thought of that. Suppose they bring Pahwa?

"They will not risk it," he answered, with supreme assurance.

"Why not? What is the risk to them?"

"It is much too crowded here, that is the risk, and unless they
wanted to identify themselves immediately as police they would have
to bring him along unhandcuffed, and he might escape. Believe me,
they will keep Pahwa secure behind their bars."

"Are you certain?"

"Positive."

"And you think we could fool them?"

Apte's courage was returning, though Natu realized now he would
have to watch his friend more carefully than he had anticipated. It
was an added burden. He half-seriously considered doing it alone,
but that might prove too dangerous. A weak ally was better than
none.

"We will *have* to fool them. And we shall. Now I want you to tell
me, Mr. Vinayakrao, what it is that brings you here to Delhi?"

"I am here on business."

"What business?"

"I make matches. My factory is in Sholhapur, and—"

"Did I ask where your factory was, Mr. Vinayakrao?"

"Well, I have to explain to you, don't I, why I am here?"

Natu shook his head, and patiently pointed out that if he said too
much it was almost as bad as saying nothing. "Sometimes it is even
worse, my friend. It sounds as if you have memorized a statement.
You must not appear too eager. After all, you are here for an hour or
two of relaxation during your hard day's work, and these people have

[24]

come to disturb you with questions—they have not even told you why! As an honest businessman, you naturally feel annoyed, put out, perhaps slightly indignant—not too indignant, not insulting, remember." He went on explaining it the way a stage director might set the mood for one of his actors, pacing slowly before Apte as he spoke, gesturing now and then at the air, pausing to taste the warm beer. Despite his anxiety, his state of near panic, Apte could not help admiring Natu's ingenuity. He could be or do anything, Apte thought, for it was more than admiration he felt for his friend, it was closer to reverence. Natu offered him another drink, and they started again.

"Matches? Very interesting, Mr. Vinayakrao, a most necessary industry for our new nation."

"Yes, of course, I think so too," Apte said, getting into the mood of their game.

"Most, most necessary. But why have you come to Delhi? You are not born around here, are you? Excuse me if I ask what seem like personal questions please."

"That is quite all right, sir. I have nothing to hide. I am an honest businessman. I always pay my taxes."

Natu smiled appreciatively at this bit of improvisation and nodded.

"Oh, but you ask me why I have come here? Well, you see, in my business sulphur is practically the most essential item. That is, I mean, aside from wood, naturally. You cannot make matches without wood, you understand, but the government does not bother me as regards my supply of wood. However! When it comes to sulphur, I must procure government license, you see, and so I have come here to appeal for special extension of my permit, which has expired!"

"That is not bad, Vishnuji, not bad."

"So I am not as stupid as you thought, eh, Natu?"

"Mmm. But tell me, Mr. Vinayakrao, why does a big businessman like yourself stay in such a dismal place as the station retiring room?"

"Oh, it is most flattering of you, sir, to call me 'big,' but I assure you I do not have money to waste on your fancy Delhi hotels, and anyway, this is quite excellent for my modest needs, you see."

"And how long will you remain here?"

"I must leave tomorrow, but I hope I will be permitted to remain here in peace and quiet until then. I was just now taking my mid-morning nap as you knocked, sir, and since I have a busy afternoon ahead of me I hope you will excuse me if I lie down again now."

"Yes, of course, we are going at once. Thank you so much for being as cooperative and patient as you have been with us, Mr. Apte."

[25]

Natu smiled warmly and held up his hands in the traditional namaste gesture of parting.

"Not at all, sir," Apte said, responding with his raised palms pressed together. But before he could lower the palms, Natu had gripped them both in a hand that locked around Vishnu's fingers like the steel jaw of a manacle.

"Idiot! You just gave yourself away! I called you *Apte!*"

"Oh, that is right, I am sorry."

"I don't ask for your apologies," Natu said, releasing the fingers with a gesture of disgust. "If we fail because of your stupidity you can save your apologies for Guruji! I am sure he will appreciate them! I will tell him that you meant to do the right thing, but you were simply too frightened and nervous! We will both explain that to him, eh?"

Apte lowered his head. He tried not to cry, but he could not help himself. It was unmanly, he knew, but he could not fight back the tears which ran from his eyes as though they were shallow tanks in a monsoon deluge. He felt the sick, gnawing shame of his own inadequacy sharper even than the dull, deep fear which had enveloped him since he had drawn the broken matchstick.

"I am not worthy of this mission, Natu," he whispered.

Natu did not hear him. He had paced to the other side of the long room, as far from Apte as he could get, less from disgust with the other's failure of the test, than from the suddenly overpowering urge to go away, to go to—no! Just to be alone, that was all he wanted. Any change would release the tension which had drawn him like a taut wire till he felt he was losing control of his temper, losing his patience, ready to snap. He had not meant to bark at Apte again. He had certainly not meant to frighten him by invoking their leader's name. Apte was bad enough, livid enough with fear, as it was, so that to remind him that their punishment for failure would be no less severe than their punishment for success was at this point unnecessary. Perhaps even dangerous, he thought, for he had no illusions about his friend's strength of character. He had seen men go to pieces in less trying circumstances. Each individual like everything else had its boiling point and its melting point, up to which it retained one shape, beyond which it became something else. Guruji had taught him that. If Apte cracked now, if he started ranting or could not stop crying, then he would not only have to go on to the garden alone this afternoon. He would have to kill his best friend first. It will be no less than

Guruji would expect of me, Natu thought. Somehow that helped to soothe him.

"Natu, I am not worthy, you must release me," Apte implored. "It is not too late. We shall go to Katuk. He will accompany you."

"Katuk has lost his aim," Natu reminded him. "Katuk is too old."

"Then Shankar will do it," Apte begged. "Shankar is younger than I am, Natu."

"He is too young," Natu explained, patiently, calmed by the thought of Guruji's approval of his decision. "Shankar has never fired a pistol. He is our servant, have you forgotten?"

"Parchure then. Natu, please, you must help me."

"We must help each other, Apte."

"Yes, yes, anything you say, I will do it, only—"

"You must come with me to the garden—"

"No!"

"—at four o'clock this afternoon, we shall arrive at the caretaker's house—"

"Please, I will be your slave! I will care for your brother all my life, Natu. I will give him everything I own."

"—and then we shall wait there together for one hour, Vishnuji. You and I shall wait for him there together—"

"Natu, my hand will tremble! See how it is trembling now. Look, I beg you. Listen to what I am saying. Why will you not listen to your Vishnuji, Natu?"

"—and we shall leave the small house when we see him approaching the prayer ground," Natu continued, a strange brightness animating his eyes, a quality of perfect calm and assurance giving his words so comforting a tone that Apte no longer tried to interrupt their flow. "Then we shall walk toward him together, Vishnuji, and we shall greet him as all the others do, humbly bowing to him, though he is the cursed devil incarnate, the worst traitor our motherland has ever known, we shall bow to him and smile our greeting, Vishnuji, and then we shall shoot him until we have no bullets left in our guns."

The tears continued to flow from Apte's eyes, but they no longer pained him with their scorching sting. He felt no pain anymore. He was suffused suddenly with a glow of satisfaction, by a glimmer of the joy of anticipated achievement such as he had never known before. Natu's hands braced his shoulders, in a grip gentle yet firm.

"We shall do that together, Vishnu, and our Teacher will bless us for it through an eternity of peace and liberated contentment, and our countrymen of every generation yet unborn will remember what we shall do today with infinite gratitude and boundless love."

Natu leaned forward gently and touched Apte's furrowed brow with his lips.

"Do not be afraid, my brother," he said.

"I will try to be worthy, Natu." Still he could not altogether stop trembling.

The retiring-room manager returned shortly after eleven to tell them that it would not be possible to rent the room another day.

"I will pay you for a full day," Natu told him, "and promise you that we shall vacate in four hours."

It was a great temptation, and the portly civil servant looked genuinely sad. "If it were my own mother, Mr. Narayanrao, who will occupy this room at twelve hundred hours, let me tell you frankly, I would keep her waiting on her baggage in the corridor! Not for the money, mind you, but to accommodate a gentleman, yet what you ask is impossible. The family of the director of our Eastern Railway is arriving at eleven hundred fifty hours on the Calcutta Mail, and if they do not find immediate space available when they get here, let me admit to you in all confidence, my good man, that though I have a record of unmatched service on this job for thirty-seven years, I have little doubt but that I will be transferred to Nagpur tomorrow!"

It was futile to argue, for to a Delhiman Nagpur was the same as Siberia to a Muscovite.

"Very well, we shall be out by then," Natu told him.

There was little enough to be packed. Everything they carried fitted easily over their mats inside the canvas bed rolls. The guns they tucked into their money belts strapped around their waists. Their loose-hanging shirts totally obscured the weapons from view. When they had finished dressing they carefully inspected each other.

"All right," Natu said. "Let's go—you first. Don't wait for the lift, take the side stairway, and get the first small cab you see. I will follow in one minute."

"Suppose they are outside?"

"If anyone stops you, ignore them. If they persist, be polite, but continue walking—go toward the platform instead of the exit. If there are a few of them put down your bed roll, and light a cigarette. When you find an opening run for the nearest crowd—they will be afraid of hitting too many to start firing. Keep running till you are sure you have lost them. If you have to get on a train, leave at the first stop. Meet me at the gardener's house at four. Is that clear?"

"I think so," Apte said. "I must make a cigarette to have ready." He was too nervous to keep the tobacco steady long enough to roll up the paper.

"Give it to me," Natu ordered. He deftly closed the roll and licked the gummed edge. Then he made another for himself.

Apte accepted the cigarette with mute gratitude. It was much firmer and neater than the ones he always made.

"And one thing more," Natu cautioned as they hefted the bed rolls onto their shoulders. "If you should be taken prisoner—"

"I would tell them nothing, Natu."

"No, that may not be possible, Vishnuji. They have learned from the English dogs how to make people talk, and silence would only intensify their search for me. Tell them—after a decent period during which you refuse to speak—tell them that our plan was to do it to-morrow."

Apte nodded, yet seemed reluctant to leave.

"Natu, what if they should catch you, and not me?"

"When you get into the cab, Vishnuji, count to one hundred—slowly. If I am not in sight by then, go—and do not forget what you must do this evening. God will help you."

"Burrai, Natu," Apte said. It was their own people's way of saying, "Till we meet again."

"Burrai, Vishnuji."

Natu closed the door behind him, and began counting, slowly. When he had counted to fifty, he opened the door again, and hurried out into the corridor flooded with late morning light. For an instant he was half blinded, so dazzling was the glare, after two days in semidarkness. He almost collided with a passenger racing toward the central stairway, then recovered his equilibrium and started off toward the side exit.

"Mr. Narayanrao! One moment please!"

He recognized the manager's voice, but did not pause to answer or look around.

"One moment please, if you will, sir!"

Unconsciously, instinctively, he accelerated his pace, acting as though he were deaf. A train must have just arrived for there was a motley crowd of veiled women, naked children, and men burdened down with their worldly possessions, sweating and fretting as they advanced toward him, clogging the corridor with their useless forms.

"Stop! I must have a word with you, Mr. Narayanrao!"

[29]

As he reached the advancing crowd, several of the children tugged at his trouser legs and held out their dirty palms, crying for baksheesh. With his free hand he caught one of them by an ear and threw him aside. The child screamed his pained protest, bringing a babble of indignation down upon his head from a few of the women. One of the men asked angrily, "What is the rush, babu? Another train will be along in five minutes!" He ignored all of them, but instead of opening a path for him they jostled their bodies against his as he moved, and it slowed him down.

Then he saw that an elderly station attendant stood directly in his path, grinning a toothless grin, but apparently determined not to move aside.

"Manager Sa'ab calls to you, Sa'ab," he announced in a tone of sickening servility and meekness, belied by his obvious determination to block Natu physically, at least to try, if he did not stop of his own volition.

Natu hesitated, inwardly cursing the stupidity, the insensitivity, the wretched insignificance of every miserable one of them, from the imbecile beggar child to the senile old man, who looked as though he would keep grinning through a sound thrashing, but he realized that he had aroused far too much attention. Another minute of this, he knew, and he might well be surrounded by a hundred gaping goons who had nothing more urgent or compelling to do with their lives than to stop and stare at the first argument or public distraction which caught their eyes and ears. Free entertainment for them, the urine-covered scum, he thought, halting and turning to confront the panting spectacle of the manager's ubiquitous form.

"Well?" Natu asked, relieved somewhat to see that the manager ran after him alone.

"Your room key, Mr. Narayanrao! You have not returned it to me."

So that was all he wanted! Natu almost burst out laughing, but there was no time—he had lost count, yet it was at least sixty, possibly seventy, since Apte left the room.

"It is on the chest of drawers," Natu told him, hastily.

"You are sure?" the manager asked.

"Yes, yes, sure!"

"Come, let us look and see!"

"I am late for my train! Do you think I would lie to you?"

"What train? You have told me all morning that you wanted to stay in the room till fifteen hundred hours."

[30]

Damn the petty bastard, Natu thought, he forgets nothing! He looked quickly behind him. The grinning attendant was hardly two steps away, and now another wretch had come up to his rear, curiously watching the free public show. The side stairway was in sight, and at its foot the exit, Apte, the taxi—it was too dangerous a run, for he could see that the stairs kept vomiting up their human refuse from the platforms below.

"All right, come," he said, doubling back, practically running, half crushing another of the children as he bolted through the crowd again, reaching the room, opening the door, going directly to the one piece of Victorian furniture, on top of which he had left the cursed key.

"Here! Are you satisfied?"

"There is no need to lose your temper, Mr. Narayanrao," the other explained with saccharine solicitude. "The regulations specify, you see, that I must personally see to it that every occupant—"

Natu brushed past him. He started counting again, but stopped when he reached the stairs. Everyone was coming up. He was obliged to cut his own path in the opposite direction, shouting, pushing, cursing. He might as well have been yelling at bricks left to dry across a country road—the only thing to do was to kick them aside. Where did they come from, these droves of human cattle? What did they expect to find at the top of another flight of stairs except more of their own impoverished, bedraggled selves, moving aimlessly from one station to the next, from one locked door to another, from one overcrowded city to its more crowded neighbor? Was anyone left in the villages to push the ploughs, and irrigate the rice? Or would the infectious madness of motion keep them dancing like dizzy dervishes till they all dropped dead of exhaustion? He felt as though he had moved through the surf against a back-washing tide by the time he reached the bottom step, and now the full impact of just how many of them were milling around there struck him audibly as well as visually, a cacophony of chaotic clatter ringing dizzily through his brain, a solid wall of sound it seemed, something palpable and massive and deafening, composite blend of the roar of fifty thousand voices competing all at once with the belching, bellowing thud and clatter of locomotives and colliding cars, of horn-blowing cabs, and braying cattle.

Apte was nowhere in sight. Ridiculously enough he started counting again as he peered inside every small cab on the virtually unmoving double line snaking out toward the full white blast of the naked noonday sun. When he reached one hundred, he stopped. He looked around in every direction for one last, impossible try at finding his lost companion needle. Then he opened the door of the nearest empty, and jumped onto the torn leather of its vacant rear seat.

The bearded driver immediately lowered his yellow meter flag, and flashed a betel-stained smile in Natu's direction.

"Where to, Sahib?"

"Drive ahead," Natu told him, seeing it would take some time just to reach an open crossroad. "I will direct you as we go, Sardarji."

"Very good, Sahib. Is it your first visit to our capital?"

"No," Natu replied with finality.

It was three minutes before noon.

2

Acting Superintendent Das, of the Political Department of the Home Ministry of the Central Government, was a singularly unimpressive-looking young man. His casual manner, slight frame, and boyish face made him appear, even at second and third glance, more like one of the millions of unemployed failed-B.A.'s who walked the streets and filled the coffee shops of India's major cities, than like the highest-ranking policeman in the nation. He was in fact so anonymous a personality and power that at times he wished he were a bit better known, at least among the lower echelons of those employed in his own service. For he had been stopped by no less than three uniformed, baton-carrying police in the short distance between the front door of Parliament House and the second-floor office of P. K. Shankaracharyarao. Each of his interrogators had skeptically studied his I.D. card, and had looked him up and down several times before smartly snapping to attention and raising his baton in salute. Ordinarily so admirable a display of tightened security would have pleased Gopal Das, but today he was in a hurry. The delays only rankled. He opened the unmarked paneled teak door without bothering to knock.

The soft carpeting of the outer office swallowed Gopal's footsteps. Seated along the wall opposite the secretary's desk were half a dozen suppliants, their Congress caps in hand. At this hour most ministers' offices would be empty, Gopal knew, but there was always a line-up waiting for a word with P.K. As leader of the Party he held more political plums in his ample pockets than any of his colleagues, including the Deputy Prime Minister. At times like this Gopal wished he had half as large a force of loyal and dedicated assistants at his command as P.K. did, though no one knew the actual dimensions of Shankaracharyarao's army, not even his own secretary. The old boss kept the real list in his brain alone. His memory for names and faces was phenomenal. And he never forgot a favor, never forgave a foe. He was a formidable power in the land. He was practically an institution.

"Is P.K. alone?" Gopal asked the secretary.

"Yes, sir, but he has just begun his midday meal, and—"

"This is urgent," Gopal said, going directly to the inner door.

"But sir, he never—" the secretary insisted, alarmed, jumping up and running after him, reaching out as though ready to grab hold of the acting superintendent's arm. He was not quite fast enough. Once again Gopal admitted himself without knocking.

P.K. had half raised a dripping handful of rice and curds to his open mouth, when his attention was so rudely diverted by the opened door, the inrushing figure of Das, and hard upon his heels the breathless form of his secretary. He stared at them without blinking, then calmly completed the act of transporting his fluid mixture to his face, sucking his fingertips clean before pulling them out.

"I told Shri Das you were eating, sir, but he insisted," the secretary explained breathlessly, "on seeing you before I—"

"Quite right, quite right of him!" P.K. shouted, dismissing the secretary with a slight backhand wave such as he might have used to brush a fly from the air before his massive face. Everything about him was massive, head, body, hands, mouth, eyes, even his voice. He spoke as though from an election-eve platform on which the microphone had just given out. "I am at your service at any hour of the day or night, Das, remember that. Feel free to come in here at any time. Never mind knocking."

Gopal did not miss the trenchant tone in which it had been spoken. He cherished no false illusions as to P.K.'s opinion of him. Nor did he bother to disguise his own feelings. Ordinarily he went out of his way to steer clear of this man, but with the Prime Minister in Amritsar, he could think of no one better to turn to. If only *he* were here today, Gopal thought disconsolately, realizing at the same instant, however, that though the Chief worked himself like five men, he was still only one. It was a big country, after all, and he was needed in a dozen different cities practically daily now, especially now. He would return from Amritsar tomorrow, of course—but tomorrow might be too late.

"Sit down, Das. Make yourself at home," P.K. suggested. "Why don't you join me in a bit of lunch? I will have my secretary bring another tray."

"No thanks, P.K."

"So you have already eaten?"

"No, but I haven't the time right now."

"No time for food? What are you saying, my good man? Nonsense! We must keep ourselves alive, Das, remember that. We must keep our bodies alive, or everything will collapse around us. For men like us, eating is a public duty!" He was seated on the huge armchair behind his massive desk, his legs tucked up on the seat, the bare toes and sole of one foot visibly resting on the other bent knee.

"P.K., we must prevent Bapu from holding his prayer meeting this evening," Gopal said quickly, because there was no time for small talk.

"What do you say, Das? Speak a little more clearly please, I don't follow. Sit down, I tell you. It gives me indigestion to see you shifting from one leg to another that way."

Gopal rubbed the flat of his palm slowly over the top of his bushy hair. He rubbed the hair only from back to front, smoothing rather than ruffling it. It was an unconscious gesture, the one outward betrayal of how nervous he really felt, how strenuous an effort it was for him to control his body and moderate the tempo and tone of his voice as much as he managed to do. It was no good trying to bludgeon this man into action, he knew, for next to the Chief he carried more weight than any member of the government, since its Cabinet had been chosen from the Party he directed. But more important than that was his long-standing attachment to Gandhi. He had been among

[35]

the first to recognize the political potential of Bapu's program of boycott. He had thrown himself wholeheartedly into the noncooperation movement from its inception, and with him went his vast family with all the landowning prestige and power at their command. Gopal suppressed his impatience, and sat down.

"Let me explain, P.K.," he said softly, slowly. "I am convinced that they plan to make a second attempt on Bapu's life this evening. I feel, therefore, that it is imperative for us to go to him immediately and persuade him that under no circumstances must he appear at the prayer ground at five o'clock."

He waited for some response, but since P.K. continued to eat without pause, he decided to explain his entire plan at once, adding, "Or, alternatively, if he proves adamant about holding the meeting despite our warning, then I must insist that he allow us to take proper security precautions."

"Which would mean what?" the heavy dark head inquired, looking up innocently, as though it were the first time he had heard that phrase used in his life.

"At least two men preceding him, and two following. The number we plant in the crowd need not be brought to his attention, but I must insist that he have a minimum escort of four from the moment he steps out into the open to the moment he returns from the garden. I repeat, however, P.K., that it will be much safer to cancel the meeting altogether, and I suggest that we don't even mention the alternative unless he positively vetoes the idea of calling it off."

"No, he won't hear of that, Das."

Gopal took a long breath before answering. It was not fear of losing his job that made him swallow the insults and invective that suddenly clamored for release. Gopal knew perfectly well that were it up to P.K. he would never have been made acting superintendent to begin with. He knew, moreover, that of the fifteen leading police officers whom he'd summarily discharged from the service on his first day as superintendent, at least ten had been appointed on the personal recommendation of P.K. He also knew that since that day hardly a week passed in which P.K. failed to submit a retaliatory memo of grievances against his department to the Prime Minister. He knew, because as soon as the Chief read those letters he passed them on to Gopal with the pencilled notation in one corner, "Another testimonial for your collection!" It was not self-interest that made Gopal politely pause now, but rather the overwhelming, excruciating, all but unbearable realization that though he was privileged with the job of protecting the greatest, most saintly, most important life in a world of some two and one half billion mortals, he felt as he had in those horrible nightmares of his childhood that he was crossing a field where a tiger was racing headlong in his direction, teeth bared and saliva dripping, yet his legs were paralyzed, he could not run. Only in the nightmares he had always dimly sensed he would awaken. But this wasn't a dream, and Gopal feared that unless he could convince P.K. to do everything in his power to assist him, something much worse than the most horrible nightmare could in fact occur.

"Naturally you know him much better than I do," Gopal conceded softly, "though from what little personal contact I've had with him, I know how stubborn he can be. But we must try our best to get him to call it off, P.K. We've never been as certain about any of their plans before as we are about this one, and—"

"But *how* are you so certain, Das? And *if* you are," the broad flat-nosed face, hard enough to have belonged to a prizefighter, grinned derogatively, Gopal saw, as P.K. added, "if you *are* so certain, then there should be no problem now, should there?"

"As to your first question," Gopal responded flatly, recognizing that P.K. was determined to interrogate him as though he were a raw detective just returned from his first assignment, "I finally got the truth out of Pahwa, the prisoner we had taken on the twentieth, after staying with him in his cell most of last night. I finally got him to tell everything. Naturally they had expected to succeed on the twentieth, but in case of failure they had agreed to try again, not immediately, because they feared it would be too dangerous. Their plan was to return to Bombay first, to disperse and stay hidden one week, then to come back and strike again on the first auspicious day. Before coming to see you I had my men round up fifty astrologers. All of them were asked the same question—'When is the first auspicious day for embarking on any important venture after January twenty-seventh?' Twenty-three of them answered January thirtieth, without further questioning, after they consulted their charts. Five insisted on January twenty-ninth, but naturally we don't have to worry any more about yesterday. The other twenty-two needed more precise information. We told eleven of them that the important venture was the murder of an evil man, the other eleven we told it was the murder of a saintly man. Of the first eleven, nine came up with January thirtieth, two with the twenty-ninth. All eleven of the second group insisted there was no auspicious day for murdering a saintly man, so we changed the question to conform with that given the others. Eight said the thirtieth, one the twenty-ninth, two February first."

Gopal paused to catch his breath. He had not slept more than four hours any night for the past ten, and he was beginning to feel it. How does the Chief do it, he wondered, at almost twice my age! Not that he was vain enough to compare himself often with the man who had taken him from his post as assistant deputy commissioner of one of the smaller provinces, and catapulted him into the chair of national commander of the Force. Gopal hastily glanced at his wristwatch. Twelve-fifteen! A quarter of an hour already wasted!

"I am glad to see you have worked with the characteristic thoroughness we have all come to expect of you, Das," P.K. remarked, buzzing for his secretary.

Gopal watched that heavy finger press its full weight upon the desk buzzer, and almost jumped up in his eagerness to get started. At last I've gotten through to him, he thought, anticipating that P.K. would call for his car now. They would be closeted with Bapu in five minutes. He stared anxiously at the door, wondering why the secretary was so slow in arriving.

"I have finished with this tray, Ramu," P.K. said, as soon as his secretary appeared. "Bring my fruit now."

"Yes, sir. Dr. Shah has just arrived, sir, and the Viceroy's attaché called to remind you of the reception at two. Will you wish to go home first to change for that, sir?"

"Ah, yes, yes, of course—uh, what does Shah want?"

"Um," the secretary glanced nervously at Gopal, and seemed to lower his voice. "His, uh, brother-in-law—"

"Yes, yes, yes," P.K. interrupted. "I have no time for him today! Tell him to make an appointment—next week, you take care of that. I cannot be bothered right now!"

"Yes, sir. Thank you, sir."

Gopal watched with a sinking heart as the door closed entirely. P.K. had nothing more to inform his secretary!

"No peace, no rest, Das! Work, nothing but work," P.K. groaned. "I'm getting too old for this job. I wish there were someone qualified —but never mind my own problems. Where were we? Yes, I remember—the auspicious day. But look here, I don't doubt your astrologers, yet how can we be sure that your informant didn't just invent the whole story to try and frighten us? He may have been trying to impress you by showing his willingness to be of service, after all. You

[38]

know how these people are, Das; they think if they tell us something we consider important that we may be more lenient with them."

Gopal did not answer immediately. A sickening feeling, a kind of nausea, had suddenly gripped his stomach, sending currents of pain through his skull, currents of apprehension which carried a message too horrible for him to translate even to his own silent thoughts. It was a warning message conveyed by the flat watery eyes of the big man whose words sounded so hopelessly inept and amateurish that he could not accept them at face value, could only interpret them as a form of code if they were to make any sense whatsoever. But he was afraid to decipher it. He erased the idea instantaneously from his mind.

"No, sir," he insisted, "I'm convinced it isn't just that. I've been with Pahwa almost constantly during the past ten days. You'll have to accept my word for it. He wasn't just trying to save his own skin this morning."

"Your word is certainly good enough for me, Das," P.K. answered, pushing himself away from his desk. "Of course I accept your word, but I have to be sure, you understand!"

Nimbly unfolding his legs, he stood and strode stiffly to the wall of windows, which opened onto the red sandstone balcony. In the spacious court below a marble fountain shaped like a lotus was crowned with a bubbling umbrella of crystalline water, its diaphanous spray holding a rainbow. Radiating from the fountain in all directions were mango-tree-shaded paths comfortably provided at intervals with cushioned wrought-iron benches painted white. There were two lotus ponds filled with goldfish, and a manicured grove of lavishly fruit-adorned orange and lemon trees. It was a setting conducive to calm judgment, a proper antidote to impetuosity, a visual sedative for mollifying rash impulses. P.K. was not insensitive to its alluring charm, nor was he indifferent to the comforts of his elegant office. After a quarter of a century of struggle, of bleak prison life, and more arduous labor while at liberty, who would have been? He was human after all, and there were limits to human sacrifice. There were limits to human patience, to the deferment of normal pleasures, the surrender of simple luxuries. He had done more than his share already, given far more than most in his dedication to the nation's cause, the cause of freedom, of independence. His reward was meager enough, coming as late as it did. At most there were twenty years left for him, probably closer to ten. As yet he had enjoyed no period of true rest. In fact he had labored harder in the past sixteen months to rebuild the Party machine, which had all but disintegrated from disuse during the war, than he'd ever worked in his youth. Late into each night he had labored, conferring with local leaders from every province, personally visiting remote towns and villages, splicing the lines of organization that had been broken, reweaving the net that covered the country, the net he alone could throw out and haul in. No one else could have done it, not the Chief, certainly not Gandhi. They had neither his talent, his patience, nor his desire to do it, for such things were beneath them, petty, mundane, compromising, unworthy. He knew they all thought him a hack, a dull-minded ward heeler. The Chief was too much the intellectual for such matters, the theoretician, the international statesman, author and darling of the *haut monde*. Bapu was the dreamer—what did he care about Party machinery? He considered all machinery evil by definition! Leave the dirty work to P.K., they said. Let P.K. manage it! Well he did, and where would any of them be now without him?

He stood silent with his back to Gopal, staring down at the garden, one fist locked in the other hand behind the lower curve of his spine. He did not relish the thought of going to visit Bapu today. Not after the bombshell statement Gandhi had issued yesterday evening, the statement P.K. heard of for the first time when he read the newspapers with his bed tea this morning. The humiliation of not having been consulted first was almost as hard to take as the insane idea itself—as though any modern nation could exist without political parties! No, right now Bapu was the last person in the world he wanted to see. If he would only play his saintly role as all other ascetics did, in silence! Why did he have to keep shooting off his mouth, continually erupting like a volcano, innocently pretending that he simply spoke as a private person, as any other citizen had a right to speak, as a weaver and a farmer. Oh, that was magnificent—weaver and farmer he calls himself, P.K. thought, nothing more! He marvelled at the man's deceptive simplicity, his naïve ingenuity, his incredible ability to manipulate the hearts and minds and actions of hundreds of millions of people by a word, a gesture, a slogan, a crackpot idea! Yet he denied he had any power or influence, just talked off the top of his head as though what he said today would not appear as the lead article of every newspaper tomorrow! It was exasperating, infuriating! Only this morning P.K. had decided that from now on the best way to handle him was to leave him alone, ignore him entirely, pretend he did not exist, and pray he would either decide to shut up by himself, or else that enough men of sound common sense would realize he was getting senile, and eventually whatever he said would be forgotten, and they could get on with the job of tackling their real, and urgent, problems. Now if he went running over there, what would the reporters write? He could visualize the banner headlines, P.K. SEEKS MAHATMA'S ADVICE! BIG TWO CONFER AT GUPTA HOUSE! Just thinking of it made him wince.

"Look here, Das, we can't keep bothering him every day with these alarming reports. You know how old he is. We don't want to frighten him into having a heart attack. My God, that would be a national calamity!"

Gopal could not speak, because he simply refused to believe what he was thinking, and yet he was afraid that if he spoke he might betray that horrible thought.

"Of course you understand what I mean, don't you?" P.K. continued rapidly, because he did not like the way this police puppy kept staring at him, he did not like it one bit. "You realize that I am thinking only of his health, which is delicate enough as is—"

"Sir, it is twelve-thirty," Gopal said, rising. "If you refuse to accompany me, I'll have to go there alone."

"Did I say I wouldn't accompany you?"

"No, sir, you didn't, but it's getting late."

P.K. did not like to be reminded constantly of the time. Couldn't Das see that he had a watch of his own strapped to each wrist? Would it be possible to go there without being observed by the reporters? He no sooner thought of it than he dismissed the idea as fantastic. He could not lie down without having someone note it any more. If he felt like taking a drive through the city or a walk along the river it was news. Fat chance of driving to Gupta House unobserved!

"But if you're so sure it will be tonight, why can't you fill the garden with your agents, and line his walk with them? Why must we trouble him with these details?"

Gopal shook his head wearily. His deep-sunk, black-ringed eyes looked their forty years, though nothing else about him did. He clutched the worn leather case with his right hand—a zippered paper container or old book bag it looked like, held carelessly under his left armpit, the way a student might carry his notes or textbooks.

"If Bapu insists on holding the meeting," he explained slowly, more from exhaustion than patience this time, "he will also insist on leaving it open to anyone who takes the trouble to attend. That means three to five hundred judging from past attendance this month. Even if I had fifty men to deploy—and I don't have twenty-five—I couldn't guarantee his security in that garden. Even if he lets us flank him with two men front and rear, that won't make him bulletproof, P.K., and I expect that tonight they'll try bullets, since they missed with the bomb. Now will you come?"

P.K. took a deep breath, strode back to his desk, and stood leaning upon the buzzer with his closed fist, his bricklike jaw clenched firmly as he kept watching the smug face of the acting superintendent. I'll have your job for this, if it's the last thing I do, he swore silently.

The secretary entered the room so swiftly that he almost dropped the silver platter piled high with mangoes, oranges, and bananas.

"My car, Ramu! Have it waiting for me at the back door."

"Right now, sir?"

"Of course right now!"

"But you have an appointment with the Minister of Agriculture in five minutes here in the office, sir!"

"Cancel it! And take that stupid fruit tray out of my sight!"

Flags flapping over its front fenders, the Bentley slid like a padded panther past the sentry box guarding the precinct of Parliament House. The soldiers flanking the gate snapped to attention and smartly presented arms, but P.K. did not even glance at them. He was busy adjusting the white hand-spun cotton cap squarely on top of his massive head, smoothing down his black hair in the back once the cap was in place. He wore a plain white achkan, and had hooked the stiff collar closed before leaving his office. His thick neck was still unaccustomed to the collar, and whenever he ate he would open it, but now he was on display again. They circled the Viceroy's mansion, and turned down the broad boulevard, which still retained the name of Kingsway. Midway along its regal path rose the triumphal arch commemorating the victory of British arms in the First World War. The landmarks of the era of colonial rule which had ended less than six months ago were still very much apparent. Few things changed overnight, and to P.K. it seemed little longer since British Imperial sovereignty was transferred to the newly created Dominions of India and Pakistan. One long night of feverish anxiety and desperate labor for all the Messrs. Agitators who now found themselves wearing the weighty caps of Administrators. Just when they had almost given up hope that it would happen in this lifetime—the roaring lion timidly, suddenly backed away. But with freedom came partition. No sooner were boundary lines drawn than millions began crossing

[42]

them, Hindus and Sikhs fleeing from Muslim Pakistan, Muslims racing toward it. P.K. glanced through his window to the west. There just a few hundred miles away was the Nation that had never existed before. He shuddered inwardly at the thought of those few hundred miles he knew so well, flat alluvial plain hardly broken with a single hill, the few there were gently sloping enough to move an armored division over, a natural super-highway, which for the past three thousand years had provided invading armies with such easy access to Delhi. He stared at the clear, azure sky over the treetops to the west as though half expecting to see the smoke of their artillery, the banners of their infantry, the glistening wings of their air force. He knew their internal problems were as debilitating as his own nation's, yet instead of consoling him it only made his fears seem more probable, since what simpler way was there to solve internal disorder than to invade a hated neighbor? But the puffy white cushions in the sky were mere harmless clouds. Not a plane was in sight. He turned to look out the other side, but Das's face ruined the view for him there, so he decided to look at the neck of his aged chauffeur, visible through the glass partition.

It was more than a mile from P.K.'s office to Gupta House, the private residence of C. H. Gupta, where Bapu lived whenever he stayed in the capital. Not that he wasn't offered ample quarters in Parliament House, in the Viceroy's mansion, or in any one of the complex of public buildings where all of them lived, where it was so easy for them to see one another, where high gates, a battalion of crack riflemen, and an army of plainclothes police afforded perfect security. Such quarters were not only offered, he was begged to accept them. "But Gupta is my friend," he always answered. "He would feel slighted if I did not stay with him." What could be done with such a man?

The soft-rolling vehicle turned up a side street, past the new temple on the palm-fringed road, along the low shrubbery of the garden, an imperfect floral wall broken in a dozen places by the pilgrims who let themselves in and out of the meetings through these convenient short cuts. Just the sight of that hedge made Das shudder. How do you secure a garden like that one? They nosed into the driveway, by a gatehouse beside which two unarmed, barefoot servants were squatting and arguing with each other so busily that they failed to notice the car till it was practically past them, and then only half-heartedly got to their feet. An alert guard, Gopal thought bitterly!

The chauffeur had run around the rear of the car and opened the door before Mr. Gupta's porch servant had started down the low flight of steps. Gopal waited for P.K. to squeeze past him, then emerged into the blanket of heat, which hung with the silence of the place like a shroud of impending doom dropped from heaven itself.

The reporters were at them even before the front door could be shut. A statement, P.K.? Any statement. Say something, it didn't matter what. From such lips the most inane remark about the weather was news! Was he smiling, frowning, scowling, the ones in the rear asked the more fortunate bloodhounds up front. What did he say? What? "No statement." What? "He said he has no statement to make!" Ah, no statement! What do you suppose that means? It's obviously a top crucial visit if he says nothing about it! Yes, yes, big news!

The pack's yelping was smothered by the closing portals of the spacious library retreat, where their host stepped forward to greet them. He was a small, elderly man, a skirt of silver hair ringing his otherwise bald brown head. He wore a simple collarless shirt of white hand-spun, loose-hanging dhoti to match, and open-toed slippers. No jewels, no ostentation, no pretense about him. Those who did not know he was one of the world's wealthiest individuals would never have guessed it from looking at him.

"Welcome to my humble home, gentlemen," he said, gracefully raising his clasped hands before his face as he greeted them. "You should have called to let me know you were coming. I would have waited outside on the porch for you."

"This came up suddenly," P.K. explained, perfunctorily returning the greeting, dropping his own hands after they had risen little above his midsection. "Didn't know I would be here myself ten minutes ago."

"Of course, I understand. You wish to see Bapu?"

"Unless he's sleeping—or eating," P.K. answered.

"No, no, he has given up the midday meal entirely," Mr. Gupta explained, sounding more like a private nurse than his nation's foremost industrial capitalist. "He says it makes him feel better if he eats less during the warmer hours of the day."

"Oh, is that a fact?" P.K. responded, with apparently genuine interest in this latest of the great man's dietetic experiments. Gopal noted that he did not expound his own contradictory theory about food to Mr. Gupta, and what was more startling perhaps, that he even moderated his tone of voice, almost matching the polite softness of Gupta's speech.

[44]

"Yes, I have tried it myself now, and do find it quite salubrious," the other replied.

"Well, I shall have to look into it," P.K. said.

"But I do not mean to detain you, gentlemen, for I can imagine how busy you both are," he said, with a separate nod toward Das. "If you will be so kind as to follow me please."

He personally led them through the vast establishment, simple, yet revealing in an *objet* here, a silk screen there, a painting, a chair— none of them arranged for effect as in a museum but all museum pieces—something of the financial status of their owner. They were only the faintest clues, however, for all of them were products of an era of Gupta art-collecting long since past, dying in fact with his wife almost twenty years ago. C.H. himself took no interest in the things money could buy, never even noticing them, it appeared, as he moved softly and humbly, head lowered, through one precious chamber after another. Finally they came to a small room at the very rear of the house. Mr. Gupta removed his slippers, leaving them outside that room before he crossed its threshold. P.K. and Gopal did likewise.

He was seated on the bare floor inside, the rimless glasses perched midway along his prominent nose, his torso covered with a rough shawl of cotton spun and woven by his own hands, the bald head bent in concentration on the small wooden spinning frame, which lay on the floor beside him. His right hand turned the flat wheel steadily, his left held the raw cotton ball up over his head, and between the two was the fine line of thread he made so expertly. He steadied the forward end of his compact wheel frame with the big toe of one foot, keeping the other foot tucked under his loincloth. He had made that himself too.

"Bapuji, there are guests to see you," Mr. Gupta announced softly, reverently keeping his hands folded and bowing quite low as he spoke.

"Gupta, do not bend over me as though I were an image of stone in a temple," Bapu said, continuing to spin with the steady even rhythm so essential to the production of a good thread. "Come sit here beside me, and see how well this little machine does."

"I see it does very nicely, Bapuji," his old comrade remarked, sitting down on the floor.

"I will give it to you, if you will make use of it," he said, the broad, toothless grin so childlike and endearing that one could not help smiling in response.

"No, no, it would be wasted on me. It seems I can never find time for spinning."

[45]

"But if everyone of us would spin one hour a day," Bapu explained, as though all of them, all the world in fact, had not heard him say it a thousand times before, "then there would be no shortage of clothing in our country. No one would have to do without."

"Namaste, Mahatmaji," P.K. interrupted, stepping closer, as if anyone could have missed seeing his enormous body from ten times the distance. From the turn their dialogue was taking, however, he feared that the cotton mill industrialist and the hand-spinner were about to start a debate on the relative merits of machine-made cloth and homespun or cottage industry goods. "Mr. Das and I have come to see you on most urgent business, Mahatmaji."

The smile did not fade from the gentle face, as the eyes peered impishly over the glasses now, first at the massive man, then at his boyish attendant. He nodded his mute greeting, but still continued to spin.

"Mr. Das, as you know, Mahatmaji, is our acting superintendent—"

"Perhaps I should close the door first," Gopal suggested.

"Do not bother," Bapu said. "It will only make the room uncomfortably warm."

"What we have to say is quite confidential, sir," Gopal explained.

"I will leave you alone then," Mr. Gupta said, starting to rise.

"Stay, Gupta, I have no secrets from you, my friend."

"Naturally," P.K. added, "Das did not mean that we wanted you to leave, C.H. We all trust you as much as ourselves, I assure you."

"You are both much too kind," the self-effacing host whispered, settling back. He knew, of course, as well as they did, that the Independence Movement, the Party, the Nation, were as heavily indebted to his pocketbook as to their labors and talents.

"The trouble is, Mahatmaji, if we leave the door open someone may hear us from the hall, you see." P.K. spoke to him slowly and elaborately as if he were hard of hearing, or rather dull.

"Close it if you like," the old man conceded. "I myself have no secrets."

"Thank you, Mahatmaji," P.K. said, rubbing his hands together nervously till the door was secured. "I do not have to preface what we are about to ask of you with any explanation of how all of us feel about you, of how precious you are, not only to us personally, but to the entire nation, in fact to the whole world. You are our guru, our master, our philosopher, and treasured guide. We would all be lost without you, for we think of ourselves as your humble servants—"

"Then why do you never listen to me, Shankaracharyarao?"

[46]

P.K. moistened his lips, and nervously ran one finger under the cutting edge of his closed collar.

"Believe me, Mahatmaji, whenever it is humanly possible we listen."

"Good. Then after you leave here why not call together your Working Committee, and propose to them the dissolution of the Congress Party? As general secretary your recommendation would carry much weight, surely more than that of a private person like myself." Now he turned to Gupta, inquiring in the most naïve of tones, "Why should we let ourselves become divided by politics, after all, now that we are a free nation? We are plagued by too many divisions already."

P.K. felt his collar choking him. He unhinged it, opening the top button of his achkan in the same frenzied motion. He had heard it directly now from the lips which had issued that maniacal statement he read in his morning papers. His collar was wide open, yet he still felt himself choking.

"Mahatmaji, your suggestion is impossible! We all appreciate your advice, but I did not come here to discuss this matter. Please, let us say no more of it!"

The smile faded from the wrinkled, toothless face. The old man jerked at his wheel too swiftly, breaking the thread. He deftly repaired it with the fingers of one hand, and continued his spinning, saying nothing now.

Gopal Das, sensing it had been a mistake to ask P.K. to accompany him, heard himself saying suddenly, "Bapu, your life is in danger." Then he stopped, because that brought those infinitely gentle, tenderly compassionate eyes directly into focus upon his own, and he felt boorish, unworthy somehow, inept, afraid of having spoken too harshly, too overtly, of having frightened him perhaps, the way a forest fire would frighten a fawn.

"But it has always been, my child," he said.

"Not this way," Gopal continued, driven to say more not so much from his deep sense of duty as from a deeper sense of love. "There is a plot to assassinate you tonight. We are positive of it. They are fanatics, well-organized, determined, desperate men. They plan to kill you this evening in the garden during your prayer meeting!"

"God forbid," Mr. Gupta uttered, so shocked by the news he had been unable to control himself. Visibly trembling, he touched his fingers to his mouth.

"No, no, my friend, you must not be afraid," Bapu said, putting down his cotton, and touching Gupta's shoulder with his hand. "Do not tremble so. We must forget fear."

"I apologize for being so blunt," Gopal said, directing his remarks to both old men now, "but there is very little time."

"That is why I personally have come here," P.K. added.

"Of course, and there is no need to apologize," Bapu told them. "It is I who must thank you for troubling yourselves."

"Don't mention it," P.K. said, grandly. "We consider your safety our highest duty. As soon as Das told me of the plot, I said, 'Come along, we shall warn Mahatmaji at once!'"

"What will we do?" Mr. Gupta asked faintly. "How can we stop them? Who are they? Why should anyone want to—to destroy *him?*"

"They are the same people who threw the bomb," Gopal explained. "They belong to the Poona Society of Nation Saviors—"

"Oh yes, yes, I know them, the beasts," Gupta whispered between clenched teeth.

"But why do you call them 'beasts,' my friend?" Bapu asked. "They are our brothers, remember."

"No, if they can think of killing you, they are no better than the wolf and the jackal!"

"They are no better than Pakistanis!" P.K. shouted.

Bapu flattened his palms to his ears, his face contorted in pain. "I will not listen to such talk," he said, only lowering his hands when they had fallen silent. "Forgive me, my friends, but I cannot stand to hear my brothers blasphemed, neither my Pakistani brothers, nor my Indian brethren. Their souls are as imperishable as ours. They too have been touched by God. If they wish to destroy me it is for my sins, not for their own."

"What are you saying, Bapuji?" Gupta asked. "It is no time for talking in riddles."

P.K. let his hands fall against his sides with an exasperated motion of futility, and turned his back to them. Gopal stared at the old man incredulously, trying his best to understand.

"But where is the riddle?" Bapu asked. "Do you not believe in the law of karma, my friend?"

"Certainly I believe in karma," Gupta said, for which devout Hindu did not? "What has one thing to do with the other, Bapuji?"

"Everything in the world," Bapu said, smiling, for he was a born teacher and loved to make simple what others seemed to find so complex. "What is the law of karma, tell me, other than that we are

[48]

what we deserve to be by virtue of what we have been and done in our past?"

"Well, of course, we all know that," Gupta said impatiently.

"Yes, you see, all of you understand, and that is why I say if someone wishes to kill me it is not his fault, but my own, for it is my own former sin which bears such terrible fruit. If I am killed violently it is because I have failed . . ." He blinked his gentle eyes several times, and tugged thoughtfully at his drooping lower lip. "I have come to think more often in the past few months of how grievously I have failed."

"Must you start that again?" P.K. asked angrily.

"So many innocents slaughtered by the partition," the old man intoned, more to himself it seemed than to any of them. "Still no peace in sight, no homes for the immigrants—"

"Were we to blame for partition, Mahatmaji? We tried to hold out till the last possible moment! Didn't we? What has happened to your memory? It was their fault, the children of Allah, those greedy Muslims, and the British who always practiced divide and rule! What could we do? And who started the war in Kashmir? Were we the aggressors who raped and plundered, coming down from the hills and desecrating our sacred motherland? Why must you torture yourself and all of us with your impossible conscience?"

"I blame no one, Shankaracharyarao," he said softly. "I only say what I feel."

"You are too hard on yourself, Bapuji," Gupta told him. "You have done more than any human being could possibly have been expected to do."

"No, I have failed, and if I am killed it will be the reward I deserve." He picked up his cotton again, and turned the wheel slowly.

"C.H., what is the use of speaking to him?" P.K. asked in utter exasperation.

"Bapu," Gopal said, squatting to his haunches so that he could see every careworn line, and every glistening bead of sweat on that face so singularly ugly that somehow it appeared beautiful, the way a gnarled tree or a weatherworn rock or an unkempt field left to cover itself with wild growth was endowed with beauty by virtue of its genuine quality, its totally true and pure character, the essence of its distinctiveness, its unadorned Self. "Please call off your prayer meeting tonight."

"But how can I? My friends have already started to come. It is a long walk for many of them."

[49]

"We will notify them," Gopal said. "I personally will see to it that they are all notified, and I will have them driven back to their homes if they are tired."

"Most of them do not have homes as yet."

"We will drive them back to the camps if they are immigrants."

"Why should you go to so much trouble and expense? We are not a rich nation that we can afford such luxuries."

"Bapu, we can less afford to be without you," Gopal answered.

"You have a good heart, my child, but you are mistaken if you think my life is worth any more than the life of the meanest peasant or sweeper servant. If you have so much money to spend, please spend it on houses for the millions who live in the fields under the sky."

"I am not authorized to spend it on them, Bapu, but it is my job to assure your safety."

"Why should a bright young man like yourself be wasted on such a job? God watches over us."

Gopal clenched his leather bag till the blood drained from his knuckles. He had to convince this man somehow, though he was no match for him in such disputation, and yet—

"What is that you clutch so tightly, my child?"

"This case?"

"Yes, why have you held it so long? It must be a heavy burden. Give it to me, I will put it aside for you."

"No, that is all right," Gopal said, rising quickly, so that the case was beyond his saintly reach.

"What do you keep inside it?" Bapu asked.

"Just a few of my things—nothing important."

"From the way you hold onto it one would think you had your most precious possessions there. Tell me, for you know how curious old men can be, what is inside?"

"My gun," Gopal whispered, unable to meet the kindly eyes any longer, holding his tongue with his teeth.

"Mahatmaji, Das is our acting superintendent of police. He must carry a gun," P.K. explained, still speaking to him as to the simpleminded.

"But if no one carried a gun, Shankaracharyarao, then no one would have to fear being killed by his own brother, and surely as a Brahman you have learned that nonviolence is our highest religion."

"I have learned it too, Bapu," Gopal said, his face burning with the shame of this great man's unspoken reprimand, "but I was born and raised in Bhopal and when I was a small boy I watched the bandits come out of the hills to our village, Bapu, and my father who was the headman and a saintly man, not as saintly as you, but a man who had never raised his hand in anger to any of us and who had done no wrong in his lifetime and committed no crime or sin that any of us could see, my father went to meet those bandits with his hands folded in a greeting of prayer, and he too had said, 'Ahinsa paramo Dharma ahe,' and as he said those sacred words they filled his body with their bullets and he was dead before any of us could reach him." Gopal bit his tongue hard when he had finished, and turned aside. "Excuse me," he whispered, quickly, "I am overtired, I'm afraid. I lost control of myself."

"Never mind," P.K. said, "we are all getting short-tempered now, and wasting valuable time. I must be at the Viceroy's reception at two, and I don't like to think of how many people are waiting in my office by now. Mahatmaji, you are no child, so we cannot scold you. We cannot order you about. For your own sake, and for your motherland, will you listen and do as we ask, or will you persist in your stubbornness?"

"Call it off," Gupta said. "I beg of you, Bapuji, do not hold the meeting tonight."

He stopped spinning, and sat hunched over, listening for the other voice, the one which had come to him before, never to tell him what he should do, but only to warn him against certain actions. His "inner voice" he called it, though he sensed that it did not just come from inside himself. He listened very carefully, for sometimes it was so faint that he could hardly understand, but then if he waited it came back again. Nothing. He shook his head slowly, for it said nothing.

"Do not fear, my dear friends," he said at last. "Love will conquer hate. Trust in love, it will protect all of us. It is truth. It is God. Do not fear for me."

"All right, we have done our duty," P.K. said, sighing deeply, as though in relief.

"If you won't call it off," Gopal hastily injected, seeing that there was no moving him, "at least permit me to walk out in front of you with another man, and to place two others directly behind you."

"But my granddaughters walk with me," Bapu said, mildly. "They are my crutches, eh, Gupta?"

"Yes, yes," the old industrialist said, suddenly rubbing at his nose with the sleeve of his shirt, unable to stop blinking his eyes.

"Then allow us to walk in front of them," Gopal added, doggedly.

"But you will only block me off from my friends' vision, and sometimes I think many of them come simply to have a good look at this funny face."

It was of course true, Gopal knew, for seeing the god was enough for most of them. They came to do their darshana. It mattered little if they heard what was said, or understood what they heard.

"Then let me walk behind you," Gopal tried as a last-ditch effort at maintaining some shabby semblance of security.

"You are welcome to do so, if you will leave your case in the house," Bapu told him.

"I would be of no use to you without my case."

"Then it is not you, but the gun, which would walk with me, my child, and I have dedicated my life to war against the gun up until now. I will not try to save my life by surrendering to the gun this late in my day."

They bowed their farewell greetings. He was spinning again before they had all left the room. They could hear the faint music of his wheel growing softer as they retraced their steps along the hall, and started back through the long house.

Driving past the garden, Gopal Das saw that the first of them had already arrived. Rag covered they came, walking all the way, some ten, some twenty or thirty miles, starting before dawn so that they would be here when he emerged from the temple, for any place in which he lived was holy ground to them, and no journey was too long, no trial too arduous, if at the end of it they could but see his face, touch his toe, or hear his voice. The homeless and illiterate, the barefoot and diseased, the strange wild-haired ones, their faces covered with ash in their robes of saffron or loincloth nakedness, mothers carrying their babes, peasants with their rag turbans all but obscuring their sunbaked faces, old and young, vigorous and frail, they came to Bapu, their "Little Father," their leader, their god. He alone was the magnet whose magic could lure them so far.

"I knew we'd be wasting our time," P.K. muttered, as he settled back in the car.

"I think I better get out here, and walk around the garden a bit before returning to my office, if you don't mind," Gopal suddenly decided.

"Do what you please," P.K. told him, signaling his driver to stop.

"Thanks for the lift," he said politely, and soon he had merged with them, with Bapu's people. He felt much better in their company, though he realized that some among them might not have come to worship.

3

Once the taxi pulled clear of the station, Natu directed his driver to turn right and then left and left again. Satisfied that no vehicle was following, he told the driver to go straight ahead—toward the new city.

"Anywhere special, Sahib?"

"Connaught Circle," he said, though the Palmyra Palms had not left his mind since reading that caption in the newspaper. But going there was impossible! It was out of the question. Even if she had come without her husband—at a big hotel like that he would be recognized immediately. Every desk clerk, probably every room boy, in the city had been alerted, shown his picture, or at least informed of his description. Perhaps Rani herself was under observation. For all their discretion, someone by now was bound to suspect. No, it would be too dangerous. He dismissed the idea of going to her as soon as it came to tempt him. Nothing remained to be said; anyway, nothing else could be. One more goodbye would not make it easier.

But why do I even think of her, he wondered angrily, scratching her name from his memory as he lit a cigarette and leaned back to stare at the passing world outside. Merely being alone with four hours to kill, that did not alter his mission in the slightest. Evasion of duty, escape from the imperative of his obligation, neither idea so much as crossed his mind. He was temporarily free, of course, and alone. Whatever happened to Apte, Natu knew he could not hope to see his friend again until four—if then. Yet there was no point worrying about Apte, since caught or free there was nothing to be done, no possible way of contacting him.

No, I must do nothing, Natu thought, but remain alive, and un-discovered, and wait for the time to pass. That was all freedom meant to him now. It seemed strange to have dedicated his life to the attain-ment of such a goal, really a Western sort of luxury, an unnatural luxury. For he was now Dinesh Narayanrao, affluent businessman, alone in the big town—perfectly free. The irony of it made him smile. There was a game they had played as children, the what-would-you-do-game, they called it. What would you do if you had all the time and money you wanted, and no one was there to order you around? Come on, Natu, you say—what would you do?

He had never really told them, because he sensed they would laugh, so he said what they all did. He would buy a big farm, he said, and a house in the city too, and a hundred fine cows, and twenty servants, and he would keep two wives, one older, more experienced woman to cook the food and run the household, and one blushing virgin of twelve. According to their religion that was not immoral as the Eng-lish missionaries tried to teach them. It was a luxury, not a sin, and if you could afford to care for two women, where was the crime in it? Wasn't it better than leaving a poor girl to starve, or worse still to live out her life without a man and babies to worry about? Baburao, as every one of his intimates knew, kept three wives. Some of the boys said they wanted a harem of fifty, but Natu suspected that would only be twenty-five times the trouble of two. But he didn't even want the two, nor the farm, nor the big house—not most of all. What he really wanted was to be an officer in the Army, but he never told them that.

The cab stopped for a light at the foot of Chandi Chawk, the Silver Market, and there beyond the maidan, filled now with the tents and

[54]

fires of refugees from Pakistan, who made the open field their home, rose the redstone battlements of the great fort Shah Jahan had built, salmon-red in the sun, the saffron, green and white of her tricolor proudly held aloft by the breeze. The moat alone was a hundred yards wide. You had to hand it to the Mughal bastards, he thought, they could build a fort. Before the light changed a jeep rolled out the path from its main gate, and swerved onto the road just ahead of them. For the fort was more than a tourist attraction. It still housed the Delhi Army command. A Sikh private drove the jeep, and ramrod-stiff at his side was a brigadier, pips gleaming from his shoulder epaulets, black baton braced under his armpit, visor cap cocked to precisely the right jaunty angle. Just the glimpse of him sent an involuntary shiver along Natu's spine. Though that was a dream long since forgotten, it always came back when he saw one of them. What would you do, Natu? I would join the Army, he thought, and become a general. . . .

The camp was several miles from their home in Poona, yet he did not mind the walk, it never tired him. He found it purely by accident, one day when his mother had sent him alone to her maternal aunt's house to see if she would give them a lime. She was a wealthy old woman and owned a big house with a yard in which there was a lime tree, and sometimes when they visited her in the summer she would give them a lime to take home as a present, and then they could all have limbupani, his favorite drink. If they went to visit her too often, though, she would act very grouchy and complain about the pains in her legs and back, and would give them nothing. But his mother said, "Natu is Maternal Aunt's favorite. If we send him to her alone she will give him a lime, watch and see!" He was seven then, and sure he could find the way, but he took the left turn instead of the right off Lakshmi Road, and because he did not see the house he went on and on until he came to the camp, and that was when he saw the general. At least he thought at the time it was a general, because he had never seen so much brass and brightness on a man's body before, on three bodies in fact, for three men were walking toward him together, laughing and joking the way soldiers do, all of them as big and beautiful as gods, and surely as strong. He was so awe-struck at the sight of them that he stepped off the pavement entirely and stood in the road as they came nearer, and then he simply watched them in naked wonder, with so much love and sheer surprise in his eyes that one of them shouted to the others,

[55]

"Well, what have we here, lads? A new recruit, eh?" That called forth a volley of laughter, so loud he was convinced they were gods, for no one he knew ever laughed like that, only softly in whispers if they laughed at all, since laughter was disrespectful, or people might think you had enjoyed some sudden good fortune.

"What's your name, lad?" the biggest of the gods asked.

"Natu," he whispered.

"There's a smart fellow for you, Gilpatrick, knows his own bloody name he does, eh what? Where's your home, Natu?"

He was too dumbfounded to tell them, too thrilled to realize that they had actually stopped to surround him, that one of them had gone down on his haunches before him and even messed up his messy hair with a godlike hand at least four times the size of his father's.

"Cute little bugger, isn't he? Lost are you, boy?"

"I think so," he managed to whisper, because by now he was sure that Maternal Grandaunt lived nowhere near here.

"Tell us where yer headed, boy. We'll point you in the proper direction."

"Why don't we adopt him, Tommy? Make 'im the bloody mascot of the Regiment. 'Ow's that for a corkin' idea now?"

"Do pipe down, blast ye," the other said, "or ye'll scare the pup. Now come on, laddy, tell us what's yer destiny."

Then he decided, though he could not articulate it yet, that it would be to follow after them for all time, to march in their gold-strewn path wherever they might lead, to wear the brass and shining leather straps they wore, to carry the short stick they carried like the scepter of a king, and be strong and brave enough to laugh out loud like a god. It was all he ever really wanted from that day till the dawn of his seventeenth birthday, when he walked to the camp for the last time. That morning after his prayers and bath he went to the kitchen to tell his mother. She was busily fanning the charcoal fire with the loose end of her dull sari, a slight, silent woman, tending as always without complaint to her limitless household chores.

"Matabai," he said, surprised at the huskiness of his own voice, for he had not felt sad or nervous, "I must be leaving you now."

Intuitively she seemed to sense his meaning. She left the fire to choke in its own sluggish gray smoke and came to peer up at his eyes.

"What does my son tell me?" she asked.

"Today I will become a soldier," he said.

She searched his eyes a long time for some indication that he was joking, but she knew him too well to misread the earnestness of his voice. At last she whispered, incredulously, "But our family has never produced soldiers."

"Yes, I know that, and I have thought of it, and for a while because of that I had decided against it, but now I know it is in my blood, Matabai, and I cannot help it. Someday I will become general, and then you will be much proud of me."

"May God forbid it," she whispered. "What are you saying, foolish child? Please do not speak of this any more."

"It will pain me if you do not approve, Matabai, but I will not change my mind, for I have made a sacred vow, and this morning I must go to the camp."

"Your father has approved of this?" she asked.

"I wanted to tell you first."

"Ah, then you have not yet asked his permission," she said, the color returning to her sudden sallow cheeks.

"I will go with his permission—or without it."

"Hush," she said, touching a stern finger to his lips. "It is sinful even to think of disobeying your father! He is our lord and master, my child. Speak with him if you must, but do not be disrespectful or God will punish your insolence."

"Do not think ill of me, Matabai. I cannot help what I do." He kissed her forehead, then had to move swiftly from her embrace, for her arms clutched firmly at his own, as though she would prevent him from going by force alone.

His father had just finished his bath and placed the sacred thread back over his right shoulder and under his left arm as Natu approached him with clasped palms. Since the death of his child bride they had not often spoken. Though his father had saved him from punishment, Natu suspected the old man never forgave him the crime of lawful lust. Not that his father had ever been a communicative man.

"I must speak with you, Dada."

"You see I have not finished dressing."

"Excuse me, but I cannot wait. I am leaving now"—he swallowed but did not allow his eyes to fall before that rigid glance—"to join the Army."

There was no visible change in his father's expression. Despite his advanced age he was still a sternly upright figure of a man, firm, though short, rigid in his bearing as in everything else, a Brahman among Brahmans, calmly confident of the primacy of his role, one of the class specially selected by the cosmic order of things to serve as a

[57]

priest of his clan, a god among men, preserver of the ritual of the sacred law, keeper of the word revealed at the dawn of all eternity to his direct ancestors and no others. He was not a wealthy priest, nor a particularly famous one, yet wealth and fame meant little to him. His major concern was with salvation. What did that have to do with wealth or fame?

"I have not finished dressing," his father repeated. "You will wait for me in the front room."

"All right," Natu said. He did not wish to argue about petty matters now.

His younger brother caught hold of him a few steps from their father's bedroom door.

"What does he say? What does he say, Natuji?"

"He is still dressing."

"Didn't you tell?"

"Yes, yes, of course, I told him!"

"Well, what does he say? Will he let you do it?"

"I have told you I will do it if he lets me or not! Stop tugging at my shirt, you fool, do you want to tear it off my back?"

"He will prevent you, Natuji."

"If that is all you have to say to me, better go outside and leave me alone!"

"Why do you yell at me, Natuji?"

"I am not yelling at you! You are the one who makes too much noise!"

"But what have I done? I am on your side."

"Yes, yes, that is a big help to me! Now what are you doing, you fool?" His brother had turned away and started biting his thumbnail.

"I will miss you, Natuji."

"Now you sound like a woman!"

"Please do not laugh at me," the boy asked.

"Listen, when I am general I will drive you all over in my carriage!"

"Will you truly? I would love that, Natuji! You must promise you will not forget to do that!"

"Balu!" his father's voice ordered. "Go fill the water jug for your mother!"

"Yes, Dada," the boy answered timidly, going out to the kitchen.

Natu was surprised to see that his father not only wore his shirt now, but had placed the red silk pagdri over his shaved scalp, and the long silk scarf around his shoulders. He even carried his walking stick with the gold top, the one his father had bequeathed to him, handed down it was said for ten generations in their family. And he wore not the open-toed chappals, but the elegant red shoes with the turned-up pointed tips.

"You wished to speak to me," his father said, leaning both hands upon the top of his walking stick set firmly before him. "What is it you wish to discuss with me?"

"I am leaving now to join the Army, Dada, and I ask for your blessing."

"There are no soldiers in my family," the old man said, as though no further statement were required of him.

"Please try to understand, Dada. I would not be happy chanting mantras at a wedding or over a funeral pyre."

"What has happiness to do with anything? It is your privilege, your duty, to serve God! As a Brahman for the families—"

"Dada, I have given much thought to my career. I know I will make a good soldier because it is what I love, and someday I will become general—"

"Silence!" Visibly shaking, the old man lifted his sturdy stick with both hands and held it threateningly over his son's head.

Natu shrank back, raising one arm in a gesture of defense to ward off the blow, which did not fall. Instead his father lowered the stick, pounding its metal-shod bottom against the stone floor.

"How dare you talk of defiling my line with military service? You are a Godse! You are my eldest son! You will inherit the duty I have been blessed with, which your great-grandfather's great-grandfather—"

"I do not wish to anger you, Dada—"

"Then say no more of such foolishness, Naturam!"

"Give me your blessing, Dada, for I must leave at once."

"I do not hear you," his father said, turning aside, the color of his face matching in its hue the blazing silk of his stiff scarlet turban with its shark's-fin-like top.

"Dada, I don't want to hurt you—"

"Save yourself the trouble of speech. I cannot hear what you say."

"Please, Dada, try to understand that I am not leaving now to spite you or to hurt you."

Yet he hesitated. He waited. He tried to move in front of his father's line of vision so that at least their eyes would meet for a parting gesture of recognition. To no avail.

"Will you not—wish me luck, Dada?"

No, not even that, not so much as a single kind word!

[59]

"Burrai, Dada," he said at last, leaving the screen door to slam itself shut as he hurried away at a run.

The old man waited stiffly without moving. Then his wife came to stand at his side, weeping and wailing. "Has he really gone? Oh, my baby, my Natu!"

"Gone?" the old man repeated numbly. "Gone where?" Then he fell down.

Natu knew every banyan tree along the way, every roadside shrine, he even knew the number of steps it would take. The sun was just starting to rise, but he could have found the way in total darkness. The tinkling bells of buffaloes coming in for their milking sounded like a welcoming bugle to his ears.

It was his favorite hour of day, this interval between the first light and the sun's burning emergence over the purple hills, the coolest, sweetest hour of all. The crescent moon still reigned above and the fragrant dew crowned each blade of grass along his way, while curling up over the edges of every house roof were the dancing veils of smoke pouring forth from the kitchen hearths, like the arms of ten thousand nymphs of the night running away before the sun could capture or destroy them. Running as he ran from the house which tried to stifle his soul, and crush his spirit, to the freedom and glory of a world his fathers had never dreamed of, to the adventure of travel to the far corners of the earth, to the comradeship of the camp, the thrill of battle and surging blood, the stirring music of the bagpipes and the band. For more than a year he had counted the days, often wondering if they would ever pass, those torpid intolerable days of endless nothingness, those replicas of yesterday's drab routine whose promise for tomorrow was always the same sorry story. Desire to escape had become so intense he could taste every morsel of it, till even sleep had abandoned him and the nights which had once been a refuge of oblivion became longer than the days. Yet now it was over.

Two Gurkhas guarded the gate, tough tiny men of the North, with their flat Mongoloid faces and narrow eyes. They watched him suspiciously as he approached, perspiring from the long run.

"I have come to enlist," he announced.

They did not appear to understand English, so he repeated it in Marathi, but their faces remained immobile as before. They are stupid, primitive people, he thought, and wondered why the British relied so heavily upon them in the Army.

"I must go inside to see officer sahib," he said, pointing toward the green wooden bungalow beyond the barbed-wire fence, but as he stepped forward they each jerked an arm out stiff, blocking his path with their rifles which crossed at their bayoneted tops. It was done so swiftly that he scarcely had time to draw his body back from the glistening steel blades.

"What's wrong with you?" he shouted. "Are you trying to kill me?"

But they told him nothing, so he decided to wait for one of his friends to come along. He had many friends in the Brigade by now, mostly Sikhs and Punjabis, even a few English, though they were usually too busy to stop for a chat. The Gurkhas had always been suspicious and sullen. When he was general, he decided, he would have no Gurkhas in his army.

"Sardarji," he shouted, recognizing one of the Sikh soldiers he had talked with before, walking past beyond the fence. "Tell them to let me through, Sardarji, I want to enlist! It is finally my birthday!"

"Oh, good! First class! But it is too early. The recruiting office does not open before ten!"

"Ten o'clock? Why so late?"

"Who am I to say?"

"Can I not see the officer before then?"

"How is it possible?" he asked with a shrug, and walked on.

Natu squinted at the sun. It was no later than seven, possibly seven-thirty. There were no coffee shops in the camp area where you could just sit around without ordering something. There was nothing to do but wait at the curb, and count the minutes now as he had counted days before. No hours had ever seemed longer.

The one good thing about waiting was that before ten the Gurkhas had been relieved by tall, wide-eyed, and friendly guards, who not only understood him, but were willing to answer his questions as long as no officers were in sight. They told him about their African campaigns in the World War, about the sea whose color was wine, and women whose breasts were both satin and stone at the same time, and about heroes who singlehanded destroyed entire companies of the enemy. There was no limit to the wonders they had known, for they were soldiers. Then one of them said, "Come along, I will take you to the officer sahib."

The fan turned slowly inside the green bungalow and Natu tried to make the waiting time pass by blinking his eyes enough to count the revolutions. Then he tried to estimate the numbers of hairs on the burly officer's bare arms, and the number of papers piled so high on his desk. He was a most busy officer Natu could see, and he did not become angry waiting, but only felt a sudden dryness in his throat,

[61]

and a wetness in his palms. He stood very straight and firm, the way he had practiced standing at attention, though no one seemed to notice him in the muggy low bungalow. Finally the officer stared at him flatly and asked in a dry nasal tone, "What have we here?"

He smiled, then quickly erased it from his countenance, and saluted as he had often practiced when alone in his room. The officer neither smiled nor returned his salute.

"I have come to enlist," Natu said huskily, keeping his fingers up against his forehead, though his arm had begun to shake.

"Never mind the salute, if that's what it's supposed to be. We don't salute uncovered, and you certainly don't at this point. Step closer here! Let's have a look at you!"

"I'm sorry, sir, yessir," he said, wishing his knees would stop wobbling.

"Age?"

"Seventeen today, sir."

"What year were you born?" came the instantaneous reply, for the officer looked as though he did not believe it.

For the life of him Natu could not remember.

"Speak up!"

Desperately he had begun counting years backwards, and instead of getting firmer his knees seemed to melt entirely, then he said the year, and felt like a total idiot.

"Name?" And after he heard it, the officer knit his bushy brows till they closed in a firm line over his long nose. "What caste is that?"

"Chitpavan Brahman," Natu proudly announced. There were no higher castes in the country. His knees felt firmer suddenly.

"Sorry," the officer barked, "no openings." He lifted a file from the top of a large stack of papers and started studying it.

At first Natu thought it had been another question which he missed hearing. He waited respectfully, apprehensively, trying not to make himself appear so stupid. He hoped the officer would ask him the year of his birth again. How could he have forgotten that? But the officer continued studying the file as though he were not there, then set it on top of another stack and took down the next file.

"Well, what is it now?" the flat nasal voice asked, those pale blue eyes peering through him.

Natu wanted to smile, but those eyes were too cold, and they froze the smile in his mind before it could reach his mouth.

"Why do you keep standing there?" the officer asked.

He did not understand. An icy numbness spread across his forehead sending a cold wave of fear through his insides. If only he could see one of his friends, but everyone in this room was a total stranger to him, and the tall bearded Sikh guard was moving toward him for some reason he could not understand.

"I want to enlist," he said.

"Are you hard of hearing?" the nasal voice asked. "I told you there's no room."

"But surely somewhere in such a huge army—"

"No, not for your kind," the officer said, his grin revealing two front teeth capped with gold, a mask more hideous than that of Kali, Goddess of Death, with her tongue drenched in blood and her necklace of skulls. "We learned in the Mutiny what Sepoy Brahmans do with our guns, boy! There's not one of you ain't born with a knife in your heart waiting to bury it in one of us! Now get out of here."

"I have come to enlist," Natu repeated, because he could not believe this officer truly meant what he said.

Now the officer was standing, and the Sikh guard who told him to do what Sahib said was gently nudging him toward the door. Still he did not understand that his interview was ended.

"Leave me alone," he shouted at the guard, rushing back to the desk. "I must join the Army! Today I am old enough! I am fit, you will see! Give me your test!"

"Put him out," the officer ordered dryly.

"Let go of me! Stop it!" His feet kicked out desperately for the substance of the floor which was no longer beneath them. His arms burned in two viselike grips which stopped the flow of blood through his fingers. Suddenly the sun pierced his eyes, and still he could find nothing solid against which to brace his feet. Then his back smashed against the concrete road, and he lay as though paralyzed, facing the fragmented sun pouring down through the gold mohur leaves. He felt no bruises at first, only the frigid numbness and the burning shame. . . .

The cab passed under the arched portal of the Old City Gate. Natu flicked his cigarette butt out the window, and as though scratching his stomach felt for the comforting firmness of his gun.

Beyond the gate a vista of open plain suddenly appeared as if they had stepped from a house door onto a long rolling lawn. Flecked sparsely with buildings and ruins of stone the approach to New Delhi presented a dramatic visual change from the cluttered confinement and bustle of the old city, providing a panoramic image of the region's hoary heritage, of a succession of kingdoms founded to flourish and die here on the baked red earth where only decaying monuments mutely testified to dreams and hopes, to aspirations and actions long since swallowed by the sandstorms blowing up from the Thar. Far above the ruins vultures circled slowly, lured by the campfires of the refugees who made their homes in and around every tomb of the past, clinging to these monuments like ghosts in the graveyard of history. From the comfortable distance of his cab, Natu watched the aimless wandering of their skeletal, emaciated frames, searching in the stone rubble for something to eat, scratching the sand for a dry root, competing with the scavenger dogs and the screeching agile monkeys and rib-bellied cows too sacred to consume. I will avenge you, my brothers, he thought. I will destroy the monster who gave your lands and your homes to the Muslim tiger, and who still wants to give more. Yes, he actually wanted to give them more! "It is unworthy of a great nation," he had said, daring to use the word *unworthy*, "to fail to fulfill her promises and pay her debts to her neighbor in their entirety."

We shall pay them, Natu thought, never fear, my brothers, we shall pay them! In proper currency, in the specie they deserve, we shall pay them for every Hindu mother raped, for every Hindu baby whose head they smashed, for every Hindu home they defiled with their beef-stained hands, for every Hindu God they shattered since they first came to plunder our sacred soil a thousand years ago, for every inch of the motherland they have robbed from us, one day we shall pay them back. But first we must liberate ourselves of him, the cursed incarnation of Aurangzeb, of Mohammed, and their blood-hungry demon God. First we must cleanse our soil of that grocer's son.

"Which hotel, Sahib?" the driver asked.

"Just take me to the Circle."

"I have good hotel for you, very cheap, Sahib."

"No, no, I have business to care for first."

"If Sahib wants woman, that can be arranged," the enterprising driver persisted. "Very nice young lady, Sahib, very cheap."

"So you have many occupations," Natu said, wondering if another of them was to work for the police.

"Yes, sure, Sahib!" he replied proudly.

"Not interested," Natu told him.

"Nice clean Punjabi ladies, Sahib?"

"I said no," yet unwittingly his eyes focused on the ankles barely revealed under the trimmed border of a sari moving slowly across the street in front of the stopped cab. The light changed and Natu noticed two girls walking in the shade of the tree-lined boulevard of Kingsway as they drove on. Their brown midriffs alone were exposed, the rest alluringly hidden under the sari's loose drape. It was a lovely garment, but he knew how deceptive it could be, concealing a multitude of sins, from obesity to knock knees, all deftly disguised by the billowing flow of the sari's shimmering cloth. Suddenly he realized that almost everywhere he looked there were women alone. Not just girls or their grandmothers, but willowy women in the full bloom of life, with luxurious braids of black hair reaching to the small of their backs, simply strolling the streets unescorted. How many were refugees from the Punjab, walking this way in search of money rather than digging among the ruins for discarded food or inedible roots?

His pulse quickened. There was something of Rani about each of them, some characteristic so distinctive of her, an arched brow, a hand gesture, a way of walking, the angle at which a head was tilted. He knew every mannerism, every trait, every peculiarity of hers. They were all indelibly carved on his consciousness. He could no more easily forget her than he could stop breathing. In his deepest sleep she was there. "We are one person," she had told him once, only then he had not believed it really.

"You can stop here," Natu ordered the driver. The cab veered to the curb beside an overhanging movie marquee on the Circle. The Sikh jumped out, and placed his bed roll on the sidewalk for him. Natu paid the fare, and two annas extra.

"What can I buy with two annas today, Sahib?" the driver asked with a scowl.

"Give it back then," Natu said. "I will buy something!"

The Sikh pocketed the coin, got back inside his small vehicle, and rode away. Natu hurried from the glare of the sidewalk to the shade under the arcade, which swarmed at practically any time of day or night with droves of tourists, office workers, and peddlers hawking their wares. No sooner had he joined the peripatetic current of midday shoppers and aimless idlers, than he congratulated himself on the wisdom of his choice of a hideaway. It was less crowded than the station or Chandi Chawk, yet certainly safer than the former, and much closer to his destination than the latter. He could, in fact, walk to the garden from here, and until then he was just another fish in the cosmopolitan ocean of the new city's busiest market and entertainment place. Peddlers adorned the base of each arcade stanchion with chaotic displays of their wares, ranging from bolt silk to hairpins, from magazine racks to black market cigarettes imported from Turkey, England, and America. Each of them called to him as he passed, some reaching out to practically stuff their merchandise into his arms—Look, take it, try it, Sahib! Buy from me, I have the cheapest, the best—you say what you will pay! The cigarette venders alone were independent, seated calmly beside their treasure trove of cartons of Chesterfields, Lucky Strikes, Camels, and Players No. 3. They knew the scarcity of their commodities here, and the foreigners spoiled them, paying whatever outrageous price they asked. Some merchants found no room for a permanent display, so they circulated with the crowd, dragging a box under one arm, holding up a ballpoint pen in the other, or a package of razor blades, or some chewing gum. Along the inner wall of the arcade were the elegant shops, windows replete with carved and polished statues of ivory, with hammered-brass trays, long-snouted pitchers, and bowls from Rajasthan, with the embroidered white shawls of Kashmir, gold-heavy saris from Benares, silver-trimmed hookas from Afghanistan, and thick matted rugs from Iran, displayed in such lush profusion that instead of rare luxuries they almost seemed commonplace items, yet their owners, supremely conscious of their princely status in the world of commercial enterprise, remained at a dignified distance from their doors, patiently seated far within the recesses of their shops like spiders who had woven well and could wait secure at the center of their magnificent webs. Elegant restaurants lured with their olfactory displays, wafting curry and condiment odors from exhaust fans that rattled over their entrances. There were sweets and pastry shops as well, and the ubiquitous coffee shop. Thanks to governmental subsidy, the latter had become a national institution. Natu passed one halfway round the Circle, and decided it might be a good idea to sit down.

A cloud of smoke hung over the crowded tables, and at first he thought there were no empty seats in the large room, but a waiter directed him reassuringly toward the rear, and as he pushed his way back the occupants of one table rose to leave. They were all men, mostly in open-collared European-style shirts, though a few were loyal to the collarless homespun. Those who wore tailored shirts, however, let the tails hang loose over their khaki shorts or dhotis. The only women in the room were Westerners accompanied by escorts with ties and light jackets. Most of the loiterers were students who spent their days here, or office workers who came for a drink after lunch. He saw no police, only a few soldiers.

The boys at the table beside his were talking politics.

"I say we must do as Bapu tells us," one high-pitched, intense young man shouted, pounding the table with his negligible fist. "We must dissolve the Party now that we have our freedom, or it will strangle us all to death!"

"Be quiet or they will throw you in jail, and your mother will have to bail you out!"

"I want to go to jail!" the young man protested. "Our Prime Minister has spent ten years of his life in jail!"

A small boy cleared the empty glasses and cups from Natu's table, and spread the dirt more evenly over its top with a brown rag. From over Natu's shoulder a bony arm deposited a murky glass of luke-warm water on the table in front of him. He sipped at the water, fixing his stare on the big-bosomed white woman seated in a booth along the wall. Her thin dress plunged in a V-line to below the divide of her breasts, ample enough to be locked together in a visible line by the brassière whose shadow he could discern through the almost transparent silk.

"Black or white?" the waiter asked.

"Extra white," he ordered, meaning a lot of cream for his coffee.

"Hot or cold?" asked the waiter.

"Cold," he said. He felt an almost irresistible impulse to walk over to their table and greet her escort first, then turn to her and jam the cold muzzle of his pistol between her breasts and fire the gun. He could not help smiling at the thought of her facial expression. Perhaps she would say, "How dare you shoot me—a white woman!"

"Naturam Godse!"

He did not react. He had trained himself not to react to that name, but instinctively every muscle in his body contracted and he was ready to kick back his chair, turn over his table, and make a dash for the door if necessary.

"Natu, it is you, isn't it? Of course it is! Great! I thought it was you all the time, but what's become of your lip brush, man? Say, what are you doing here anyway? I heard you hated this big town! Hey, come here, Dhoble, pull up a chair, I want you to meet an old friend of mine, Naturam Godse! And don't tell me you never heard of him, or you'll just prove you're an illiterate!"

There was no bluffing him, Natu could see, so instead of trying he hoped that no one within earshot of the table was a plain-clothes man, as he greeted his former college classmate and Poona neighbor, Bal Dev. He nodded to the one named Dhoble.

"Say, this is like old times," Bal said. "How many hours did we sit together in Poona coffee shops, heh, Natu? I tell you what, man, give me one rupee for every hour, and I can stop working today! How is that for a bargain? But stop trying to change the subject, man. What are you doing here anyway? It looks to me as though you are hiding out! What do you think, Dhoble, should we report him to the Minister?"

"It may win you a promotion," Natu said softly.

Bal found that a very good joke. He slapped Dhoble's back, encouraging him to join in the laughter. "He is quick-witted, I tell you! A promotion, you see! Oh, that is excellent, man. Listen, I could use a promotion. Everyone else is getting them these days, I tell you."

"Where are you working now?" Natu asked the loud-mouthed intruder.

"Same department—Finance. The trouble with me is that I am too good, I tell you frankly. I just figured it out, man. If you are unable to add up a column of numbers they make you a minister immediately and then you don't have to do anything but go to cocktail parties and deliver speeches! No fooling, that is the secret to success! That is why I expect Dhoble to be promoted very swiftly, heh, Dhoble?"

He burst out again in raucous laughter. The waiter set a tall foamy-topped glass of creamed coffee before Natu.

"Say, that looks good enough for me to have another," Bal decided. "Two more of those, waiter!"

"We should get back," Dhoble reminded him.

"Don't let me detain you," Natu volunteered.

"Nonsense! If we are late enough they will promote us both, Dhoble! Anyway, how often do I get a chance to see Naturam Godse?"

There must be some way, Natu thought desperately, to make him stop shouting that!

"Do you realize that he is the greatest journalist Poona has produced since Kelkar! I'm not talking about his ideas, because he knows what I think of them—too wild, you see, too radical. He wants to change the whole setup overnight. Am I wrong, Natu? Stop me if you think I am being unfair to you! But when it comes to style, Dhoble, ah! I have always maintained that when it comes to style there is no match for Natu—"

"Tell me," Natu interrupted in time, "how far is your office from here, Bal?"

"I will take you there as soon as we finish our coffee, don't worry! It is quite close, you will see."

"No, no, I didn't mean—that is, I don't have time right now."

"Nonsense, do you think I will let you get away from me? For the rest of your stay, you are my guest here in Delhi. Where is your hotel? What's this, don't tell me you are carrying a bed roll? Excellent! Then you have no lodging yet! You will sleep at my place!"

"No, I couldn't do that."

"What do you mean? It is settled! We have plenty of space! You should see the apartments they give us, practically free of charge. I tell you, freedom is a wonderful boon to this country!"

"You are too kind," Natu said, "but—"

"Nonsense, man, I tell you it is all arranged. You will eat dinner with us tonight."

"No, that is impossible."

"But why? Oh ho-ho-ho, I see that gleam in your eye! I know what you are planning, you devil! Oh, so that is it!"

Dhoble held out a pack of cigarettes and Natu was relieved to take one.

"Come on, admit it," Bal said. "Who is she this time? Dhoble, I tell you he puts us both to shame, this one. Lock up your sisters when he comes to visit you! Come on, Natu, you can't keep any secrets from your old friends, they know you too well!"

"No, it isn't that, but I am here on assignment, and—well, there isn't enough time to do everything. Next visit I will be sure to write you first."

"Listen, Natu, you don't have to keep that secret from me, I tell you! If that is what you want there is no problem. In fact with you staying with me it will make it easier all around, since I will just tell my wife that I must take you out to show you the sights. And, man, I tell you there are some beautiful sights!"

"So life is not all dull figures for you," Natu said, sorry as soon as he said it that he had yielded to the temptation, for this time Bal doubled over with laughter, attracting more attention than before.

It was not easy to get rid of them. After they drained their glasses Bal wanted to order another round, but Dhoble's good sense and professional diligence prevailed, and fortunately, for all his bravado, Bal Dev was not devoid of a bureaucratic measure of discipline. Bal made him promise of course to come to his house at least once before returning home, and proudly presented his card, on the back of which he wrote the address. Natu breathed a sigh of relief as he watched them go, but Bal turned at the door to wave idiotically and direct fresh attention to him.

"No, I say the only thing to do is dissolve the Party!" the high-pitched voice at the next table was still shouting, and fortunately that heated argument must have killed some of their own conversation. Still Natu realized it was not safe to stay here any longer. He remained seated only until he felt that Bal Dev had had time enough to disappear in the crowd outside.

He picked up his bed roll and walked calmly to the door. Instead of hurrying away when he reached the arcaded street, he stood for a moment against the building next to the hinged side of the door. It opened almost immediately, a mouse-faced young man rushed out and looking quickly in each direction as though in search of someone he was following. Finally he turned to confront Natu directly, and was so startled he gasped, but then composed himself, stepped closer, and smiled a secretive smile.

"I am yours to command, master," he whispered. "Guruji and our motherland are one."

Natu did not recognize him. Not that he could possibly know every member of their Society personally. That was too much to expect even of Guruji now that close to one hundred thousand had enlisted in the more than two hundred nationwide branches.

"Trust me, master," the youth continued. "I could not help overhearing your name, and though we have never met I have worshipped you since I was old enough to read your pamphlets—"

"What is it you want?" Natu interrupted sternly.

"You must not stay here. We have been sent out to warn you if we could locate you. They are planted all over the Circle. This spot is too dangerous! You must come with me."

"I haven't the vaguest idea what you are muttering about! Whatever your business may be you better go about it, and stop bothering me!" Having said that loud enough for anyone who passed them to hear it, Natu picked up his bed roll and started walking back in the direction from which he had come under the arcade. Why do I hold onto this cursed bed roll, he wondered, feeling suddenly inhibited by it should he have to break off at a run. Yet where could he leave it without arousing suspicion? And who would bother stealing such a tattered old thing if he just set it down and did not watch it while he purchased some useless article? He realized now that he should have left it at the station, or in the cab.

"I beg you, master, listen to me!"

[70]

"Are you still following me? I told you to go about your business!"

"Katuk has sent me," the youth whispered.

He looked reliable enough, gaunt, burning eyes as though fired by a fever of the soul, timid yet intense, an unemployed graduate or matriculate perhaps, the typical raw material for their cadres. Yet looks were deceiving.

"If you don't stop following me at once," Natu warned, "I will report you to the police!"

It did not seem to frighten him.

"Please, master," he whispered, "there is no time to waste. They are watching us already!"

There were of course people watching them now, the street venders, the idlers, the jobless who circled the Circle all day in search of some scurrilous livelihood. Natu walked ahead. The bed roll was not heavy but was awkward to carry because of its bulk, and he did not want to draw more attention to himself by holding it up on his shoulder, so he kept bumping into people. Impulsively he decided to put it down, glancing around as he did so. His shadow was still there dogging his trail just a few paces behind. Without the encumbrance he could move more swiftly. Then he noticed a beggar boy racing beside him, holding the bed roll on top of his head.

"I carry for you," the beggar shouted, pointing at the luggage on his head.

Natu waved him away, but the boy was determined to prove his worth.

"You keep it if you like," Natu said. "Go home!"

"I carry for two annas only," the boy said eagerly, for he could not seriously believe that anyone would give him such a magnificent present.

"No, no, you take it. Now leave me alone!"

"One anna, Sahib, whatever you like to pay is all right!"

There was no point arguing with him and starting another scene. Yet now he had a regular entourage! He could not have drawn more attention to his movements if he had set out deliberately to do so.

I must get away from them, he thought, and just then caught sight of the garish movie marquee ahead. There were seats in four price ranges. He went to the booth selling the second most expensive tickets, not wanting to sit alone with the Europeans and Americans in the rearmost two-rupee stalls. He paused at the undulating curtain across the entrance, and saw his young shadow rush over to the one-rupee booth he had just left, fishing out a handful of bills in his eagerness

[71]

to pay for the ticket. Had Katuk suddenly become so generous with his help, or was some other source paying for this job?

Merciful darkness enveloped him, a cave filled with the roar of a sound track which at first seemed like a wobbly siren screeching but was soon distinguishable as an Oxford English voice expounding the tragic evils of drink. He fumbled swiftly past a row of cramped knees till he reached a vacant seat, and sunk as low as possible onto the wooden folding chair.

". . . Homeless and without funds Krishna continues his desperate search for alcoholic beverage, tempted now to steal by the lustful desire which has already cost him his job in the accounting office, ruined his marriage, destroyed his only son, and estranged him from his closest friend. . . ."

A woman in the row ahead was crying audibly, for indeed as the screen showed, Krishna, the hero of this didactic short, was a pitiful creature, unkempt and shabby, hovering now outside the liquor store, obviously torn between the temptation to steal the vile bottles on display and fear of arrest. Finally he succumbs to temptation, dashes in, pilfers a bottle of Johnny Walker Red and does so amateurish a job that he can't even get the cork out before the police have him securely in tow. Off he goes to the district lockup, another victim of the curse of foul drink.

"Remember the words of our nation's saintly father," the Oxford commentator boomed. "You cannot build a sober country without sober citizens!"

Advertisements for Coca-Cola, Parle's Orange Smash, and Mukherjee's Ice Cream followed the short. The sound track groaned to its end like a hand-turned victrola all played out, and suddenly the lights came on. There was an intermission between the shorts and the first main feature.

Natu cursed his luck, and glanced about furtively. Patrons were yawning, stretching, smoking, standing, and heading for the exits and the sweets counter beyond the curtains in the courtyard outside. Sure enough, two rows back he saw his young friend, who nodded, it seemed, as their eyes met.

"Do you think liquor is so bad as that?" a woman's voice next to him asked.

He had not noticed her before, though now he realized that in the close-packed row their legs were touching. Her face was coated with a thick layer of cream and pale powder, daubed with rouge at the cheekbones. Her eyes were ringed with mercury. The painted red tilak spot on her forehead was flecked with silver so that it glistened.

So they even sit next to you in the cinema house in this city, he thought, for no respectable lady would have spoken to a stranger in a public place.

"I like to drink now and then," he said, eyeing her bodice.

"I always say if it is good enough to offer to our gods, why not taste it ourselves?" she responded.

"Yes, why not?" Lightly, almost imperceptibly, he increased the pressure of his leg against hers. She did not draw away. Then as though alerted by some sixth sense, he looked around again, and noticed them moving down the aisles from the rear of the crowded house. To a less experienced eye they would have appeared innocuous enough, four men walking singly down each aisle, scanning faces in the audience as though searching for a lost friend, but in the otherwise chaotic discord of helter-skelter movements they stepped with the precision and coordination of a team of athletes moving abreast down a broad field to their opponents' goal post. Natu knew very well who they were.

"What is wrong?" she asked him.

"Nothing," he said, touching her elbow with his hand. Still she did not draw away. "Come, let us go outside for some refreshment," he urged.

Sensing his urgency, she rose at once and preceded him past the row of grudgingly averted knees. He continued to hold her elbow so that anyone could see they were a couple, that he was not alone. They reached the exit a few rows ahead of the slowly advancing line of face searchers.

"You are hurting my arm," she said.

"I'm sorry." He released it as they emerged from the building.

"You do not want refreshment, do you?"

"No. Have you any conveyance?"

"My cycle is with the others in the shed," she told him.

"Do you live very far from here?"

"Not very," she said, studying his eyes, trying to read their full meaning.

There were no taxis in the cinema yard, just the refreshment stand and the bicycle shed. He was afraid to walk to the street alone. The mouse-faced one caught sight of them.

"Come," Natu said, gripping her elbow again. "Which is your cycle?"

[73]

She led him to it, and unlocked the chain, removing it from the spokes of the rear wheel.

"If you hug my waist firmly," he said, "you will be all right on the back rack."

"I know," she said, "but where are we going?"

"Direct me to your home," he told her in so firm a tone of authority that she did not even attempt to argue.

"Master," a harassed voice cried, "where are you going?"

"I will not *warn* you again," Natu told him. "Stop following me, and get out of my way!" Meekly he stepped aside.

Pedaling up the alley to the street, Natu only hoped that whoever they left waiting out front would not think it too strange to see a man riding a woman's bicycle.

But no one stopped them. He had to pump hard with so much weight on the luggage rack, though he did not mind that. He did not even mind the heat, for he was a child of Maharashtra and could pedal long hours under a far fiercer sun without tiring.

It was only after they had gained momentum, joining the stream of small taxis, pedicabs, and Lambrettas circling the oval road, that he realized her arms were locked around his money belt. Her fingers could hardly have helped feeling the outline of his gun.

4

Purushottamdas Katuk removed his glasses and absent-mindedly rubbed the lenses between his stubby fingers. He did not wear the glasses to correct his vision, but rather for cosmetic purposes. They gave his round face a more benign and dignified quality, a scholarly rather than terroristic aspect. It was an idea he had picked up during his visit to Germany before the war. Most of the top Germans he had known wore rimless glasses, so one day he purchased a pair. The only thing sinister about Katuk's appearance was his facial skin, so deeply and thoroughly pitted that it seemed once to have contained a thousand eyes all of which had been gouged from their sockets. The more orthodox considered this legacy of Katuk's smallpox a special sign of divine favor, marking a soul purified by ordeal.

"And did you have something to drink?" Katuk asked.

[75]

"Of course we had tea," Vishnu Apte reported miserably, wishing now that he had not been so weak as to run here to Katuk's hideout instead of remaining on his own.

"Nothing stronger than tea, is it?"

Shankar, who stood at the door, his narrow-browed head as formidable as a giant ape's, his naked wrestler's torso glistening like oiled mahogany, grinned broadly as though there were nothing more humorous than this interrogation of Apte which had been going on now for more than half an hour.

"I don't hear you, Apte. Speak louder," Katuk ordered.

"My head is splitting open," Vishnu pleaded. "Let me try to get some sleep, will you?"

"Is it something you had to drink which bothers your head?"

"Never mind *me*. What will we do about Natu?"

"I ask the questions," Katuk reminded him softly, replacing the glasses carefully on his nose and flashing that frozen grin which revealed his perfectly white teeth. He never dirtied his mouth with pan or tobacco. "What is it you were drinking, please?"

"We had a bottle of beer—that is all," Vishnu muttered.

"Just *one* bottle?"

"One bottle each!"

"Ah, *each* one of you had a bottle of beer, is it? So that makes *two* bottles, yah?" His slight German accent was an affectation Katuk employed only among trusted friends, where it earned him the prestige of foreign experience without the onerous overtone of British influence. "But tell me, Apte, did I not order you to drink nothing intoxicating today?"

Shankar emitted his idiot's giggle.

"Yes! Yes, that is what you ordered, but Natu wanted beer so I got him beer! Now what are you going to do to me for it?" Vishnu clenched his fists and jumped to his feet. "I tell you the police have captured Natu and all you can do is waste a lot of time asking me stupid questions! I should never have come here in the first place!"

"That is correct, Apte," Katuk informed him. "That is also something you were told not to do, but now you are here, sit down and keep your voice low please. Remember we are not alone in this house."

"Why don't you say something, Parchure?" Vishnu asked, appealing to the skeleton-thin young man who sat huddled into himself on the daybed, his bony face masked behind the black aviator glasses

[76]

he always wore. "Tell him to stop bullying me, will you? Is it my fault if they have captured Natu?"

"Oh, leave him alone, Katuk," Parchure said. "He is right, if they have Natu we are in trouble."

"When I want your advice I will ask for it!" Katuk snapped. "I am in command here, and you will take my orders—all of you! Our Leader has given me full responsibility for this mission, and I will not have it fumbled because of your stupidity—" His voice had become too shrill. He stopped and waited for his temper to cool. It was not the first time on this project that he had lost the control on which he had always specially prided himself. He had decided long ago that men who hoped to rule their own nation, and perhaps someday the entire world, would be obliged first of all to gain absolute mastery over their passions, to eradicate impulse entirely, to function with the cool precision, the undeviating exactitude, of a highly tooled and well-lubricated machine. Most of his countrymen had never learned that simple, yet basic, premise. They were volatile, sloppy, and stupid. Even those who were as strong as Shankar were like animals, and so, like animals, they were enslaved by the English, who had no passion in their blood. But the English not only lacked passion, they lacked imagination as well, and ambition. The wealth of America had saved them from utter annihilation, yet the Germans had exposed England's vulnerability, and next time they would not be saved. Katuk liked to think of that next time. It would come in the night while all of them slept, and before they would awaken . . .

"Shri Katuk, please excuse me if I disturb you," called the owner of the house, tapping softly at the door. Shankar opened it just enough to allow the timid little man inside his own room. He too wore glasses, but they were thick bifocals and even with them on he seemed to stumble about as though he were unable to see the floor in front of his feet. "Gentlemen, gentlemen," he said, bowing his greetings nervously to each of them, "I am afraid I am disturbing you?"

"It is the guests who disturb the host, Krishnaji, not the other way round," Katuk told him politely.

"No, no, you have honored me in gracing my home. I hope your accommodations are satisfactory?"

"Most satisfactory," Katuk assured him, wondering if there was some special reason for this visit and the Honorable Krishna Bhumi's obviously distraught condition, or if it was no more than his usual oversolicitiousness and congenital anxiety.

"Perhaps you would like tea now?" Krishna Bhumi asked.

"No, it is much too early."

"Yes, yes, it is too early." He massaged his hands like a nervous waiter hovering over a table from which he expected a substantial tip. "I could bring some fruit?"

"Please do not trouble yourself," Katuk said.

"It is no trouble! Whatever my humble household can offer—"

"We are quite full," Katuk told him firmly.

"Yes, yes, I see. You are quite full. Good. I am glad that you are feeling comfortable."

Yet he remained there nodding and smiling at them, shifting his weight nervously from one bare foot to the other.

"Is there something you wish to tell me, Krishnaji?" Katuk finally asked, knowing his host well enough to realize that if it was something unpleasant it might take him half an hour to say without prompting.

"Yes," Krishna Bhumi said with relief. "There is someone here to see you."

"Who is it?"

"I—I do not know him. He—he is a policeman."

The last word brought Apte and Parchure both to their feet, though Katuk, to his own satisfaction at least, did not move.

"I told him—I—I said I did not know if you were here or not," the Honorable Member of the central Assembly from Nasik stuttered, sweetly smiling at the grim faces all around him, and nodding stupidly. "Should I— If you wish, I could tell him you are resting now, and—and that he should come back later?"

Krishna Bhumi knew enough about the activities of his leading campaign contributors to realize that the appearance of a policeman in search of them was possible cause for alarm. But he was always careful to ask nothing about the details of their work, and grateful that no one found it necessary to tell him anything which would disturb his conscience. He had a large family, and was a deeply religious man. He did not seek influence and money for himself, but merely for the sake of his children.

"Did he say *why* he wants to see me?" Katuk asked calmly.

"That he did not say. Should I—perhaps I could ask him?"

"We can go out through the rear bedroom," Parchure said, "but we better hurry."

Katuk noted his host's alarmed expression at this undignified suggestion of flight, and silenced Parchure with a swift, angry stare.

"My children are playing in the bedroom, Shri Katuk," Krishna

Bhumi reported apprehensively. "I do not want to frighten them."

"Of course not. My friend was only joking. We have no reason to wish to run from the police—now that we are a free country."

"Yes, yes," his host agreed, somewhat calmer.

"That is an unfortunate habit which some of us still retain from our long era of foreign rule, isn't it, Parchure?"

The skeletal head did not answer.

"Yes, yes, we are now an independent people," the Member from Nasik said, encouraging himself with that pleasant reminder. "The police are our servants. If you like, Shri Katuk, I will send him away."

"We do not wish to be impolite, Krishnaji."

"No, certainly we should never be impolite, and that is why I have disturbed you with this message. You are a true gentleman, Shri Katuk."

"But let me trouble you to ask our visitor his name, Krishnaji."

"Yes, yes, of course, I forgot that he told me his name—Brijain, he said it was. Of course, I should have told you at once, excuse me."

"That is quite all right," Katuk said, much relieved. "We all forget things, Krishnaji. Please do send him in, and we will see what the poor fellow wants."

Their host left the room after more bowing and nodding.

"Have you gone out of your mind?" Apte asked, gripping his gun.

"Put that away this instant!" Katuk ordered. "Sit down and be silent—you too, Parchure! Not a word from any of you, understand? Any further insubordination will be called to our Leader's attention for disciplinary action."

Sulking silently they obeyed. When the policeman entered the room he did so with clasped hands in humble namaste, his tassled red turban snug between his upper arm and uniformed torso. Krishna Bhumi was happy to be allowed to leave them alone. After the door closed behind him, the policeman looked cautiously at each of the other faces, then questioningly at Katuk's.

"Speak up, Brijain," Katuk said. "Don't worry about them."

"Even behind prison bars a bird will sing," the policeman whispered.

So Pahwa had finally cracked. Katuk's impassive moon-shaped face revealed none of the emotion he felt, none of the passion which continued to plague him, the apprehension, the anger, the disappointment stronger than anything else, for Pahwa was his special disciple. Pahwa of the melancholy eyes, the soft full lips, the firm hairless body, was his alone, and at his insistence over Natu's strenuous protest, Pahwa had accompanied them. He sensed the mocking scorn in Parchure's eyes, though he could not see them through the black glasses. He read the reprobation in Apte's stare. Shankar merely looked bewildered.

"That was to be expected," Katuk said at last.

"The song has roused the sleeping ones," Brijain continued in his peculiarly cryptic manner.

"Yes, yes," Katuk said distractedly, wondering if they had marred his face, if they had raised long purple welts on his soft body, wondering how harsh the torture had been. Visualizing those tender bruises, those pain-seared spots all over Pahwa, he felt mixed with revulsion a tingling pleasurable sensation, a warm stirring inside of himself as he imagined his fingers caressing those blood-filled bubbles of flesh.

"I have risked much to tell you," Brijain continued.

"Our Leader will be informed of your devotion to him," Katuk promised.

The policeman, who had gone down on his haunches, stared at the ceiling, cocking his ear in Katuk's direction as though it was waiting for other words to be spoken.

"Our Leader does not forget those who have served him faithfully," Katuk added, wishing this bearer of ill tidings would leave as swiftly as possible. "Have you any further message to convey?"

"My wife is in the family way again, Sahib."

"Then God has blessed you. Let us hope it is a boy," Katuk told him as though he did not understand why Brijain had suddenly voiced this autobiographical tidbit.

"Yes, God gives the child, but his father must support him, and now costs are so high, Sahib."

"Our Leader will see to it that your child is taken care of, Brijain, do not worry."

"There is much expense already, Sahib."

Katuk knew he was lying, but it was no time for pinching rupees, and though the mission had to date cost them more than twice the anticipated budget, its successful completion would promptly replenish their treasury.

"I have very little money right now," Katuk said, "but I would like to help you meet your expenses. Here." He had extracted a crumpled ten-rupee note from his money belt, and held it out for Brijain to take.

The policeman glanced at the magnitude of the note, and stared uncomprehendingly at Katuk's placid face. He made no attempt to accept the offer.

"Well, how much do you want?" Katuk asked curtly.

"It is for you to say, Sahib," he responded unctuously. "We have just been ordered to search the city for you—"

"Do not threaten me, Brijain," Katuk whispered.

"You misunderstand me, Sahib."

"I say do not threaten me."

"I only mention that to indicate how dangerous it has been for me to come here."

Katuk was pleased to notice that Shankar had moved a step closer to the small man's rear. By simply allowing himself to fall forward without another step the giant wrestler would be on top of the squatting figure, and his neck could be broken before a sound would emerge, but it would be difficult to dispose of the body without alarming Krishna Bhumi or one of his family. Katuk preferred to avoid such unnecessary complications if possible.

He extracted a second ten-rupee note from his belt, placed it on top of the first and held out his hand again. Brijain hesitated no longer. He pocketed the notes swiftly, replaced his bright turban, and left with a polite bow.

"I would not trust that scavenger dog," Parchure said after the door closed again.

"Yes, yes, Katuk," Vishnu Apte added, "what is to prevent him from reporting us now?"

"Don't be fools," Katuk told them, "why should he give up a steady income to report us?"

"He may earn more by doing so," Parchure pointed out. "I say we must leave here immediately."

"I will decide when we shall leave, Parchure."

"Let us take a vote," Apte suggested.

"You will do as I say," Katuk countered. He looked at his watch. It was only one o'clock. "I am not ready to leave yet. Shankar is not ready either, are you, Shankar?"

"Whatever you say I will do, master," Shankar told him.

"Then Vishnu and I go alone," Parchure said, rising.

"Sit down, schoolteacher," Katuk ordered. "You are not in your classroom now."

"Trap yourself if you wish," Parchure said. "Vishnu, are you coming?"

"What is the good of staying here any longer, Katuk?" Apte pleaded.

"Let him stay if he likes, Vishnu. What is that to us?"

"So you are independent, schoolteacher, yah?"

"I am not stupid enough to wait for them to trap me, if that is what you mean, Katuk."

"I have never been trapped—"

"There is a first time for everything, Katuk! You had never missed with a bomb before, had you? And you had never been wrong about picking a man either, had you? Isn't that what you said when Natu told us that Pahwa was too raw for this job? Well, now you have missed, haven't you? And you were wrong in your judgment, weren't you? And this time I say you are wrong again, only this time I do not wait till it is too late to find out! Get out of my way, Shankar, I am leaving," the volatile Parchure shouted.

Katuk shook his head negatively and closed his eyes. Shankar would not move without his order, he knew, yet what if Parchure were right? What if Brijain had rushed out to report them at once? Perhaps they were coming this instant. Perhaps in five minutes it would be too late for escape. Katuk wavered, yet to follow Parchure at this point would mean voluntary surrender of his command. It would in effect be his own admission of what he suspected they were all saying behind his back, that Katuk is getting too old for this sort of field work, Katuk is losing his touch. Well, he was determined to prove to Guruji that age had enhanced his value to the Society, that the wisdom of experience meant more than all of Parchure's book learning, and was as valuable as Natu's literary talent. For Purushottamdas Katuk had neither education nor talent at his disposal. His one natural endowment was physical strength, and as a boy he learned its value. He learned it could win him respect from classmates who laughed at his ignorance, or made fun of the pockmarks on his face. Learn to toughen your fists and your fists shall make you free became the practical ethic of his life. While the others grew thin and pale poring over past examination questions and answers, Puru swam in the Mula and worked out in Mankar's gym, wrestling on the pounded dirt floor, which slammed against your back like an ebony paddle and flattened out your lungs at each throw till you lay there gasping and quivering like a fish flipped onto a trawler's deck. The Mankar brothers made him their special toy, lifting him clear over their heads and twirling with him till he was too dizzy to keep his eyes open, then throwing him down so hard they seemed to expect

[82]

him to bounce up like a rubber ball. The gym was his classroom. He went there every day, for he had enough studious friends who would alternate at answering "Here, sir," when his number was called before the college lectures began. None of the professors bothered learning any of their students' names, and the system worked perfectly all year until examination week at the very end. Katuk tried to take his examinations only on the first day. He thought perhaps that common sense would be enough to earn him a passing grade, but when he read those first questions on Wordsworth, and Coleridge, and Tennyson, he knew it was hopeless, and by the same token he realized that he had done the right thing, for what did he care about Englishmen and their poetry? It was wasting their youthful energy and time on such nonsense which had kept his countrymen in bondage so long. The English taught their own boys how to ride horses and shoot, but all they taught the Indians was poetry and bookkeeping so that they would become docile clerks too timid to raise their voices before the Sahibs.

After that first try, Katuk never returned to the examination room. His failure was a blow to his father and his uncles for they all hoped he would graduate and then pass the Bar exams too, so that with a barrister in the family the eternal fear of litigation might be dispelled, and the rupees would roll in once he managed to build up a reputation among the wealthy landowners. "The law is power," his father always told him. "Once you have mastered the law you will have the key to all problems." Katuk knew better. Real power he knew was in the fist, in the bicep, in the pectoral, in the bomb. But he did not learn of the bomb till he met Guruji. That was before the First World War. Less than a year after he had been thrown out of college, he was offered his first "scholarship."

That morning at seven he went, as he did every day, to Mankar's for a prebreakfast workout. The gym was in the heart of Poona's old city midway along the alley named after the Mankar family, an ancient Maharashtrian aristocratic clan whose scions had turned from agriculture to bodybuilding. The gymnasium was actually the inner courtyard of one of the clan's ancestral homes, and like every other building along the alley its front was a drab stucco wall with a formidable solid wooden gate totally protecting the world of the household beyond from the prying eyes of pedestrians and the intrusion of migrant sacred cattle.

Katuk entered through the small door within the larger gateway, opened only for vehicles or during a festive celebration. The old gate-keeper inside the passageway nodded in recognition of this familiar face, and lay back on his straw mat again. A few of the stalwarts were already doing their pushups and deep knee bends out in the center of the courtyard, but the Mankar brothers were standing to one side talking with a venerable Brahman, much too elegantly attired for exercise, whom Katuk had never seen here before. The eldest brother motioned to him, calling him over.

"This is the one I have been telling you about," the senior brother explained to his guest as Katuk respectfully approached them.

Katuk had rarely seen so impressive a mustache as this gentleman's, the thick black hairs extending well beyond the limits of his face, bright with oil and curled up smartly at the ends to such sharp points that they looked as though they would pierce your finger if you dared to touch them. His eyes were like flaming coals.

"How old are you?" he asked, not bothering to introduce himself.

"I have just passed twenty years," Puru told him.

"What sort of work do you plan to take up?"

"I don't know yet."

"Isn't it time you decided? Or do you have a wealthy father?"

"No, it is not that—but—"

"But what? There are plenty of jobs in government service. Why don't you take up something like that?"

"I don't like to sit all day," he said, which made the old man laugh, but made him feel even more awkward than before in this obviously important person's presence. The Mankar brothers, he noted, were careful not to interrupt this man, and looked at him, it appeared to Katuk, almost with reverence. Yet they revered practically no one.

"The government has plenty of standing positions available for healthy young men," the mustached mouth snapped, suddenly serious again. "I'm sure you would qualify for one of those."

"Maybe," Puru conceded, "but I don't know, I just don't feel like working for the white people."

"Why not? What is wrong with them?"

"I don't know," he shrugged, feeling uncomfortable under this rapid-fire questioning, half wondering if this man might actually be a high official somewhere despite his attire. "I don't like the way they treat us."

"Why is that?"

"Well, they think they are like—like gods."

[84]

"And you don't think they are?"

"Of course not. They are just white people."

"But they rule over us, don't they?"

"Well, that is because most of us are still weaklings."

"You too?"

"What do you mean?"

"Are you a weakling?"

"I can take care of myself," Puru said, not without a surge of pride.

"That remains to be seen," the old man said, nodding to the Mankar brothers to indicate he was ready for the demonstration.

Katuk had not been warned before, but was told now that as far as the Mankar brothers were concerned he was ready to take his final examinations in the course they had been giving him. The other stalwarts who had been working out when he arrived were to administer the tests, since all of them were former graduates. The first exam was in wrestling, and his opponent was a much taller and heavier young man, who seemed eager to begin the match. Katuk stripped down to his loincloth and took his time about massaging the oil onto his body. He knew it was a test all right, though he had no idea of what the reward for passing it would be. But he liked to wrestle. He liked the feel of another man's body in his arms. He even enjoyed the pain when he was losing, though he no longer lost very often. Circling as he approached the other, Katuk looked for his weakness but saw no excessive flab or obtruding bone, only well-oiled muscular flesh, and the neck, like his own, practically nonexistent between the lumbering body and shaved head.

Katuk made the first pass, but his opponent's greasy arm yanked itself free, and the momentum of his forward lurch left him vulnerable for a neck lock. It was a stupid opening, and in his eagerness to join battle he had fallen into one of wrestling's classic traps. Luckily he had the sense to keep his head low enough to catch the forearm with his jaw, rather than taking its full grip on his neck muscles alone, but he could not maintain his stance, and went down under the formidable weight which now lay over his back. He felt his opponent's warm breath against his ear, and the slow but steady locking of that arm around his jawbone and neck. He dared not open his mouth, but kept his nostrils fully distended as he panted air through them, and stared with bulging eyes at the mocking grain of the pounded dirt scarcely an inch below his face. He did not try to move. He relaxed his entire body instead, except for his jaw and neck which he kept as rigid as possible. He lay that way for what seemed like an hour, but was less than a minute, till his opponent whispered, "Through?"

It was like the signal he had been waiting to hear, for at its sound he pushed off the dirt with his stomach, his legs, and his arms, carrying the huge body aloft with him, till he was high enough to flatten one foot upon the ground and use it as a lever to flip both of them over. He could not have done it a second time had he missed at first try, but his prolonged pretense of submission had caught his antagonist just enough off guard to induce him to relax momentarily. With their positions reversed and Katuk's arms free at last he quickly broke the headlock, turning the arm which had tortured him clear around till it was pinned against its owner's back. There were no rules against armlocks at Mankar's gym, and Katuk was ready to keep moving it higher until it would break off like the wing of a dressed chicken on a carving plate.

He did not waste any breath or energy asking his opponent if he was ready to give up, and though the other grit his teeth and fought hard he finally uttered the agonized groan:

"Enough!"

Katuk released the arm instantaneously, jumped away, and walked back toward the old man and the brothers Mankar. The sweat rolled freely with the oil off his dark dirt-stained skin, but he was smiling as he approached them, for he did not misread the approval in his teachers' eyes. But it was the burning coals over the mustache that he watched with the greatest interest. There was an intensity to those eyes that he had not seen in any others.

"That will do," the old Brahman said, blandly. "How soon can you be ready to leave for England?"

"But how can I afford to go to England?" Katuk asked, amazed.

"You have just now won your scholarship which will pay for your passage," he was informed. "How soon can you be ready?"

"I can be ready tomorrow," Katuk said, even before he realized that he still had not the vaguest idea of what he would be expected to do once he got there.

It was, however, closer to a month than a day later before he climbed the gangway of the P & O liner at Bombay and headed for Liverpool via Suez. There had been papers to procure, medical tests to take, clothes to purchase, and people to meet and speak with. There were young men in Nasik, in Dhulia, in Ahmednagar, all of whom he had gone to see at the Mankar brothers' instructions, all of them past graduates of the gym, who had spent a year or more in

[86]

London already. They taught him how to make change in shillings and pence, and gave him the names and addresses of some people they had met abroad, and tried to explain where Kensington was in relation to Westminster and the City of London, which he found most confusing, but other than that they revealed hardly anything to him of what they had done in London. "Dhondo will train you," they said, uttering that name as though it were bound to mean something to him. The first time it was mentioned, Katuk asked who Dhondo was, and was simply told, "He is our guru." He had meant to ask then, but what does he *teach*, when somehow the conversation shifted back to geographical trivia. Thereafter whenever Dhondo was mentioned, Katuk felt too embarrassed to reveal his ignorance by pressing the question of this well-known individual's identity or occupation. He came to visualize Dhondo as someone like the aged Brahman who had interviewed him for the scholarship, a venerable and shrewd old bird. He rather liked the mysterious character which his future work had assumed. It appealed to his adventurous spirit, as did the prospect of distant travel. Even his parents, once they overcame their initial qualms about the pollution involved in journeying across the dark waters, began to look at the bright side of their wayward son's "scholarship." "An education in England," as his father put it, "is always an asset. Be sure to study some law there!" His mother of course worried about his diet, and the lewd women he might meet. "Remember you are a Brahman," she told him at least once every day. The Mankar brothers sternly reminded him to keep exercising.

Katuk made no friends aboard ship, and took most of his meals in his cabin. It was a long and lonely crossing for him, but fortunately ended soon after he decided that his eyes could endure no further sea-filled horizons. The boat train to Victoria failed to revive his spirits, however, for his feet could not adjust to the constraining vises of his first pair of real shoes, and his neck chafed at the starched white leash it was suddenly obliged to wear. Then too, ever since they had passed Gibraltar the sun had disappeared, and now the damp soot-suffused atmosphere of his dismal compartment and the slate-gray vistas he watched racing by outside made him wish he had never left the friendly comforts of home to come to such a godforsaken miserable land as this one. He would surely have started back on the next train were it not for the fact that the thought of another three weeks at sea was even worse than the prospect of lingering awhile where he was. Thoroughly depressed, disheartened, and despondent, Katuk stood beside his steamer trunk on the center of the platform, and waited as he had been told to do for someone to pick him up. Everyone else seemed to know exactly where they were going. Everyone else had friends or relatives there to greet them, yet he did not even know the name of the messenger who was supposed to be waiting. Ten minutes passed, twenty, a half-hour—the platform was practically deserted. A new train was arriving. . . .

"Are you Katuk?" a slender young Indian asked.

"Yes, of course!"

"Good. Sorry to be so late, but it was unavoidable. Porter here!" He snapped his fingers, and the porter brought a dolly for the trunk. "You will have to surrender your ticket at the gate, Katuk. Come along."

The messenger did not appear much older than himself, and had no muscular development to speak of, Katuk noted at a glance. He looked somewhat feminine in fact, for his black hair was quite long, his facial features delicate, and his eyes rather misty behind luxurious lashes. But his gait was distinctly masculine, as was his voice. Katuk wondered if he too was here on a "scholarship," but had no chance to ask until they settled back in the carriage and started off toward Highgate, which was the address given to the driver.

"Yes," the young man told him, "I have been here now for five years."

"As long as that?"

"There is much we have to learn, Katuk."

"Oh? What do you study?"

"A little of everything."

"I see. Law?"

"Yes, that too," he said, "but mostly chemistry."

"What is chemistry?" Katuk asked, for it was not one of the subjects taught at the college he had attended, and he had never heard the word mentioned before.

"It is a science of matter."

"Oh, I see, it is a science." But he suspected that the misty eyes were not deceived by his sudden pretense at knowledge.

"A most important science," his guide explained. "Tell me, Katuk, do you know anything about bombs?"

"About what?"

"Hmmm," the young man answered, frowning. "I see we shall have quite a bit to teach you, but never mind that now. Let me point out some of the sights here."

There was something about his tone, about the authoritative manner in which he spoke which suddenly reminded Katuk to ask, "What is your name please?"

"Just call me Dhondo," the other replied. . . .

"I warn you, Katuk, tell this fool to get out of my way!" Parchure shouted.

"Do not insult Shankar, schoolteacher," Katuk told him, opening his eyes languidly. "And do not make so much noise. I am in command, not you."

"Guruji will be informed of this," Parchure threatened, "if any of us escape this trap alive!"

"Yah, I will inform him, don't worry. I will tell him his schoolteacher is a coward."

Before Parchure could answer there was a gentle knock at the door.

"Shri Katuk," Krishna Bhumi called, "one of your servants has just returned and asks to see you."

"One moment please, Krishnaji," Katuk answered, then rising and going over to Parchure, he asked more softly, "Will you sit down by yourself, or must I order Shankar to hold you down?"

Parchure trembled with rage, but knew it was futile to try to fight these wrestlers. He sat beside Apte. Katuk opened the door himself to admit the mouse-faced little man who had trailed Natu. Out of breath, he reported what had happened.

"Then Natu is safe," Apte shouted joyfully.

"Let him finish," Katuk insisted.

"But that is all, master."

"You mean you did not follow them?"

"How could I follow them, master? I had no bicycle."

"You could have taken a taxi!"

"There were none empty, master."

"Who was she?" Katuk asked.

"I do not know, master."

"So you have no idea who she was, and yet you made no attempt to find out where they were going, yah?"

"But master, I tried—"

"Be silent! That is not enough to try and fail, do you understand! Get out of here and do not come back unless you bring him with you or can tell me where he is staying."

The mouse-faced youth hurried away.

"Buttock of a bullock," Katuk whispered as he left.

[89]

"But, Katuk, at least we know he is safe!" Apte repeated.

"Ah, so now we hear from the other intellectual," Katuk said, clasping his hands behind his back and pacing off the small room like a trapped tiger. "Are you so sure, Apte? How do you know who this woman is?"

5

Her room was in an apartment project which had been erected not far from the Circle before the war. Like most buildings in the city this one looked older than it was. The bricks had started changing color in uneven streaks and patches of white, the concrete steps had settled irregularly, opening diagonal cracks, the plaster, incapable of withstanding the alternating impact of extreme moisture and dryness, flaked off and peeled everywhere, and the dirt was ubiquitous. What should have been a perfectly good and relatively new structure appeared a tottering wreck, barely fit for habitation. Climate and custom had taken their toll, and the Western architectural import had by erosive mutation become a hybrid eyesore.

Natu followed her to the second floor past a barricade of screaming children and squatting adults. The shrivelled women, he noticed, eyed her as though she were a tax collector or a leper. The loitering young men watched her graceful ascension with a different sort of passion in their eyes. She greeted none of them, staring fixedly at her painted toes as she climbed each step, gingerly avoiding the banana peel, mango pits, and shallow puddles of urine. She let herself into the apartment, then turned and invited him to follow.

One of her roommates was preparing to leave as they entered, viewing her rear in the wall mirror.

"Is that you already, Sheila? Back early, you lucky girl," she said, adjusting the drape of her sari, appraising him swiftly and adding, "Lucky *indeed!*"

"Come," Sheila told him, quickly taking his arm, "my room is behind the kitchen."

"You might at least introduce people!" the other shouted.

"Double lock the door when you leave," Sheila called back, drawing aside the curtain before her own room, and whispering to him, "She is very lightheaded, that one."

It was a modest room, but much cleaner than the rest of the house. There was a large bed, a dressing table with an unframed jagged-edged mirror balanced against the wall on top of it, and one over-stuffed armchair. On the walls were brightly colored pictures of the gods, Krishna fluting to the lovely milkmaids, Lakshmi rising out of her lotus, Brahma flying over the sun on the back of his giant swan, the whole pantheon of lesser deities hovering in the background with their luminous eyes and hourglass figures, the men almost as voluptuous and alluring as the women, who but for their melon-shaped breasts could hardly be differentiated from their male consorts. On her dressing table was a small ivory figure of Ganesh. He picked it up and stared fondly at the elephant head, covering the smooth pot-belly with his thumb.

"But you are not from Maharashtra, are you?" he asked.

"My home was in Punjab," she explained, which he had assumed.

"Yet you worship Ganesh?" It surprised him, for this second son of Shiva was the leading god of Natu's region.

"My husband was Maharashtrian," she said.

"Your husband?"

"He was killed in the riots," she explained. "Last year we—" but she did not continue. The painted mask of her deeply lined face had momentarily lost its gay expression, then as though remembering what she was, it falsely brightened again. "Let me make us a drink," she said.

[92]

"How many of you live here?" he asked.

"Four—three others and myself."

The front door slammed. They heard the lock clicked shut a second time by the key outside.

"Now are we completely alone?" he asked.

"Yes," she said, somewhat furtively.

"Will the others come back soon?"

"They might."

"With men?"

"Perhaps."

"Where is the servants' exit?"

"Behind the washroom."

"Where is that?"

She showed him. He opened the rear door and looked out to see where the back stairway went. Two servants were asleep in the yard below. He returned and locked the door from the inside.

"We leave it open for the sweeper," she said. "Why do you lock it?"

"You can open it again after I am gone."

"Why are they hunting you?" she asked.

"You need not be afraid," he said. "I will not remain here long."

"I have not asked you to leave."

"Just a few hours," he said, taking the remainder of his money from his belt, putting back twenty rupees, which would be more than enough for later, and handing her the rest without bothering to note the sum.

She looked at the roll of tens in disbelief, started counting them, but soon stopped, and looked at him again with eyes made bright by a sudden upwelling of tears.

"It is too much," she said.

"Never mind," he told her.

"I—I cannot repay you for this in a few hours."

"How do you know how much I can drink, eh?"

She moistened her lips with the edge of her tongue and moved toward him, extending her arms over his shoulders, parting her lips slightly as she brought them closer to his. She closed her eyes and stood there before him waiting for him to make use of the merchandise he had purchased at so generous a price.

Natu gripped her arms and gently but firmly pushed her away. "That is not why I gave you the money," he said.

This time she was too perplexed to speak, and merely stared at him as though he were truly mad or marvelous or something of each.

"Why don't you get us that drink," he suggested.

She brought gin and quinine water. The first glass had no effect on him, not even a cooling one, for there was no ice. He had taken the soft seat on the stuffed chair, which felt strange to his body accustomed to stone floors. With seats like these he could more easily understand why the wealthy grew so fat. There was no reason to get up and walk around, and their beds were the same, floating platforms of cotton and down, the cushioned world. There is the cushioned world and the stone world, he thought. It would be a good title for his next editorial, but then he remembered that Naturam Godse would write no more editorials. He held out his empty glass to her.

"Do you want it stronger?" she asked.

"It does not matter."

"Do you want chapatis with it?" she asked.

"If you have some."

"I can make them for you."

"Do not bother."

"It will not take long. The charcoals are still burning."

"As you like," he said, tucking his feet under his thighs. The trouble with a stuffed chair was that there was no room to properly fold up your legs on it because of the restraining arms. Not that you really needed to fold up your legs on such a chair, for there was a back to it after all and an ample cushion underneath, yet habits break slowly. The second drink had no more than a filling effect. The gin remained in the stomach, and only moved later to the head. But gin never really bothered him, no matter how much of it he drank. Nasik whiskey was different. Of course, there was no Nasik whiskey in the North. There was really only one place to get Nasik whiskey.
. . . He had told her that the third time she visited the Press. Or was it the fourth time? Those initial visits were so brief he could not keep track of them any longer. She always said she was just on her way to meet someone, her husband or a friend, just passing by and thought she might pick up the latest copy of his paper while she was there, and simply say hello again. She didn't seem to mind the way everyone stopped working when she entered his office, the way they all stared at her, the typesetters, the copyboys, his editorial assistant, even the messenger at the door who usually never raised his eyes from his toes until Natu had pounded the bell on his desk half a dozen times. For no other woman came there alone, not even Dr. Mrs. Indira Bharve, the indefatigable sociologist who drove around

Poona on a motorcycle in her one-woman crusade to prove the utter and intolerable emancipation of her sex. Rani Mehta simply walked past them all, not as though she were crashing so well-established and exclusive a club for men only that there was no need to post this first rule of membership on its gate, but rather as if the New Light Press were her goldsmith's shop or her kitchen. She was either without pride and consciousness of her place, or else so proud and supremely self-confident that it never occurred to her to doubt that her presence was welcome anywhere on earth. After her second visit Natu decided it was the latter which explained her brazen behavior, and felt all the more attracted to her because of it. By the third visit (or was it the fourth?) he too ignored the gaping inquisitive eyes of his subordinates, and found himself not at all unnerved by her appearance in the sanctuary of his professional estate. In fact, he enjoyed her company, and went so far as to ask his assistant to leave them alone, and to see to it that they were not disturbed unless some urgent matter vital to the existence of the Press demanded his immediate attention. . . .

"Why don't you sit down," he suggested, though he liked the way she looked standing, for she was a tall woman and the light coming from behind outlined her slender figure in silhouette through the soft blue of her sari. Her shoulders were broad, her hips ample enough, and but for her small breasts she might have been the model who posed for the Parvati in a Shiva temple nearby.

"I really must be going," she said, now that they were alone.

"Too bad you are so busy," he said, without conviction.

Her skin, remarkably fair, so much so that he wondered if there were English blood in her ancestry, flushed to a darker hue, and she explained, "It's just that I happen to have a luncheon date at the Club."

"The Club? Which club? Excuse my ignorance but I do not belong to any clubs, you see. My skin is too dark."

"The Racquet Club," she explained, sitting down. "I don't belong either. My husband does."

"Ah yes, the Champion." She said nothing, but caught the edge of her lower lip between her teeth, and seemed so despondent he felt obliged to try to cheer her. "Can you get Nasik whiskey at that club, eh?"

"Well, they have practically every kind of drink," she said, "but I don't think I ever heard of—*Nasik* whiskey, did you say?"

[95]

"You mean you have never *tasted* Nasik whiskey?"

"No, I don't think so." The faint glimmer of a smile brightened her expression. "Is it good?"

"It is *unique,*" he said, "but come now, you are fooling me. Surely you have relished it many times."

"But I have never heard of it till now."

"Is that possible? I had thought of you as so—so well-traveled, so cosmopolitan."

"I have visited seven countries," she said, smiling openly.

"Yet you have lived without Nasik whiskey," he said earnestly, almost tragically. "How unfortunate. Of course, it is still not too late, I suppose."

"I should hope not," she said. "Where do they sell it here?"

"In Poona? Oh, you could not find it in Poona," he explained gravely. "I thought possibly so exclusive a place as the Racquet Club might have some, but you say they don't?"

"No, I'm sure they haven't."

"No. Well there is really only one place to get Nasik whiskey that I know of." He hesitated saying it, for he was by no means certain, and despite his self-assurance in such matters he did not like to be rejected; perhaps because of his good fortune with others he was more anxious to succeed with her as well. He did not want to frighten her off by too early an advance, yet timidity often proved more deadly than rashness. He tried to read the message in her eyes, to anticipate the answer he might expect. But why has she come here in the first place, he thought suddenly. "We could go there next Tuesday if you like. The Press is closed on Tuesday, and I have nothing special planned."

"Oh?" She fidgeted nervously with her sequin-covered purse, and caught her lower lip again. She looked like a small girl when she did that.

"We could meet on the bus," he said, quickly adding, "I would take you on my motorcycle, but you know how people talk—"

"Of course, they have nothing else of interest to do!"

"It's not too bad a ride," he said. "We could take the six-twenty bus, which will bring us to Nasik before eleven. It will be rather warm by then, but there is another bus which leaves for Trimbak in the hills at eleven promptly, and that is quite comfortable. We can have our lunch at Trimbakeshvar—there is one particular place I know which serves excellent Nasik whiskey."

"It sounds as though you must do this quite often, Mr. Godse."

"I have been there before," he said evenly.

She lowered her eyes, and before she could compose herself sufficiently to say anything further, his assistant knocked and barged in with a handful of fresh copy.

"Natu, these must be approved at once," he said.

"Well, read them!"

"I have," the other muttered.

"Good. What is your opinion?"

"My opinion?" He had been with the paper since its inception six years ago, and had worked on other journals twenty years before that. In experience as well as in age he was Natu's senior, yet he never thought of relying upon his own judgment as final in anything since he was after all only assistant editor. "I—well, I think they are all right, but—"

"But nothing, Ganesh! You must learn to assume more responsibility around here! I cannot be bothered with every petty detail all my life. If you approve of them—let them run."

The assistant looked worried. "I will read them over again," he said nervously.

"Good. Do it outside," Natu told him.

"Yes, yes, thank you, Natu. Excuse me." He hurried away.

She had stood up, and walked toward the outside door.

"I really must go now," she said. "I've taken too much of your time already."

"Six-twenty then at the terminal on Tuesday?" he asked.

"I can't remember what I promised someone to do on Tuesday. I *think* it was Tuesday—"

"I will be going in any event," he said. "It has been too long since I have tasted Nasik whiskey. Come if you are free."

"All right," she said. "Goodbye."

"That is too long a word," he told her. The next few days seemed longer still.

There was always a crowd at the bus terminal. For some people it was home, and as the glow of dawn's heavenly fire spread the gap between hill-painted horizons, the humbler flames of several family hearths flickered along the platform and mothers warmed the tea while their children watched with such intense solemnity that one might have thought they expected a magic genie to rise from the spout of a battered brass kettle. The buses were huddled together like patient elephants half under the shed, their hulking rear ends still shrouded in the valley's shadow. Several uniformed drivers and fare collectors bustled about officiously, big with the sense of belonging here, like landlords strutting around their property. But most of the people were passengers waiting their call to get on board, rubbing their stiff hands together in the bracing cold which several thousand feet of elevation imparted to the plateau valley after the sun went down, even in the hottest months of April and May. By July it was quite cool at 6 A.M., and Natu had decided to order a cup of tea. He drank it inside the small waiting room, eagerly scanning the faces in the crowd as he did so. He recognized a few of them, but not the one he was looking for.

At six-ten a khaki-clad collector, his chrome coin container strapped jauntily over one shoulder, his ticket and paper money box securely held under one arm, peered into the waiting room, and shouted, "Nasik bus loading! Hurry up for Nasik!" There was a mass exodus from the room, peasants burdened down with bundles especially eager to squeeze through the door as swiftly as possible, convinced that the bus would leave before they could get outside. Natu ordered another cup of tea. It was bitter, but warm, and what anxiety he felt had nothing to do with the bus.

At six-twenty there was no sign of her. Had she gone directly to the bus? He decided to go out himself now, for the schedule was relatively well observed. The monsoon thunderheads rose like massive turbans above the Western Ghats, but the wind had brought none of them over the valley as yet. It would be a perfect day—if she comes, he thought. Two buses were loading. The one for Sholapur had just begun, but the Nasik bus was practically filled. The driver and his ticket collector were busy securing the luggage piled on top of the roof. Inside there was the usual predeparture turmoil, the arguments over window seats, the struggle for extra hand-luggage space, the cries of babes in arms who wanted freedom to explore so fascinating a new aspect of the world as the inside of a bus, the frenzied last-minute check of possessions. "Where is Balu? Where is Balu?" one hysterical mother screamed. Someone found him crawling under the next row of seats. The woman who had seemed on the verge of suicide for fear that she had lost her darling infant began beating him furiously as soon as he was restored to her arms. He wailed with equal fury. Natu walked halfway through the bus, and searched the faces in the rest of it. She was not there.

He went outside again, and looked around.

Panting from their exertion the driver and collector climbed down the rear ladder of the bus, nodded their greetings to him, and got inside. After much groaning the motor caught, and the rattling warm-up began. The collector secured the rear door, and came back to stand on the steps up front.

"Do you come, Sahib?" he asked Natu.

"I am expecting someone," he said.

"We are late now, Sahib."

"People are still coming," Natu told him, sighting a family which had started to run their way. They had one suitcase too large to fit inside, so the collector had to climb the roof again. But it was almost six-thirty now.

She will not come, he thought, finally admitting to himself what he had begun to fear several days ago when she no longer appeared at the Press. Stupidly enough he had begun to wait for her every day, and when by late afternoon she did not arrive he felt not only distracted but became short-tempered, snapping at everyone who stepped into his office, even at Vishnu Apte. "What is it, Natu?" Vishnu had asked only yesterday. "Why are you so nervous and upset, tell me?" And now on his one day off instead of going to Bombay where any of a dozen women would have greeted him like a Maharajah in his own harem, he was standing like an idiot, half-frozen beside a rattling idiot-filled old bus which was supposed to have left for Nasik, of all places under the sun, ten minutes ago! It was not only preposterous, but humiliating as well. To Yama's hell with her, he decided.

"Sahib, do you come? I must close this door!" the collector yelled above the accelerated roar of the motor.

Then a taxi arrived, and she stepped out before the driver could open his door to assist her.

"Of course I am coming," Natu shouted at the impatient attendant. "But don't close the door yet, you idiot. Can't you see that lady is also going to Nasik?"

He saw to it that she found a seat, but rather than take another some distance away, stood in the aisle at her side. He knew none of the people on the bus, and did not mind standing there. In fact he rather enjoyed it, for the road was bumpy and the driver somewhat reckless so that every few minutes he would be hurled against her or else she would practically tumble off the seat onto him. Each time that happened they would apologize, but he somehow suspected that she did not mind such unavoidable contact any more than he did. It was an exciting ride in other respects too, as a bus ride always was. They were detained by the usual herds of sheep and goats along the way, and by one particularly stubborn group of black buffalo, who proved so intransigent about moving aside for a helpless horn that the collector himself was obliged to get out and slap at the upjutting pelvic bones of the great lethargic beasts, whom he cursed most affectionately, yelling "Move over, Mother, I say! Damn you, Auntie, get out of our way!" There were monkeys too. At one roadside stop an exceptionally bold chimp tried to hitch a free ride, jumping onto a window ledge, then deftly using his tail to snatch a banana right out of a young girl's hand. It was a fine trick, though the girl and her family were too indignant to appreciate it. Off the ticket collector went again, but the culprit retreated to his perch on a banyan tree and nonchalantly sat there eating his banana, while the irate collector ordered, "Give it back, you scoundrel! Give it back, I say!"

Rani laughed without inhibition, flattening her long-fingered graceful hand against her chest and throat, and looking up at him with so carefree and infectious a smile that his misgivings of the past few days and hours were erased at its impact, and he was tempted then and there to promise that he would always love her.

The rain caught them twice before they reached Nasik. Hanging like smoking curtains across the road ahead, huge pellets of bountiful moisture beat a welcome rhythm on their rolling drum and those who sat by the windows gleefully held out their hands and arms to catch the refreshing manna of the monsoon's gift, the blessed water without which nothing could live very long in this otherwise parched and barren plateau. Beyond the rain clouds the air was swept clean of dust and dirt, trees glowed with their new crystal garlands, the earth exuded its most fragrant smell and opened its million mouths wide to swallow the intoxicating potion. "Pani, pani," adults and children alike uttered in joy.

"To them it is Nasik whiskey," he stooped to say in her ear.

"Better," she said. "What is your Nasik whiskey made from anyway?"

"Ah, first you must try it," he answered with a mischievous gleam in his eye.

Like so many of India's cities Nasik was famed for its temples and Brahmans, but for little more. Flanking the Godavari River, its spired stone monuments to the Godhead in varied forms were places of pilgrimage to the orthodox from all over the land. Next to Mother Ganges no river was held more sacred and if the Brahmans of Benares and Poona were kings and princes of the Hindu faith, those of Nasik were its leading barons and earls. But by the time they reached Nasik the sun had cleared the highest peaks and their hovering clouds, and hung like a naked broiler coil over the oven-hot plain below. And by the time they emerged from their bus and found the one scheduled to leave for Trimbak at the Godavari's source in the hills, it was completely filled with passengers standing already half the length of the aisle.

"When is the next bus?" he asked the driver.

"Three-thirty."

"None before that?"

"This one, if you are willing to stand."

"I don't mind standing," she volunteered bravely.

"No, no," he said, "it is more than an hour's ride." He was moreover tired of standing by now himself. "We shall rent a car," he told her, fingering the bills in his pocket, hoping he had brought enough money. There were three empty cars parked outside the terminal. They drove only to and from Trimbakeshvar, all large vehicles, built with added seats in the back so that up to nine people could fit inside one, thus reducing the per capita cost. Natu glanced about casually as they approached the massive automobiles, hoping to catch sight of a group who looked affluent enough to be willing to share the luxury drive with them. But it was a weekday, and none of the Bombay business crowd were around. In fact, there was no one in the vicinity of those cars but a beggar woman, a few stray dogs, and the Muslim drivers who sat on upholstered seats at their polished wheels like mighty moneylenders squatting over their treasure chests. He tried not to let her see how concerned he was about so petty a matter as the fare.

"Which car do you prefer?" he asked her debonairly.

"It doesn't matter to me, Natu. They all look alike."

"Well, you never know," he said. "Some of these cars are more run-down than others, and since it is a steep climb—better let me check. Sit there on the bench a moment. I'll talk to the drivers."

"You needn't bother," she said.

"No, no, it will just take me a moment," he insisted, feeling idiotically petty, and cursing Apte for the grudging pittance he was paid. She obliged by going back to the bench without further argument.

"Look here," Natu said in a tone of strict confidence when he reached the first driver. "What is your best price for two up to Trimbak and back by eight this evening?"

"That is sixty rupees, sir," the fat-cheeked fez-wearing son of Allah replied.

"Are you crazy?" Natu asked, keeping his voice low. He had precious little more than that in all his pockets.

"It is the standard price," the driver explained.

"We'll see about that," Natu said, indignantly, going directly to the neighboring vehicle.

The second driver wanted sixty-five, arguing that his was a heavier car than the first and used more petrol. Then he generously came down to sixty, but Natu had already left him for the final port of call in what was becoming a nightmarish kind of storm.

"Sixty," the last driver announced after Natu had stated his desires.

"I don't have it," Natu said in desperation.

"How much do you have?"

"Forty-five," Natu told him, though a few minutes ago he had sworn to himself that forty would be his outside limit.

"Petrol alone costs me thirty," the driver insisted.

"Well, how much profit must you make on me?" Natu asked, beginning to lose his temper.

"But it is a steep road, my friend. Much wear and tear on the motor, remember."

"And if you leave it standing here under the sun all day?" Natu asked, wondering why he had been so stupid as to suggest the trip to Trimbakeshvar in the first place! She was obviously content to come away with him for the day in any event, and for sixty rupees he could have bought an ocean view in the Taj Hotel.

"For you fifty-five, my friend," the third man, who seemed more enterprising than his competitors, whispered.

"Not one rupee over fifty!"

"All right, get in," the driver answered, so quickly that Natu suspected it was a conspiracy in which all three drivers were partners.

"That last car seems sturdiest," he told her, returning to escort her back.

"It's such a big car," she said, "isn't it terribly expensive? I really wouldn't mind standing in the bus."

"Nonsense," he said, "who ever heard of a queen standing in a crowded old bus? Anyway, it's only money."

She enjoyed the drive so much that less than halfway up he forgot the exorbitant cost entirely, and decided it was only proper that he should be riding this way, with a Rani at his side.

"Look! A wild canary," she pointed. "Did you see him, Natu?"

"I have found a more lovely bird to watch, my Rani." He placed

[102]

his hand upon hers, but she drew it away after hardly a moment of contact, pointing out some flowering tree to him.

"What is that called?" she asked.

"Rani Mehta," he said.

"So you don't know either. Someday I must buy a book and learn the names of every flower and bird. Isn't that a noble ambition?"

"Everything about you is noble, my darling."

"You mustn't call me that," she said, looking frightened.

"Why mustn't I?"

"Because—well, because it is—so intimate a term."

"That is how I feel about you," he said.

"But you hardly know me, Natu."

"I know the most important things."

"No you don't. You couldn't possibly. I don't feel I know anything about you, except in a most superficial way, really."

"Then you must ask questions," he said. "I would keep no secrets from you."

"Were you ever married?" she asked.

"Yes," he replied, but now it was his turn to look out the window. They had started up the narrow ridge, and he could see the mudhut villages embraced by their shallow stone walls below, frail islands of primitive society in an ocean of millet-sown plain and barren badland, the compact cells on which the superstructure of urban and industrial and political life ultimately depended for its vital sustenance. It was on one such primal mud island that he was born, and there he had returned for his wedding.

"Is she still—?"

"No, she died within a week of our marriage. That was many years ago. I have not remarried since. Do you want to know her name?"

"I'm sorry," she said. "It's none of my business, I know. Please don't be angry, Natu." Gently she covered his hand with her own.

"Your hand is cold, Rani."

"Poor circulation," she explained, smiling.

"Warm heart—isn't that what they say?"

"I don't know, is it?" She lowered her eyes.

"Why are you so sad, Rani?"

"What makes you ask that?" She looked as startled as though he had walked into her bedroom before she had a chance to put any clothes on.

"It is in your eyes," he explained. "I saw it the first time we met."

[103]

"How could you see anything out there in that garden?"

"I could see enough. You can tell me what is wrong."

She searched his face with childlike intensity, the way an infant who understands no words probes the visual world for some unspoken key to its meaning.

"No, I hate people who do that," she said at last, "cry all over the first shoulder they find, unburdening themselves to every stranger. . . ."

"I am no stranger, Rani."

"Of course you are," she said, drawing her hand away, strangely distant again. "I shouldn't have accepted your invitation today. I didn't plan to. Even this morning when I woke up I had no intention of coming—"

"But you *did,* because instinctively you knew that we belonged together. Why are you afraid of admitting it, Rani?"

"I wouldn't have come if I were afraid of you."

"It's yourself you fear. You're not happy with your husband, isn't that it?"

"Please don't expect me to answer such questions, Natu. It's too soon. We don't know each other."

"Why must you keep repeating that? You talk as though time had some magic power," he said, almost angrily. "Did you learn that from your travels to the West? Perhaps you read it in some English novel, eh? Nothing is further from the truth, I tell you. People can live together for a hundred years and know nothing of each other's real nature. Name and form are not reality, my darling, only veils to distort and disguise the truth, which we see in a flash of insight that transcends all external appearance, or else we die without seeing it."

"You *are* a mystic, aren't you?" she said. "I felt that in your editorials, especially when you write about our nation."

"I don't know what I am," he said, and the bitterness with which he spoke surprised him as much as it worried her. Then they both stared silently at the awesome spectacle of ragged stone cliffs and plummeting gorges as the heavy car groaned in low gear up the tortuous shelf road on the mountain's edge, up to the sacred spring high in the living rock where the Godavari River was born.

"Do you wish me to drive to the temple?" their chauffeur asked as they reached the small town nestled at the fanlike foot of the last and highest peak, which rose like the back of a giant's chair to obscure the sky before them.

"Just beyond the temple," Natu told him, "there is an eating place—"

"Ah, you wish the hotel!" the driver said, too conspiratorially.

"Yes, yes," Natu said, explaining to her, "it is the only decent place to eat here."

But she did not seem to have become alarmed, and kept looking at the peak ahead. "How magnificent," she said softly. "It is so stark and splendid."

"The people here believe that mountain is the Mother Goddess, and the river her hair," he explained.

"What a lovely idea, and the air is so delightfully cool. I love it here," she said. "Thank you for bringing me."

"Wait till you taste the whiskey before thanking me."

It was not much of a hotel. On the ground floor was the dining room, and above that half a dozen small rooms. Only a few of the tables were occupied when they entered. There were more waiters than customers, and the owner, a somewhat corpulent man with rolled-up shirt sleeves, who sat on a stool beside the cash register chewing a toothpick, jumped to his feet when he saw them, shouting:

"Naturam, where have you been all these weeks? Hah, it is good to see you again—and the lady also. I do not think I have seen her before, is it?"

He led them to a table with much pomp and fuss, calling over a few idle waiters, spreading a new cloth for them himself.

"The mutton curry is excellent," he announced.

"It is the only thing they serve," Natu told her smiling.

"I see you are well acquainted with this place," she retorted.

"Naturally. It is not the Racquet Club," he said. "Look here, Karve, bring us a bottle of Nasik whiskey first of all!"

"No, but it is not necessary today," the owner said proudly. "I have begun to keep beer and Scotch now."

"Never mind, I can drink beer and Scotch anywhere. I tell you it is Nasik whiskey we want!"

"You *prefer* Nasik whiskey, Naturam?"

She covered her lips with her fingertips to keep herself from laughing aloud.

"Of course I prefer it," Natu said, disgusted with this fool who had ruined his surprise by now, but determined to carry out his promise. "Would I order it if I didn't want it?"

"Whatever you say is all right with me," the bewildered owner

[105]

shrugged. "Nasik whiskey, of course, is there," he muttered, going away to fetch a bottle of the foul stuff.

"Oh, my God, what *is* it?" she sputtered after tasting the slightest sip.

"I told you it was unique, eh. Ah! There is a drink for you!" He emptied his glass, but could not quite manage to keep himself from coughing.

"How do you stand it, Natu? It's the most vile drink I've ever tasted. Won't it kill you?"

"Who knows what will kill us, my dear. So you don't relish it, eh? Well, that shows you how wrong I can be in my judgment of women —that is, women's taste, I mean."

"Perhaps in both," she said.

"Perhaps. But come, let us get some food to go with our drinks. Karve, bring on your curry, will you!" He started pouring himself another drink, but paused midway to ask her, "Or are you a vegetarian?"

"No, I have all the vices," she said.

"Excellent. Let us drink to them, shall we?"

"All right, but I will drink my toast with water, if you don't mind."

"And it is such good whiskey," he said sadly, smacking his lips as the burning fluid passed into his gut. "I think they use Jowar grain mostly, blended with some Bajra, but actually the important ingredient is Godavari water. They take it from the spring as it flows from the rock; that is the secret, you see."

"Let us hope they keep it a secret," she said. "Why do you drink so much?"

"Much? Surely you do not call two glasses of such fine whiskey *much,* do you?"

"No—if that is all you will drink."

"But we cannot waste this excellent bottle," he said, turning it full around. There was no label.

"That is what I mean by much."

"Ah, so you are worried about me. Well, that is certainly a good sign. I must drink to that—to your tender concern for a stranger! How is that for a toast? Tender concern. Do you feel that for all strangers, Rani, or only for certain special strangers?"

"I wish you would stop making fun of me, Natu. It's really very childish of you, you know."

"Is it? Well, perhaps I am a child then. Would you like to mother me?"

She averted her eyes, and nervously smoothed out the cloth in front of her place.

"Have you any children, Rani?"

"No."

It was several years since he had read of the Champion's wedding, though he could not remember how many. That was the big event of the Poona social season, of course, for Maginlal Mehta was considered the best catch in town. Natu had never taken any interest in such nonsense, but now he wondered what had gone wrong.

"I've been too busy for children," she added. "There were so many places I've always wanted to see."

"Yes, of course," he said.

"Once a woman has children she becomes a slave to them."

"Yes, yes, I understand."

"You don't," she said. "You're like all the men in this country. You think that a woman only deserves to live for her family. I can tell that is what you think, isn't it?"

"For most women it seems to be enough."

"Well, I'm not most women. I never have been."

"Then you are perfectly happy, Rani?"

He was surprised to see her take another sip of the whiskey.

"I don't know anyone who is perfectly happy," she said. "Do you?"

He could think about that while the waiter set their plates before them, and brought the tray of condiments. The service was Western style, since most of the customers who came here were from the fast Bombay crowd. Natu did not mind using a fork, when he saw that she preferred to use hers.

"No, I don't," he said, watching the steam rise from his mound of rice, meat, and vegetables. "Of course I have never considered happiness a particularly desirable goal. I shouldn't really have asked you that. What I meant was—are you satisfied? Perhaps *content* is a better word?"

"As much as most people, I imagine," she said, picking absent-mindedly at her food with the prongs of her fork.

"Or as little?"

"All right, as little. And you?"

"I have never been content," he said, and poured himself another drink, and finished it before continuing. "And I never will be as long as we remain slaves."

"Yes, I expected you would say that."

[107]

"Oh? Then you must find me very boring if you can read my thoughts."

"No. I find you very puzzling, Natu."

It flattered him, so he magnanimously said, "But I am very simple really. All men are simple compared to women. You are the puzzling ones—you especially."

"Do you really mean that? Strange—how at times you act as though you know all about me, and something you say makes me feel so—so transparent, or just the way you look at me sometimes, as though I were covered with glass . . ." She caught her lip with her teeth.

He pressed her fingers firmly with his own. "I only look at you that way because I love you, Rani."

"Our food is getting cold," she said, and would not raise her eyes to look into his again for what seemed like much too long a time.

He drank more than he should have, not because he liked the whiskey—it was too bitter and strong to like—but because he needed something to give him the courage to ask her. He never needed courage in Bombay, but though she had accompanied him here he felt uncertain, almost shy. At one point he started to ask her, but then the blood rushed to his face. She seemed too innocent.

"What is it?" she asked.

"Never mind," he said.

"What time is it, Natu?"

"Two-thirty."

"We must start back soon," she said.

"We will take the eight-fifteen bus from Nasik," he told her.

"But that will be too late. I told my husband I would be home by eight."

"By eight? Why did you tell him that?"

"I had to. He has invited some friends to our house."

"That is impossible," he explained. "We would have to catch the four o'clock from Nasik, which means we must leave here any minute."

"Yes, I know. I should have told you before."

"Yes, you might have told me!"

"Don't be angry with me."

"Oh, why should I be angry?"

"I don't know why, but I can see you are."

"You are most perceptive to see that!"

"Please don't shout that way."

"Who is shouting? What reason have I for shouting? After all I have had my lunch, eh? What difference does it make whether or not I have any dessert?"

"But we have had des——," she began, then realized what he meant, and turned crimson, then dead white. "If that is what is angering you, Mr. Godse, I can assure you there would have been no dessert no matter how late a bus we would take!"

"Ah, I see!"

"I hope you are sober enough to."

"Never fear, Mother, I am perfectly sober—now."

He snapped his fingers for the bill, and after glancing at the total, handed the waiter ten rupees, and told him to keep the change.

"Why are you leaving so early?" the owner asked in alarm. "Was something wrong with the service?"

"Not the service, Karve, the company."

"Ah, too bad, Naturam," the other replied sympathetically.

If she heard it, she gave no indication of having done so, walking out before him, and gazing once more at the impassively magnificent rock pile. The driver started up his motor at Natu's signal, and came around to open the door for them.

"Will you go see the temple now?" he asked.

"The lady has no time for that. We go back to Nasik."

"But I am willing to wait for you until seven as we agreed, sir," he said, indicating that the price would be the same whether he drove them back before then or not.

"You are a generous man," Natu replied, trenchantly.

"That is quite all right, sir."

Sarcasm is wasted on this bastard, he thought, but the real anger he felt now was not directed toward the driver. It was not even aimed at her, but rather at himself, for having been so colossally stupid in the first place. It was so expensive a walk up the garden path that he would even be deprived the satisfaction of confiding in Vishnu about it, for it made him look too absurd to be funny.

He said nothing to her on the trip back, but sat glumly in his corner, and stared vacantly at the scenic wonders outside. The money-grabbing bitch, he thought, over and over in his mind, until it spun there like a broken record, throbbing against his brain with the Nasik whiskey's poison. When they reached the bus terminal it was even hotter than it had been when they started up, and worst of all they had forty minutes to wait before the bus was ready to leave for its Poona run. She had said once in the waiting room, "I did enjoy our outing, Natu," and another time, "I am sorry if I led you to expect something different." But he merely looked at her when she spoke as though she were a creature from Mars, trying to contact him in a language he had never heard before.

No rain fell to relieve the oppressive heat during their bus ride home. The crowded old hulk rattled across the naked plain like a tin can dropped down the rocky ledge of a desert slope, and though he had a seat, the combination of heat and jolting was more than his tender stomach and head could stand. He had to ask the driver to stop along the road, practically fell off the bus as he descended its few steps, and was hardly outside before he began throwing up. She is no doubt watching and laughing, he thought, as he squatted before his own poison in the ditch. She has been laughing at me all day, he told himself, resolving as he stepped back onto the vehicle under the curious gaze of the ticket collector, driver, and everyone else, that though he might live for a hundred years he would never take that bitch out again. . . .

"Do try one," she said, holding the plate of chapatis before him.

He folded the unleavened pancake in half, then once again the other way so that he could lift it off easily and fit one end into his mouth. The tan wheat was saturated with clarified butter, which he licked from his fingertips after he finished the cake.

"Not bad," he said. "Do you make puris as well?"

"My husband liked puris," she told him, "but I would have to prepare the dough for them now."

"These will do." He took another, and handed her his empty glass.

The third drink relaxed him. It did not go to the head, but seeped soothingly down his arms and legs, opening tired pores in his blood vessels and muscles the way a warm bath opened the pores of the skin. She knelt on the floor in front of him, leaned her cheek against his knee, and slowly caressed his calf with her adroit fingers.

"You are tired," she said. "Why don't you lie on the bed? Then I will be able to massage you."

"Is that all you will do for me?"

"I will do anything," she said, too eagerly, too readily.

"You should learn to be more reticent," he advised her.

"I do not know that word," she said, bewildered.

"That is the trouble, Sheila."

"I have had little schooling."

"Yes, I expect you were married too young for that."

"No, I was fourteen before I married."

"All of fourteen?"

"Yes, my father did not own much property."

"Have you many children?"

"God has taken them back," she whispered.

You mean the Muslims have slaughtered them, he thought, but he did not say that to her. "I seem to be ready for another drink," he said.

"You can drink much," she said.

"Too much do you think?"

"No, no, I did not mean that!"

"So you will not mother me," he muttered, more to himself than to her.

"I did not hear you please."

"It is just as well."

The fourth drink stirred him. It was as though the other three were awakened by its impact, as though they had been waiting for it to come and transform them all from insipid warm liquid into an intoxicating beverage that ignited his brain, and sent currents of desire through his hitherto languid body. He removed his shirt and unhooked his money belt, rolling the gun in it neatly and putting the roll under his shirt on the floor beside the chair. Her eyes widened at the sight of the pistol, though she had known it was there.

"Have you ever used it?" she asked.

"During the war, many times."

"Oh, you were in the Army. I see."

"Yes, something like that."

"One of my brothers is in the Army."

"Here?"

"He is in Kashmir now."

"That is good."

"I have received no letter since he went there."

"He is too busy to write."

"Do you think it is very dangerous for him there?"

"Never mind about your brother. Why don't you massage me? Come."

"You are very firm," she said, placing her hands upon his stomach, moving them slowly up his ribs, then down under his arms, the fingers probing gently against the flesh, the palms leaning down into the relaxed muscle fibers, her hands moving in large circles at first, then turning inward as she traced two invisible spirals over his torso, then all but stopping as she edged her hands lower, pushing the gathered cloth at the top of his dhoti loose, gripping the wings of his pelvis tightly at first, then running the very tip edges of her fingers over the ridge of that obtruding bone, till he felt his blood rushing there in response to her fingers' call, till the warm, intoxicating surge of inner fluid throbbed through his hips and tingled his thighs in an almost painful ecstasy of passion.

"Rani," he whispered, reaching out to stroke her soft hair, rising on one elbow, and looking into her eyes, which stared at him flatly, with a dull look of incomprehension and surprise.

"You do not like me to massage any more?" she asked. The dumb simplicity of her words, the dead flatness of her gaze, hit him like a bucket of ice water, and all the intoxication which the fourth drink had brought suddenly dissolved.

"Better get me some more to drink," he ordered, though he could not help thinking that perhaps he had had enough to drink by now. His hand would have to be steady today, and it would not do if his vision blurred. He tightened his dhoti, dropped his legs over the edge of the bed, and tried to stand up, but felt too lightheaded and had to sit again almost immediately. He looked at the face of his wristwatch, but saw two faces where there should have been one. Both faces informed him that it was one thirty-five.

"Here is your drink," she said.

6

Gopal Das remained in the garden outside Gupta House only long enough to decide where he would post his men once the crowd began to thicken. He drew a rough sketch of the layout, sitting on the grass and using his briefcase to support the paper. Bapu's path ran the length of the garden down its middle, and his small platform was only a few yards from the far hedge opposite the porch. There were trees on either side of the platform, but unfortunately none of them were sturdy enough to take a man's weight, or he could have placed a sharpshooter in each. The older trees were really too distant to take such a risk from, for the crowd would be dense, Gopal knew, and then of course, no matter how excellent the marksman, that kind of medicine might prove more fatal than the disease. The bullets meant to save him might stray into Bapu himself. He could put a few men on the platform, but not until Bapu settled down there, for it would be more than disrespectful, it would be sacrilege, to have them mount the outdoor altar before the high priest. The only structures in the garden were the gardener's hut and the well. The gardener was friendly enough and did not object to his coming inside to look around there. One small window faced the platform from a rear corner, but its line of sight was less than five feet above ground level, and would surely be obscured by many backs and heads by the time the meeting started. To post one of his men there might merely be wasting him. Of course, ideally he would have liked to put men everywhere. Yet were there enough to go around? Gopal marked every opening in the hedges with a cross at its approximate position on his sketch, drew a circle for the well, a rough square for the gardener's hut, folded the paper, and zipped it inside his case.

Outside the garden, across the street from Gupta's new temple, he saw a parked taxi, and recognized the Sikh driver as one of his department's recent recruits.

"I am occupied, Sa'ab," the driver said sullenly.

His flag was down and the meter humming, but Gopal was not fooled by that. "Home Ministry—Criminal Division," he told the plain-clothes man, letting himself into the back.

"Forgive me, sir," the driver said briskly. "I did not see it was you."

"Quite all right. But please hurry."

The taxi started off before he had uttered the last word. Gopal almost regretted having unleashed this Sikh entirely with that command, however, for though he was a fine driver he almost caused several collisions weaving from lane to lane, and startled a few policemen by totally ignoring their traffic directions. He did not even stop at the Ministry's gate, but came to a screeching halt in front of the steps, which was after all a bit risky, since the guards would have been perfectly within their rights to have taken a shot at his tires. They were apparently alert enough to recognize that this was no ordinary taxi, though Gopal was pleased to see that at least one guard had started running after the car, and only stopped when he recognized the passenger who got out.

"Better take it a bit slower going back," Gopal told the driver. "Many thanks."

"My pleasure, sir," the Sikh said, saluting.

His office was on the third floor, but Gopal did not wait for the lift. His doctor would have scolded him for it, but he suspected that most of his colleagues' heart attacks came from too little exertion rather than too much. They all blamed the climate of course, but he had served under enough Englishmen in his life to know better. The healthiest individual he had ever known was Mountstuart Malcolm, District Superintendent of Police of the Central Provinces, who galloped at least ten miles before dawn, was practically the only man to walk the streets of Nagpur between eleven and two, and always led his raids into the Bhopal hills at the hottest time of day and year when the most desperate bandits were fast asleep. Some people attributed such vitality to the special character of English blood, but Gopal had pushed himself hard enough to explode that myth. Then too there was always the Chief. But it was hard to convince aging and potbellied ministers and secretaries that what they really needed to do if they hoped to live longer was to speed up instead of slowing down. He had tried telling them that for a while. They called him a crank.

Entering the office, Gopal found his deputy waiting. A tall, white-haired figure, handsomely erect, Frank Ramamurti stood gazing out the window. His rugged, square-jawed face and steely blue eyes might easily have belonged to a movie idol rather than a professional policeman. He turned as the door slammed, nodding his mute greeting.

"Frank, just the man I wanted," Gopal said, opening his briefcase and removing his sketch of the garden before sitting down at the desk. "Pull up a chair, I have something to show you."

"There's lunch on that tray, Chief," Frank said, pointing to a platter of tanduri chicken he had ordered an hour ago.

"Not now," Gopal muttered, taking a cigarette from his desk box instead, but lifting his phone before pausing to strike a match. "Ask Bose and Munda to report here at once, please," he ordered into the phone, then hung up and turned to his deputy. "There's my security plan of Gupta's garden. How does it look to you, Frank?"

"Looks like you've plugged all the holes," Frank said. "But where do you get the plain-clothes men to fill them?"

Lighting his cigarette, Gopal took a long, hungry drag. "We'll use every agent we've got," he explained.

"Chief, better read what I've left on your desk," Frank suggested glumly. He pointed to some papers now lying under Gopal's briefcase.

Gopal glanced hastily at his deputy's weekly report, then curiously, almost with annoyance for the interruption, at Frank's handsome Anglo-Indian face. "I'll read this tomorrow," he said, tossing the report aside.

[115]

"I wish you'd read it now, sir," Frank replied. "You'll see it shows that more major crimes have been carried out in Delhi during the week we've had practically the whole force on the assassination than in any two-month period before—"

"I've seen the figures, Frank," Gopal interrupted, wearily.

"And you plan to use even more men in that garden tonight, sir?"

"Yes, I must."

"They'll hang you for it, Chief."

"What are you talking about, Ramamurti?"

"They've been waiting to ruin you ever since you made a half-English Christian your deputy," Frank explained.

"I picked the best damned policeman I could find in this wretched country for my deputy," Gopal countered, "and I can assure you or anyone else who's interested that if there was a Hindu, Sikh, Muslim, or godforsaken Animist half as good at the job of maintaining law and order—"

"I haven't done much of that this past week—"

"Never mind it now, Frank. After tonight you'll have all the men you need."

Frank pushed away from the desk and strode back to the window. Folding his arms over his chest he narrowed his eyes to stare at the white glare of the southern horizon. His English father had been commissioner of police in Madras, and though he could not bequeath his illegitimate son his surname, he had given Frank his looks and his mannerisms, his professional pride. Deputy Superintendent Ramamurti was one of the few men in government service who still wore a linen jacket and starched white shirt and tie to work every day. There were indeed many people, Gopal knew, who considered Frank a relic from the era of colonial rule, one of those crutches from the past which the nation should throw aside as quickly as possible.

"And if they don't try again tonight, Chief?"

"I'm convinced they will, Frank."

"But what if they don't?"

"If they don't try tonight, they'll surely try tomorrow."

"And if not tomorrow the next day. And if not then, the next—"

"All right, I can count!" Gopal snapped. He rubbed the back of his neck with a sweating palm. The hunger pangs in his empty stomach sent throbs of pain through his temples, pulsating pain which settled somewhere behind his eyes and made him wish he could simply close them and leave them closed for a few hours. Sleep had

[116]

never been so rare a luxury before. Momentarily slumping forward he covered his face with both hands.

"Chief, I know what you're up against," Frank said, leaning close to Gopal at the desk so that he could say the unpleasant things he had to in a much milder tone. "But we should be returning men to regular duty instead of taking more of them off. The city's practically wide open already, Chief—larceny, kidnapping, murder— Every thug in town knows what's going on! Soon the word's bound to spread to Calcutta, Madras, Bombay—every criminal in the country will buy a ride to Delhi. Read my report if you think—"

"I know it, Frank! But it doesn't matter," Gopal blurted irately. "We've got to save him!"

Frowning, Frank turned aside. He shook his head negatively. "If Gandhiji won't do anything to protect himself, Chief, double the force we've got won't make any difference."

"It must! He's the prophet of a higher kind of human existence. We can't let him be destroyed by violence," Gopal insisted, though he had covered his face again and seemed unaware of Frank's presence now.

"Chief, you need a rest."

"Nonsense," Gopal said, slamming his desk top with his palms as he got to his feet, standing up stiff-armed against the desk. "I want every man you've got in that garden by five, Ramamurti, and see what the devil's keeping Bose and Munda so long, will you!"

"Yes, sir." Frank waited, but there were no further orders. He hesitated, as though about to speak, then changed his mind and left abruptly.

Gopal locked his jaw and stared at his outspread fingers flattened on top of the desk. He had just those two hands, no more. Only the gods had all the fists they needed. Frank was right, of course; if an assassin was really determined to do it, ready to trade his life for Bapu's, even a hundred agents in that garden couldn't guarantee anything. How many others were there like Pahwa, Gopal wondered, ready and willing to trade their useless lives for a saint's? *My own people*, he thought bitterly. *My own gentle Hindu brothers.* There was a time when he had believed that everything Christian, white, and Western was evil, everything Hindu, black, and Eastern, good. It was so simple and flattering to believe. Everyone he knew believed it, so obviously it had to be true. At least it had seemed that way till he was sixteen, till his final year at Nagpur High School. . . .

Even the meager portion of rain annually allotted Nagpur during June, July, and August, did not fall that year. Each day all eyes scanned the western sky in vain for the clouds that simply *had* to come. Yet none came. The ploughed and seeded earth remained dry. The rivers and water holes became shallow green-covered basins of fetid moisture, then black-stained mud bottoms, and finally parched sand. The cattle were first to die, lingering patiently at the bottoms of the river beds and watersheds, where they went every morning in their dumb brutish manner, trusting that the water which should have rushed soothingly neck-high in August would miraculously appear to quench their ceaseless thirst. Then gradually they succumbed, first the eldest and scrawniest, next the newborn who found no milk in their mothers' dried bellies, and soon after that the best of them. Cows, bullocks, and buffaloes marred the fields and city streets with their distended carcasses, legs stiff and brittle to touch, dried tongues outstretched. Only the vultures and dogs grew sturdy that year. By September the migration of villagers began. Every day they straggled into the big city, entire families, still clinging to ragged bundles of material possessions as they collapsed on the street, never to stir again.

It was the first real famine Gopal could remember, and though some old people said that in 1918 the famine and epidemics had been much worse, he found it difficult to imagine how anything could be worse. Every night the sky was obliterated by smoke rising endlessly from the cremation grounds. Still more corpses littered the streets, some for days before they would be dragged away by the over-burdened untouchables to the overcrowded pyres. The stench of death and decay hovered with the smoke as a rainless cloud of horror over the doomed dry city. Epidemics of typhoid and cholera followed.

"The white men have brought this upon us," everyone said. Gopal listened and nodded. He belonged to the Nagpur Student's Association at school, and when the famine was worst they would meet every evening in the dormitory to discuss its causes and solutions. Their leader was an older boy, who did not attend the high school, but who always carried a book in his hand and knew much more than any of them about everything. His name was Manu, but some of Gopal's friends said that was not his real name, only the name he assumed in public so that the Englishmen would not know who he was. They said, moreover, that he had been to London, and had graduated Oxford with First Class Honors, and that he had passed the Civil Service examinations with the highest grades, but then refused to take up his appointment out of sheer defiance to show the English how little he cared for their honors and money. Gopal had never asked Manu whether the stories about him were true or not, for that would have been insulting. Anyway, he believed them. Everyone did.

"Naturally, as students we ask, 'What are the causes of this famine?'" Manu began, that evening, the hollows of his face and eye sockets black shadows in the eerie glare of the kerosene lamp on the table behind which he stood. They huddled close to one another on the floor of the dormitory common room before him.

"'What are the causes?' we ask. The answer is simple enough. The English have bled our country dry! Yes, my brothers, it is that simple, the foreign vultures who rule us have stolen your food and mine, and so we must starve! We had no famines in this land before the white people came here! I do not ask you to take my word for it—read what our Grand Old Man has written! You see this book in my hand, it is all here in print, I tell you, thoroughly documented—these are the facts! *Facts,* I say—not I, it is what Dadabhai Naoroji has said many years ago!"

At the mention of that patriarch's name there was a stir among the audience, then a cheering round of applause, for who had not heard of Dadabhai? Which of them was so stupid as not to have recognized the name of this saint among patriots, who had served three times as president of the National Congress?

"Our wealth has been transported beyond the seas, my brothers! Each year for two hundred years uncounted millions of rupees—yes, you have heard me correctly—I said *millions!* Millions upon millions robbed from our motherland! Stolen by the plunderers, who have brought us their Bible in return! When they came here we owned the land and they owned the Bible, now they own the land and tell us to take the Bible!"

He was a brilliant, clever fellow, you could not deny it, Gopal thought, laughing with his classmates and comrades. They gained courage and renewed hope looking at each other's faces as they laughed.

"I am glad to see you can still laugh, but is the death of our parents and brothers truly worthy of laughter, tell me? Today alone two hundred bodies have been carried to the sacred ghats for burning! That is right, I said *two hundred!* How long can such a state of affairs be allowed to continue?"

There were cries of "Shame, shame" from the group.

"I say we must take action, brothers! We must liberate our mother-

[119]

land from this octopus which has crawled out of the ocean and seeks to strangle her! We can stand idly by no longer, while the missionaries preach patience and brotherly love, while the white bandits bleed us to death with their so-called rule of law! Law indeed! It is the law of the jungle they have brought us, with themselves as the tigers and lions! I tell you that unless—"

The murmur and nervous gesturing from the audience made him pause and look toward the door. "Pundit" Jackson, the principal, was standing there, a squat dishevelled figure of a man, his hair unkempt, his collar, as always, curling up over the unpressed lapels of his unpressed jacket. His knowledge of Sanskrit had won him the gratuitous title of "Pundit," which somehow stuck.

"I am sorry to interrupt this way," Mr. Jackson said, not to anyone in particular, "but what I have to say won't take very long—if I may?" He looked to Manu for some indication that he would yield the floor, but Manu returned his glance with stony silence, so the Pundit simply continued, addressing his remarks to the boys: "I've just learned that the central government's finally declared us a famine area—"

There was some snickering at this report of so belated an official recognition of reality. Pundit Jackson waited for quiet before continuing.

"—which means, of course, that food shipments are now on the way here, scheduled to arrive tomorrow morning in fact."

This time it was a less hostile murmur of excitement which buzzed across the large room, and the small man's face brightened in response.

"Yes, it is good news, isn't it? I don't know precisely how large the first shipment will be, of course, but the D.S.P. just rang me up, you see, and he seems to feel it should be quite substantial, rather too much in fact for his staff to handle right off. Which is why he called me, and why I'm here now. The more volunteers we can find to help move the grain, the faster we'll be able to get it out to the villages, you see, and naturally—"

"Ah, excuse me for interrupting you, sir," Manu broke in. "When you say *volunteers,* am I correct in assuming that you mean there will be no payment for this work?"

"Yes, that's correct."

"That is what I assumed. I merely wished to clarify that point for the sake of some of the others."

While Manu said that in as slow and meaningful a manner as

possible, Pundit Jackson dragged out a large handkerchief and wiped the back of his neck and forehead.

"I'm sure I don't have to tell any of you," the principal continued, "just how urgent a need for grain exists right now throughout this entire district. What I'm here for now is to ask all of you to go to the railroad terminal tomorrow morning instead of to your classes. I'm declaring the school closed until this job can be handled, and I trust you'll all take advantage of this opportunity to help distribute this food as fast as possible. I plan to be at the station myself tomorrow at eight. The sooner we get at this the quicker we'll get it done. Are there any questions?"

"You aren't authorized to *order* any of us to do this unpaid work, are you, Mr. Jackson?" Manu asked.

"Certainly not."

"I didn't think you were, but I just wanted to make the point clear for the sake of the others."

"I see," Pundit Jackson said, rubbing his stubbled chin. "No, I can't *order* my schoolboys to do this sort of work. Shouldn't want to if I could, for that matter. This isn't the sort of job that needs to go begging, I should think, at a time like this, not if any of you with eyes in your heads still have energy enough to do it! I don't know who you are, sonny, and I don't rightly care! No, I'm not ordering you, lads. No, Heaven help us—no. Good night."

He was not an eloquent man, but the sincerity of his words and the glimpses of passion he revealed impressed Gopal, who whispered to his neighbor, "I will go, won't you?"

"Before continuing with my talk which has been interrupted this evening," Manu said, after Pundit Jackson had gone, "I wish to comment on what is clearly an attempt by the white rulers to use our labor in order to help them do what there would have been no need to do if they had never come here in the first place! This is just one more example of the slavery they have tried to impose upon all of us with their shrewd tactics of divide and rule! It was by divide and rule that the Romans managed to control their empire, and the British have studied these lessons carefully. . . ."

Despite Manu's advice that they boycott this latest governmental attempt to enslave them, Gopal and several of his friends walked to the station the next morning. Not many of the other students joined them, however, for by nine o'clock only ten boys had appeared.

"Well, I suppose that's the lot of us, lads," Pundit Jackson said, with a weary sigh. "Not much of a showing, but never mind, we'd best get cracking."

There were three freight cars filled with grain sacks. The police had sent about twenty men, the Army a company. There was a missionary school in town, and its staff was also there. By noon the cars were emptied, and after lunch they started loading carts destined for the villages. Gopal was not accustomed to such heavy work. He had to pause a while after moving each sack. Standing in the shade catching his breath he watched Pundit Jackson and the missionaries, all dressed in their regular suits, doing the work of coolies. They were white Englishmen and Christians, yet they worked that way so that black peasants, who were Hindus, would not starve to death. Trying to equate what he saw with what Manu had told them last night was most puzzling. That evening he felt more exhausted than he ever remembered feeling, but he went to the common room eagerly anticipating to learn from Manu the answers to many questions which disturbed him now.

"Can't you see they have shipped this food because they are afraid we have become too strong," Manu told him, before the lecture began. He spoke with the same self-assured tone of complete conviction, which had always impressed Gopal before, and which alone had been sufficient to stifle his questions.

"But the food will save lives," he persisted this time.

"For what?" Manu asked sardonically.

"For what?" Gopal did not understand.

"Precisely. For what will these wretched lives be saved, tell me? No, let me tell you. They will be saved from immediate starvation so that they can continue to slave for the white bloodsuckers and starve gradually."

"But without the grain we brought them today," Gopal insisted, "I am sure that many peasants I have seen with my own eyes would be dead tomorrow."

"And what of it?" Manu asked. "They would be born again the next day or next month. Are their lives so precious that we should weaken ourselves to save them, when all that we do by saving them is help to save the British raj as well? If enough people died tomorrow can't you see that those who were left would rise as one man and throw the white dogs back into the ocean where they came from?"

"And then?" Gopal asked.

"Then we shall be free, my brother. Why do you look so confused? It is very simple, believe me. Do not waste your strength again helping them do their coolie labor—you are a Brahman, after all, aren't you?"

"Yes, yes," Gopal said, listlessly going to take his seat on the floor as Manu cleared his throat noisily and began his lecture.

The next day there was no school again, but instead of returning to the railroad station, Gopal remained lying on his cot. His arms and back were stiff, but that was not why he stayed on the cot. He simply had no reason to get up. He kept thinking about what Manu had said, and the logic of that argument seemed too sound for him to refute. What did it matter, after all, if anyone lived or died? Life in the abstract was nothing of value, was it? Life under any terms? The goal he had always been taught to seek was escape from life and its tortures. Moksha was release from the chains of existence, release from passion, release from all striving. After his father had been shot by the bandits, his eldest brother had taken the family away from their village, and brought them to this big city, yet for what? His mother soon died of her grief. She had shaved her head, discarded all her jewels, and day by day they watched her frail body languish, till one morning she did not rise. He had cried then, but his brother told him how wrong it was to cry at such a time, for the tears of loved ones only added karma to the departing soul, and would make its journey toward salvation that much longer. "Let her go," his brother said. "Let her go in peace." Yes, he thought, let us all go. Was that what Manu meant by freedom? He often wanted to ask about that word, but it was so commonly used that it never really occurred to him he did not understand its meaning. The nation was fighting its "freedom struggle," he knew well enough, but if freedom was moksha then why was it necessary to struggle? And if it was necessary to struggle then did that not make freedom a foreign concept? But if it was foreign, then, why was the struggle directed against foreign rule and its ideas? Or were the ideas good, and only the rulers bad? The more he tried to untangle things the more confused they became.

Gopal slept intermittently all that day. He got up only to relieve himself and to drink some water from the earthen jug that stood at the far end of the long dormitory. He did not bother to go down for his millet cakes when the servant came to sound the meal gong. It was almost a week since the school had run out of rice and curds, and the millet alone tasted like wood pulp, so he did not bother with it. He lay half-asleep, suddenly falling off in the heat-heavy windless atmosphere, jolted into wakefulness by a bad dream, finding his body covered with sweat, smelling the smoke of the dead as he sat up and peered about him at the slumbering forms of his classmates. So the day dragged on, an indeterminate mixture of conscious and unconscious dreams, of questions unanswered, of fears without form, of sudden sharp images of dead bodies half-consumed by their pyres' flames rising up to glare at him with skinless skulls and teeth blacked by smoke. He screamed, covering his face with trembling hands, and woke up. No one seemed startled, though a few of the boys turned their heads in his direction. His entire body was trembling now, and he thought it was still the dream, and lay back again saying nothing. His bones ached at every joint, but he thought it was the strain of the work he had done yesterday, so he told no one. Even after the sun set and a breeze had begun to stir, he continued to sweat profusely. He thought it was merely the heat.

The next morning Gopal was too weak to leave his cot. His thirst had become unquenchable, but he felt too tired to walk to the water jug. He tried to call his neighbor, but his voice was like a single thread of sound, which could not be heard. Then he realized something was wrong, so he forced himself to his feet. Then he collapsed. The fever lasted ten days in all. For the first five it continued to rise. On the fifth night it reached one hundred and five. That was when the nurse told Pundit Jackson, who had come to visit him in the hospital, "He is going through the crisis now. If he lasts the night, we should be out of the woods, I expect. Of course, you never know with typhoid, do you?"

"Suppose not," Mr. Jackson said dejectedly, though he quickly brightened. Gopal remembered it with a clarity that amazed him later, for he could hardly remember anything else that happened during the preceding days. He could not even remember being brought to the hospital. "But we can't afford to lose this one, you know, nurse. He's one of my best lads, you see. Be sure and keep an eye on him tonight, will you?"

"I'll do the best I can, Mr. Jackson." She was a gray-haired Englishwoman, and looked very tired.

"Yes, be sure and do that," the principal said, coming over to rest a hand on Gopal's arm. "And don't you give up, lad, you hear! Don't you let any bug get the better of you now! I'll be in to see you in the morning."

Somehow after that Gopal sensed he would not die. He stopped wanting to die. He felt suddenly that his life mattered. He had no idea of how it mattered, of what he would use it for. It was enough to know that someone really considered it worth the trouble to come

[124]

here and urge him not to give up. "One of my best lads," Pundit Jackson had called him. He fought hard that night to merit such praise. . . .

The door opened, followed by hasty knocking, more an afterthought to courtesy than a request for admission to the superintendent's office. Inspectors Bose and Munda entered the room.

"More tough luck, sir," Chittaranjan Bose began, barging in first and pulling up a chair near the cigarettes, taking one as he spoke. "We spotted one of them entering the Circle cinema an hour back. Almost nabbed him, but the blackguard positively vanished! Clever lot, blast them! What we need is more men, sir! Enough to throw a net over the entire city. Start at the outskirts and move in together, the circle of diminishing radius technique. Don't you think that a good idea, sir?"

"Oh, yes," Gopal said. Leave it to Bose to come up with some theoretically brilliant idea! His mind was as quick as his tongue. "Only we have neither men nor time enough for that now, so we'd best forget it and do what we can. Now this diagram—"

"But, Sir—"

"Chittaranjan, are you going to leash that Bengali tongue or do I have to tell Munda here to do it for you?" Gopal asked.

Moti Munda grinned broadly. He was a short man, but his fists were the largest in the Force. They had been toughened by the mountains of Ladakh, which he'd climbed daily as a boy. His broad flat face revealed the Mongoloid strain in his blood. One of those fists swallowed the bowl of his pipe as he removed it from his mouth to chuckle at Bose's ill-disguised anger.

"I'd like to know where our nation would be without its Bengalis," muttered Bose.

"Let's get to work," Gopal suggested, tracing the lines on his sketch as he spoke. "This is the garden hedge. Here's the path he uses, that's the platform. It's one hundred paces from the rear porch to the platform, and I want both of you stationed along that path—"

"We can cover him better," Bose injected, "if one of us walks right ahead of him and the other—"

"He won't permit it," Gopal snapped.

"Oh. Well, that's a jolly big help," Bose said.

So are you, Gopal thought, though he knew Chittaranjan meant well. Besides he was too good a marksman to discharge today. Gopal lit another cigarette.

[125]

"Mmmm," Munda remarked, studying the diagram intently. "Perhaps from on top of the platform we would be in better position to see."

"But anyone up there's a sitting duck," Bose argued.

"I agree, Moti," Gopal said, "that the platform gives us the best range of vision, and I plan to get up there myself as soon as Bapu does."

"Mmmm," Munda nodded, dragging on his pipe. "Why don't you let me take the platform, Chief?"

"Thank you, Moti, but—no, I'd rather be . . ." Gopal shrugged it off. It would have taken too long to explain why he wanted to be as close to Bapu as possible for as long as possible tonight. "I'll do the assigning," he simply said.

"But what if they throw a bomb again," Bose insisted, "and this time it lands on the platform, sir? I should say we can afford to lose an inspector rather more readily than a superintendent! Why not let Moti *or* me take the platform?"

"And here I thought he's been gunning for my job all this time," Gopal said, with a wink to Moti.

"Blast your bloody jokes, sir! The least we can do is put it to a vote!"

"Now look here, Chittaranjan, just because this country of ours is a democracy that doesn't mean my department has to become one! I'll guard the platform. Anyway," he sighed, sobering suddenly and rubbing his palm forward over the top of his head, "I doubt that they'll risk another miss with the bomb. I expect tonight they'll try with a gun."

"Yes, I think a pistol," Moti agreed.

"Bengalis would keep tossing bombs," Bose said.

"These are Marathas," Gopal reminded him.

"Well, I shouldn't be surprised if *they* wouldn't use the knife," Bose suggested. "Half-civilized people!"

"That *is* what Shivaji would have used," Gopal conceded. He hadn't thought of a knife before. What else had he neglected to think about? "Whatever they use we've *got* to stop them! We can, and we will! Moti, you stand here, just a few yards from the porch. They may try it as soon as he appears, though somehow I—no, we've got to expect everything. Keep after him when he passes you, Moti; try to stay as close behind him as you can, closing toward the platform, but don't trap yourself by coming too far along. Remember we've got to cover him going back as well as coming out!"

"Understood," Moti said.

"Chittaranjan, I'll want you here at midpoint, and I'll wait just in front of the platform till he reaches it, then I'll climb on top behind him. Going back we should try to keep relatively the same positions. Clear?"

"Roger," Bose said.

"Good enough. Now let's set our watches. He's always on time; at least we can be sure of that. He'll emerge onto the porch at five sharp, but we'd best get near our positions in the garden by four. It is now precisely—" he paused, watching the slow sweep of his second hand, "seven minutes to two!"

They set their watches and rose to leave.

"Before you go," Gopal added, "Chittaranjan, you'll be responsible for getting the police net rigged as soon as possible. One hundred men should do it, but I want them to cover the area in depth, is that clear? At least one man at every road and alley for three blocks around. And make sure they understand that if a shot is fired, the net closes—nobody leaves the ring till we pass the word."

"Roger."

"Have a walkie-talkie standing by to alert the riot squad if necessary. Moti, they're your job. See to it they know what we're up to. We don't want this thing getting out of control. I don't imagine we'll need any heavier artillery, but in case we do—" Gopal paused. He had devoted so much of his energy and time to thinking about how to thwart this assassination plot that he had not really allowed himself to contemplate the possible aftermath of failure. Yet what would become of order in the city, in the entire nation in fact, should its Father be shot tonight? A chill of apprehension seized him. He had witnessed too many riots ignited by far less volatile an explosive. "I suppose I'd better contact the Army people myself. All right, have we forgotten anything?" he asked, coming around the desk to stand directly before them.

"Not that I can think of, Chief," Bose said.

Moti nodded in agreement.

"We meet next in the garden," Gopal said, extending his hand, first to Munda, then to Bose. "Good luck, men."

7

"We are most patient, Shyama," the Maharaja said, placing the areca palm nut carefully under the sharp blade of his silver cutter and slowly squeezing the handles together within one fist till the brown nut split into several pieces. "We are most patient, as you know, but there is a limit to our patience, just as there is a bottom to our pocketbook." He always referred to himself in the plural, and in view of his weight alone, not to speak of his royal lineage, it was hardly surprising.

"Your anxiety is perfectly understandable, Maharaj," Shyama Prahlad told him. "Perfectly understandable." He himself was a big man, though seated so close to His Highness Shivaji Rao Nulkar II, the Honorable Dr. Prahlad looked almost diminutive.

"Please let us make ourselves clear, Shyama, it is no longer a question of anxiety. We are becoming *annoyed*." He continued fragmenting the areca nut pieces while he spoke, his bulging eyes fixed upon them as his bloated fingers placed them again and again under the guillotine of his cutter. "We are getting *tired* of listening to that man telling us how much money we owe the Pakistanis, Shyama. We do not wish to *hear* such things any longer. Why must we continue to *listen* to such foolish talk?"

"I am assured Your Highness will not be disturbed by such seditious scurrility much longer," the honorable doctor announced softly. A gold-uniformed attendant stood far enough away in the sitting room of Delhi's plush hotel apartment so that there was really no fear of his eavesdropping, nonetheless Shyama Prahlad was careful to keep the volume of his voice quite low. His Highness did not, however, bother to train himself at so late a stage in life to speak in whispers. He had been among the leading lights of the more than five hundred maharajas who traded their princely states for handsome government pensions when independence was granted several months ago. Unlike many of his royal colleagues, Shivaji Rao did not retire to the Riviera, however, but remained close to his people. He did not forget his grandfather's promise to reunite them someday under his noble line's standard.

"Who makes you this assurance, Shyama?"

"I have heard from Guruji today, Maharaj," the white-bearded, saffron-robed Member of Parliament replied. He was leader of the rightist splinter group opposition in the central Assembly.

"We have been promised much by Dhondo in the past, Shyama. Dhondo makes many promises." Satisfied that he had ground the nut into as many minute particles as was possible, Shivaji Rao extracted a fresh betel leaf from his silver pan box, and poured the nut chips onto its center from his ample palm. Dipping into the small compartments of his silver box with pinched fingertips, he then spread clove, cardamom, and coconut onto the leaf, over which he smeared just a stain of opium paste with his small finger. The last ingredients were finely flattened leaves of silver and gold. It was truly a pan fit for a king, and would have cost one hundred rupees in Bombay. His Highness folded the betel leaf's edges neatly around the precious contents so that the final package was shaped as a triangle. He rubbed a bit of fluid lime over the leaf's outside, like glue used to seal a parcel, stared admiringly at his handicraft for a moment, then popped it into his cavernous mouth. Bovine-like he continued chewing the stimulant throughout the remainder of his conversation with Shyama Prahlad.

"Guruji is a selfless saint, Maharaj," the venerable doctor replied.

"Selfless? Perhaps, Shyama. Who is to judge human motives, after all? As for 'saint'—the word has been corrupted so far as we are concerned. Our people bestow that title too readily on charlatans—and much worse, on traitors as well. They speak of the Muslim-lover as a saint too, do they not?"

"The undiscerning do, Maharaj."

"Yes, the *cattle* you mean. Well the cattle will always be cattle, Shyama. They were born to be whipped, but nowadays instead of whipping them, politicians worship them. Now that you are a politician, Shyama, forgive us if we offend—"

"Please, Maharaj, you know I agree."

"It is the inevitable consequence of suffrage, Shyama. You exalt the herd by giving each ox a vote. Then instead of leading the herd you must bow before it. You must let it trample over you, because you have surrendered your sovereignty to the majority of the oxen's hoofprints. That is the meaning of democracy, Shyama. Remember it. Do not let yourself be deceived by other high-sounding definitions."

"I am not easily deceived, Maharaj," his visitor replied. "But Your Highness need have no fear. This foreign import will never take firm root in our country. Our classical tradition is one of *royal* rule, not the mob rule which government by the whim of the 'demos' implies. Our young men's minds have been spoiled by reading too many foreign books, but it is all a temporary infatuation. We shall return to the wellsprings of our tradition. We shall bathe again in the ever-fresh fountain of our own past, Your Highness. It will not take long, Maharaj."

"You are a wise man, Shyama. We are pleased with your wisdom, but words alone achieve nothing."

"I have come to inform you, Maharaj, that the words are about to be translated into action," Shyama Prahlad whispered, leaning far forward in his chair, stroking the long silken hairs of his beard, which gave his face so prophetic an appearance.

"When?"

"This evening, Maharaj."

"Or so Dhondo claims!"

"This time he promises, Maharaj."

"Last time he also promised!"

"They will not fail again, Your Highness."

[130]

"We hope you are true, Shyama, for as we indicated earlier our pocketbook is not bottomless. We can afford to support no more failures. Our expenses have been excessive these past few months, and now your government speaks of reducing our pension in order to pay the infidels who have robbed our ancestral domain!"

"I do not consider this transitional administration *my* government, Maharaj."

Shivaji Rao studied the star, trapped within the dark sapphire of his largest ring, from various angles, extending his open hand before him, then closing his fist, then caressing his silk-garbed thigh. He appeared totally absorbed by the moving star on his thumb.

"My government of Ramaraj is yet to be reborn on our sacred soil, Majesty," Prahlad continued. "But its birth will depend on you."

"On us? We find that most interesting, Shyama. Elucidate."

"When the news of what is about to occur this evening travels like brush fire across our motherland, Maharaj, it will release all the pent-up frustrations of our people and will serve as a signal and a guide indicating to them how they should act toward the Muslim-appeasing traitors who have forgotten the sack of Somnath and Mathura! It will warm the blood which has grown cold and sluggish in three hundred million hearts, Maharaj! It will kindle imaginations which have been dulled by Western clichés about constitutionality and legal procedures. In a word it will—ignite! For several days, possibly weeks, passion will reign, chaos will be unleashed to do its purifying duty! And when it has become apparent that this administration is powerless to act, I shall rise in the Assembly to propose its dissolution. As a *temporary* measure, mind, I shall suggest a caretaker government under the direct and forceful control of someone whose personality and heritage place him above party factionalism and petty partial loyalties, someone who can serve as a symbol not only of temporal unity for our population but of divine justice as well, someone whose divinity flows in his regal blood—Your Highness."

Shyama Prahlad left his seat, and sank gracefully to the carpet in front of the massive potentate. His obeisance brought his forehead to the perfumed and painted toes of Shivaji Rao's extended right foot. It was not the first time he had thus vowed his allegiance to the former monarch. During the interwar years he had served Shivaji Rao as prime minister of his principality. In 1946 they both decided that his services might prove more useful if he stood for election to the central Assembly. When independence and partition together conspired to strip the Maharaja of his royal estate less than a year later, the wisdom of their decision concerning Prahlad's career was tragically confirmed for both of them. Shyama had not wasted his year in office. His eloquence, classical erudition, and seemingly endless source of income, had won him the backing of forty-three members of the Assembly. Though most of them did not belong to his small party, all met periodically at his home, and voted as he advised on major matters of legislation. Their number was, of course, too small ever to carry a vote of no-confidence, yet with the somewhat larger leftist opposition far less unified in purpose, they represented the leading potential alternative to the Congress administration.

"We are pleased by your devotion, Shyama, but what makes you think the government will seriously entertain your abdication proposal?"

"Two things, Your Highness," he replied, returning to his chair. "First—the breakdown of order will make it obvious to everyone that emergency action will be required. This breakdown will come so suddenly that no one else will be prepared to suggest an alternative solution. Secondly, by making my measure a temporary one, I shall win the support of many members of the majority who would otherwise chafe at the idea of abandoning democratic principles. Needless to say, once you are in power the latter expedient will be forgotten."

"We do not question your astuteness, Shyama, but have you not forgotten the Army?" Shivaji Rao asked, glancing now at several of his other rings. One of them was a large ruby surrounded by ten fragments, all set in white gold. He liked that almost as much as the star sapphire. "Surely you do not expect the Army to sleep through all of this—this chaos you describe?"

"Certainly not, Maharaj, but so much of the Army is presently engaged in Kashmir and garrisoned along the new borders that the South has practically been denuded. It is there that the rioting will be most intense, led by Guruji's Hindu clubs! What is our military command to do, Maharaj? Will they draw back forces from the Muslim enemy to fight their Hindu brothers? It would be suicidal! Yet if ordered, you say, they will do so, and of course I agree—but who will issue such an order? The Prime Minister personally might be foolish enough—he is after all Hindu in name only, but dare he take this responsibility alone? I think not. He is impetuous to a point, but I have watched him carefully enough to know he is a practical politician as well. He has some idea of the power of our religious appeal, and he is not altogether ignorant of the firm roots of our cultural heritage. These things will make him pause, as will his natural predilection to study every aspect of every major problem till his mind is practically paralyzed by contradictory arguments—"

"Yes, it is the curse of all liberals, Shyama. They have no true principles, so they make reason their god, and then wonder why he invariably abandons them. But continue, continue!"

"Thank you, Maharaj. Allow me to say how much your humble slave is impressed by your cogent comments and questions."

"We have not entirely confined our study to the arts of rule and war, Shyama," Shivaji Rao said, with a tight smile.

Shyama Prahlad moistened his lips to speak, when the telephone rang. The attendant, who might have been a statue for all his prior movement, instantly came to life, striding across the room to the end table on which the phone rested within easy reach of His Highness' arm.

"Yes?" the turbaned guard answered. "Yes, madam, one moment please."

"Tell her to wait till we call," Shivaji Rao said, before his guard even announced who it was.

"His Highness will call when he is ready, madam." He nodded mutely. "Yes, madam, I will." He hung up. "She asks me to inform His Highness she is hungry, Your Highness." He bowed and returned to his post at the other side of the room.

Shivaji Rao ejected a red mouthful of saliva into the silver spittoon at his side, and chewed the remaining pan more vigorously. He gestured to Shyama to proceed.

"At any event, Maharaj, I feel certain that the Prime Minister will not initiate drastic action before consulting his Cabinet—and there, as you realize, more sensible minds prevail."

"We realize they are more sensible, Shyama, but how favorable will they be inclined to feel about accepting us as even their *temporary* sovereign. It was they who deposed us, remember, not the Prime Minister alone."

"Quite so, Maharaj. Quite so, *but!*" He touched one upstretched finger to his furrowed tan brow. "The past six months have taught them much! They have taught all of us, yes, but some had more to learn than others. The devout and the orthodox who should have known better, but were fools enough to believe they could hurl a fragment of the motherland to wolves and expect the wolves to be sated with it have learned that a scavenger's appetite grows upon the food it devours. Since the invasion of Kashmir many slumberers have awakened. I have heard them open their hearts and pour forth their regrets in private—*too late,* they imagine. We shall show them it is not too late! I have already prepared the soil with a few, who would not have listened silently to anything I said six months ago, but who stand now with their heads bowed and hear my words without arguing. In the next few days before I rise publicly to announce my resolution I shall speak to others still more influential."

"We are pleased to learn of this, Shyama."

"Your Highness' pleasure is his slave's reward, but though the sun shines on the soil no grain will sprout without water."

"Our pocketbook is not without a bottom."

"From a handful of seed, Maharaj, many cartloads of grain may be reaped."

"We have already planted many handfuls."

"Tonight Guruji promises the first harvest."

"Exactly where will Dhondo fit into all this, Shyama? What position does he visualize for himself in our caretaker state?"

"Have no fear of Guruji, Maharaj."

"We fear no one, Shyama, but only because we trust no one."

"Your Highness is truly heir to our classical wisdom, but Guruji has no personal ambitions."

"All men have ambitions."

"Guruji has passed beyond aspiration, Maharaj."

"Then why has he labored so hard to develop his Society?"

"So that our religion will not be destroyed by Muslims, Christians, and atheists, Maharaj."

"Yes, of course, that is what he claims, Shyama." Shivaji Rao turned his head slightly and emitted another stream of blood-colored fluid, which hailed against the inner wall of the spittoon. "You are a wise man, Shyama. Tell me, who is the most dangerous enemy?"

"The most dangerous enemy, Maharaj? To whom?"

"To anyone, Shyama. It does not matter."

"But surely it matters, Maharaj, for the enemy most dangerous to one man may be the staunchest ally of another, is it not?"

"No, Shyama, the *most* dangerous enemy may be your staunchest ally—"

"But surely, Maharaj—"

"Never interrupt us, Shyama!"

"Forgive me, Maharaj."

"Your most dangerous enemy may be your staunchest ally," repeated the massive Maharaja, whose stomach, even in the soft deep

[134]

chair into which he was wedged, rose like a balloon high above the upholstered arms, *"if* he professes to want nothing for himself."

The Honorable doctor smiled uneasily and stroked his beard.

"You, for example, Shyama—"

"Me?" He uttered it involuntarily, then clamped his jaw shut, for Shivaji Rao had not finished.

"You, Shyama, have healthy ambitions, which you have never tried to disguise from us."

"I admit I have many faults, Maharaj."

"Why call them *faults?* None of us are beyond temptation. King Rama himself was often tempted, and he was the incarnation of divinity as all sovereigns are. We too recognize our human attributes, Shyama—never mind telling us we are perfect! We know that, but we also know we are imperfect. You desire power, Shyama, but simply to look at you anyone can see you have no craving for wealth. Another man desires wealth, a third women, a fourth opium. Faults? Not at all. If they were we should be more guilty than anyone, yet as divine sovereign we are free from guilt as long as we do not ignore the desperate need of our people for the beneficence of our personal guidance and rule."

"I crave power, Maharaj, only to be able to serve you more effectively."

"Careful, Shyama, do not profess to be too selfless. One so-called saint has already brought us near to ruination, while the other labors to destroy him. The question, Shyama, is will Dhondo try to destroy us as well someday?"

"But we are his friends, Maharaj. You have been more than a friend—you are his patron, sire. And it was your blessed father who gave him the funds to proceed to England when he was hardly more than a boy. I fail to understand, Maharaj, why you think Guruji will ever repay you with disloyalty or—or worse?"

"But we do not think it, Shyama—yet. It has only crossed our mind that someday he *may,* and we wish to caution you concerning so grave a possibility. You realize it is a possibility now, don't you?"

"I had never thought of it as one, Maharaj."

"Of course. Dhondo is too clever for that, which is precisely what makes him so dangerous, Shyama. How much will you need?"

"Ten thousand is enough to begin with, Maharaj."

"You think we are made of gold, Shyama?"

"Before the moon is full once again Your Highness will sleep in the palace now occupied by the English Viceroy."

[135]

"Who is to do this first harvesting this evening, Shyama?"

Dr. Prahlad nervously curled the ends of his beard before answering. "Naturam Godse, Maharaj."

"The drunkard?"

"But, sire—"

"Ho—no, no, Shyama, say no more! Save your breath. Why waste your valuable breath?"

"But Guruji swears—"

"Let him swear till the stars turn green. What do we care for such nonsense? So he still trusts that big mouth, does he? This is the heartening news you bring us, is it? Refresh our memory, Shyama, how much did we pay Dhondo's drunken disciple six months ago to do this very thing?"

"Be reasonable, Your Highness—"

"We did not ask you whether or not we are reasonable!" Gripping the arms of his chair, his cheeks puffed out from the effort, like a battleship launched from drydock, Shivaji Rao Nulkar II pushed himself forward, and somewhat miraculously, before falling through the floor on his stomach, rose to his feet. The clock, which had just chimed twice, shook on the mantelpiece over the fireplace as the room seemed to vibrate ever so slightly. Shyama Prahlad had been sure to get to his feet before the sovereign stood upright. "Was it not ten thousand rupees then?"

"Yes it was, Maharaj, but this time—"

"So it was ten thousand? Our memory is improving, but help us a bit more, Shyama. Remind us, will you, of what Dhondo's journalist friend did with all that money?"

"Your Highness, the plot then was premature."

Still breathing hard from the exertion of standing up, Shivaji Rao spoke as though he had heard nothing from Shyama Prahlad, ignoring the latter entirely. "We seem to recollect that he stayed in this very hotel—three weeks comes to mind, but perhaps it was longer?"

"Two weeks and two days, Maharaj."

"Ho, only sixteen days, was it? And how many gallons of champagne did he consume in those sixteen days? No, don't bother telling us. We do not wish to be reminded of failures. There have been too many failures. We have given our final rupee to Guruji's young friends." He snapped his fingers. The guard rushed to his side, bowing. "Call my—acquaintance. Tell her she may come up now."

"I beg of you, Maharaj, permit me to explain—"

[136]

"Shyama, we are weary." He closed his eyes and touched the back of his hand to his brow. "We must rest now."

"I have been promised, Maharaj, that Godse will not live to fail a third time," the white-bearded ascetic whispered into the regal ear.

"Unreliable people should never be employed a *second* time, Shyama, but our head is throbbing now. Please, no more!"

". . . yes. Very well," the guard concluded softly, "if you must." He replaced the phone on the table.

"What does she say?"

"If His Highness will excuse me, she is powdering her nose and will come as soon as she finishes, Your Highness."

"Is that so! Well, well!" Shivaji Rao paced impatiently to the fireplace, and stood drumming his fingers on the mantelpiece.

Dr. Prahlad realized that his audience had come to an end, yet he also knew that if he left empty-handed now and if nothing spectacular happened this evening, his party might long remain bereft of its major source of support.

"Should Godse fail, Maharaj—I do not believe he will—but *should* he, I say, for you have taught me today to think of even the least likely as possible," Shyama whispered, moving as close as he dared to the massive back whose width almost obscured the fireplace, "I shall feel obliged to assume direct responsibility for *the very urgent* matter, which I have left in Guruji's hands up until now. Does Your Highness hear me?"

"We do not yet hear you quite clearly," he answered, without turning around.

"What I mean to say, Maharaj, is merely what you have been telling me many times, that I find it intolerable to listen to a man who pretends to be a devout Hindu urging poor Hindustan to pay so many millions to a bloodthirsty neighbor. After all, where could such money be found unless—unless someone should get the idea of introducing a bill to rob our own royalty of their much-deserved pensions? Is my voice clearer, Maharaj?"

"We are not entirely deaf, Shyama."

"The longer this man continues to talk the more real the possibility of such a bill would seem to become, is all I wish to state, Maharaj, so that if Guruji's friend fails— How shall I put it? When one ax handle breaks, another must be found."

"You are rich in metaphors, Shyama."

"But otherwise poor, Maharaj."

Shivaji Rao moved his bulk slowly around. He liked the diamond ring least of them all. There was nothing particularly aesthetic about it, no special beauty of cut or setting, nothing at all remarkable except for its weight—ten carats. He eased it carefully off his middle finger. For a moment it stuck at the knuckle, and Shyama Prahlad raised his hands as though ready to tug.

"Perhaps you would like the finger as well, Shyama?"

"No, no, Maharaj, your slave merely wishes to help if he can."

"There!" He pulled it free, and smiled to see how rapidly his old friend was curling the edges of his beard with both hands. "It is worth fifty thousand rupees. You will have no trouble getting twenty for it immediately, but see that it is not wasted, Shyama. It belonged to our grandfather." Shivaji Rao deposited the ring in the cupped and waiting hands, which shook slightly till they closed firmly around the precious gift.

"The grandfather's ring will return the grandson his realm," Dr. Prahlad promised, kneeling again, this time to touch the royal toes, not with his forehead, but with his lips.

8

"Shall I tell you a secret?" Naturam asked her.

"Yes, I love secrets," Sheila said, bending over him to blow lightly against his ear and neck.

"Why are you doing that?"

"Men like it—I thought."

"Well, I don't—it tickles."

"But that is what it is supposed to do," she said. He was the strangest customer she had ever encountered.

"How can I tell you a secret if you tickle me?"

"I will listen carefully," she promised.

"You must not tell anyone else!"

"I will not."

"Do you swear by Ganesh?"

"Yes, why not?"

"Say 'I swear by Ganesh never to repeat what I am about to hear.'"
She said it.

"Now if you break your vow he will destroy you," Natu said, sitting up on the bed.

"Please do not look at me that way," she asked. "It frightens me. Let me get you some more gin."

"Do you not want to hear my secret?"

"I do not think so—no."

She was so obviously superstitious it made him laugh, which only frightened her more, but then he realized what he had been about to do and it worried him.

"Better make us some tea," he suggested. Then watching her walk away the motion of her hips enticed him, and he said, "Come back here."

"What is it?" she asked, returning timidly.

He pulled her down onto the bed, and pressed his mouth against hers.

"Wait, let me undress," she said.

"Do not speak," he told her. He closed his eyes and found her lips again. They were soft and yielding. Her mouth opened too quickly. He kept his own lips firmly closed and pressed them very tightly against hers.

"Please. You are hurting me," she said.

"I told you not to speak, damn you!" He jerked away and pushed her aside gruffly. She lay with her back to him, rubbing her arm where he had gripped it too hard.

"What are you doing now, stupid?" he asked.

She had begun to cry. She was apparently a rank amateur at this business.

"Make the tea," he ordered. "You are not paid for tears."

"Sorry," she sobbed, sniffling as she went to the kitchen.

It was not her fault entirely, he knew. It always ended that way with the others. Always pain and tears for them. For himself only contempt, disgust, a sense of futility, of wasted effort. Rani alone was different. If I could see her just once more, he thought. Even for one hour. There had been so few hours for them, it almost seemed to be worth the try. After Trimbakeshvar, of course, he had been sure it was finished forever. He had returned to his job with a passionate dedication that even Vishnu Apte found impossible to accept. . . .

"Are you trying to kill yourself, Natu?" Vishnu asked, combing back his hair carefully as he entered the dim office. "Why must you work so late tonight? Tomorrow is Tuesday, did you forget?"

"Listen. How does this sound, Vishnu?" Natu asked, setting his pen aside, and picking up the paper blackened with scratch-out lines, cross-hatching, and interlineal scrawling. " 'Mr. Jinnah has finally revealed himself,' " he read, stooped over the desk, caught in the yellowish glare of a single small bulb dangling from a wire above him, " 'and we are glad of it. In fact, we applaud his frankness! We wish to thank you, Mr. Jinnah, for admitting that the Muslim League is dissatisfied! Certainly they are dissatisfied. This is exactly what we have been saying all year long'—no, I think it is better without 'long' —'exactly what we have been saying all year!—' "

"It sounds fine, Natu," Apte interrupted, "but why must you write this at ten o'clock at night when we will not be able to publish it until Wednesday anyway?"

"Bah! It's no good!" He crumpled the much-worked-over page and tossed it at the basket. It missed and rolled stupidly across the floor. "It lacks fire. There is no punch to it, Vishnu!"

"Natu, what you need is a rest! You must listen to some music, and that is just what—"

"Words can be music, Vishnu. They should be if they are right. They should stir the way music does. They should arouse the soul —Guruji's words do that. He is a poet, you see, but I am—"

"Listen to you, you are becoming morbid again! What is wrong with you these days, Natu? Our circulation is climbing steadily!"

"Is circulation all you worry about, Vishnu?"

"All *I* worry about? I am not the one sitting over my desk every night till I fall asleep there! Look here, I have purchased tickets for the concert tonight. Come, they have started already."

It was the semi-annual cultural highlight of Poona. For years in his youth he had never missed a performance. They began at sundown and played till dawn. People came and left any time in between, but he used to remain there all night. He never fell asleep either.

"No, I must finish this editorial," he protested.

"You will write it in an hour tomorrow, Natu. The concert will inspire you."

"All right—maybe it will," he decided.

The hall was crowded by the time they walked over. It was not far from the Press, and was used ordinarily as a hostel for out-of-town visitors, but during concert weeks no one but the musicians was permitted to live there. It was a large old wooden structure and several hundred people, mostly young men, were seated on the floor in front of the players. There were benches along the sides and back of the cleared rectangle used by the musicians; those were reserved for minor dignitaries and their guests, wealthy landowners, barristers, college presidents. Some of them brought their wives.

"Come, let us get up close!" Vishnu urged, pulling his sleeve.

"Stop dragging me, will you! Do you want me to step on people!"

"Hsst! Quiet!" the more attentive music lovers said. Not that it was ever a passive audience, but there are cranks everywhere. Actually the listeners made almost as much noise as the instruments. They kept time to the tabla with the flats of their fingers slapped against the upturned soles of their feet. They clicked their teeth, smacked their gums, and uttered such expletives as "Va, va!" "Shabash!" and "Tsangla!" It was part of the performance, in fact, and were no such appreciative responses forthcoming the players would have felt insulted, ill appreciated. A concert, after all, was something to be enjoyed, not mourned over. It was a place to meet friends as well, and several of them waved to him, indicating there was ample room on the floor beside them, but Apte always liked to sit close enough to the musicians to smell their sweat.

"Come, I see Baburao!" Vishnu said, shouting, "Baburaoji!" before Natu could stop him.

"Quiet! Quiet!"

"Ah, Apte, Naturam, come along! Plenty of room!" He was seated near the end of the bench on the tabla side. Next to him was Rani, and on the other side of her, the Champion. "Squeeze closer, everyone! Make room for Apte and Godse!" The entire bench was his entourage, and they all willingly obeyed.

"Vishnu, why crowd them? There is room here on the floor!"

"Come, we cannot insult Baburao," Apte insisted, grabbing his shirt again.

"Quiet, will you! Sit down! Hssst!"

It was hardly an appropriate place for an argument.

"Let Godse sit next to me, Apte," Baburao ordered. "Come, Godse, stop acting like a shy bullock. What do you think of my tabla player here? He is great, isn't it? Va, va!"

The young man with the double drums grinned gratefully, and accelerated the already mounting tempo of his swift naked palming on the taut rubber-centered leather skins.

Their eyes met before he sat down. Staring full at him, she puckered her lips ever so slightly. He sensed it was a kiss communicated to him from the far side of Baburao's ample torso. Yet he could not be certain, for almost instantly she concentrated her full attention again on the music. He pretended to do the same, but that silent greeting had transformed him. It was as though she had thrown the switch that turned on all the lights of his soul.

"Shabash!" he shouted, slapping his thigh, starting to beat the time there with his tingling fingers. The artists were first-rate. The sitar, of course, set the pace, its polished gourds echoing the haunting wail of its many strings as the plaintive evening raga told its tale, that of the tragic love of Pururavas for the heavenly nymph Urvashi, who remained as his bride only so long as he kept his vow never to show himself before her naked. "Embrace me three times a day," she told him when they married, "but never lie with me against my will." It was truly a song for the night, and the strings filled the hall with its eerie melody of love half requited. The standing tamboura's tonic drone provided a background of melancholy as the lovers were separated by a bolt of lightning, which illumined the naked Pururavas in full view of his divine bride. She vanished immediately, and the rhythm of the tabla portrayed the frantic search of her distracted husband as he scoured hill and vale, river and stream, in the all but hopeless task of finding her again. One day he stopped to weep beside a lotus-covered lake filled with swans. Urvashi, who was one of the lovely creatures on the lake, pitied him, and momentarily assumed her human form to tell him to go home, saying, "I have vanished like the first of dawns. . . . Friendship is not to be found in women, for they have hearts like jackals!"

Recalling the epic tale, Natu felt less elated with Rani's long-distance kiss (if it was a kiss!), and concentrated his thoughts instead on the long descent from Trimbakeshvar. The raga ended in a crescendo of rhythm and counter-rhythm improvised by sitar and tabla, a vibrating dance too fast to keep in time with, too high-pitched yet sustained, almost too nervously furious to believe. The tabla player's fingers moved so swiftly they could not be seen. His mouth was open wide. Sweat streamed freely off his face. Then he gasped and flattened both hands over his small drums. It was finished. The audience clapped, whistled, screamed. The musicians smiled and bowed, then rose to take a break.

"Ha, that boy is great," Baburao said. "I have discovered him, Godse!"

"They are all good," Natu said.

"Aren't you glad you listened to me, Natu?" Apte asked, still applauding, though his palms were sore.

"Did you enjoy it, my dear?" Baburao asked Rani. "And what does the Champion have to say? Speak up, Maginlal, so we can all hear you!"

"All I can say," said the Champion, "is that I'm glad that tabla man doesn't play tennis. He's got a devastating swing!" Like so many Parsis, Maginlal Mehta dressed and sounded more English than Indian, but it was not affectation, and his famous smile revealed an open, boyish nature at once winning and disarming. In spite of himself, Natu could not dislike him.

"You have met Mr. Godse, haven't you, darling?" she asked. "He's our famous nationalist editor."

"Yes, of course," the Champion said, smiling genially. "Good to see you again, Godse. I say, it is getting late, isn't it, Rani?"

"But the concert is just beginning, Magin," she protested.

"So it is, of course, but—"

"Don't tell me you are running off on us again, Mehta?" Baburao complained. "Where can you play tennis at this hour?"

"I did promise Jemsetjee I'd stop by the Club before midnight, you know, dear. He wants to discuss the Australian match, and well—"

"Go if you like," she told him, "but I hope you don't expect me to accompany you?"

"No, certainly not, Ran! But you're sure you won't mind?"

"Why should she, Mehta? I will take good care of her, don't worry! But I am the one whose permission you require to leave since I paid for your ticket!"

"It has been great fun, honestly, Babu. Many thanks, old chap, and tell you what . . . Perhaps I can buzz back here later—"

"You'll be much too exhausted, dear," she said, as a thoughtful wife might. "Anyway, if I know Jemsetjee he'll keep you talking till three in the morning. Never mind making a special trip back for me. Baburao can drop me home, can't you, Baburaoji?"

"Leave her to Baburao, Mehta," he said. "Go, go on!"

"You're both angels! Thanks, Ran!" He tapped her arm before going, a sportsmanlike tap such as he might have bestowed on a vanquished opponent after jumping the net and saying, "Good game, old sport!" He tapped Natu and Vishnu just the same way as he walked past them, flashing that winning smile.

You cannot really hate a man like that, Natu thought, watching the lithe handsome figure hurrying toward the exit. It was too bad in a way. It made everything that much more difficult.

Then the music began again, and sitting down, to his surprise he found not Baburao, but Rani right beside him. "Oh, we seem to have changed our seats around, haven't we!" she exclaimed, as though it was a surprise to her also. Her smile radiated perfume, and like the silent kiss seemed to reach out toward him. "Are you still angry with me?" she asked. Her lips were moist and trembling.

"Not really," he said, surprised not only by the words, but by the huskiness of his voice.

"Please don't be," she told him. "Do try to understand."

Her sari was pale rose, edged with gold. The tight bodice over which it was softly draped was flaming red, clearly outlining the high full curves of her breasts, more nearly the breasts of a young girl than a mature woman. She seemed in many ways like a girl, timorous, almost faunlike, yet at the same time more bold and independent than any woman he ever knew. He could think of no other woman in Poona, for example, who would have risked remaining in a public place after her husband had gone, except for Dr. Mrs. Indira Bharve, but no one really thought of her as a woman. She belonged to that small select third sex of "public-minded" women, who were so unattractive to begin with that men merely considered them eccentric, not immoral. But no man could look at Rani once without turning to eye her a second time. And she knows it, damn her, he thought, she knows it all too well.

"There is a fiddler for you, heh, Naturam!" Apte said, clicking his tongue.

The fiddle had joined the trio, and now took over for its solo, a runaway gypsy melody of pathos and humor. The instrument rested against its player's tough stomach, rather than being propped between chin and shoulder. The bow danced over the strings horizontally, instead of at the more nearly vertical angle common in the West. Gravity thus added its pull to the impact of bowgut on strings, conspiring with body resonance to do strange things to this violin's tone color. The player bent over his bow like a sawyer determined to cut through the sound box or die trying.

"Are you busy tomorrow?" she asked, pretending to flick a speck of lint from her sari as she turned toward him.

"Tuesday is my day off," he said in a noncommittal tone.

"I'm driving into Bombay," she added quickly, busily adjusting the drape of the cloth which passed over her shoulder. "Would you care to join me?"

Baburao had glanced in their direction, and Natu coughed into his fist, and again concentrated, it would appear, most attentively on the music. Yet he barely heard it now. He hardly even saw the players, though he stared wide-eyed directly at them. His better judgment told him not to get involved with her again. Remember your resolution on the Nasik bus, Naturam, he thought. Remember Trimbakeshvar! Of course if she drove there would be no exorbitant taxi fares, would there? But what sort of excuse would she make to her husband so that he would allow her to drive alone to Bombay? Or wasn't she going alone? Wouldn't that be fun—just the three of them? He was prepared to expect almost anything of her at this point.

He took out his handkerchief and rubbed it around his nose and mouth. "Are you going alone?" he asked, coughing to cover it.

"Of course," she muttered, making him feel like an idiot.

"All right," he said, deciding that if the drive down were anything like the last drive they'd taken together, he would find plenty of other congenial company in the big city. He always enjoyed himself in Bombay.

"Take the train to Khirdki," she said. "I'll come by the station there about nine."

"See here, Godse, stop monopolizing this woman," Baburao said, not without a trace of jealousy. "She is in my charge, remember!"

"Mr. Godse was just explaining this raga to me, Baburaoji," she told him, lying in so innocent and professional a way that he could not help admiring her talent, though he cautioned himself never to forget that she was so expert at such things.

No further words passed between them that night till she left about twelve with Baburao and several of his other guests.

"So nice to have seen you again, Mr. Godse, and you too, Mr. Apte," she said politely, formally, daintily, lifting her sari slightly as she walked past them.

"If I know these two," Baburao said, laughing heartily, "they will remain here till dawn!"

"Yes, and why not?" Apte responded.

But a few minutes after they had gone, Natu began yawning.

"I think I have had enough music tonight, Vishnu," he said.

"But I thought you were just beginning to enjoy it!" Apte replied sadly. "What has come over you nowadays anyway, Natu?"

"Maybe I am just getting old, my friend." He yawned again and rose to leave.

Khirdki station was two local stops from Poona. The third-class ticket cost only four annas. The ride took barely ten minutes. He had timed it to arrive just a few minutes early, and had not even begun looking for her as he strolled off the platform toward the space where taxis and cars were waiting. Then he saw the small Austin back away and swing around to cut off his path.

"Want a ride?" she asked, smiling.

"That depends on where you're going," he said, jumping in the other side. "I'm going to Bombay."

"Then you're in luck, sir, because that happens to be just where I'm going." Her lips threw him another kiss. This time there was no mistaking it.

"Are you only so generous with those at long distance?" he asked.

"I haven't the vaguest idea what you're talking about, sir," she answered, releasing the hand brake and letting up the clutch too suddenly. They got off to a jerky and sputtering start.

"I hope this isn't the first time you've driven this vehicle," he exclaimed.

"Don't be silly," she said, grinding the gears a bit as she shifted into high. "It's the second!"

"Maybe we should take the train," he suggested, only half joking.

"And I thought you were a fearless man, Mr. Godse." Her laughter ceased when she had to swerve sharply and only narrowly averted taking some flesh off a cow. "Stupid beast! Why can't he make up his mind which way he's going?"

"Obviously because he's a she. Shall I drive, Rani? I'm not too experienced, but I have handled one like this before."

"That's the most insulting thing you've ever said to me, Natu!"

"Give me time. I can do better."

"Don't you dare, or I'll stop right in the middle of nowhere and let you walk home!"

"You have a lovely temper, Rani."

"That's silly. There's nothing lovely about a temper. I know mine is awful, but I can't help it."

Her eyes were fixed on the road ahead, and his on her sharp profile. Her hair was pulled back stiff and straight off her high round forehead and set in a bun at the nape of her neck, which was long and gracefully curved.

"Your neck is like a swan's," he told her.

[147]

"It's not, either. It doesn't have any soft feathers on it."

"I like it better the way it is." He touched the pale flesh with his fingertips.

"Please don't do that," she asked. "I can't promise to keep us from going off the road if you do that."

"Then why don't you stop," he suggested.

"I thought you want to go to Bombay."

"I'm in no hurry."

"But I am," she explained. "I have an appointment with my doctor at eleven."

"Are you sick? You don't look it."

"It's not exactly visible," she said, which didn't help much.

"Aren't there enough doctors in Poona?" he asked.

"Not my kind."

"Oh? What kind is that?"

"Neurologist."

"But you aren't cra——" He did not quite stop in time.

"Crazy? You needn't be afraid to say it, Natu. I know that's how most people think of anyone who goes to a neurologist. It's really quite generous of you to think I'm not. I suppose I should be flattered, shouldn't I?"

"I shouldn't have said that," he insisted. "I don't actually know much about—neurologists." But why did people go to them he wondered, staring at the traffic on the road ahead, a train of grain-laden bullock carts, and a few milkmen cycling back to their villages, empty tin cans swaying suspended from their handlebars.

"You wouldn't think twice about going to a doctor for a fractured leg or arm, would you?"

"Of course not," he said. There were bells on the tips of the lead bullock's horns. They sang as he jogged along, shaking his head proudly.

"Your nerves can be fractured just the way a limb might be," she explained. "I suppose that's what's happened to mine."

"That's too bad," he said.

"You needn't sound so sympathetic," she said.

"I'm just not the sympathetic kind."

"I could have guessed that! Perhaps I'd better stop or we will have an accident." She had started crying.

They rolled off the soft shoulder into the ditch beside a barren field. He was surprised at how silent it became when she shut the motor. The only sounds were her sobs and the voice of a cricket. She fumbled about in her purse. He held out his handkerchief.

"Thanks," she said, taking it. "Now I'll look a mess, won't I?"

"I won't think so," he said, reaching beyond her neck to the silk of her saried shoulder, bringing her closer as he leaned toward her. There was a silent plea, a faunlike fear in her eyes. Be gentle, they seemed to ask. Her lips were small, firm but mobile. She trembled at the touch of his mouth against hers. She seemed like a young tree caught in a high wind, fluttering like a bird held in his hand. He caressed her naked midriff, his hand moving slowly toward the soft underswell of her breast.

"No, God, please!" She wrenched herself away, holding him off at arm's length. "Please, Natu, no more!"

"What is it, Rani?"

Her face held a story of mixed joy and pain which he could not decipher.

"I told you I must get to Bombay. He's a very busy doctor. He can only see me one hour a week."

"We can go in a few minutes," he said.

"*I* can't turn it on and off so easily, Natu. Please! Try to be patient with me, can't you?"

"If you find me repulsive, Rani—"

"Oh, you foolish foolish boy," she said, laughing and crying, ever so gently caressing his cheeks and neck. "How can you even think that? Natu, you must never never think that. Will you promise me never to think it?"

He gripped one of her wrists and brought her palm to his mouth, kissing it warmly.

"Isn't it terribly obvious that I love you?" she asked. . . .

"Don't you want the tea now that I've made it?" Sheila asked, holding out the cup for him.

"Ah, yes, the tea? Yes, yes, tea is very sobering. Thank you, my dear. Sit down here next to me, Sheila. Tell me all about your life," he said, sipping the hot milk-flavored brew.

"My life? It would not interest you."

"Tell me anyway."

"What is there to tell?" she shrugged. "My life ended with the partition. If I had been stronger I would have ended it then, but—you see how I am?"

"We will avenge you soon," he promised.

[149]

"Avenge? I do not know what that is."

"It is to pay back in kind, Sheila. We will pay back the Muslims in kind for all the deaths and damage they have caused."

"But that is too late," she said, pinching the edge of her faded sari.

"They will be made to pay dearly," he vowed, ignoring her total lack of concern or anticipated joy at his promise.

"Is the tea warm enough?"

"Yes, yes."

"If it is not sweet enough I have more sugar."

"No, it is quite all right. Have you no interest in politics?"

"It is not a subject for women," she answered. "It is too deep."

"Not for all women," he said, though there was a time when he agreed with her entirely.

"One of my friends can read," she said, after a while.

"Truly?"

"Yes. Sometimes she buys the newspaper and reads out loud to us. She tells us which movies are playing."

"That is most useful," he said, thinking how odd it was that he should have to spend so much of this day in the company of a woman like this one. Yet he had been lucky to find her, otherwise they might have caught him by now. It was *lucky,* wasn't it?

The tea made him sweat. It seemed to flow from his pores as quickly as it passed into his stomach. The trickles of moisture crept down his armpits and between his legs. One slow drop moved along the muscle fold of his belly where his money belt had been. He suddenly touched his naked stomach and jumped up.

"What is wrong?" she asked, startled.

"Where is it?" He gripped her arm fiercely. She screamed. "WHERE IS IT?"

Then he remembered. He got up and rushed to the chair. He picked his shirt up off the floor. It was safely wrapped in his belt under the shirt. He stared at its black silent muzzle, breathing heavily as though he had just run a long distance. She had not touched it.

She remained on the bed, too frightened for tears, slowly rubbing her wrist where his fingers had left their rude imprint.

"This is good tea," he said, draining the cup. "Is there more?"

"I will make more—in a minute," she said.

"That's a good girl," he said, handing her the cup and sitting down again in the soft chair, where he could keep his eye on the gun. He kept looking at the muzzle wondering how it would feel if it were pointed at him, if it were held very close to his face and he were

[150]

staring into it, and suddenly it came alive, and the metal pellet slashed into his flesh. He wondered if it would burn, or sting. Perhaps it would feel like ice, he thought, remembering how the touch of ice against your flesh was like fire for an instant. He wondered how long it would take to die if the gun was fired very close. He had often tried to imagine what it would feel like. The closest he could come was sleep. You are there on your pad in the room in the world. You are breathing and have toes and arms, and then you are gone. . . . He could not see the muzzle anymore. My eyes are closed, he realized, that is why I cannot see it, but I know it is there. He opened his eyes just to check. It was there. He closed them again. His eyes were very tired. He decided to rest them, just for a moment or two. I must not sleep, he told himself. It was too late for sleep. He was so tired that he might sleep too long. But it is all right to rest, he decided. I can keep my eyes closed and rest without sleeping as long as I think. I cannot sleep if I keep thinking, just as I could not think if I were dead, that is why I cannot conceptualize death. Yet the real I will not perish, but must live to animate another form, unless what I do today will liberate me from rebirth forever.

But then I would never see her again, he thought. That residue of desire alone would assure rebirth, for release could come only when all desire was sated. And there was so much more that he wanted! "That is why I love you," she had said. . . .

"But what I want isn't any different from what millions of others want, Rani," he said, looking up from her lap at the long sturdy limb of the banyan tree above them with its many finger roots reaching back toward the soil.

"Yes it is," she insisted, stroking his temple with her infinitely tender touch. "Most people want to be comfortable and happy. They have no divine discontent in them. All the other men I have ever known were like that—except for one." She drew her hand away, leaned back on her arms for support and looked out toward the bay and the Bombay skyline far beneath their perch in the park atop Malabar Hill.

"Who was he?"

"A boy," she said. "Very much like you, really. How old are you, Natu?"

"Thirty-six."

"He was just eighteen," she said, "and it isn't so remarkable to be that way at eighteen, I suppose. At least it's a lot harder by the time you're thirty-six."

"You loved him?"

"Oh, yes." She caught at her lower lip with her teeth, leaning over him again, and cupping his face in her hand, pressing it more firmly against her stomach. "Yes, Natu, he was the only one I ever loved—till I met you."

"Including the Champion?"

She frowned and closed her eyes. For a while he thought she would not answer. She had a strong sense of guilt about her husband, he realized, and it was as though every mention of his name came as a painful jab at her conscience.

"I'm very fond of Magin," she said finally. "He's a very good person, a lot better than most, I think. . . ."

"But?"

"But nothing. Did you expect me to cry and tell you how horrid he's been to me? Well, he hasn't, if you're that interested. He's never said a harsh word to me all the years we've been married—not once! And I haven't exactly been easy to live with."

"No, I don't imagine you would be, Rani."

"Oh? Am I that awful?"

"Not awful . . . Strong-willed, independent, stubborn."

"Guilty, your lordship," she said, "but are those things so bad to be?"

He set his jaw firmly and watched a blue jay perched snugly midway along the branch. He did not feel like arguing with her now. He felt like taking her to one of the cheaper hotels he knew so well, one of those places scarcely five minutes away where questions were never asked at the desk as long as you paid your four rupees before walking upstairs. He had suggested it during lunch, after she had finished with her examination—or whatever one did at the neurologist's—but that only made her cry again, so he suggested the park instead, and for the last hour all they had really done was to talk. I am definitely slipping, he thought; not that he minded talking to her, but it was, after all, Tuesday.

"Well, are they?" she repeated stubbornly.

"For a woman, yes, as a matter of fact," he said.

"Perhaps I've given you too much credit after all," she said. "Please let me get up, Natu."

"Certainly." He lifted his head, allowing her to move back and stand up. She walked gracefully to the low balustrade and stood there watching the view. He plucked a few handfuls of grass and tossed them aside in disgust. Half the day had been wasted but there was really still time to visit one of the brothels, yet to his own confusion he realized that he did not want one of those women. They never argued the way she did. They never asserted their independent wills, never tried to thwart his demands on their bodies. They were in good measure the classical ideal of Woman, loving, obedient, submissive, like perfect domestic animals. Yet he did not want them, he wanted her. He went to her side at the balustrade. She did not move or utter a syllable. She seemed more distant than the city below, its tumbling cascade of white and pastel shaded flat roofs rolling downhill amidst the palm mops and the mango trees to the crowded old tenements stretching off toward the fort and the harbor, more distant than Chaupati's white sand and the black scars of teeming slums that looked from afar like patches burned over and devoid of life, somehow more distant even than the fringelike docks and the tiny toy ships waiting their turn off at anchor in the sparkling blue bay, with its ring of islands rising like hippos' backs against the horizon.

"What happened to the boy, Rani?"

"Which boy?"

"The one you loved."

"Why? What difference does it make to you? I'm just a piece of flesh to you, aren't I?"

"No."

"No? That's surprising. I thought that was all a woman should be —as far as you are concerned at least."

"I've never known any other kind, Rani."

She had wrapped the sari under her arms, pressed close to her stomach, yet she trembled as though she were freezing.

"Are you cold?" he asked.

"No. Of course not."

"Please don't cry again."

"Don't worry, I'll spare you that. I realize how sensitive you are, and I wouldn't want to spoil your fun, though I'm afraid I've spoiled another holiday for you. Would you like to drive back, or should I drop you off someplace and go on alone?"

"I'd like to stay awhile longer, if you would."

"Oh, I'm in no rush," she said, "but I should think it trying for you to have to put up with the company of a strong-willed, independent, and—and—"

"—stubborn woman," he prompted.

[153]

"Yes, thank you. I almost forgot what I was."

"—whom it just so happens I love very much," he added. "You did forget that part."

"Did I?"

"Yes."

He did not say the rest, which he meant to say, that he wanted to hold her fragile body forever in his arms, that he wanted to sleep with her not merely because it was flesh that he longed for, but because he wanted that as well as everything else about her, her smile and voice and tears and trembling, her flattering estimate of his value as a man, her flashes of lovely anger, her pride, and the lonely need which had cried mutely to him from their first fleeting moments together in Baburao's garden. He said none of it, but he thought it with every fiber of his spirit, and somehow what he thought was conveyed, or perhaps it was written like destiny's mark, which the old people claimed was indelibly stamped on every infant's forehead; perhaps it was so clearly visible on his face and in his eyes that she heard it all· anyway, for after looking at him hardly an instant she opened her arms and wrapping them fiercely around his body pressed herself full against him as though a hurricane wind had blown her there, resting her head firmly upon his chest and imploring, "Oh, Natu, Natu, my darling, we must never never never fight and argue. There is so little time for us, Natu, we must not waste it arguing."

His hands moved greedily over her back before closing around her, closing so tightly about her slender frame that they reached to the soft flesh of her breasts.

"I love you, Natu," she kept repeating, kissing his shirt-covered chest in rapid pecks as though it were sprinkled with crumbs and she was a bird who had landed there. "Will you get very tired of hearing me say that? I love you."

"I will let you know if I get tired," he promised, her body like a flame against his skin, searing the length of him with an almost blinding passion of desire. "I would like to consume you, Rani. I wish I could devour you entirely so that we would not be two people—"

"Not two people," she whispered, looking up at him, a glaze of passion misting her eyes. "There is only one person here . . . only one."

"We must go into the car," he said, feeling that if they stood there much longer he would surely fall.

"All right." She sought his hand with her own and led him quickly across the grass patch to the waiting Austin. Except for some children and their ayahs, and a few elderly people seated on the stone slab benches, the park was deserted. It was too far a walk from the slums or tenements to absorb the countless overflow of either.

But there was really no room in the car, no matter which way they tried to turn, till at last he said, "It is no use. The English automakers are a practical and cold-blooded people! Like the rest of them."

She laughed exuberantly, and lay her head against his shoulder. "This is enough for me, Natu, just to be close enough to touch you."

He could not bring himself to make a similar confession, but decided against raising the matter of a hotel room again. It had made her feel "cheap," she said at lunch.

"Tell me every single thing about yourself, Natu. I must know everything about your life."

"That is a long story," he said, "and you still haven't told about your—boy."

"What shall I say about him? He was an ardent revolutionary. He quit school and left home when he was fifteen to follow Gandhi. He joined the first Satyagraha and was killed in a lathi charge in this city."

"Yes, that is what happens when you try to match their violence by turning the other cheek," he said.

"But he felt it was the only way since they have so much power."

"We will have more power soon."

"Then you do not believe the Mahatma is right?"

"I thought you have read my editorials, Rani."

"No, I have, but—it is something I have wanted to discuss with you."

"He is no mahatma," Natu told her, his tone, his facial expression, everything about him changing so suddenly that it surprised her, almost frightened her. "He is a traitor."

"Natu, what are you saying? You should not jest that way!"

"But I am not jesting!"

"You *must* be! You're far too intelligent and sensitive, and—"

"Let us not talk anymore of him."

"All right," she agreed, for she did not want to argue again either. "But you will admit, whatever his weaknesses, that he is the greatest leader our nation has ever produced, won't you? Surely you would admit that?"

"Guruji is far greater."

"Who?"

"Dhondo Kanetkar! Haven't you ever heard of him?"

"The author of *Independence or Nothing?*"

"Yes, and many other books. He is our teacher, so we call him Guruji."

"Our?"

"The members of a society I belong to."

"Which?"

"It does not matter."

"Does that mean it is secret, Natu?"

"More or less."

"Oh. But is it dangerous for you to belong?"

"Not particularly."

She sat up alarmed. "It is, isn't it? I can tell from your voice it is. Do try to be careful, my darling!"

Her sudden anxiety made him laugh. "I am really quite safe, as you see!"

"Yes, right now you are," she said, turning his face toward her own, running her fingers through his hair, looking at him as though he were made of snow in the sun. "You are safe now because I can watch you and take care of you."

"Ah, now you wish to mother me again."

"Yes. Always. I have adopted you, can't you tell?"

"Who gave you permission?"

"You did."

"Is that so?"

"Yes. You have never stopped me from doing anything I wanted to you. You let me sip your champagne the first time we met, don't you remember?"

"And from that you have taken it upon yourself to adopt me?"

"Yes, of course!"

"You are a strange girl, Rani. How old are you?"

She did not turn away from his stare. "I was thirty-seven last month."

Vishnu Apte and his other friends would have called her a squeezed lemon.

"That is too young to be my mother," he said.

"We will not tell anyone else, all right?"

"Perhaps in that case . . ." He kissed her tenderly.

"But you must not kiss me as though I am your mother!" she insisted, smiling.

"Ah, you are a tigress, are you?"

"Of course, can't you see how sharp my teeth are?"

"No—let me see!"

His lips reached hungrily for hers, seeking the fulfillment in a kiss which his body had thus far been denied, groping for the consummation her fear had prevented. They lost track of time, locked in the tortured embraces whereby their mouths alone could meet, yet neither of them willing to draw away, till he finally buried his face against her breasts and she hugged his head to her calling, "Natu, Natu. How can you be so perfect for me, my Natu? What has made you so perfect?"

"I must have all of you, Rani," he said.

"I am yours entirely, my darling."

"But I must have you."

"Try to be patient, till we can find a way—a way that is not—horrible."

"It could never be horrible with you."

"Anything sordid is horrible. . . . Going to a vile hotel wouldn't be right somehow, and—I want it to be *just* right with you, Natu. I want everything to be just right—with *us*."

"If that is what you want," he said. "I can wait."

"But now you must talk to me. You must tell me everything about yourself. Will you?"

"It is hard to tell everything, Rani—even of what you have not forgotten."

"Yes, I know what you mean. Do you know what I think, Natu? But first you must promise not to laugh."

"I promise," he said, laughing. "Now I will not laugh anymore."

"I think—you will think this is silly and very vain of me!"

"Not if you never tell me!"

She laughed and bit the tip of her fingernail like a mischievous child. "I will say it anyway," she decided. "I think we are really very much alike—"

"And is that so surprising?"

"Let me finish! Only—only you do the things I have not got the courage to do."

"What makes you think me so courageous?"

"You could be arrested for some of the things you write!"

"Perhaps," he conceded, "but the English are too shrewd to arrest me. They have learned by now that nothing makes a newspaper so popular in this country as the arrest of its editor. So I am really quite safe."

"But they could arrest you for the other things you do—in your society."

"What do you know about that?"

"Nothing, except that if it is so secret you cannot even tell me the name—then it must be illegal."

"Perhaps." He gnawed off the end of his nail and spit it out the window. "But we have not done enough. It is very difficult."

"Liberating a nation is not an easy task," she said.

"That is true."

"You must have patience."

"Yes, I know, but sometimes I feel—"

"What?"

"I—I don't know how to say it."

"Can't you even begin?"

"Well, it is—it is that I feel so much—hatred."

"Hatred?"

"Yes, sometimes I will see an English officer or a magistrate or a smug businessman, and—you know how they can look at us—"

"I am not sure I know," she whispered, timidly touching her lips as though they were in pain.

"—with that cold, glassy arrogance," he explained, groping for words that could never express the knotted core of bitterness he often felt, "that I-spit-on-you contempt so many white people are born with—"

"Natu, you needn't tell me if it is painful."

"Not painful," he told her, "perhaps impossible. It is as though the only way I could say it would be with a knife—or a gun."

"Shhh! No more, my darling."

"They think we are not good enough to use their guns."

"It is upsetting you—never mind now."

"That is why they will not take us in their Army. They would not take me, you know!"

"Natu, it is getting late. I think we should start back. Natu—it is getting late!"

It is getting late! He woke with a start. The sweat saturated his body. His eyes felt bleary. His head was sluggish from the heat. He kept blinking his eyes as he looked at the pistol wrapped in his money belt. My God, I fell asleep, he realized.

[158]

It was two-thirty. He held his wristwatch to his ear to be sure that it had not stopped. The dim ticking brought a relaxed smile to his lips. He could not have slept more than a few minutes. He shook his head briskly, and rubbed his knuckles into his eyes.

I must wash my face, he decided, getting up.

"Sheila," he called, "where are you?"

He went to the kitchen and found no one there.

"Sheila?"

The washroom was also empty. He bent over the tap and cupped some water into his face, then bent lower and let it pour out onto his head. It was warm from the pipes, but served to revivify him. There were no clean cloths in the washroom with which he could dry himself.

"Sheila!" What the devil had become of her?

He looked into every room in the large apartment. He finally found something to use as a towel, but Sheila was nowhere.

He returned to her room, and quickly dressed himself, checking his gun to make sure the bullets were still there. It was useless to look for his money, he knew, but he rifled her possessions anyway. There were a few cheap bangles and some beads, but not one dirty two-anna piece. Serves me right, he thought, for trusting that bitch.

But where had she gone? Recalling the terrified look in her eyes after the last time he had gripped her wrist, he suspected it was fear rather than anything else which had made her run away. But how could he be certain she would not go to the police? Most of them knew what she was anyway. Wherever she went, he knew that it was no longer safe for him to stay in her apartment. Even if one of the others returned with a client and found him there alone it would be dangerous.

I must get out of here, he decided. The more difficult decision to make, however, was where to go until four?

9

Yet he knew before leaving the building precisely where he would go. He knew though he dared not even admit it to himself, for even that silent admission would have been enough to make him reconsider. He would have reflected then on the time, on the risks involved, on the stupidity, the absolute futility of the venture. He would have asked himself why he was doing it then, what he could possibly have hoped to gain from going there, what he expected her to say? He would have asked himself questions he could not have answered, not sanely, no matter how hard he tried to fabricate, to rationalize, to invent excuses or reasons. There were no reasons, none whatsoever. He was going because he had to go, because he had to see her, because he had to try at least even if he could not see her, even if she was out, or standing there at Maginlal's side. It made no difference to him now. None of it made the slightest difference, not the risks, or the dangers, or the futility. She was there within reach, and he was free. If he could have found a telephone he would have called, but it would have taken as long to find a telephone, and it would have been as dangerous surely as going in person. The only telephones were in large offices, in banks, in hotels, in wealthy private homes. He had merely to think of telephoning to reject that idea.

Outside Sheila's building people looked at him as though they had been warned he carried a gun. They seemed to shy away as he approached. They whispered as he walked past. When he stopped and turned, they stopped whispering suddenly. They peered at him with frightened eyes. He wondered if she had cautioned them. Even the scrawny ragged children who usually dogged his steps with outstretched hands and imploring cries were strangely silent and timid. He almost wished they would bother him, but none of them did.

There were no taxis in sight, not in either direction in this residential district. He walked slowly at first, anxious not to arouse further suspicion, but the more distance he put between himself and her apartment building, the faster he moved, till he was practically running. Then his breath came too fast, so he slowed down again. It would not do to use up his energy now, yet infuriatingly enough no taxis appeared, not even a motor-scooter, not so much as a rickshaw. Try to walk half a block in this city when you do not want a vehicle, he thought bitterly, but that did not help any. Yet now that he had decided, it was so late, every second seemed so precious, much too valuable to waste in such aimless wandering. He was not even sure if he walked in the right direction—perhaps her hotel was back the other way? He had never been here long enough to really get to know this cursed city—this city built by the white men for their cursed imperial capital.

For block after block he passed elegant private homes, set far back from the sidewalks, back behind neatly trimmed lawns enclosed with low fences of fieldstone or cement, protected from prying eyes by high hedges of lush foliage, green and fragrant, comforting and cool. Who lives here, he wondered, now that the English are gone? He had always thought of such places as white people's homes. Perhaps some still were, though surely not all he passed, not even most of them. Now they belong to the white black people, he thought, hesitating in front of one of the finer homes to catch his breath again. There was an orange tree on the front lawn. Just a few yards from where he stood ripe fruit dangled surrealistically from branches that seemed too small to bear the weight. Surely such a home would have a phone. He could see a dark bespectacled head watching him from behind the steel-barred window of the house. He was tempted to go inside, to appeal to this man who was obviously the owner, one of his own countrymen, saying, "I am Naturam Vinayak Godse, patriotic liberator of our motherland—let me use your phone!"

Then the front door opened and a servant came out to squat on the porch, holding a long stick across his lap, like a watchdog in waiting, sent by his master to guard the oranges.

"So that is what you think, you pig, that I have come to steal your oranges," Natu said aloud. Then he spit onto the lawn, and walked away quickly. It was all most of them cared about, their piddling possessions, their petty property, which they hugged the way beggars hugged their bowls, the way scavenger dogs hugged a bone. A roof over their heads, food in their stomachs, and money buried beneath the floor, that was enough for them. The spark of cosmic fire had gone out in their puny souls. They thought of God as an image made of stone, hidden from heaven in the dark vault of a temple. They thought it enough to propitiate Him with flowers before dawn, to bribe Him through some priest no less venal than themselves, to celebrate His glory with a gluttonous feast. Natu hated them for it. He despised them. He felt no pity for them, only hatred, contempt, disgust. He would show them all soon enough what it was to be a man, what it meant to have the power of divinity inside a human body, what courage and courageous dedication to duty truly meant, as he had learned it from Guruji. He would teach it to all of them. Natu heard the motor-rickshaw before seeing it. The khaki-colored three-wheeler puttered noisily toward him. He lifted his arm. The driver brought his taxi-scooter to a neat landing at his side.

"Palmyra Palms Hotel," he ordered, crouching and jumping onto the seat behind the dirty plastic shield to the rear of the driver. The noisy little vehicle lunged to a vigorous start. Leaning back, holding the straps hanging to either side of his seat, Natu closed his eyes. I will try to prove worthy of you, Guruji, he swore, refusing to think now of where he was going, refusing to allow himself to ask why. It was more important, he felt, to remember now what his guru had told him. . . .

That night his professor of literature at Deccan College invited Natu to his bungalow, explaining, "I have asked a few people, Godse. I think you will enjoy meeting them." It was the first such invitation he had received in three and one half years at the College, where the social distance between faculty and students was nearly as great as that between Brahmans and Shudras in the world outside. He was so startled at the invitation that it took him some time to reply. "I trust you are free, Godse," Professor Bhat finally had been obliged to add.

"Oh yes, yes, certainly! Of course!"

"Good. Let us say nine-thirty," the good man concluded, disappearing before he had time even to utter a word of thanks.

Natu's dinner that evening, as most every evening throughout his college career, had consisted of a cup of weak tea and a homemade cigarette. He had eaten his meal at lunchtime in the Lakshmi Restaurant off campus where students were given a special weekly rate of one rupee for which they were permitted to consume as much rice and vegetable curry and as many puris as they could at any one sitting daily. He was usually too hungry by midday to defer eating till dinner, but now he wished he had done so since he would have to stay up quite late. The hunger was easier to tolerate when he went to bed at nine.

All the faculty bungalows beyond the cricket field looked alike. He snooped about until it got so dark that he feared it was much later than nine-thirty, though he had no watch, and finally he decided to knock at the door of one cottage where he could hear several voices, among them, it seemed, Professor Bhat's.

"Well, Godse, you're early," the professor said, opening his door. "Never mind. We needn't stand on ceremony. Come in, come in."

They were still eating, gathered in a circle on the floor of the living room, three other men, two who were as physically robust as the third was emaciated. Only the thin man looked up as he entered the room. The others were too busy consuming their rice and curds.

"This is Naturam Godse, Guruji," Professor Bhat said, returning to his place at the thin man's side, "the one whose essay I showed you."

"Come over here and sit next to me, Naturam," Guruji said, as though it were not the first time they had met, as though it were rather a long-awaited reunion, a son's return to his father's side. His voice was mild and warm, his deep-set eyes warmer still, in contrast to the drawn and line-ravaged face that looked like the erosion-worn delta of an ancient river. "I see you are hungry, Naturam."

"No, no, I have eaten," he protested.

"Ah, but how long ago? Is there enough left in your kitchen, do you suppose, for our young friend, Bhat?"

"I am sure there is, Guruji."

"Please do not trouble yourself, Professor," Natu insisted, but Professor Bhat was already on his feet and calling orders to his wife.

"Do not worry, Naturam," Guruji confided. "It is no extra burden for them. My stomach is not yet accustomed to much food, so I have taken only curds. You will be given my portion."

"That is very generous of you—Guruji," Natu said. "May I call you that?"

"Please do."

"Have you been ill?" Natu asked. "Is that why you cannot eat much?"

He sensed it was a stupid question when the robust man sitting on his other side looked up and laughed. The blood rushed to his face and he felt like an idiot.

"You will become ill if you laugh while you eat, Katuk," Guruji warned the other quietly. It was so mild yet effective a reprimand that Katuk sobered at once, and Natu felt not only gratitude, but immediate respect and admiration for the man he intuitively accepted as his guru. "I have not exactly been ill, Naturam, but the rations I have received for the past sixteen years in Mandalay Prison were not meant to stimulate my appetite."

He said "sixteen years in Mandalay prison" with no greater emphasis than he might have used in speaking of a weekend in Nagpur, which was why it took Natu so long to react, but when the words finally registered in his mind he got so excited that he could do nothing but stutter, "Sixteen? But then—then you—you must—you must be—Dhondo Kanetkar!"

"Ah, then you have heard of me?"

"But who hasn't? I have read every single line you have ever written," he hastened to say in an excess of exuberance. "I have read them twice!" Actually he had only read a few one-anna pamphlets.

"Good. In that case I need not burden you with any elaborate exposition of my views. I did not think I would have to, Naturam, after reading your own excellent essay 'On Revolution.'"

"But that was nothing. . . ." This time pride rushed the blood to his cheeks.

"Permit me to be the judge of its merit, Naturam," Guruji insisted. "You have considerable talent, and what is of greater importance, a passionate love for your motherland. Each is a gift in itself all too rare, the combination far more so. But here is your food. I must not distract you while you eat."

He no longer felt the least pang of hunger. He could not have cared less for the well-stacked tray set before him if it had been placed there half an hour after he'd finished two similar portions at Lakshmi's. Dhondo Kanetkar, the greatest revolutionary his people had produced since Lokamanya Tilak, their greatest poet bar none, the only man who had ever received a life sentence of deportation to Mandalay and endured long enough to win royal pardon, which brought him home more as a god reborn, more as a legend of heroism, than a released convict, had not only spoken to him kindly, but even complimented him. He was afraid to talk, afraid to look up, afraid it would prove to be no more than a dream of glory beyond his wildest dreams, beyond anything he ever dared imagine in the wakeful darkness of his dormitory when hunger deprived him of sleep, and when he envisioned himself a mighty soldier, not in the Army which rejected him, but in the forces of light that would march to liberate his mother from the chains in which she wept.

"Guruji, it appears that your flattery has robbed our young poet of his appetite," Professor Bhat said, not quite flippantly enough to disguise his own envy.

"You are mistaken, Bhat. I flatter no one. I have told Naturam no more than he deserves. Whether or not he shall deserve higher praise, will be for him to decide. Come, Naturam, do not let your food get cold. Young men should have hearty appetites!"

"My greatest hunger is to serve you, Guruji, in any way you will allow me to."

"I see you are no less eloquent in speech than in writing, Naturam."

He could not meet those eyes at all now. He felt he had been too bold, as though he must have sounded too sure of his ability, too brazen. He felt like a fraud, for who was he after all to think himself worthy of serving a man like Dhondo Kanetkar? He had written his essay one evening in a fever of passion, in a frenzy of anger, disgusted with the futility and ineptness of his own existence. It had been a momentary expression of fantasy, an exercise in imagination, a release of some hidden spring of wishful longing which was no more typical of his actual thought and behavior than the histrionic statement he had just uttered so impulsively was a true expression of his usual feeling. His greatest hunger was for food, and when that was satisfied, for women. Before that it had been for a uniform and a gun, but when that avenue had been closed to him he had sulked back to his home, only to find his father sick with grief and disappointment, only to face a future as barren and boring as all the long years of his adolescence had already been. He had turned to school for the lack of anything better to do, not for any positive goal he had in mind. The truth was that for most of the hours of most of his days he had nothing in mind, at least nothing beyond some petty and generally futile plan for satisfying either of his mundane and immediate cravings.

"I wonder if you have any idea of the dangers and difficulties involved in our work, Naturam? Wait, do not be so eager to profess your undying devotion to danger! I am not unaware of its attractions for young blood, especially blood as ardent as your own—"

There was an intensity, an almost hypnotic quality in the slow cadence of his voice and the unwavering penetration of his gaze, which seemed to pierce the veils of guile and subterfuge by which individuals protected their innermost thoughts and fears, their self-doubting and misgiving, from the superficial vision of others. Natu could not help feeling that it was dangerous to think anything unworthy under the eyes of such a man.

"No service should be lightly undertaken, Naturam, for all are demanding and exacting in greater or lesser degree, but that of the revolutionary is unparalleled in the hardships it imposes. Wait. Hear me through before you speak, and do not think I exaggerate, for I am not trying to test your boldness. If I did not believe you were bold I should not have had you invited here to begin with. But boldness is one thing, courage another, and courageous dedication to duty still a third.

"Many people possess the boldness which is the raw material of courage, only the raw material, mind you, because courage is no gift of nature. It is a product of training and experience, a compound quality if you like, the blend of natural endowment and testing, just as steel is the resultant blend of iron and coal. Iron is your boldness, Naturam, it is there in the soil of your nature. It is hard, dark, and brittle, and indispensable too, of course. But steel is tougher, more malleable, harder than iron, more useful. Where can you dig for steel, tell me? Nowhere. Why? Because it simply does not exist in nature, just as courage does not exist in man, until it is fashioned, that is, until through the fire of experience with the added ingredient of training it emerges out of boldness, transformed molecularly, modified in its basic structure, a new and more potent power at your disposal. But it is still only a tool, an adjunct, an aid. Once it is fashioned, the important question is how will it be used?"

The words flowed without pause or effort, with no fumbling or

[166]

halting utterance to break the spell of their effect upon him. And spell it was, for he listened rapt and attentive as though he understood entirely what his mind could barely grasp, not to speak of digest, what he absorbed rather than understood, what he felt was true rather than knew to be. In his seven semesters at college, Natu had heard more lectures than he cared to tally, invariably read in prose carefully polished beforehand, but none had ever stirred him as did this improvised monologue. Professor Bhat's lectures came closest, but even they were like food already chewed and devoid of its juices, passed along as tasteless pulp for his students to digest.

"This question of use brings us to the final stage in the transmutation of a bold and ardent young man into a professional revolutionary. At this stage your new product goes to work. Your courage is harnessed to dedication to duty, not the English duty, Naturam, not the partial and insipid Western concept of duty as responsibility, obligation, or loyalty to job, family, country, or what have you. *Our* duty—dharma, the sacred law of our eternal religion, Naturam, that is what I mean by duty. It calls for no less than the highest capacity of which you are capable. It seeks no grudging offerings one hour each day, no puja of the flowers you have picked in your morning stroll about the garden, no sacrifice of one tenth of your wealth, or one half. Every object you may possess is too paltry an offering. You must be prepared to sacrifice your life, nothing less is acceptable. Your life and all its years, all its unused moments and hours, all its untasted pleasures and desires. Can you understand what that means?"

"I think—I am trying to understand it, Guruji."

"It is wise of you to hesitate before professing you do, Naturam. Let me try to help explain what it will mean. You are now twenty-two, I understand. Your wife died soon after you married. Under ordinary circumstances, if you choose practically any other career, it would be quite natural to expect you to remarry as soon as you were in a financial position to do so. If you enlist in my service you must forget marriage entirely. The revolutionary cannot be tied to either wife or children. He must be free to move anywhere without prior notice, to risk anything without fear of family reprisals or sentimental anxieties. No doubt that is an obvious point which has occurred to you, but I wish to make your prospects as clear as possible."

It had not occurred to him at all. He stared at the meal which had been set before him by Professor Bhat's wife, and this seemingly apparent contradiction disturbed him. He looked at the professor, and then at Guruji in so perplexed a manner that the latter could read his unspoken question.

"I see the presence of your good professor has confused you, Naturam, but he is no exception to the rule I have stated. He is a trusted confidant and ally. No, he is more than that to me—he is a friend," Guruji explained, turning to rest an emaciated hand on Bhat's knee, "for which I cherish him dearly."

"I am honored to do whatever I can, Guruji," the other replied.

"But he is not one of us, Naturam, for some time ago when I explained to him what I am telling you now, he had the wisdom to recognize, and the good sense to admit, that he would not be capable of making the requisite sacrifice."

He said it without malice or derogation in his voice, yet Natu could not help feeling the implied contempt for Bhat's frailty incorporated in the bland explanation of his quasi-revolutionary status.

"In addition to wife and family, of course, you would have to abandon any occupational ambitions you may have formulated," Guruji continued. "Naturally you will do some work, depending upon your talents, but whatever you do for purposes of social deception, let us say, your career, your profession, remember, is always that of the revolutionary, and none other. You may be asked to do many different jobs, or you may be allowed to establish a reputation at one. In any case you will be expected at all times to subordinate your sense of loyalty and obligation to your work and employer to the higher loyalty I demand of all my disciples. Furthermore, if you desire personal fortune I must caution you against committing yourself—"

"I have no such ambitions, Guruji."

"Not now, perhaps, but you are very young now. In ten years, let us say, or twenty, you may be tempted to change. Hear me out, Naturam, and think carefully about what I say. I pride myself on my judgment of men, and I judge you to be no person of ordinary ambition or petty temptations, but you alone know the inner recesses of your soul. Search carefully there. Look well before you leap. I ask for no commitment tonight. Think over what I have told you. It is hard to do, but try to imagine a future without the daily companionship of wife and children, devoid of any prospect of material gain or personal comfort, always threatened with the possibility of arrest, of deportation—and, yes, of sudden, violent death."

Guruji paused, watching his face closely for a reaction expressing fear or the faintest trace of apprehension, but Natu felt neither. None

[168]

of the dreadful prospects Guruji mentioned disturbed him. Arrest, deportation, violent death were words of glory, not of terror, to him. They were goals to be desired rather than shunned, as far as Natu was concerned, now that he had been singled out, personally selected by Dhondo Kanetkar as worthy material for becoming a professional revolutionary. The mere sound of that title excited and impressed him—professional revolutionary! He had often thought he was destined for some very special and adventurous role in life, something out of the ordinary rut of a clerk's existence or a businessman's drudgery, some job in which his inchoate cravings and unarticulated ambitions would be afforded full opportunity for expression, in which his capacity for hatred and love could be utilized to the utmost. In his sophomore year at college he had answered Gandhi's second national call for nonviolent noncooperation. He had been among the first to stop attending classes. He had eagerly broken the law against manufacturing salt after the Mahatma's thrilling march to Dandi. He had courted arrest without flinching, but then, just as he had done a decade earlier, the general called off his own army when victory seemed closest to their reach, when the jails were so crowded that the English were running out of men with which to guard them, when the people were so excited that it appeared as though one final mass charge would rout the enemy entirely, when noncooperation spread like a forest fire over the human tinder waiting to burn bright. At that very moment the unpredictable Sadhu suddenly reversed himself, and ran off to conclude his pact with the Viceroy and then to attend the Round Table Conference in London. Cooperation was restored, the leaderless army disintegrated, the jails opened again on the larger jail of a nation still in chains. With his classmates, Natu returned to school and the dry-as-dust boredom of lectures that had no relation to life. By now he had all but abandoned his faith in a future any more exciting than Lakshmi's vegetable curry. Neither arrest, deportation, nor violent death seemed anywhere as horrible as a life of dullness, dullness, and more dullness. His eyes only grew brighter with joy as the picture Guruji painted assumed darker and more dangerous hues.

"If after all I have said you are still not deterred, Naturam, let me finally warn you that should you join my service there can be no turning back. The vows my disciples must take are taken for life. No one may change his mind suddenly and resign. A few have tried—it pains me to have to say it but I want you to ponder this point fully conscious of its meaning—a few have tried in the past quarter century to run away. One got as far as Austria. He changed his name,

[169]

married a German woman, and no doubt thought after five years that he had eluded us entirely—"

Katuk laughed at the mention of this renegade whom he had tracked down in Munich, and who was still listed officially by the police there as a "missing" person.

"We can dispense with the details of his death, Naturam, as we shall of a former disciple who ran as far as Tokyo. I do not say these things to frighten you, but merely to underscore the seriousness of our purpose and the full extent to which I hold my disciples to their lifetime vows."

"Yes, I can understand that, Guruji."

"Good. And is your greatest hunger still to serve me, Naturam Godse?"

"It is, if you will have me," Natu said, without faltering.

Dhondo Kanetkar narrowed his eyes as though he were trying to see something very far away, despite the fact that he continued to stare hypnotically at the young man's face.

"I shall be here again two nights from now, Naturam. Return then at the same time, and let me know if your decision has changed."

"It will not change."

"I will not hold you to that promise now, but what I shall ask you to promise is that you will speak of nothing I have said to you to anyone."

"I promise."

"Wait. That you will not so much as mention that you have seen me here—"

"Yes, I swear it."

"—or either of my disciples. Your professor invited you here this evening to discuss your writing, and that is all. Do you understand?"

"You can trust me, Guruji."

"I think I can, Naturam, but we shall see. Go now, and think over what I have told you. Burrai."

"Burrai," Natu repeated, rising to his feet. He was halfway across the cricket field when his hunger reminded him that he had not touched the tray of food left so long in front of his nose. . . .

Swerving suddenly, the rickshaw left the road, and turned up the semicircular path toward the entrance of the majestic hotel. The sight of that white-pillared portico, of the red velvet carpet adorning the central portion of the long, low marble steps leading up to the revolving door, of the high-windowed massive structure above, looming like

[170]

the wall of an ocean liner, awesome and impervious, sky-obliterating, over the small boat of his rickshaw, rudely jolted Natu from his reverie. But it was too late to turn back. He was tempted to tell the driver to keep going, yet before he could manage even that the motor had stopped, and the gold-turbaned doorman had focused his most haughty, disapproving gaze upon this shabby excuse for a taxi and its uncouth occupant. The worst thing he could do at this point, Natu instinctively realized, was to run.

"I won't be long. Wait," Natu instructed his driver, stepping out of the doorless vehicle as calmly and casually as he could.

Above all, Natu realized, he would have to appear perfectly at ease, thoroughly relaxed. The informality of his attire would present no problem as long as he acted at home here. For all anyone could tell from his simple clothes alone, he might be a member of Parliament, even a minister. His manner, of course, could betray him. Status in the last analysis was a state of mind. He understood all this, yet once he reached the topmost step at the level of the doorman, he hesitated, and all but exposed himself entirely. The lackey, dressed like a raja, had been watching him in so curious and contemptible a way that Natu almost felt obliged to acknowledge his existence by saying something like, "I have come to visit Mrs. Mehta, who is staying here." It would have been a fatal error surely, alerting this human decoration to the fact that anyone callow enough to inform him of that probably did not belong.

Without so much as a nod or a smile in the doorman's direction, Natu strode to the revolving door, and found to his relief that instead of trying to stop him, the raja placed a gloved hand on the edge of one door blade, giving it a gentle whirl before Natu could exert himself by pushing. The high-ceilinged lobby was overpowering in the grandeur of its design and the ostentation of its décor. The Palmyra Palms had been built by a Swiss firm in the heyday of imperial glory, shortly after the capital had been shifted to Delhi. A crystal chandelier, larger than most village homes, dangled ominously over two long sofas and a dozen or so stuffed chairs midway along the cavernous expanse between the entrance and the marble staircase at the far end of the lobby. Thick Persian rugs brightened the floor. Huge vases of bronze sprouted palm trees, set around pillars adorned with creepers painted gold.

Natu hoped to find a crowd of guests or visitors inside. He had planned to drift unobserved among them, perhaps spotting her there on one of the expensive sofas. But none of the seats were occupied, and the only people he saw were men standing alone, some in uniforms less flashy than the doorman's, others in formal black with bow ties. They were all employees, each one a potential enemy. Instinctively he thought of stepping back to the protection of the revolving door. He thought of running out while it was still turning. He could be in his rickshaw before anyone had a chance to react to his intrusive presence. Let them think what they liked of him. Let them think him a robber or a madman. As long as he left peacefully, having done no damage, they would not bother racing after him. They would not even bother reporting his appearance to the police. Then he would be free and alone again! He was sorely tempted, for now the incredible risk of what he was doing fully dawned upon him. No action of Apte's this morning had been nearly as dangerous or stupid! For all he knew the tall man approaching him this instant was the superintendent of the C.I.D. himself. He looked at least that important in his tuxedo, with the black silk lapels. What is wrong with me, Natu thought. *Why don't I run?*

"May I help you?" the tall man asked quietly.

Now it was too late. Natu tried to moisten his lips with his tongue, but there was no saliva in his mouth. It was too late to run, yet he could think of nothing to say, absolutely nothing. He simply looked around vaguely, distractedly, idiotically, frozen by fear at the sudden appreciation of how vulnerable he had become. He sensed that he would not have had enough presence of mind or courage at this instant to even draw his gun if the other man gripped his arm and said, "You are under arrest!" But instead of saying that, the assistant manager merely repeated his question, though in a slightly more imperative tone.

"I was to meet Mrs. Mehta here," Natu said at last, amazed to hear himself saying it, "but I don't see her."

"Mrs. Mehta? Ah yes, of course," the assistant manager said, smiling. "She must be in her room now. Do you wish to call her?"

"Very well," Natu managed to say, nodding, hoping this man would lead him to the phones.

"You know where the phones are?" the other asked, ever so slightly motioning to one side of the vast room with his finger.

"Certainly," Natu replied, though he could see no house phones where the man pointed, in fact he could see no reception desk at all! It was so stupid a pretense that he wondered angrily why he hadn't said, "No, please direct me," instead. Surely there was no harm in admitting that he was ignorant of the location of their phones, while to be caught in such an obvious lie if he could not find them now would only arouse suspicion. Though the manager backed off politely, Natu felt he continued watching. There was nothing to do but walk toward the corner he thought the other had indicated.

After a few paces he saw the side passageway leading to the desk, opposite which was a shelf with two phones. A bearer was talking with the desk clerk, but as he approached they became silent. They stared at him boldly. He kept his back to them once he reached the phone.

"Mrs. Mehta's room," he whispered into the mouthpiece.

"What is the number please?" asked the switchboard operator.

"I don't know."

"Hold on please!" She sounded annoyed.

From the corner of his eye he could see that the bearer had moved clear of the desk and now stood watching him. He shifted his weight slightly, just enough to turn his back to those prying, hostile eyes, but then he could see the sullen desk clerk's face! Why was the operator so incredibly slow? He stared at his wrist—it was almost three.

"Hullo, hullo," he said into the phone. There was no answer, only buzzing and muffled chatter, as though that idiot woman, wherever she was, had stopped to talk with a friend!

Then it occurred to him that even if Rani was in her room Maginlal might answer. Or even if she answered, Maginlal might be within hearing distance! He was about to hang up. Suddenly he heard a long ring, and then as though in a dream that soft familiar voice said, "Mrs. Mehta here."

"Rani," he whispered, surprised to find that his hands trembled.

There was a long pause. Was she trembling? Was she too breathless to speak—or—or had she hung up? He thought he heard a click.

"Rani?"

"Yes?" It was so faint a whisper he flattened his palm against his other ear to try to hear better, though there was no noise in the lobby. "Is it you, Natu?"

"I must see you, Rani."

This time there was a still longer pause, but he waited. "Where are you?" she asked. The phone made her sound so distant.

"In your lobby."

"Oh? But I had no idea—"

"Are you alone?" he asked. "I must see you."

"Yes, I am alone," she said.

[173]

"Then tell me your room number?"

"But—"

"Will you tell it to me, or must I ask at the desk?"

Still she hesitated. Then she whispered the number, and saying no more she hung up.

10

"Yes, send him in," General Ashok K. G. Singh told the intercom box on his desk, switching it off with a sigh and wondering if he would ever find time today to finish reading the latest report from his field commander in Srinagar. "Good afternoon, Das," he said, coming around his huge desk and extending his hand in greeting.

"Afternoon, General," Gopal said, shaking the firm hand, impressed as always to find that no matter when he barged in on Ashok Singh, the general looked as though he had just shaved, showered, combed his hair, and put on a freshly tailored full dress uniform.

"Why don't we sit over here, Das," General Singh suggested, guiding his visitor to the large leather sofa under the upraised wall map of Asia. "What can I get you to drink, old chap?"

"Thanks, I think nothing, General."

"Nothing at all?"

He sounded so sad that Gopal relented. "Some water perhaps, sir."

"Of course, but let me put a bit of Scotch in it, old chap, and then you needn't worry about any bugs, you see," the general said, raising the top of one end of his desk, which opened like a piano, extracting the decanter of Scotch, a thermos jar of water, and two tumblers, and returning to set them down on the coffee table in front of the sofa. "Don't recall if I ever told you about the time I was campaigning along the Kistna, and damned near died of cholera because I had to drink the wretched water without anything to purify it!"

Gopal smiled politely. He heard that story every time he came to this office, which was why he had gone to the Minister's office first, but the Defense Minister was at the Viceroy's reception and that wouldn't be over until three-thirty.

"There we are," General Singh said, holding out one of the tall glasses and settling down with the other. "Cheers!"

"General, there may be some trouble this evening," Gopal said, after just tasting a sip to keep Ashok Singh company.

"You don't say? What sort of trouble?" Though it was twenty-five years since he'd graduated from Sandhurst, the general had never lost its accent.

"I'm not sure," Gopal explained. "I think another attempt may be made on the Mahatma's life today."

"You don't say? Yes, that could mean trouble, couldn't it?"

"It could. I just wanted to alert you, General."

"Why yes, glad you did of course, but see here, Das, if you know about this—possibility—"

"Naturally, I'll do whatever I can to stop them."

"Of course you shall, yes, but look here, old chap—can I get you another? No? Do help yourself when you're ready. I'll just freshen this one up a bit. . . ." He leaned forward and refilled his glass with equal proportions from each container. He was a large man and could absorb a substantial quantity of alcohol without showing the slightest sign of it. "What I mean to say is, why the devil can't *we* do something about him before anyone else does?"

"I'm not sure I understand what you mean by 'do something,' General," Gopal replied evenly. "What exactly did you have in mind?"

"Well, nothing *exactly,* Das. Haven't really given it much thought, you know." The general unbuttoned his breast pocket and extracted a thin cigar, offering it first to Gopal, then took out a campaign ribbon he kept in another pocket to use its pin for puncturing the rounded end. Rolling the cigar between his lips a moment to moisten the tip, he removed his silver lighter from his trouser pocket and dragged at the flame till his head was wreathed in a small cloud of smoke. He held the cigar at arm's length to study it while considering the problem of what to do about the Mahatma.

"I suppose we might arrest him," Ashok Singh finally suggested.

"Arrest *him?* Are you serious, General?"

"Yes, quite! Not that we'd call it that, of course. I imagine 'protective isolation,' say, would be a much neater way of phrasing it." He rolled the cigar contemplatively between his fingers. "No, better still—we could rush him off to Simla and tell the press his health's broken down. Rest cure in the hills and all that!" The general looked pleased with his idea.

"I'm afraid he wouldn't hear of it," Gopal said.

"Oh, I'm sure he wouldn't!" The general winked broadly.

It was meant as a flattering sign of intimacy, Gopal knew, but instead of flattering, it only disturbed him. It frightened him, really, because he knew as well as Ashok Singh did just how much power the two of them had at their immediate command. Power in the abstract had always frightened him. Perhaps that was why he had worked as hard as he had to gain some direct control over it, to attain a position from which he could see that it was used properly instead of being abused by unscrupulous men. He often worried about his definitions of "properly" and "unscrupulous," moreover, for he knew how tempting it was to operate with two sets of definitions, one for himself, the other for everyone else.

"Fact of the matter is, of course, Das—and I'm sure you've noticed much as I have, dare say we *all have*—he *hasn't* really been too well of late, has he?" General Singh's bushy eyebrows rose and remained stiffly at attention, giving his handsome face something of a startled and worried expression.

"He hasn't?"

"Certainly not! Come now, Das, you know perfectly well what I mean! Why if anyone else said a quarter of the things he's been mouthing these past few months you'd have had him in the lockup as a dangerous anarchist—or worse! You know perfectly you would."

Gopal frowned and stared at the golden fluid in his glass. No matter what he thought of Ashok Singh's opinions he had always admired the man's frankness. The general could invariably be relied upon to say what everyone else might be thinking. It pained Gopal to listen at times, never quite so much as right now, but the truth he knew was often painful, and though he felt like doing it, he would not simply dismiss the general's argument by storming out of his office in a rage of righteous indignation. He held no cow or human being sacred, after all, and if falsehood could not be refuted in argument, perhaps it was not falsehood.

"No, General. I disagree. Bapu's said nothing for which I would jail him. He's a philosophical anarchist, of course, I wouldn't argue about that, but how can you call a man who has made nonviolence the guiding star of his ethical existence 'dangerous'? He wouldn't crush a mosquito and you know it."

"But that's *precisely* what's so dangerous about him, Das. We are at war, you know. Read that blasted field report from Kashmir that I've been trying to get through all day if you doubt it! I only release *their* casualties to the press, of course, and if I give any at all for our side it's put euphemistically under 'missing in action.' Missing, my foot! We're fighting some tough boys up there, Das. I wish to God half my men were a match for those Pathans, bloody scoundrels that they are. Call them whatever you like, old chap, they're *fighters!* Weaned on rifles most of them, taught to ride a horse before they could walk! If I didn't have five effectives in the field for every one of those blighters I tell you quite frankly, Das, we couldn't hold the Vale for a week! Oh, I know he's Christ and Buddha wrapped in one, don't think I'm not aware of it, old chap! Let him go up there and tell it to the Pathans is all I say, and if he won't do that, let him keep quiet!"

The general drained his glass and refilled it immediately.

Gopal drank more of his own highball than he intended. He put aside the glass and lit a cigarette.

"But look here, old chap, I don't have to tell *you* what we're up against these days. We all put on a good show for the newsreels, but let's stop fooling ourselves, shall we? I've told this to the Chief. I'll tell it to anyone with brains enough to understand. I'm a soldier, Das. I've been a soldier all my life, and there's been time for damned little else in it, so I do feel qualified to give my soldier's opinion of our national state of health. In two words it's damn critical, and your 'Great-Souled One' doesn't make it any better. In point of fact, and to put it bluntly, he's more than a nuisance, old chap, he's a hindrance."

"He's the greatest man we've produced in the last century, General," Gopal said quickly, feeling uncomfortably insecure before an argument that had all the fire power of an artillery regiment and all the hot urgency of a shooting war at its back.

"I'll accept that," General Singh said, to Gopal's surprise. "I'll go a lot further, in fact. I'll grant him priority in five centuries or two thousand years if you like, but it doesn't change my opinion of him, old chap. It's the fact that he is so great that makes him as dangerous as he is. There are millions of crackpots in this country who try to imitate him exactly, we all know that. They spin thread because he does. They go practically naked because he does. They even fast whenever he does. I'm not in the least worried about them, Das, because they are imitations, some fairly close I'll admit, but he's the genuine article, and there's the difficulty. They follow his lead, but he follows no one. God only knows what makes him think up most of the things he does. I won't try to explain it. These damned prayer meetings of his, for one thing! Who ever heard of a Hindu holding a prayer meeting before he got the blasted idea, tell me? *That's* what's so dangerous, Das—his unpredictability. Yesterday he tells the Party to resign, the day before he tells us to pay up our debts when he knows damn well we're on the rocks. What will it be tonight? Or tomorrow? I'm just waiting for him to come out and tell my soldiers to throw away their guns! Oh, he'll do it yet, blast him. I'm so God-awful sure of it, it makes me shudder!"

"He's promised the Chief not to," Gopal said glumly.

"Yes, I know all about that! And what if his voice tells him that's an immoral promise? Look here, Gopal, you remember what he did during the last war. With the bloody Japs two hundred miles from Calcutta he still wouldn't budge from his noncooperation stand, even with the Chief practically begging him, and the Viceroy sending me over to his ashram with my blasted maps! I sat there talking the facts of logistics to him till I felt blue in the face! Good God, Das, do you know what he actually told me? 'If the Japanese invade us,' he said, 'we will conquer them with love.' Now honestly, old chap, really!"

General Singh crushed his cigar and got to his feet. He was every inch the soldier, his barrel chest so crowded with colorful ribbons, many of them starred for double and triple awards, that there was not room for them all and some were half hidden under the flap of his left lapel. His leather belts were polished to mirror-perfection, as was the pistol holster strapped to his waist. His trouser creases were knife-edge sharp. Even his shoe buckles sparkled, as he walked across his spacious office to retrieve his ivory baton, and strode back slowly tapping it in the palm of his left hand.

[179]

"I'm no more of a Satyagrahi than you are, General, but maybe that's why his ideas sound as strange as they do to us. Maybe those of us who have no faith in them, keep them from working in practice," Gopal said, trying to make his voice sound more convinced than he felt.

"That's rot and you know it, Das. I've seen too much of war, old chap, to want any more of it, believe me. If I thought it could ever be stopped I'd gladly give my life to do it. But violence is as much a human instinct as hunger. It's as much a social instinct as religion or the family. The only thing to prevent it is fear, fear of greater violence. We'd best face it, old chap, we're in a race against time, and the sooner we forget about fuzzy-headed ideas of love and neutrality, disarmament and moral rearmament, the better chance we'll have of surviving. I don't say we will survive. I doubt that anyone will once the supergiants get to work on each other, and they're bound to, you know, but even if we forget about them for the time being, look here at this map, Das, it's all clear as geography," he said, pointing his baton at the heart of East Asia. "China won't drag on her civil war forever, you know. The Generalissimo's on his fanny right now. His army's no better than a rabble, while Mao's gets stronger every day. It may take them a few months or a few years, but I'm afraid the Commies will make it, old chap. Then we'll really be in for it. Indeed we shall, Das, you mark my words!"

Gopal glanced at his watch and stood up. He had problems enough without taking on China at the moment.

"I see you don't believe me, Das."

"Not at all, General. I hate to admit it, but I suspect you're right." He would have preferred to believe that Bapu was right, but he tried never to do his thinking with his heart.

"Of course you do, Das, because I *am* right!" Ashok Singh poured himself another drink, this time adding no water. "I'm convinced of it, old chap, and if you'll take my advice you'll do us all a service by arresting him under your powers of preventive detention right now. Bring him to the station, and I'll have a train waiting to take him up to Simla. He'll be handled like a crate of eggs, I assure you, and once he's there he'll be given free reign over my personal estate. The only thing we'll deny him is access to the press or any communication with the outside—"

Gopal was too stunned to speak. The same horrible feeling which had sickened him in P.K.'s office now all but smothered him with its impact.

"Listen to me, old chap, it's the only sensible answer to both our major anxieties at the moment. You don't want him to be assassinated; I don't want him to speak. Nor do I want him assassinated either, of course, and if you're in agreement with anything I've said you'll realize how dangerous his continued pontifical pronouncements can be. But hold your temper a moment, Das—I don't underrate your ability by one jot or tittle, believe me, old chap. You're up to the mark of Scotland Yard's best, I know that, but you won't be able to save him, Das! No you won't, not as long as he's free as a bird to go where he likes and say what he pleases. He's lost what good sense he had in the past, I tell you. He's gone too far already, and God knows he can't be stopped by reasoning with him. I don't pretend to be a medical authority, but if you want my frank opinion of what's come over him, it's senility. Shake your head as much as you like, but mark my words, if they don't get to him today, they will before long— blast it all, Das, *someone* will, and here's one man who won't be surprised, and I know a lot more who won't either!"

"I will try to forget that you have said any of this to me, General," Gopal told him.

"Don't be a fool, Das, tell every word of it to the Chief tomorrow if you like! In fact if you don't I will! I've been intending to do just that, I assure you!" He strode back to his desk and sat down behind it. "We can't run a nation very long if we all act like saints or madmen. As far as I'm concerned they're bloody close to the same thing, you know. I'm not trying to tell you how to run your department, Das. Just thought I might be helpful, old chap." He finished his drink and picked up the battle report.

Gopal clutched his briefcase and stared down at the rug. He realized what a fool he had been to even imply a threat to Ashok Singh. His officer corps thought the sun rose and set by him. No one could really frighten him, not even the Chief. He would have to be won over by argument or else he would have his way. Power made its own laws.

"General, I just couldn't do it unless—unless the Chief ordered me to," he sighed, feeling quite insignificant, wishing he could have had the confidence to allow him to agree wholeheartedly with Ashok Singh or else to tell him bluntly that he considered him a traitor and a threat to the national security. He could bring himself to do neither, though he envied the man he watched, who had the self-assurance of God.

"I hope he'll have the good sense to do so tomorrow, Das. Unless, of course," and Ashok Singh removed another cigar from his breast pocket, eyeing it for some flaw in its roll, "unless your friends anticipate us this evening, old chap. I'll alert my camps. When do you expect it?"

"Between five and six, if they try."

"Well, that doesn't give us much time to wait, does it, Das?"

"No, I'm afraid it doesn't," Gopal said, walking to the door.

11

Following the bearer across the lobby and out to the winding path that cut through the lush gardens behind the hotel, Natu found to his amazement that in spite of all their meetings since the first night he had gone to her home, he felt very much the same as he had then, like an adolescent bridegroom whose unpracticed fingers had nervously lifted the veil above his bride's lips. He had felt then like a stumbling boy, awkward, inadequate. . . .

"Please come in," she said, opening the door before he had knocked.

"I got your note," he said idiotically. As though he would have come to her home at midnight without getting it!

"I had to see you, Natu."

Mutely he stood looking around the dim, spacious living room.

There were several trophies, large silver cups and gold plaques, and a tennis racket mounted on the wall. He half expected Maginlal Mehta to walk in and greet him.

"He's gone to Australia for the match," she explained, reading his thoughts it seemed. "I've given the servants a holiday. Won't you sit down?"

"Thank you," he said, hastily lighting a cigarette. He felt like a burglar who had just broken into the jewel room of a temple.

"Can I get you something to eat?" She kept rubbing her palms against her hips, avoiding his eyes.

"No thank you," he said, "but I need an ash tray."

She brought one over, and taking it, he held her arm.

"Talk to me," she pleaded.

"I cannot talk now."

"Please try."

He crushed the cigarette and drew her down beside him.

"Have you thought of me at all since we were in Bombay, Natu?"

"I cannot stop thinking of you," he said.

"What have you thought?" she asked.

"Kiss me, Rani."

"Tell me you love me, Natu."

"I am not sure what love is," he said. "If it is desire, then I love you, Rani. I am blind with love for you—"

"No, but that is not love. Love is tender. It is a spiritual bond more than anything else—Natu, please!"

He locked her firmly in his arms and bruised her lips with his hungry mouth, forcing her down beneath his weight, pressing his greedy body stiffly against her thin and struggling frame. She tugged at his hair frantically, but he paid no attention to the pain. She dug her long nails into the flesh of his neck, trying to wound him deeply enough to force him away. She closed her teeth over his under lip, and that made him draw back, tasting the warm, fluid flow of blood in his mouth.

"Never," she said, between gasps for breath, backing away disheveled and wild-eyed. "Never—I won't ever allow anyone to do that. How could you? You must have nothing but utter contempt for me—to even think—"

"Where is the kitchen?" he asked. "I must soak my handkerchief in cold water or my lip will be a balloon tomorrow."

"Follow me. Did I hurt you badly?"

[184]

"No, it is just messy," he said, spitting into his handkerchief as he followed her through the darkened rooms.

"Why did you make me do it?" she asked.

He did not want to talk about it. He was determined, in fact, to say nothing more to her than was absolutely necessary, and to leave as soon as the bleeding stopped. If it would ever stop! He held his lip under the faucet and kept it open till he felt faint from simply watching the water turn to wine, realizing that it was instead his own blood. She was a tigress all right, but she was more than that—she was crazy, completely mad, totally incapable of knowing what she wanted, incapable of accepting what she seemed so obviously to desire just as passionately as he did. Deciding that and acknowledging it made his own behavior seem as idiotic as hers was irrational. He had wasted far too much time on her already, receiving nothing in return. Some women liked to toy with sex, he knew. They made it a plaything, a parlor game, an adjunct to their spiritual existence. For him it was as basic and real a need as food. He felt there under the running faucet that he understood her as thoroughly as anyone ever could or would, and he decided to have nothing more to do with her. Not tonight, not ever, he decided.

It took a while for the blood to clot, and by the time it did he felt like paper. He felt as though the blood had all been drained from his legs. He could hardly walk across the kitchen.

"Come and lie down," she said, putting an arm around him, holding his hand as she led him to the bedroom, totally immersed in darkness.

"You're such a boy, Natu," she said, gently caressing his forehead, tingling the flesh of his neck with her fingertips. "Such a foolish boy. Don't you know I would give you anything? Don't you know I would give you everything I possess—freely, lovingly? Don't you know that love is a gift, never to be taken by force? Why do you try to force me? Don't you know I am yours for the asking?"

Gently, ever so gently and delicately, she removed his clothes, deftly caressing him, kissing his entire body, consuming his passion, dissolving whatever pain he had felt with her lips, making him forget his resolve of a few moments earlier.

"No, don't move," she said softly. "Let me love you. Let me love you, Natu. You are all I live for. Let me love you."

Soon after the fever subsided he heard the steady tapping of the night watchman's stick on the pavement outside. The metal-shod wood was dropped in time to the Gurkha's pace as he made his rounds of the sleeping city. He was hired by the municipality to protect homeowners from thieves, but made so much noise as he walked that only the deaf could have been apprehended by him. All the neighborhood dogs joined in with their yelps and barks and howling cries, which continued for many minutes after the watchman had passed out of earshot.

"I should be going," Natu told her. "When can I see you again?"

"I don't know," she answered.

"Is something wrong, Rani?"

It took her some time to ask, "How do you mean wrong?"

"You sound so distant."

"You better be going, you said. I don't want to hold you back."

Her voice was strained, and she had turned her face from him.

"Are you—? Do you feel good?"

"Why? Don't you?"

"Yes, I feel quite good—though I wish I did not have to work tomorrow, so that I could sleep here with you—"

"But you can't!"

"No, I cannot."

"Then what is the use talking about it?" She stood up quickly and readjusted her sari. "Goodbye, Natu."

"Why do you say it that way, with such finality?"

Since she did not answer, he went to her, he touched her arms from behind, yet no sooner had they made contact than she broke away, saying, "Please—you must go."

"Don't you *want* to see me again?" he asked at last.

That was when she started to cry, and in response to his questioning could only explain, "I feel so ashamed. . . ."

The next day when he phoned and asked for her, Mrs. Mehta's servant informed him that she had gone to Bombay. No, she had not said when she would return. Each day he waited for a message, or a call. None came. For three weeks none came. Her exasperating silence was so protracted and complete that he finally convinced himself she had returned to Europe, or gone off with the Champion for the matches in Australia. Then the letter arrived that stirred in him the languid longing he thought dead, and filled him with the fever he felt the next morning as he walked over the barren white sands of Juhu toward the bungalow nestled in an arc of bending palms, where she promised to be waiting.

There was no other house in sight. The taxi had left him at a small fishing village less than a mile away, but the bungalow Maginlal had built for his bride just after their wedding was on a slight promontory, so that within a hundred yards of either side it stood there alone, with the palms, the sand, and the sea. Hardly two hours from the slums of Bombay, it was another world entirely, rich in that rarest of Indian luxuries, privacy. Until that morning Natu had not quite realized how wealthy the Mehta family was.

A white crane stood poised on one stick of a leg near the water's bubbly edge. The saline smell of the sea filled the mild December air. From somewhere behind him a gull's piercing shriek penetrated the perfect silence. Outwardly the bungalow looked deserted. There were no sandals on the porch, no bed rolls, no wicker chairs. Even the window shutters were hooked closed. There was no trace of charcoal smoke, and for a few moments Natu wondered whether he had misread her directions.

He knocked softly and waited. Then he knocked harder. The door rattled but no voice or approaching footsteps answered his summons. He knocked once again, and finally turned the knob, admitting himself.

The slanted corridor of light, stretching from the door frame like a sash across the room, fell as a spot over her legs and bare feet. She was seated on a large pillow, her back braced against the rear wall, gently caressing an Angora cat, who lay curled and content on her lap. The black silk slacks she wore fitted snugly over her thighs, ending just below her calves. Her bodice was crimson with a plunging V-neck, and its lower line exposed an unusually ample portion of her midriff. It was hardly an appropriate costume for an Indian matron. In fact Natu had never seen any woman dressed this way before, except in a Western movie. He could not help but stare at her dumbly with mixed feelings of passion and revulsion.

"Why don't you close the door," she said. "The light hurts my eyes."

He obeyed, but instead of crossing the room to her remained standing where he had entered, suddenly feeling not only an intruder and stranger in this bungalow, but as remote from her as though they belonged to different species.

"I was beginning to think you would not come," she said.

"Have you just been sitting this way in the dark?"

"Yes, I have always loved the dark," she told him.

"Did you not make any fire this morning?"

"Fire? Oh, you mean a charcoal fire. No, that is unnecessary here. We have a gas tank and burners, you see."

"I see you have adopted many Western customs."

"Many? Perhaps—but why do you sound so disapproving, Natu? Is there anything wrong with owning a gas burner if you can afford it?"

"I suppose not," he answered with a shrug, for it was not really the burner but the way she dressed that angered him, yet as he thought about it even that seemed foolish. She was not his wife or sister, after all.

"What is it, Natu?"

"What is what?"

"You know what I mean."

"No I don't. I am no mind reader!"

"Must you snap at me like that? Why are you so angry?"

"I am not angry!"

"All right, then don't tell me."

"There is nothing for me to tell! You are the one who asked me to come here! I have been traveling since six o'clock, and now I am finally here you have not even offered me a cup of tea! You did not even trouble yourself to answer my knock or come to open the door! If you must know, you act more like a memsahib than an Indian woman!"

Setting the cat on the pillow at her side, she got to her feet, and bowed before him in mock humility. "Noble Brahman, forgive my impertinence for daring to relax in your exalted presence—"

"Stop it, Rani!"

"But I am only trying my best to please—"

"Well, you aren't succeeding."

"Oh, but kind sir, I am merely—"

"Will you shut up?"

Unconsciously he had moved toward her, gripping her arms at first, then moving his hands around her back till he felt her full body against his own feverish form, but before he could close his lips over hers she averted them, pressing her head against his shoulder, whispering, "Why—if you hate me so?"

"I don't hate you."

"You sounded as though—"

"Sometimes you anger me."

"I never want to."

"I know."

"Do you—my darling?"

"I know," he repeated, and then her face turned up to his like a flower directed toward the sun, and hungrily he kissed her.

"Say you have missed me one half as much as I have missed you," she pleaded.

"Then why did you run away?"

She lowered her eyes and could not answer. He felt her trembling.

"Never mind," he said. "That is past now."

"I tried—I tried to—to forget you," she said. "Oh, Natu, I tried so very hard to forget you—"

"Yes, I have also tried," he confessed.

"Did you? And—and you couldn't either?"

"You see I am here."

"Oh, Natu, I need you—I need you so terribly. I want you inside of me—I want all of you—"

As one person they moved toward the pillow, sinking to the floor. The cat mewed and scampered away. He could hear her sharpening her nails upon the door, scratching and slithering and crying strangely like a baby. I should put her outside, damned beast, he thought, but then he forgot about the cat entirely. . . .

"That is bungalow, Sahib," the bearer indicated, discreetly stopping some distance away from it, and pointing, then smiling as he waited for his tip. But Natu had only two ten-rupee bills. He ignored the servant, and walked on toward the small cottage in a secluded corner of this hotel's tropical garden.

From behind a high wall of bamboo nearby he could hear the dull thud of a bouncing tennis ball. He could not see the players, but wondered if the Champion was among them—it made him hesitate. From the opposite direction, toward the hotel proper, came ripples of laughter and splashing. The high board was visible over the shrubs that otherwise obliterated the pool in this world of games and comfort, of relaxation and quiet. It was the foreigners' world, yet somehow he had found his way into the heart of it, and now it began acting on his single-minded resolve like acid burning through brass. Its calm security unnerved him. Here he was left alone in the midst of so much affluence, with no one apparently watching him, no one following to see that he did not destroy any flowers or steal any fruit. How long could I remain here undisturbed, he wondered. But the mere thought worried him more than the prospect of entering the hotel had a few moments ago, for he wondered in terms of days, not of minutes, yet minutes alone were left for him to squander.

I should never have come, he decided, stepping onto the porch, tapping softly on the door. He had worried only about getting in. Now he knew that leaving would be harder.

The door opened seemingly from the weight of his knuckles but once he walked inside it closed again, and turning, he saw her there leaning full-backed against it. Their eyes met as though magnetized, without moving, without blinking.

"Well?" she asked, trying to sound perfectly composed.

"I—have come to say goodbye," he said.

"Again?"

"For the last time," he said.

"Oh?" Then she caught her lower lip between her teeth and turned aside, and without facing him said in a strained voice that was meant to be casual, "You might just as well sit down."

"I do not have much time, Rani."

"Then stand—I don't care—or go if you must—" Her voice broke at that. He heard the slight gasp, like a sudden inrushing gulp of air. It was a stifled cry.

"Rani!" He had to touch her. He could not look at her from a distance any longer. He had to feel her, no matter how tenuously. She turned on him fiercely, the instant his fingers touched her arms; she swirled full about like an armature caught in the magnetic field of an energized rotor.

"What? What is it this time?" she asked, the tears already reaching her chin. "How long can you spare for me this time, Natu? One hour? Two? Surely no more than that! And how many weeks will pass before I hear your voice again? Five? Six? How many weeks has it been, Natu? I've lost count. Do you keep track of it?"

"I have been busy," he said.

"Of course, I know that! Haven't I learned that by now? I have learned it, honestly I—oh, please, please go, Natu. Please leave me alone. Don't start it again, I beg of you. Don't start it all over again. I'd just begun to—forget—oh, God!" Though she pressed the lids of her eyes firmly closed, tears continued to emerge. She walked stiffly across the room, took a handkerchief from her bag on the mantel-piece, dabbed at her face, and blew her nose. "Sorry," she said. "I shouldn't lose control like that. Do sit. Tell me how you've been?"

"As you see," he said. Then he looked at his watch.

"Oh, for God's sake, sit down," she insisted. "You make me nervous standing like that. Don't be so frightened. Magin's gone to a match. He won't be back before six."

"No, I was not thinking of him."

"Has something happened, Natu? What is it?"

"I wanted to tell you," he began, walking closer to her, though he knew it would be easier to leave if he kept at a distance. "I had to—see you—Rani, to tell you—"

"Tell me what?"

"I never thought I needed—love," he said.

"Everyone needs love, Natu."

"But I never thought *I* did." She did not jump away from his touch this time. She moved willingly closer. "Even after I met you I did not think—it mattered."

"Yes, I know."

"You do not know," he whispered, brushing her ear with his lips, inhaling the scent of her, the perfumed fragrance, but not daring to close his eyes for he felt as though he stood on the edge of the high board poised for a dive that would take him too deep to pull out of in time. "I have never wanted any woman this way, Rani."

"Natu, I love you."

"It is like—a fever."

"Yes, like malaria," she said. "Just when you think you've been cured it comes back—only stronger. Natu, kiss me."

Though they had been touching lightly it was not until now that their arms locked convulsively around each other. No sooner were their lips joined than he remembered the gun, as he felt her belly pressing against its unyielding frame. He could not back away in time. Terrified, her eyes asked the question mutely at first, before she whispered, "Why do you carry that today?"

"It is necessary," he said.

"Natu, what are you planning to do?"

"Never mind," he insisted.

"No! You *must* tell me!"

"I cannot. Rani, you have lovely eyes. They are so full of pain and sadness—"

"No, I won't let you distract me by doing that! Natu, please. You have no idea what it has been like this past month, never hearing from you, not even a word to tell me you were still alive—"

"I tried to call several times—"

"My darling, I have been so frightened for you. Where have you been? What have you done? How long have you been here in Delhi? What has brought you here?"

"It is—an assignment," he said.

"For your paper?"

[191]

"More or less."

"Why are you lying to me, Natu?"

"What makes you ask that?"

"What made you ask the first time you took me out why I was sad?" she retorted, just the trace of a secretive smile hovering about her mouth. "We understand each other too well for deception, Natu. That is why we belong to each other, haven't you come to realize that?"

He could not look into her eyes and lie again. He turned away. He sat down. "Then if you know me so well, why ask?"

"Because I love you more, and I am afraid," she said, kneeling before him, embracing his legs, resting her chin on his knee staring at his face with such intensity of affection that he was forced to lower his eyes, for fear that if he looked at her long enough he would be unable to turn away ever again. "I need you, Natu. I must have you always. You are like air for me, like blood."

"Perhaps in another life," he said, "you and I—"

"No, I need you in this life! I do not have your faith in rebirth, my darling."

"It makes no difference, Rani. It is desire that leads to rebirth, not faith."

"But why must you talk of rebirth, Natu, as if—as if—?"

He tried to shrug it off. "We never know when—or how long, my dear."

"You know—you know *now*, don't you?" She backed away from him trembling.

"Of course not."

"You do! I can see you do! That is why you said you had come to say goodbye for the last time. That is why you have the gun. Natu, what are you going to do? Where are you going from here?"

"I will tell you—tomorrow."

"But then it will be too late. Yes, it will, I can see it in your eyes, Natu. Tomorrow it will be too late, that is what you mean!"

"We have talked too long. Why don't you kiss me? I must leave in a few minutes."

"No, I won't let you!"

"Then I must go now," he said, standing.

"No—wait!" She ran to him, encircling his neck with her arms, caressing his head with her fingertips, pecking lightly, swiftly at his lips with her own, moistening her lips with her tongue, then touching his again, backing off as he advanced, averting her face, moving her

[192]

softly trembling hips ever so lightly against his body, then pressing her mouth with sudden fury full upon his lips, running her hands down the length of his back till they impulsively probed beneath the loose hanging lower end of his shirt, finding his flesh, sending currents of warm, fluid passion surging through him. They moved onto the deep rug before the fireplace, sinking to the floor, her agile hands never leaving his body, their lips no longer able to part. There was a clock on the mantelpiece. He listened to its ticking.

"I wish I had never told you I loved you," she whispered, staring up at him through eyes half closed, "so that I could say it now for the first time."

"You are more beautiful than any woman I have known, Rani."

"You make me beautiful," she said.

"And more passionate."

"That is also you," she uttered, lowering her lids entirely, puckering her lips in silent invitation.

"It is too late," he said.

"You must never leave me again, Natu. Never—"

"That is a long time."

"Not long enough."

"You are a strange girl," he said, touching the silken hair where it left her brow.

"I am yours, Natu—all of me, always."

But to his ears the ticking sounded louder now. It was three-fifteen he saw.

"Please don't move," she begged.

"I must."

She tightened her grip around his waist. For so thin a girl she had a remarkably strong grip. "Natu? Natu, I will ask Magin for a divorce this evening, so that we can get married—"

"Married?"

"Why, is it—so surprising? Why did you say it that way?" she asked, unable to keep her chin from trembling though she tried hard to sound unoffended.

She had relaxed her grip on him. He got to his feet quickly and adjusted his clothes. "I am afraid that is impossible, Rani," he said.

"Oh?" It was barely an audible cry. She covered her face with cupped hands, but they could not quite keep in the choked sound of her sobbing.

He started to leave. He had already stayed longer than he'd planned. He was not sure how long it would take to reach the other

[193]

garden—No, it was hardly that. He knew it could not take more than half an hour, with his rickshaw waiting outside. And if it took only ten minutes? Now that he was safely here, what better hiding place could he possibly find? It was fear of what she could do to his resolve that made him walk to the door, the fear of forgetting. He touched the brass knob. Still he could hear her whimpering. Somehow it did not seem fair. He had never thought of her the way he did of the Sindhi girls in Bombay. It was hardly fair to use her no differently than he used the cheapest of them.

He walked back to the rug before the hearth and touched her trembling shoulder. "Rani, it isn't that—"

"Please don't—don't feel obliged to explain!" She said it shrilly. "Please! I had no right—no right at all to assume—"

"But you did," he told her. "If I could marry anyone, Rani, I would marry you."

She sat up slowly. Her eyes were bloodshot, the lids swollen with crying. She looked so helpless, so utterly bewildered and lost, like a child left alone. "I—I don't—understand," she muttered.

"Then I better explain," he said. Taking a deep breath, he sat down again, facing her. He was not sure of where to begin, so first of all he reached out for her hands.

12

By three-fifteen, the palpitation which had begun after his morning meal became so rapid and constant that Dhondo put down his pen and tapped the bell on his writing table. His valet appeared from behind the curtained doorway even before the bell stopped vibrating.

"Tell Dr. Jivan to come at once," Guruji ordered.

The usually blank expression on the elderly servant's face changed to a look of uncomprehending panic, but habit stifled his questions. He saluted and rushed out. The younger man at the bottom of the first flight of stairs rose in alarm as he saw the valet racing down to him, bare feet under the bowed and naked lower legs taking the steps two at a time. He ignored the anxious questions of the second-floor guard and plummeted on, using the banister to help him accelerate faster. There were two young men at the bottom of the lower stairway, which was somewhat broader than the other. "Where is the fire, babu?" a wiseacre first-floor guard asked. He ignored it, and dashed to the first door, which was solid mahogany and had a steel bar six inches wide fastened to its midsection with a tongue almost a foot long extending through a slot into the wall. He deftly raised the locking hinge and jerked back the bar, then turned the big brass knob and opened the door. There were several young men on the other side, seated in a circle on the floor, rolling dice. He maneuvered around them and, panting by now, raced on to the steel gate, which opened from the middle once he unhooked the heavy chain. The guards beyond this gate were burly wrestlers twice his size. He did not address himself to them, but to the chauffeur, who was squatting behind the unpretentious street door.

"Bring Dr. Jivan," he told the chauffeur. "He wants him at once!"

The valet watched as the chauffeur ran out to the smoky glare of Bombay's Sandhurst Road, jumped into the limousine parked at the curb in front of the old three-story house, and started his motor at first try. A crowded trolley squeaked to a jolting stop, its enraged conductor shouting above his bell's rapid clanking, its passengers hanging outside almost flung off onto the road. The black limousine pulled away hardly a hairsbreadth in front of the trolley's suddenly arrested front wall. The old valet nodded in appreciation of his friend's dexterity, stepped back inside the building, locked the front door, and started his return trek upstairs.

Dhondo kept his fingers pressed to his wrist till the second hand of his watch swept its full cycle. His pulse was normal, yet the heart flutter continued, as did the intermittent spasms. He had known flutters before, but none as persistent as these. At the age of seventy he did not think it advisable to wait any longer before consulting his physician. He decided that he had done enough work on his memoirs for the day, at any rate, and left his desk to lie down on the daybed. From where he lay he could see the antique hands of the grandfather clock across the room. By now he had begun to feel a positive revulsion for those ornate iron hands, those crude stubs of spears whose naked existence on his wall had been interrupting his writing all afternoon.

No, it is not pride, he told himself again, neither pride nor jealousy. There is nothing personal involved, nothing personal.

"Doctor comes soon," he heard his valet reporting. "Something I can do—?"

"Nothing." At his age he expected there was really nothing anyone could do if his heart had decided it was time to rest.

But not yet, he thought, at least not for a few hours more, at least not before there would be time to get word. . . . Not that he *personally* craved the satisfaction.

"It is not personal," his lips just barely muttered, as he drew his bony hands along his hollowed cheeks after a particularly sharp spasm that felt like a fist closing around his heart. He almost wished he believed in prayer now. It must be comforting to fools who believe in it, he thought. But his was never the religion of devotion, the path of Bhakti Yoga. He had chosen rather the path of action. As a Karma Yogin he had lived, as a Karma Yogin he would die—but not yet, he thought. At least not till I can hear he is dead!

Is it personal, Dhondo? he asked himself. He shook his head negatively, but then another spasm gripped him and he closed his eyes. Sensing somehow that it was important for him to be sure it was not personal, he dredged the archives of his memory for some documents to support his position. Their first meeting had been in London. The month was August . . . 1914. . . .

He had come to the Victorian brownstone in Hampstead that night to talk to them about the South African struggle just concluded. Most of the permanent Indian community had turned up to listen, the business people and professionals, as well as the students. Almost half of the students lived at the old mansion, for shortly after H. H. Shivaji Rao Nulkar had purchased it they converted the top floor into a dormitory, removing all the furniture, and sleeping on the carpets, the way God had meant people to sleep.

Dhondo did not bother introducing himself before the talk started. He had taken his usual seat beside the fireplace, dressed in his dark suit with the woolen muffler he always wore, wrapped several times round his neck. Throughout the rather dull account of the final phase of the struggle ending in the agreement with Smuts, he remained so deep in concentration with his eyes closed, that he appeared to be fast asleep.

"But I did not mean to tax your patience with so long a talk," Gandhi concluded. "If there are questions I will try my best to answer them. Thank you."

The ovation was protracted. There were cheers, whistling, and floor-pounding as well as applause. Dhondo clapped politely, but stopped long before the last of the blustering business babus, who felt so guilty about their own selfish pursuit of money that they uncritically cheered every political worker, especially those like this Gujerati Vaishya with friends in influential positions. Dhondo disliked such demonstrative emotional displays. He considered them vulgar and immature. In practical terms they accomplished nothing. As safety valves for letting off steam they merely dissipated passions which should have been harnessed to direct action. He mistrusted most noisy people. Those who yelled rarely acted. Those who acted had no need to yell. True passion, he believed, was cold, not hot as most people thought of it. Emotion was hot. Bluster was hot. Emotion and bluster, like heat, were agents of diffusion. They had throughout his motherland's history scattered the energies of most of her peoples, leaving them vulnerable to conquest by every cold and unified race. The Maharashtrians alone were different. He knew enough of Gujerati, Bengali, Tamil, and Punjabi history to feel confident that his conclusion was an objective rather than a partisan one. Geography had much to do with it, but ultimately, he was convinced, the answer to the riddle of his people's singular superiority lay in the nature of their blood, in the distinctive configuration of their genes. Thanks to caste, blood purity had been preserved in India to a much higher degree than anywhere else in the world. Blood had endowed his own community with the special characteristics of passion and wisdom required for rule. He had just finished writing a book about it.

Dhondo waited for the noise to stop. He had no intention of shouting to make himself heard. He spoke very softly in fact, for then those with sense enough to care to listen would have to be even more silent, and hence more attentive.

"Your most interesting talk," he began, staring at his fingernails instead of at the guest speaker once he had caught the other's eye, "does raise a few questions to mind. You spoke at some length of the relationship of means and ends—"

"Yes, that is most important!"

"May I be allowed to finish my question, please?"

"Of course, please do. Excuse me for interrupting," he said, smiling warmly and nodding.

Dhondo did not return the smile. It was nothing personal. He did not view this unattractive individual as an adversary. Quite the con-

[198]

trary, he considered him an ally, for he was obviously a patriot, and palpably sincere, within the limits of his intellect.

"You stress the primacy of means," Dhondo continued, "relegating to the end in view a distinctly subordinate status, do you not?"

"That is quite correct."

"From the viewpoint of Christian charity perhaps," Dhondo said, looking up now and smiling to take some of the edge off his words, "your position might appear most laudable, but from my understanding of Hinduism it derives no support from *our* spiritual tradition. Yet inconsistently enough you claim inspiration primarily from our own scriptures, do you not?"

"Excuse me, but I see no inconsistency in the question you raise. No true religion is false. The tenets of one do not contradict those of another. Christ's Sermon on the Mount and Shri Krishna's message to Arjuna in the *Gita* are to my reading essentially the same. Both exalt the Golden Rule. Charity is not *Christian,* though good Christians, of course, must possess charity. Charity is an attribute of the Divine, and as such it is the common spiritual property of all mankind."

"I should like to think you are right," Dhondo began, but before he could continue he was interrupted again.

"It is not a question of whether or not *I* am right. My own opinion, after all, is unimportant. I have no illusions concerning my own imperfections and inadequacies. I make no pretense to any gifts of prophecy. I merely state what every inspired prophet and great religious teacher has said over and over again in the past. I repeat what has been preserved for any and all of us to read. God is lovingkindness. He is mercy. He is charity. He is all ethical virtue, and that is why I insist that we must be scrupulously careful that the means we employ in any struggle, in every phase of our existence in fact, be only the purest and spiritually highest. Otherwise the end we shall achieve must be something far different, something base, even grotesque. After all, how could it be anything better?"

Dhondo realized now that he was more slippery than he had anticipated. He was not deceived by any of the fine-sounding words, but he feared that others in the room who listened were. The guest speaker was certainly adept at employing the dust-storm technique in debate, and by refusing to meet a question on its own terms managed to create an atmosphere of sufficient verbal confusion to impress those who were not clever enough to see how evasive he was actually being.

"To get back to your earlier answer," Dhondo insisted. "Surely you cannot be serious in equating the Sermon on the Mount with the message of the *Bhagavad Gita?* The former calls for turning the other cheek, while our scripture is a stirring battle cry, if it is nothing else! No, let me finish please! What, after all, is the very setting of the dialogue? It is Kurukshetra, the field of war! Arjuna, our hero, has lost his courage when he sees his own relatives, his own guru even, arrayed in the front line of chariots massed against him. He lays down his arms and cries out, 'I cannot fight them!' What does the Lord Krishna tell him? 'You are a warrior, Arjuna,' he says, 'therefore, your highest duty is to fight!' Our ancestors, remember, were conquerors; the Christians' were slaves!"

There was appreciative laughter at that, followed by hearty applause. Dhondo was careful not to wait too long this time before continuing, for he was determined to tolerate no more interruptions.

"Our religion is that of the strong, Christianity of the meek and weak! Simply because the Christians grew strong enough, and we became foolish enough to allow them to make slaves of us, that does not mean we should ever forget our God-given destiny to conquer and rule our own motherland, or trade the dharma of the warrior for that of the slave. Let me add that I believe freedom so pure and glorious an end, that I have no doubt it will purify and justify any means we may find necessary to employ in reaching it."

"Bande Mataram!" someone shouted. "Long live the Mother," others repeated, and the battle cry was followed by loud cheers.

Dhondo was content to lean back, satisfied that he had imparted a proper air of militancy to what had almost degenerated into a Christian missionary sermon.

"I do not read the *Gita* as a message of war," came the soft-spoken reply, "but rather allegorically as the struggle of the soul's higher nature against the baser instincts of mortal men. I find it inconceivable, indeed immoral, to believe that so lofty and lovely a poem was written to glorify murder or violence of any sort—"

"Give it whatever personal interpretation you like," Dhondo told him curtly. "I have stated what it says."

"No, you have stated what you *think* it says. Of course, that is your privilege, but by the same token mine is to disagree. Excuse me, but I can see no point in wasting all of our time in further discussion with you, for you have obviously closed your mind—at least on this subject. Our ways are quite different, I see."

"Mine is the Hindu way. What is yours?"

"I like to think it is the way of truth and nonviolence, and I pray that neither is the exclusive possession of Hindus," he replied, but then he turned his back to Dhondo and asked if there were any questions from the other side of the room. . . .

Dhondo tried to lie very still, hoping the palpitation might stop if he did not exert himself in the slightest. He was not simply unaccustomed to illness. He despised it, as he did frailty of any kind. Barring unnatural death he had long been convinced that his body would serve him at least for one hundred years. Why shouldn't it, after all? He never smoked nor drank. He ate moderately, and with careful attention to his diet, abjuring all highly spiced or heavily greased foods. He slept no less than six hours daily, and exercised no less than two. His habits were regular, his temper always in harness. The ancient Vedic seers had lived for many hundreds of years. The reason most people died so quickly in modern times was that they longed for death, they yearned for its liberation. Their lives had no mission, their days no meaning, and once their bodies recognized both discouraging facts they simply stopped bothering to labor for ungrateful masters. They gave up life, so naturally death had to come.

As a young boy, Dhondo had decided never to give it up. He could not remember just when he decided. He suspected it was in a former life, which must have ended long before he wanted it to. Certainly in this one his grandfather had helped him. No one knew exactly when the old man was born, but his grandfather claimed to have counted a hundred monsoons before dying. It was his spirit not his age that Dhondo admired, as God-fearing yet independent a spirit as any he had ever known. Malicious gossips said he was lazy, because he knew that life was too precious a gift to waste in the service of others, especially foreigners. Just to silence the gossips he had taken the clerk's examination in early manhood, passed it easily enough, and became a scribe for John Company. Two months later he quit his office, never to return there. He packed the entire family into two bullock carts and started the long journey from Akola to Benares. "One bath in the Ganges," he insisted, "is worth more than a lifetime in service!" The trip took them nine months. Dhondo was only seven then, but he could still remember many of the wonders he saw, the mountains of pure marble, temples tall as the sun, completely covered with dancing images of God, fields green and lush as a mango leaf, elephants covered with gold, peacocks as common as crows. "All gifts from our God," his grandfather explained, "which the white people have stolen from us. Someday they'll belong to us again, God willing." It was a magnificent journey, but an expensive one, and by the time it was over their savings had run out. "We will sing in the service of God," his grandfather decided for them all. "Better His service than anyone else's!" That was how the Kanetkar family became kirtan singers, though they had not been born Haridasis. At first they were ridiculed for it. People called them beggars, instead of slaves of the God Hari, for the other kirtan singers were too jealous to teach them their songs. "Do what you were born to do!" the jealous Haridasis said. For months they were haunted by hunger. Dhondo's sister died first, and soon after that his mother. But the old patriarch lost none of his determination, and Dhondo's father was made of much the same granite. They wrote their own songs, composing them on the open road. "He is the God they call Hari," they sang, "who ripples as water through the millet grain and rice. He is the God they call Hari, who dances with the milkmaids by the moon's pure light." Dhondo clapped the hand cymbals, his father beat the drum, and his grandfather blew the conch shell announcing their arrival in a village. They sang all together, and when the performance was over, Dhondo walked around with the bowl.

Why does he take so long? Dhondo wondered. He disliked doctors no less than disease. Shivram Jivan was the only one he really trusted. He had been burned once, and that taught him a lesson he could never forget. Dhondo stared at his hands. The palms were withered and scarred, not from age alone. . . .

By that March night of 1916 he had manufactured so many bombs in the cellar workshop at Hampstead House that he was overconfident and got careless. He sensed he was working a bit faster than he should have, but the news in his package of six-week-old papers from Poona received earlier in the day had been so exciting that he was anxious to double the size of the next bomb shipment scheduled to leave for Bombay. District Magistrate Hartford and Sessions Judge Winslow, two of the most hated bureaucrats in western India, had been killed by one bomb hurled at the carriage in which both of them were riding. Not only had the assassin escaped without leaving a trace, the papers reported, but the police were totally baffled as to where or how the bombs were being produced. Since the war had started, of course, restrictions on the sale and use of any munitions, explosives, or arms within India had become far more stringent. Mere possession of saltpeter without license was a crime punishable by as much as ten years of deportation. Dhondo most enjoyed the quoted assertion by one "highly placed" government official that the bombs were made in Germany and shipped overland through Turkey to Persia and Afghanistan. War jitters and censorship had kept the story out of the English press, and for more than a month Dhondo had begun to feel that all their work was wasted effort. Now he was so elated that he surely expected at least one of his next shipments to destroy a governor—possibly the Viceroy himself. Yes, that would more than repay all his patient labor. That was the big game he truly wished for and dreamed about. He was flushed with anticipated joy at the thought of the viceregal carriage splintering sky high. At that moment he made the mistake. Perhaps he took down the wrong jar of acid. He never figured it out exactly. All he knew was that the half-finished bomb exploded, and that fortunately the explosion was so weak that it was really more reflex shock than air concussion that knocked him back.

Instinctively Dhondo held out his hands to shield his face. The only damage done was to his palms. At first even that seemed minor enough to be handled by sodium bicarbonate, in which he immediately immersed his hands and arms. The nitric acid was neutralized before it could blacken the pink flesh of his palms entirely. Two of his helpers quickly covered his hands with rags, another ran up to see if the explosion had awakened anyone on the top floor. Fortunately it hadn't. Outside all was clear. It was in anticipation of just such a mishap that they only worked after midnight and before dawn, when the fewest neighbors would be awake to hear anything.

He felt the hot rapid throbbing in his fingers, but there was no bleeding, and no severe pain. He lay down, and far sooner than he'd expected, was asleep. He did not awaken till well after dawn, but by then the pain had sharpened. Removing the bandages, he did not like what he saw. His palms were huge bubbles of flesh that looked more like stretched rubber than skin. His wrists were less swollen, but equally sensitive to touch. Purplish discoloration had started up his forearms. He knew enough about blood poisoning to recognize the danger.

Several of his Indian friends were Ayurvedic doctors. They were called for at once. Each prescribed a different herb potion. He took them all, but the only apparent effect was to make him vomit. By late afternoon the pain was unbearable. Whether he totally immersed his hands in oil to keep out the air, or left them exposed, or kept one covered and the other bare, seemed completely irrelevant. The pain defied all home remedies. It got worse instead of better. It made him nauseous, then dizzy, then faint with so intense an agony of torture that he finally insisted upon being taken to a neighborhood doctor, the nearest one they could find.

"I will say I was cooking," Dhondo explained as they left the house. "I was making—puris—remember that if you are questioned separately. I was making puris. The oil was boiling hot. I tipped the pot accident— Aieee! Hurry up, will you! Accidentally. I tried to grab it—to save it from falling. The oil poured out over my palms—I screamed, and you two came at once!"

There were several patients in the waiting room, but the nurse took one look at his hands and brought him to the doctor without even letting him sit down.

"My goodness, those are *lovely,* aren't they?" the doctor said, peering at the discolored balloons as if they were impressionistic paintings on a museum wall. "What in heaven's name have you done to them, old boy?"

Dhondo told him the story of his mishap with the puris.

"I see! Devilishly tricky business cooking, what? Hold still a bit now. Anything in that oil you were using, eh?"

Dhondo shook his head. "The pain is terrific," he said.

"I dare say it must be! Do shout if you like, old boy. I won't mind, you know. This will help in a few seconds though." He filled the hypodermic syringe with a local anesthetic and inserted the needle into the muscle of the forearm with a sharp punch that looked worse than it felt. He did the same to the other arm. "Now lie back on here, old boy, and count slowly to three hundred. By the time you've done that the pain should be gone, and then we can do a bit of something else. Lie perfectly still now, because if you move about that pain killer might not work, mind you. I'll get the things I need, meanwhile."

By one hundred the pain was considerably dulled, by two hundred he no longer felt the throbbing, and by three hundred he felt nothing below his elbows, other than a cold stinging which he did not mind at all. He was so relieved that he did not become impatient with the doctor for not returning till a few minutes after he'd stopped counting.

"How is it now, old boy?" He returned holding a scalpel, and something that looked like a pair of scissors, and a small magnet. He touched the palm with the dull end of the scalpel. "Feel anything?"

"No."

"Good! Yell out if you do, eh?"

"What are you doing?" Dhondo asked.

"Oh, just a bit of probing about. Best keep your head back, old boy, that's a good chap. That doesn't hurt, does it?"

"Not yet."

"Splendid! We are in luck, aren't we?" After each incision he lured out the metal chips with his magnet, drained off the pus, and moved on. "Do a lot of cooking for your friends, do you, Mr.— By Jove, you haven't told me your name, have you?"

"My name is—Shankar."

"Shankar, eh? But that's your first name, isn't it? Spent a bit of time in India myself, you know, as a boy— Easy now. Did you feel that?"

"No. But I would like to know, please, what it is you are doing?"

"Just trying to fix you up, Shankar, that's all. Steady on now— there! All finished with that hand. Nurse, will you wrap this one, while I get at the other? Not too tight though, we want those to have free drainage."

"Yes, Doctor."

"What did you say your last name was, Shankar?"

"I did not say it."

"No, so you didn't, eh? I will need it for my records, of course."

"Gupta," Dhondo told him.

"Well, that's a fine name, isn't it? Been in London very long, have you?"

"Not very long."

"Really? Well, I must compliment you then on your facility with English. Quite excellent, by Jove. Beginning to feel that, are you?"

"Yes. Will this take much longer, doctor?"

"Heavens no—be through in a jiffy now. Studying here, are you, Mr. Gupta?"

"Yes, I am."

"What subject?"

"What subject? Law. Why do you ask?"

"Just curiosity, you know. Do you mind?"

"No, of course not."

The buzzer announced the opening of the front door.

"What is that?" Dhondo asked.

"Steady on now! Don't jerk away like that, old chap. This scalpel is rather sharp, you know. Just a patient arriving. See who it is, will you, Nurse?"

She opened the door, saying, "Please come in."

Dhondo took one look at the tall figure who entered, and knew who he was even before the doctor greeted him, explaining, "Says his name's Shankar Gupta, but I don't imagine he's been any more truthful about that than about how he got these blasted burns."

"What is this?" Dhondo asked, sitting up and trying his best to seem genuinely outraged.

"Just what I was about to ask you, laddy," the big police officer replied.

His hands were still bandaged, but the swelling of his wrists had gone down enough to accommodate the steel bracelet used to help drag him onto the ship, which returned him to Bombay, to stand trial. . . .

Lying down had not helped really. Dhondo got up and paced across his room. One entire wall consisted of books. A separate shelf was reserved for his own writings. There were several copies covered in hand-tooled leather of each of the six books he had published: A history of Maharashtra, essays on Hindu dharma, a biography of H. H. Shivaji Rao Nulkar, an anthology of his poems, and the first two volumes of his projected five-volume history of Hindu freedom. Each of his more than one hundred pamphlets was sewn into its own cardboard folder. The published record of his trial was the tallest book on the shelf. Its jacket had a picture of his head emblazoned upon its red leather surface in gold leaf. That book had been presented to him on his jubilee birthday. In his will he specified that it was to be sent as a gift to the National Archives. His trial was, after all, a historic landmark of his nation's struggle. He carefully removed the tall book from its shelf and took it to his desk. The first fifty pages, preceding the verbatim courtroom account, were testimonials to his patriotism and sterling character, testimonials freely given by leaders from every avenue of Hindu life, many from men who had never met him, but admired his poetry and simply said that, others from casual acquaintances. Few who had been approached by the members of the Committee for Justice for Kanetkar, under whose auspices the book was published, had been churlish enough to refuse to say anything at all. One name, however, was so conspicuous by its absence that when he first noted it, Dhondo had felt offended. Now he was glad that his book was not infected by that name.

"Mahatma indeed!" he whispered, but that was followed by so intense a palpitation that his heart seemed to flip over and back again. "I bear him no personal grudge," he quickly added. God knew he had never sought personal glorification, if there was a God. Many a time in Mandalay he had wondered. . . .

"Are you God?" he asked, softly. "Are you? Have you come at last to free Guruji? Have you?"

The ropelike tail was as long as the rodent's body, a not very long or sleek body, rather thin in fact, somewhat scrawny. There was not very much to grow fat on in Mandalay's Central Jail. The pointed nose quivered sensitively.

"Why don't you chew the bars for me, God? Why do you only eat my chappals? Do you love them so? I will love you if you chew the bars. I will give you buffalo milk and coconut meat every morning and evening, my dear God. You can believe Guruji. Trust me, and I will believe in you. Do you smile, God?"

The rat bared its front teeth, and licked at its nose with a pointed tongue.

"Perhaps you would like me to sing to you, is that it? Have you learned that your Guruji was a kirtan singer? Is that why you have come to him? But I have no instruments. Will you mind if I sing without my cymbals? Are you sure not? Very well, then. I shall compose a kirtan specially for you.

> "He is Hari, whose teeth are like razors,
>   Blessed Lord of all prisoners is he,
> When he gnaws, then my bars go to blazes,
>   God of all Gods is Hari!"

The song seemed to give the rat courage. It scampered across the cell and began nibbling with incredible speed at the chappal strap whose ragged edge already bore its teeth's trademark. Guruji hurled his copy of the *Gita,* which was the nearest book at hand.

"Die, God," he yelled. "You are a false god! I am more of a god than you—whoever you may be—can you hear me? Guruji is more of a god than God! Can you hear me? Can you hear, you deaf one!" His fists closed around the blistering black bars of the high window, and he tugged against them till he had drawn his body off the ground entirely and his shaved head butted against the bars, like a horns-down bull racing toward a tree.

That was the second year, the one which had seemed longer than all the rest, because for most of the first year there was the hope of Privy Council review of the High Court's verdict, because two years in Mandalay were eternity, and the fourteen that followed were few enough to add to all that. The third year he started writing again. He was permitted all the books he asked for, all the paper he needed. He could write one letter a month, and receive two. And he could plan for the future, because he was determined to fool them. They were sure he would die there, but he was determined not to die. His sentence had been "life" and life was what he clung to, for though it might take twenty years he knew one day the doors would open if he endured. One day a secretary of state would arrive in Whitehall to find a petition waiting from the Committee for Justice for Kanetkar, and he would scratch his head and ask, "Who the devil is Kanetkar anyway?" It was for that day and all the years of freedom to follow that he lived, and waited, and planned, and planned . . . not to avenge himself. He longed for no personal revenge. It was retribution for the national insult, for the humiliation of his people and his cause which his barbarous sentence represented, that alone concerned him. . . .

"I no longer exist as an individual," Guruji muttered, "so I can feel no individual hatred or jealousy. I can feel nothing apart from my motherland's need."

But why does my heart continue to flutter, he wondered, when at long last Dr. Shivram Jivan, wiping the perspiration from his forehead with a neatly folded handkerchief, entered the room. He was a big-bodied man. His head and legs seemed too small for his massive torso. His sweat left dark crescents under the armpits of his soft white jacket. He walked briskly to the desk and placed his satchel on top of it.

"Well, my dear Kanetkar, you look quite fit. What troubles you?"

"My heart, Jivan."

"Heart? Yes, yes, there is our weak link, Kanetkar. Let me see what I can hear. Just breathe normally. That's right. Hold that in a moment—now exhale. Again please. Now normally. Now as deep as you can and hold it. All right, release. Hmmm."

The doctor straightened up and removed the stethoscope from his ears. Guruji's valet had brought over a chair for him and he sat down.

Ultimately we are all at their mercy, Dhondo thought, watching the dark, dispassionate face of his devout friend, waiting as eagerly for his verdict as though he were a justice of the High Court.

"Tell me, my dear Kanetkar, just what is it—uh—that you feel? How would you describe it?"

"The more important question, Jivan, is how would you describe what you hear, isn't it?"

"Not necessarily, my dear Kanetkar," the doctor told him, tugging at his already elongated earlobe. "There are many mysteries, as you know. The human body is one of the most baffling, I must confess. The longer I practice the more convinced I become that actually we know very little, surprisingly little, my dear Kanetkar."

It was hardly the most encouraging information a patient could receive from his physician. If the other doctors in Bombay did not find it necessary to consult Shivram Jivan on their most difficult cases, as Dhondo well realized, he would have felt more angry than upset by his friend's confession of ignorance.

"Do you feel *pain*, my dear Kanetkar? Would you say your heart gives you pain now?"

"Certainly!"

"*Sharp* pain or dull—which would you say?"

"A little of both, and constant fluttering!"

"Fluttering, you say? Mmmm, do you feel any now?"

"Of course! Didn't you hear it?"

"Sometimes it is not exactly easy to hear. Perhaps if you could point with your finger to a spot where you feel the fluttering?"

Must I do everything for him, Dhondo wondered. "I feel it all around here," he said, pointing to half a dozen spots.

"Mmm. Let me listen again please. Right here, is it? Good. Now breathe normally." After a few moments of tapping about and listening, Shivram Jivan removed his stethoscope again, and stood up. "I should like to take your blood pressure, my dear Kanetkar. Will you please lie down?"

"As you wish," Dhondo said. "What do you think it is, Jivan?"

"Let me check you a bit more thoroughly before I commit myself, my dear Kanetkar. I should remember this, of course, but tell me, your last birthday, was that your sixty-ninth or seventieth?"

"Seventieth."

"Well, seventy! A fine age, my dear Kanetkar. If you will just pull up your sleeve a bit please, then I can wrap this tire around your arm."

Do whatever you like, Dhondo thought, lying back and closing his eyes, determined to say nothing more to Shivram Jivan until the latter was ready to commit himself to at least a tentative verdict. Not that he really cared one way or the other. I do not care one way or the other, he told himself, calmly, for one should always be calm when his blood pressure is being taken. I do not care one way or the other! . . .

"As for my *personal* feelings about it, gentlemen," Dhondo explained, looking alternately at each of the three members of the Working Committee of the National Congress, who had come to visit him, "I do not care one way or the other."

"Naturally, Kanetkar," Rao Bahadur Paranjpe, senior member and spokesman for the delegation replied. "It is you who will honor the office of president, not the presidency which will honor you, after all you have sacrificed."

"It is not that, Paranjpe," Dhondo insisted. "My health is run-down, as you see, and after sixteen years away I have lost considerable touch with political affairs."

"You are far too modest, Kanetkar, but modesty indeed is the hallmark of greatness," Paranjpe said. "In any event, of course, our permanent joint secretaries and Working Committee are there to carry on the routine jobs. Your major task, naturally, as president, will be your address to our annual meeting, and there we are convinced none can rival your talents. Then too, Kanetkar, your presence alone at the head of our national movement, even though for one year, would symbolize, as it were, the indestructibility of our Hindu way of life, of all we hold dear. All we ask is your permission to allow us to nominate you at our Committee's next meeting."

Dhondo sipped his tea slowly. He had expected a larger deputation from the high command, or at least a more representative one. The three who faced him now were long-standing allies. They had sent many memorials on his behalf to the Crown. They adorned most of the larger rallies held in Bombay over the past decade and a half to raise funds for the Committee for Justice for Kanetkar. They were all excellent and influential gentlemen, but Dhondo wondered how many of the other seven members of the Working Committee would go along with them.

"As you know, Rao Bahadur, my life is dedicated to the service of our motherland. If you—and, needless to say, a majority of your colleagues—feel that my poor talents may prove to be of some value at the helm of our nation's mighty political organization, I will not shirk my duty."

"We have expected no less of you, Kanetkar, but now your words from your own lips give us fresh inspiration! Naturally, we can only speak for ourselves, but I think it safe to tell you that I am fairly positive that six, possibly seven, members of our Committee will be overjoyed at the prospect of your bold and forceful leadership finally

[210]

gaining some measure of formal recognition, which is so long over-due, if I may say."

"Definitely six, I agree!" Shet Munshi commented in a rare moment of self-assertion that obviously startled him as much as it did Rao Bahadur at his side, who silenced his timid colleague with a sharp glance.

"Possibly *seven,* as I say," Paranjpe continued, "but as you doubt-less know, Kanetkar, in matters as important as the choice of our annual president we have made it our regular policy to select our candidate by unanimous agreement only in order to prevent any cleavage within the Congress as a whole when we present our slate to the delegates."

"What Rao Bahadur is driving at, Dhondo," Kakasahib Joshi, the youngest of the trio, explained, "is that while all of us want you and feel the majority share our predilection, the fact of the matter is that without the Mahatma's approval the Committee will nominate no one."

"Very well, Kaka, you are now our spokesman!" the much-offended Rao Bahadur said, extracting a pinch of snuff from his box and inhaling it noisily.

"We might just as well admit it," Joshi said, his eyes flashing with reckless intensity. "Our whole Committee is nothing more than the Mahatma's rubber stamp! If you ask me, the most effective thing any of us can do is resign!"

Munshi sighed and nodded his head, while Paranjpe remained too insulted to try to counter so rash a suggestion.

"But surely, Kaka, if you are prepared to go that far," Dhondo remarked softly, disinterestedly, as though he were merely thinking out loud, "and if, as you say, the majority agree with you, then what prevents you from using your constitutional powers?"

"Ah, excellent! Excellent, my dear Dhondo! Splendid," the Com-mittee's firebrand retorted, rubbing his hands together gleefully as though he had just come in from a frosty outdoors. "Ask *them,* I beg you! Ask my honored colleagues. Perhaps it is a secret they will divulge to you—not to me, I hasten to add, never to me! I have asked them a hundred times already! Well, Rao Bahadur?"

"I have yielded the floor to you, Kaka," Paranjpe replied, hugging his massive bulk with crossed arms, holding himself to himself like a giant seal jealous of the prerogative which his weight gave him to pre-empt the highest rock shelf and content to sit there basking nearest the sun, aloof, inviolate.

Kakasahib shrugged in futile resignation. "What is the use," he muttered.

Cowardice is the curse of our race, Dhondo thought, seeing now as he watched them what he had seen so many times before, in so many political conferences, with so many political leaders who used the tactics of false pride, of loquacity, of whatever devious disguise they found nearest at hand, to hide the simple fact of their moral cowardice, which invariably prevented them from asserting their wills even when they knew perfectly well that such self-assertion was within their rights. They all realized it, of course, and hated themselves for it, which was why they had gone so far in his defense in the first place. But risk an open battle against the Prophet of Liberation? No, that would be asking too much of any men already seated among the elect of the shadow cabinet. They had become so accustomed to running to his ashram for advice and accepting every word as a sacred order that they feared the freedom to make their own decisions far more than any possible sanction he might impose for apostasy. What, after all, could he do other than threaten to fast unto death? Yet just the thought of it was enough to bring most of them to heel.

"Will you have another cup, Rao Bahadur?" Dhondo asked.

"Thank you, no, Kanetkar. I have stayed far too long already. Such political talk must still be a strain upon you."

"Not upon me, Rao Bahadur."

"I see." He smiled and twisted his neck uneasily. He was a moderate man in most respects, politically more nearly a nineteenth-century liberal than radical, professionally a schoolteacher, personally shy, and since the death of his second wife very much alone. He had not rushed to embrace the nationalist movement in his youth, but had courted her much later in life, when he could bring to support his suit not ardor but reputation, position rather than passion. In most ways he was Dhondo Kanetkar's opposite, yet he was Maharashtrian, and had desired to join the movement when he did for religious rather than secular reasons. He felt, moreover, that in supporting Kanetkar he was championing the underdog, and he knew that in the eyes of some of his colleagues that made him appear a bigger man than they usually thought he was. "Kanetkar, I think it only proper to say before I go that though Kaka has been far too rash and *extreme—*" He paused to look at his junior with stern reprobation under his bushy brows. "Far too extreme entirely! Nevertheless, amongst ourselves here we need not be *formal,* and consequently—" He paused to inhale another pinch of snuff.

"To put it another way, Kanetkar," the ponderous Rao Bahadur continued, shifting his weight slightly, "perhaps it would not be a bad idea for you to write Bapuji and tell him you would like to come visit with him awhile, and then—"

Dhondo stopped listening. He watched the mouth move, noted the ripples vibrating away from it over the pudgy cheeks, down the double chin, watched the delicate finger gestures so integrally a part of his countrymen's speech habits, noted the spot of cloth drawn tight by the outward bulge of the stomach's advance guard, but heard no more, and when the mouth stopped moving said nothing himself. He had made it a practice many years ago, before Mandalay in fact, to stop listening when people were stupid enough to think they were smart enough to tell him how to behave.

Rao Bahadur Paranjpe waited what seemed like a sufficiently respectable length of time, then coughed against his fist, and smiled uncertainly. "Naturally, Kanetkar, you must do whatever you think best, of course, and in any event, as I say, naturally we shall be honored to put forth your name now that you have given us permission. . . ." His voice trailed off to a grunt as he leaned forward and stood up.

"So kind of you to visit me, gentlemen," Dhondo said, clasping his hands in the reverential farewell.

"We shall put up a fight in the Committee, you can rely upon it, Kanetkar," Paranjpe promised as they walked toward the door. "It is high time your sacrifices received the compensation they deserve!"

Dhondo lowered his head modestly but said nothing. It would have been ungenerous of him to point out that no amount of compensation could pay for sixteen years of solitary exile. . . .

"Thank you, my dear Kanetkar," Shivram Jivan said, closing his bag. "Please sit up if you like. I find nothing abnormal whatever, nothing distressing at least, since, I should say, your physique is abnormally vigorous for your age. I wish my own were as good!"

"But what are these flutters?"

"You still feel them?"

"Yes!" He seemed to ask it as though they were a product of imagination to be wished away or forgotten.

"They could be several things, my dear Kanetkar. The stethoscope, of course, does not tell us very much. If you still have pain tomorrow I should like to take a cardiogram. Have you altered your diet in any way recently?"

"Not at all."

"You don't take any—intoxicants, do you?"

"Of course not. What are you driving at, Jivan?"

Shivram Jivan enumerated the possible physical causes of the flutters and pains, then asked in an offhand tone, "Has anything special been worrying you lately, my dear Kanetkar?"

"Naturally I am most distressed about Kashmir," Dhondo replied, sorry now that he had yielded to the impulse to call for aid—not that he did not trust Jivan, not that he feared Jivan. He had wanted physical assurance, and now that he had it, he wanted no more, sought no more from this man.

"Yes, of course, it is a time of great tension for all of us," the doctor agreed. "You as a public leader must feel everything more keenly—"

"I take no active role any longer, as you know, Jivan," he said, rising to indicate that he did not wish to continue the conversation.

"Ah, that is our nation's loss, my dear Kanetkar. I have often thought that of the many mistakes we have made in the past several years one of the greatest was not to have insisted that you participate in the prepartition conferences. I am afraid we have relied altogether too blindly upon the judgment of one man, and simply because you violently disagreed—"

"Why do you say violently, Jivan?"

"I—well it is just a figure of speech—"

"But as a doctor you should be most precise in your speech, shouldn't you? Let me caution you, Jivan, to remember that I have never been *violent* in my personal relations with him, or with anyone else. Violence is a form of passion, remember, and I firmly believe that passion has no place in our personal relations. I hold that as an article of my religious faith, Jivan."

"I am sorry if inadvertently I offended—"

"Not at all! I have taken no offense, none whatsoever. I simply do not wish to have my position misstated. It is a matter of public record, as you know. My entire life is a matter of open public record, Jivan, and I challenge you or any man to cite any instance, any single statement from the entire corpus of my writings or from any reported speech I have made with reference to him, which could be adjudged in a court of law as violent! What I have written and said of him has always been done without personal hatred. It has been nothing more than sober and proper commentary upon what I have

[214]

deemed the errors of his political judgment. Sober and proper, Jivan—never violent! Please remember that."

It was so unexpected and torrential an outburst that when it ended both of them stood in surprised silence, awkwardly confronting each other as though they had met quite by accident for the first time. Dr. Jivan explained that the electric cardiograph machine could not be removed from his office, and suggested again that if the flutters were still with him by morning Kanetkar should drive over for a reading. He had left several patients waiting, he added, and apologized for having to go so quickly, though by the time he went they were glad to be rid of each other.

Guruji stood before his desk and stared at the unfinished page of his memoirs, on which he had written:

By April of 1946 our choice became clear. Daily the toll of Hindus murdered by Muslim fanatics was mounting. The white sahibs gloated. The Muslim League had been their ally throughout the war. Hindu patriots alone were their enemies. Would British rifles be turned now against allies to protect enemies? Only the naïve could believe so. Only traitors to the motherland, who were not naïve, could urge others to believe so. Only traitors or madmen! Our choice was vigorous self-defense or death! Our choice was the path of blood leading to Liberation and Salvation, or the path of blood leading to Humiliation and Destruction! Our choice was Self-respect or National Surrender! We could fight and live as Hindus, or we could cringe and die in slavery. We could complete the work of total Liberation of the Mother so beautifully begun by our patriotic societies during the war, or we could abjectly surrender to her vivisection! The choice was ours alone. Seeing it clearly I rushed to Delhi to appeal to the man who for more than twenty years had been sole dictator of the Congress, at whose insistence the Working Committee had chosen a Muslim president for the year! I had written well in advance to notify him of the date and hour of my visit, but found when I arrived that he had gone to the Muslim mosque for evening prayers. Suddenly I saw that this man in whom we had put so much faith and trust no longer considered himself a Hindu! Had he gone completely mad, I wondered, or was the illness which afflicted him less forgivable than insanity?

Dhondo reread the last sentence several times, then returned to his daybed to lie down. The fluttering seemed less rapid. There were longer intervals between the painful spasms.

No, it is definitely not personal, he told himself with greater assurance now. He felt much more at ease, and was pleasantly surprised to note that in less than twenty minutes it would be four o'clock.

13

For two hours Vishnu Apte had been thinking: Now I must stand up and leave! But each time he converted his desire into words, something which Katuk said, or did not say but merely appeared to be thinking, frightened him into deciding to wait a bit longer. All his life it had been that way for Vishnu Apte, deciding one thing, then doing the opposite because someone told him to. He had rebelled only twice, on the eve of his wedding and later when he joined the Society. In a sense, of course, the second was no overt rebellion, since he told no one who would have objected to what he was planning. As for the first, he sometimes wondered if it was really an assertion of his own will as much as the acceptance of what he inwardly suspected to be his mother's true desire. She was the most devout woman he had ever known, and that night before his wedding she had gone off to the temple alone to pray for him. . . .

His father was too busy chewing pan and laughing raucously at the jokes of his four uncles to notice Vishnu leave the large room. Their woman servant in the kitchen informed him, "Bai has gone to God." She had not been told to which temple, but the first thing he noticed when he stepped outside was that the full moon had risen just above Parvati. Bathed in that pale light glow the lofty double-domed temple of the Goddess looked so lovely and serene that he started immediately toward its breastlike hill sensing he would find his mother at the top. He passed several holy men along the climb; statues they seemed at the sides of the road, snakelike hair extending wildly from their heads in every direction, Shiva's trident upright in one hand, the beggar's bowl firm in the other. Their eyes were as bright and round as the moon; their flesh, streaked with ash, was otherwise black and parched as the earth. Their noses and ears were pierced with steel rings. On their brows were three horizontal strokes, drawn in red, symbol of Shiva as Destroyer. Vishnu trembled at the sight of them, though they never moved nor made any sound. By the intense powers of their concentration, his mother had once explained, these sadhus kept the entire universe in order. He knew they were great and good men, but at night just seeing them scared him. There were no houses along the road, for this hill was a public shrine. Vishnu started to run. Then he saw some pious people calmly descending the old stone steps, which started almost halfway toward the top, and the sight of them shamed him into walking again. Besides, it was a steep climb and he began to feel winded. He paused where the stone railing began. These were the rocks the early Peshwas had laid when they first built this private temple to Shiva's consort. They were pitted throughout like the rest of the volcanic lava trap around Poona, though time and wind had softened their sharp edges. He looked back at the dim yellow lights of the city, like fireflies flickering over the plain. He searched for his own house, but could no longer be sure which it was. Most of the world he saw was in darkness. He wondered again if his bride would be as beautiful as he dreamed. They had been together only once, for their betrothal, but the veil she wore had hidden her face from him. She was very young, he knew, and her father was even wealthier than his. "My boy," his father had told him many times, "you are to be paid a princely dowry, *princely* I say!" It was all his father would tell him when he asked if she were beautiful.

The domes disappeared as he climbed higher and the crenelated outer wall loomed larger, till it seemed a rampart skirting the world's edge with nothing beyond but a moon-filled sky. Though his English teacher insisted the world was a sphere without edges to build walls around, Vishnu believed that Hindu cosmology was far more logical. Somewhere the end had to be, and there as his mother often described it to him, God had built a wall of pure marble, higher than any mountain or ocean wave. It was just an inch higher than Mount Meru, in fact, where Shiva sat on his tigerskin, though the all-seeing eye in the center of his forehead could, of course, peer over its battlements to the Suchness beyond.

The gate was just partly opened, but unguarded. He walked into the sacred garden. There were no flowers, only ancient trees through which the wind moaned its mournful melody. He listened carefully, for his mother said that when the moon was full the Peshwas' spirits returned here, to this place where their ashes were interred. The moon rippled in bone-white fragments on the scum-coated surface of the lotus pond. No lotuses rose above the floating heart-shaped leaves. There was no one in sight. He stared at the pond and wished that she might be as beautiful as a lotus. Then the wind seemed to laugh, and he looked around furtively, hurrying away from the palace where the ashes were sealed into the walls, through the small archway to the temples. There were really three temples here; the one nearest the gate and supposedly the most recent of them all belonged not to Parvati, but to her eldest son, Kartikeya, God of War, slayer of the demon Taraka. Its door was open, and Vishnu stopped before it, removed his sandals, and stepped inside. He did not expect to find his mother here. No woman was ever permitted to approach the six-headed idol mounted on his peacock chariot, yet he could not pass Kartikeya without obeisance, for of all the gods whose wrath a man might incur, none was more dangerous. He knelt before the multiheaded, many-armed figure of might, its ivory eyes blazing behind the flickering kerosene lamp, and bowed his head for fear that if he stared too brazenly the War God might hurl a spear through his eyes. He fumbled about in his dhoti, extracted his handkerchief, untied its knot, and removed a silver coin which he placed on the empty offering plate before the altar. As he did so a bell sounded from behind the god's image, and though he suspected it was a priest hidden in the shadows who rang the bell, its sudden noise seemed to him like the thunderbolt Kartikeya had hurled from a cloudless sky the night he had poured torrents of red-hot human ash on top of Taraka's demon army, and his heart stopped beating till he was safely outside again. Instead of waiting to step into his sandals, he

bent and swiftly retrieved them, rushing on bare feet to the sanctuary
of the Goddess. When he was little more than an infant his mother
had related for hours on end the story of Taraka's destruction. There
were flocks of vultures, he remembered, hanging over the demon
army in such awful numbers that they obscured the sun. There were
serpents bigger than banyan trees, blacker than charcoal, spitting
poison that fell like rain. There were jackals with hungry cries that
rumbled and reverberated off the mountains.

Vishnu saw the slight figure of a woman leaving the larger
Parvati temple as he approached it, and for an instant he thought it
was his mother, for the dark sari was drawn over the top of her
head, instead of around her shoulders, obscuring her face. Several
people were standing along the balcony overlooking the plain, but he
noted at a glance that she was not among them. Nor was she inside
the larger Parvati. He hurried across the parapet walk to the entrance
of the temple with the smaller onion-shaped dome on top. Was it
possible she had not come here, after all?

The outer hall of the temple was empty. Its darkness swallowed
him. His feet almost slipped over the dank smooth stones, clammy
cold, rubbed to glasslike polish by the soft abrasive of countless naked
soles. The inner shrine was a low-ceilinged cubicle, faintly illumined
by oil-wick lamps on either side of the seated statue of the Mother.
She was dressed in bright blue and red silks, Her hair lustrous and
falling loose to Her waist, Her lips painted red, Her eyes ringed with
mercury, their black lashes long and upcurling. She seemed real
enough to breathe. At first he thought She was alone. He heard the
faintest sniffling, and even thought that was the Goddess, till stooping
to enter the inner chamber, he saw her crouched very low on the
bare stones to one side. He knelt just a step behind her.

Without looking around, she whispered, "Vishnu?"

"Mother, why do you cry?" he asked, feeling himself on the verge
of tears. The plain dark sari covered her head as though she were in
mourning. She had never seemed so frail and alone.

"Do not ask me before the Goddess," she said. "Pray, my
son."

He bowed his head, but was too bewildered, too upset to know
what to pray for. He kept looking at his mother and wishing there
was some way in which he could console her. He was her only child.
She had given him her life. No sacrifice was ever too great for her,
no vigil at his sickbed too long for her to endure it alone. She herself
was so slight that his mere birth had almost killed her. She had not

[219]

told him that. He learned of it from his aunt, who said she had lost so much blood that the doctors all but abandoned hope, yet she lay on her sickbed whispering, "I have a boy, I have a boy," and it was that knowledge which gave her the strength to survive. "Help my mother to help me," he prayed aloud.

"What troubles my son?" she whispered, yet to him the voice seemed to emanate from the Goddess.

"I am not ready to marry," he said, not knowing what made him say it, but sensing as he did so that it was the truth he had been afraid to admit even to himself since the day of his betrothal.

"But all is ready," she said.

"I am not. Help me, Mother!"

"My son is no longer a child," she answered, her voice as faint and flickering as the lamplight.

"Help me," he begged, placing his entire handkerchief now on the offering plate.

"Come, Vishnu," she said, gripping his arm and walking slight yet strong at his side, back into the silver-strewn night.

They stood on the rampart ledge facing the plain far below, his arm pressed firmly against her flaccid breast, the breast he had so greedily drained for so long as a child. "I never once denied you, my son," she had told him. "Even when I was too sick to sit up, you lay at your mother's heart and drank the food God gave me for you. Every day for three years you took all your nourishment through your mother's heart, my child." Though her flesh was wrinkled her face possessed a spiritual beauty more perfect than that of any other face he had ever known.

"Tell me what to do, Mother," he asked.

"Why have you waited so long to speak, my son?"

"I did not want to hurt you or father."

"But your father has made all the preparations for tomorrow. Your uncles have come a great distance."

He felt hopelessly trapped.

"Are you sure you do not desire the mundane life of the house-holder?" she asked.

"I am sure," he answered eagerly.

"Let me say that when my son was born," she said, closing her eyes as though in prayer, "the Goddess told me he was not meant for ordinary things!"

"Then you will help me, Mother?"

"How can I help? Parvati alone can save you."

[220]

"But how?"

"She alone must call her disciples to her bosom. Have you felt Her loving power, my son?"

"Yes, I think so, Mother."

"It is not enough to think so," she said, rising as though the breath she inhaled filled her entire being and made her much larger. "You must *know* in your heart. You must be filled with Her radiance, permeated with Her fire, covered with the mantle of Her divine grace. You must feel as I felt when my son was born and all pain was beauty, all suffering love undiluted—"

"I am trying, Mother. I think—"

"Yes?"

"I think I can feel Her!"

"In the pure blood of your innermost heart, my child? You must feel Her here, only here," she said, placing his hand upon her upper breast, and staring at him with a pure spiritual rapture so beautiful that he could not keep himself from crying.

"Yes, I am sure," he said.

"The life divine," she whispered, "is reserved for the few. Marriage has no place in it."

"Then you will not be angry if—?"

"No mother regrets having borne a saint," she told him.

"But what will father say?"

"I have never told you," she said, "that my elder brother on the eve of his wedding felt much the same as you feel now. He was in many ways like you, Vishnu, seemingly weak but spiritually the strongest amongst us. His soul was too pure for mundane marriage. He had given himself to the Goddess as a boy, and when despite his protests my father went ahead with the plans for a wedding, in his quiet way Rama said nothing more, but the night before his wedding he simply did not come home. The next day, of course, the bride and her family were ready, but without Rama nothing could be done, could it? The dowry was returned, the pandal destroyed. My father fussed and fumed, but after a few days he stopped shouting about Rama and started praying for him. Then little more than two weeks later Rama appeared at our door in the saffron robes of a Ramdasi, holding his staff and beggar's bowl. I thought my father's tears of joy would wash away our home, and Rama, remember, was not his *only* child."

"Then I too could—"

"Hush, Vishnu, tell me nothing of your plans! As your father's

[221]

wife, remember, my first duty is to urge you to obey his every wish and command! I must, therefore, urge you not even to think of staying up here tonight, and should you decide to remain in the womb of the Goddess, where at least you would be sheltered from the raw wind, should you decide to give yourself up to Her rather than to the lame daughter of—"

"Is she *lame,* Mother?" That horrible prospect had never occurred to him—a crippled, disfigured wife! Yet why else had his father never once spoken of her beauty, only of her dowry? And why else, of course, would so princely a dowry be paid for so young a bride? What a blind fool he had been not to realize it all before now! He shuddered at the thought of how close he had come to shackling himself for life to an ugly cripple.

"Have I said too much, my son?" his mother implored, her saintly eyes overflowing again.

"No, Mother, you have saved me! You have saved me," he repeated, bending to kiss the tears as they streamed from her eyes.

"Not I," she whispered. "I have done nothing, my child. It is the Goddess. She alone can save those who give themselves to Her."

"You are the Goddess, Mother."

"What are you saying, foolish child?" she asked, but with so sweetly serene a smile that he was more positive of it than ever.

"You are the Goddess! I am your slave for all eternity."

"No. Say no more," she cautioned, touching his lips with her wrinkled finger, holding her finger against his lips as he kissed it tenderly, with all the passion of divine love he felt for her now.

"I must go, Vishnu," she said, "before I am missed. I will return here at least once each day to bring my offerings of food to the Goddess for Her—disciple."

"Do not fear for me, Mother. I am strong. I will wait here for you."

"My blessed son," she whispered. "My beautiful son."

She moved away like a spirit in the night, her sari drawn close around her face, Parvati, the Mother, Goddess of all the earth, giver of life, protector of all Her children.

Vishnu remained on the hill for ten days. Each night he slept on the dank stones of the temple's outer hall. He drank water from the well in the courtyard before dawn, then prayed facing the East and stared at the burning orange ball of the sun till its rays lashed so fiercely against his brain that he saw visions of his mother rising like pure gold before him, covered by nothing but the hair that flowed like the silk of corn over the mellow curves of her tender body. He saw other visions also, of the bride who had almost trapped him, her body twisted hideously out of proportion, her face scarred, her lips burned away to reveal jagged teeth, while from her mouth, instead of a tongue, the heads of many serpents emerged, spitting poison. Each afternoon and evening his mother came to him with food she had cooked and fruit she had picked with her own hands. They walked together along the parapet after he finished his food, and she talked of the days when the Peshwas had stood where he was standing, of Balaji Vishvanath's genius and his single-minded dedication to the nation of the Goddess, to Her alone truly. "She *is* our nation," his mother kept saying. "She is the earth, and all of us belong to Her." She told him then of his grandfather's grandfather on her side, who had been assistant land revenue collector for the last of the Peshwas, Baji Rao II, and of his father, who had served Narain Rao. "There is greatness in your blood, my son," she said. At night he would dream of those ancestors of his, living as lords in their palaces, carried on their palanquins through the countryside on the shoulders of servants, dispensing silver rupees to the poor as they passed them, meting out justice to the petitioners who ran pleading for aid, reverently praying before an image of the Goddess, whose face was always his mother's. He spent many hours watching the Goddess. He saw Her smile at him several times. Once She extended Her hand to him, and Her lips moved in silent prayer. He cried out to Her, "Mother!" He lay before Her with his forehead pressed against the damp stone. Each day his mother brought a rupee for him to put into the offering dish. He became friendly with the priest who cared for the temple, a small old man, who said, "The Goddess is God!" whenever they met, his eyes turned so far upward that the pupils could not be seen, only the whites. He was always chewing pan.

Vishnu Apte had many spiritual experiences on the hill, but by the tenth day he was too homesick to remain longer. He had become so filthy that he could not stand his own stench. His body had broken out in sores and rashes, which he could not help but scratch, and several of them had begun to suppurate. His scalp itched constantly, and his hair when he looked at his reflection in the lotus pond appeared to him to resemble that of the holy men along the road. He missed his friends, moreover, and school would be starting again soon. His wedding had been arranged during the spring recess, but that was only two weeks long. That afternoon he unburdened himself to his mother, and ended by placing his head on her lap and crying, "I

[223]

cannot stand it any longer. I cannot stand it!" He felt ashamed of his weakness, but was relieved to hear her finally say, "The Goddess must wish for you to return to your home. Wait until it is dark. Come to the rear door."

Soon after the sun was down, Vishnu started his descent. He walked at first, but then began running as fast as his feet would carry him. He could think of nothing but a bath with heated water, clean clothes, a hot meal, and the luxury of sleeping again on a charpoy instead of on stone. He was panting so hard by the time he reached his house that he could not knock at the door until he had calmed down slightly. But even before he knocked his mother opened the door for him and cried out, "Vishnu! Vishnu, my son, God has sent you home to us!" She kept howling and crying till his father appeared in the kitchen.

"So you've come home, have you, you scoundrel," his father shouted; then, trembling with rage, he ran to get his stick, but when he raised it over Vishnu's panic-paralyzed head, his mother flung herself against her husband's massive hulk, screaming:

"Beat me, if you must! Spare my son, I beg you!"

"You put him up to it, I suppose," he shouted, pushing her aside, and landing so solid a smack on Vishnu's shoulder that he yelped and sobbed uncontrollably, falling to the floor. "Scoundrels! I should kill the both of you," his father raved, "making a laughingstock out of me! Throwing away a princely dowry! Get up, you blithering imbecile," he ordered, "and go wash yourself!"

But he was too frightened to get up. . . .

It seemed to Vishnu now that Purushottamdas Katuk was his father, for each time he told himself I must stand up and leave, he shrank back at the mere sight of Katuk's pocked face. Yet in joining the Society, Vishnu thought he had once and for all asserted his manly independence, liberating himself entirely, though covertly, from patriarchal domination. Guruji he thought of as God, and that was different. His father was neither a pious man nor a patriot. His father was a businessman, and as such, the orthodox considered him something of a traitor to his Brahmanic birthright, but if ever they sneered in howsoever circumspect a manner, he told them, "I pay others to pray for me. Worry about your own salvation!" He did not retain the land he had inherited, as his brothers did; he knew that in so crowded an agricultural country all land was preposterously inflated in value, so he converted poor soil and baronial prestige for silver enough to buy a comfortable home in the city and a press on which to support it. His brothers all considered him a mad wastrel, but he knew his own people better than any of them. "A Maharashtrian will go without food three times a day," he said, "but his hunger for printed matter will never let a press in Poona go bankrupt." Actually several presses went bankrupt every year, though Poona did attract more intellectuals than any city of India, with the possible exception of Calcutta. But Ganesh Vasudev Apte's press flourished. His secret was honesty. He never overcharged, and he never cheated a customer. He even saw to it that by the day he had promised delivery, whether of cards announcing a wedding, or of a book, or a newspaper, the goods were ready. People accustomed to every manner of fraud, and every excuse for delay of delivery, were so shocked and delighted by Apte's honesty that his reputation spread with legendary swiftness and embellishment. He soon had more orders than he could handle, but instead of turning them away, or succumbing to the temptation to lie as his competitors did, he bought out a press on the verge of collapse, and doubled his output capacity. He gave himself ungrudgingly to his business, and even brought two of his brothers to his aid, leaving the less industrious two to their genteel pride. He kept abreast of the latest improvements in printing techniques by ordering manuals from England, and paying a young professor of English to help him decipher them. Thus recognizing his very real debt to the English it was not possible for him to get any more excited about independence than he had about God. He had more business than he could handle despite the existence of English competitors. "I never mix politics with business," became his standard answer to anyone who wanted to know why he was not more outspoken a patriot. "Some of my best customers are Englishmen," he explained. As Vishnu got older his fear of his father was diluted with shame. His spiritual experience had taught him that the Goddess and Her nation were inseparable. His most devout desire was to serve them both, or rather the one in its two forms. Yet his father obviously cared for neither. His mother alone understood, and they spent more and more time together in long talks about religion and politics. One day in the middle of a particularly deep and philosophical discussion about the identity of both, his father had barged in on them unexpectedly, found her pressing his hand to her heart, and fumed:

"How long are you going to keep clinging to your mother's bosom like an imbecile? It's time you went to work, Vishnu. College is just fuddling your head and giving you too much time to lay around the kitchen. You come to the Press with me tomorrow morning, you hear! I'm not going to live forever."

Though the business of the Press was no less awful than he feared it would be, Vishnu happily found, one day when his father was out taking orders, that the opportunity he had long been waiting for came knocking at his office door. . . .

"Come in," Vishnu shouted, quickly pushing the page on which he had been doodling under the stack of proofs he was supposed to be correcting. To give the impression of total absorption in his job, he did not look up until he read through an entire sentence and noted deletion of a word in the margin. "Yes, please?" he asked, smiling politely at his young customer.

"I have not come here on commercial business," the young man announced, "but in behalf of our motherland. What I have to say will not take much of your time. May I sit down?"

"Of course," Vishnu said, rising to offer his own pillow, and dragging over another for himself. "Our motherland, you say? My name is Vishnu Apte."

"Mine is Natu."

"Natu what?"

"Let us dispense with further introductions for the time being," Naturam told him, elaborately adjusting the drape of his dhoti after crossing his legs. "It will be sufficient for you to know that I am here as the personal deputy of Dhondo Kanetkar."

"I see," Vishnu said, his eyes growing larger with awe. His visitor's bearing and manner impressed him immediately as that of a highly spiritual person. "Kanetkar the terrorist," he added, for that was how his father always spoke of him.

"The *patriot*," Natu corrected him. "To the white people he may be a terrorist, but to our people he must always be worshipped as a patriot."

"Yes, excuse me, it was a slip of the tongue. He is a very great man, of course. I have read of him often."

"He is our greatest living hero," Natu explained blandly.

"I see. You would say he is our *greatest*?"

"Certainly. Who has spent longer in prison than he?"

"I see. That is true, yes."

"Since I have many calls to make today," Natu said, "allow me to come directly to the point. Your press has been selected for the privilege of contributing to the Dhondo Kanetkar Jubilee Fund."

"The Jubilee Fund?"

"Of course. You are aware, I am sure, that Dhondo Kanetkar will celebrate his sixtieth birthday this October, are you not?"

"Oh, I see, yes," Vishnu said, impressed by how much this young man, who did not appear much older than himself, obviously knew.

"Naturally," Natu continued, "no amount of money can adequately indicate how grateful all of us feel to Shri Kanetkar for the sacrifices he has made for our motherland, but the purse of one lakh of rupees which is being collected for presentation to him on his birthday will serve as a token of his nation's esteem."

"As much as one lakh, you say?"

"It is really quite little. I am sure you realize that there are more than one hundred thousand people who would be willing to contribute one rupee each—"

"Yes, when you put it that way," Vishnu agreed.

"—but unfortunately we do not have the manpower or time to visit so many potential contributors, Mr. Apte, so we have selected patriotic citizens of substance like yourself for more generous contributions."

"Yes, I see," Vishnu said. "Of course, my father would have to approve anything concerning money."

"But when I asked to see the manager I was directed to you," Natu responded.

"Well, you see, he is out at the moment, and when he goes out I sit in his office," Vishnu explained sheepishly.

"I am sorry you did not inform me of that sooner, Mr. Apte." Natu rose to leave. "When will your father be in?"

"But please do not leave yet," Vishnu asked. "I could make a very slight contribution from my own earnings, of course—say ten rupees, and then—"

"Ten rupees will be quite acceptable," Natu told him, sitting down again.

"—when you speak to my father he may give you much more, of course, but I must warn you that he is quite ignorant of politics, and does not appreciate the spiritual character of our motherland's struggle; however, thanks to my mother I have become aware of many things, and I am most eager to help in any way I can."

"I can see your heart is in the right place," Natu said.

"Perhaps my mother will contribute some money of her own as well."

"Good."

[227]

"And my uncles. I will ask them, and our neighbors, who are very keen about politics—"

"You have the right spirit, Mr. Apte."

"Thank you, Natu. But how can I reach you, please, in order to give you the money when I collect it?"

"I will come back here tomorrow, if you will tell me the best time to see your father."

"Very early in the morning is best."

"Shall we say eight?"

"Yes, that would be excellent."

"Very well then—"

"But wait, let me give you the ten rupees." Vishnu pulled out his handkerchief and untied its trusty knot. His money was folded up very small inside. There was a five-rupee note, four ones, and enough silver to make up the last. He felt very good handing it over to the deputy of Dhondo Kanetkar. "It will honor me to be of more help in the future," he said.

"I am sure that can be arranged, Mr. Apte."

"Thank you," Vishnu said. "I will try to have much more for you tomorrow."

And he did. In fact, by October he personally had collected nearly one hundred rupees, and had provided the Society with at least an equal amount of free printing to help induce others to contribute. He did it all without consulting his father or asking his permission, by giving more of his own time to the Press and working far more efficiently when he went there. Indeed he became so efficient for fear of being caught that instead of suspecting him, his father trusted him with more responsibility and rewarded his duplicity by making him independent manager of one of his presses. Shortly after that he met Guruji for the first time, and was given the opportunity to devote more than his money to the Cause. . . .

Looking directly at Katuk, Vishnu clenched his teeth and stood up. "It is three-forty," he announced. "I must go now."

"You have time, Apte. You should not reach the garden until four. That is less than ten minutes to walk from here. Sit down."

"I will walk slowly."

"You are nervous? Yah, I see you are nervous."

"If you walk too slowly you will arouse suspicion. It is safer to wait. Sit down, Apte, I will get us tea."

"I cannot sit any longer!"

"All right, what of it? If you are so brave, Katuk, here! Take it, and go yourself!" he shouted, holding out the pistol.

Parchure snickered. Katuk made no effort to accept the weapon.

"Well, Katuk, will you take it—or do I go?"

Shankar pressed his back against the door.

"Be sure you are so bold at five," Katuk told him. "Let him pass, Shankar."

Vishnu left them without another word. He could not understand why he had come to fear and hate them so. As fellow disciples of Guruji were they not, after all, his closest comrades? Yet he only felt that way about Natu. Katuk and Shankar frightened him. There was nothing spiritual about them, but Guruji's was to be an army of the spirit. Its power was not in numbers but in faith, in dedication to duty, in devotion to the Mother and her land. That alone was what Vishnu could give his life for. He walked the streets feeling terribly weak and isolated. If only he could find Natu it would be so much easier, for Natu's strength was like his mother's had been. It was the strength of knowledge harnessed to faith. Vishnu's faith was unknowing. He could never sustain it long by himself. It required replenishment at the source of inspiration, and after his mother's death Natu had become that source, for Guruji was too remote, too busy to be bothered with his continuing need for nursing.

I need you, Mother, he prayed. Help me!

He walked in the general direction of the garden, toward the now descending sun. He moved slowly, pausing to look behind him every few paces, wondering if Katuk had sent Shankar to follow. Yet where could he run, or hide? Where can anyone hide, he wondered. Then he saw Jantar Mantar, the weird public ruins of the outdoor astronomical observatory built by the eighteenth-century Rajput Raja Jaisingh II. He stared unblinking at the stone and concrete relics, the gigantic astrolabes and celestial hemispheres, the flight of concrete steps rising in supreme isolation toward heaven, looking more like the approach to a building that had somehow been vaporized than the entity it was meant to be.

Unconsciously Vishnu was drawn to the ruins, to the tall steps especially. They are the steps of God's temple, he thought, unable to resist a now compelling need to climb them. He did not look back as he climbed, only upward, up that ladder of narrow concrete to the dome of cobalt above, the most majestic and beautiful tower of any temple he had ever seen, veiled now with the fine gauze of cirrocumulus, the high protective curtain delicately drawn across his

[229]

mother's face, though he sensed he could see her smiling down at him.

Vishnu paused before climbing the last step. His head had begun to feel strangely light. His balance wavered. He stiffened his body instinctively. The sickening wave of vertigo passed. He stood on the upper platform now, perfectly erect, eyes blinking into the sun. Then he dropped to his knees and covered his face, crying out, "Please, Mother, help me!"

He had not courage enough to look down.

14

Leaving his office at three forty-five, Gopal decided to
drive by his home before going on to the garden. He had not intended it before, but his talk with the general had depressed him. Besides, he had not been home at all last night, and told himself that
he would stop by to say hello out of consideration for his wife, not
merely as a tonic for his own spirits. At any rate his house was really
on the way.

Next to sleep or a warm bath Gopal found nothing quite as restful
as a leisurely drive. Floating through them at moderate speed imparted to the city's governmental and residential areas an aura of
comfort and security which, however deceptive, was at once soothing
and reassuring. Stately trees and substantial sandstone and white
buildings stood as comforting reminders of natural and social en-

durance and continuity. Whatever personal tragedy or unexpected change a day or an hour might bring, they would survive it. They would endure over the same earth, under the same sky, and though the earth ran with blood and the sky was covered with smoke, the same trees would offer their shade, the same buildings their room. We shall pass, Gopal thought, but they will remain, as Jantar Mantar has remained for so many years.

Driving by the ancient monument park he saw the figure of a man slowly ascending the stairway to nowhere. What are your dreams and hopes, he wondered, what are your fears? He would never know, but could not help wondering if perhaps in that person's heart and mind this day seemed as crucial and critical as it had come to seem in his own. Then he tried to imagine how many thousands or millions of people felt much the same way about what might happen to them today. Yet even if all of them were right, would the total impact of what happened affect any of the trees or buildings he saw? They will neither cry nor crumble, he thought, and it was soothing just to think that.

His house looked much the same as all the others on the quiet block, a flat-roofed one-story stucco building set behind some fifty feet of lawn. They had planted an orange tree, but no fruit appeared as yet. The elephantine leaves of a banana tree half obscured the front porch. The scarlet-purple tentacles of the bougainvillaea bush climbed tenaciously up the front wall. He could hear his son's voice from inside as he approached the porch.

"Mama, look at me! Look at me!" the inexhaustible Balu was shouting, and just as Gopal entered the living room, he saw his four-year-old completing a forward somersault on the floor.

"Shabash!" Gopal said, applauding.

"Dada, did you see? Look, I will do it again!"

Kamala was helping their daughter dress her dolls on the daybed. Her silent greeting was a smile full of tenderness and warmth, but she knew better than to try to race her daughter to his arms.

"Daddy's home! Daddy's home! Hurray!" Sunanda cried out, flinging herself up at him with all the possessive power of a demoniacally jealous woman of seven, whose first and only love was her father. She kept kissing him noisily, till he finally managed to set her back on her own feet, and to extricate his neck from her spindly arms.

"Poor darling, you look exhausted," Kamala said, taking his hand

and pressing it with secretive affection. They never kissed in front of the children.

"I feel a bit," he said, tousling Balu's hair as the boy clung to his leg, trying to drag himself higher by clutching at Gopal's skin. "Ouch, that hurts, son!"

"Daddy, let's play elephant ride!" Sunanda screamed, jumping up and down and dragging at his back.

"Now, children, leave your father this instant!" Kamala ordered, clapping her hands to capture their attention. "Can't you see that he's much too tired to play with you right now? Sunanda, take your brother out back and play with him in the yard. Each of you may take one banana if you get outside before I count three. One—"

They hesitated just long enough to decide that from the look on their father's face and the sound of their mother's voice it would most probably be no play now *with* the banana, or no play without it. They raced toward the dining room.

"Two," Kamala intoned, and though Balu, who loved bananas more, was already through the kitchen, Sunanda stopped to peer back at them and ask, "Will you play with us after we finish our bananas, Daddy?"

"Once I say three it will be too late, Sunanda! Thr—"

She scampered off at top speed.

"—eee!" he shouted, finishing it for her with a smile, taking both her hands and sitting down on the edge of the studio couch. "My dear, we could use you in government," he said.

"The children are taking bananas," their servant reported anxiously.

"I told them they could," she reassured him.

"Will Master want tea now?"

"I'll have to go soon," he said.

"But surely you can spare a minute for tea, Gopal. Bring us both tea, Mahar," she said.

He disappeared as silently as he had come.

"Try to slow down, darling. You'll simply wear yourself out at this rate, you know you will. I don't mean to scold, Gopal, but—I was so frightened last night. I kept dreaming about you, and—are you all right, my dear one?"

"Of course I'm all right. When are you going to learn to stop worrying, Kamala? I've told you a thousand times I'm too stupid to get hurt. And what has become of my kiss, tell me?"

"Oh, you are as crazy as Balu," she said, leaning toward him with open eyes, then closing them as she opened her lips against his,

[233]

searching gently along his cheek with her fingers, caressing his brow and touching his eye to be sure its lid was also lowered.

"Can't you lie down just for a little while and rest?" she asked. "Just for an hour?"

"Impossible," he told her.

"But why? Can't anyone else in your silly department do any work without you? Must you do *everything*, Gopal?"

"Absolutely everything," he said, wondering how after ten years of marriage and two children she managed to look as fresh and trim as she had on the day they were wed. Most women indulged their passion for sweets as soon as they found a husband, and let themselves go entirely after their status was enhanced by the birth of a son, but Kamala looked more like Sunanda's elder sister than her mother.

"Now you're just making fun of me, Gopal!"

"Would I do a thing like that?"

"Yes, always! But how can you expect me to know anything about your work if you never tell me about it?"

"But I tell you everything I want everyone to find out, don't I?"

"I don't care," she said, turning aside as though ignoring him. "I have secrets of my own!"

"Do you?"

"Yes! And instead of telling you, I think I'll just let you be good and surprised when you find out!"

"Do you mean about your mother coming?"

"How did you know? Oh, that Mahar! I'm going to thrash him—"

"Don't blame him, poor fellow. I've a better agent who's much closer to you, you know."

"But Sunanda promised me faithfully!"

"And she most faithfully intended to keep that promise, my dear, but she is a woman, after all."

"Oh, what treachery!" She tried to look very stern, but then smiled. "You aren't angry are you, darling? She's missed the children terribly."

"Of course I'm not angry."

"Anyway I hoped that while mother was here you might take a short holiday—even four days would be enough. We could go to Dilwara, just the two of us! Could we, Gopal? It's so lovely there now, not nearly as cold as the north. Do say we might be able—please!"

"That would be fun," he said.

"Oh, it would be glorious, darling!" She clapped her hands together and leaned her upper teeth against the upraised fingertips, peering at him as though to see if he remembered their last visit to the Rajasthan hill resort as vividly and beautifully as she did. "You could write and ask for the same room, Gopal."

"We could afford a better place now—"

"Oh, but we would *have* to stay in the same room! I wouldn't want any other!"

"We'll see," he said, smiling.

"Men have no hearts," she said, pouting, but then Mahar entered with the tray of tea and assorted sweets, and she swiftly changed from a sentimental girl to an efficient matron, telling him where to set down the tray, and tucking a loose stand of her hair back in its proper place before pouring, then selecting her husband's favorite sweets and bringing the plate of them and his tea over herself.

"I suppose we could try for the same room, if you're not afraid of freezing again," he said, accepting her offering.

"I expect you would let me freeze now," she said, because the only time they had been to Dilwara together had been on their honeymoon. At least they had called it their honeymoon, since it was the first holiday he'd been granted after their wedding eight months before. She remembered no frost, though they'd used every blanket at night and her cheeks were burning cold when the first light seeped into their small room. All that week she had glowed with an inner warmth, fired by her secret furnace, as she'd called it. They would walk all morning in the hills, over trails that seemed to exist for their use alone, discovering hidden lakes and the deserted castles of Rajput princes who only came there in the summer months. But the Jain temples were more magnificent than any castle, pure white marble carved so intricately it looked like lace, vibrant with dancing girls so ingeniously drawn from their prisons of stone that they seemed to smile more broadly as you watched them, seemed ready to fly with a tempting whirl of their ample hips down from their ceiling perches and into the arms of every admiring male. She had held him very close to her as they walked through the temples. Recalling that week she felt very old.

"You won't have time, will you?" she asked.

"It's hard to tell right now. I might next month."

She could see he said it only to cheer her. "I'm afraid I sound terribly selfish, darling, always talking about holidays."

"You don't always talk about them, Kamala."

"I really don't mean to," she said, apologetically. There was just less and less it seemed that she could talk to him about. "Is this—job you're on very dangerous, Gopal?"

"Not for me," he said, sipping the tea.

"For the nation?"

"I think so," he said, wishing he could say much more.

"Mommy, we finished our bananas!" Sunanda announced, running over to stand between her father's knees. "Yummy, sweets! Can me and Balu have some chiwara, Mommy?"

"Dada, watch me," Balu called out, placing his head on the floor. "*Can* we, Mommy?"

"You may have some milk if you like, but no sweets," she said.

"Please, please, Mommy!"

"I said no, Sunanda, you'll spoil your appetite again. It's too near your dinnertime."

Gopal looked at his watch. It was five minutes to four.

"Must you leave already?" she asked.

"In a minute—yes," he said, helping Sunanda climb onto his knee. "Will you be home tonight?"

"I hope so. Now what do you want, you demoness, a pony ride or an elephant ride?"

"An elephant ride, an elephant ride!"

"All right," he said, putting aside his cup and plate, and getting down to the floor on hands and knees. "Up onto the howdah with you! Be quick about it!"

"Hooray! Balu, look I'm going for an elephant ride!" she screamed, climbing onto his neck.

"Hold tight," he warned, swaying slightly the way an elephant might have as he stood up. "Here we go now!"

"Hooray, hooray!"

"Dada, me too, me too," Balu demanded.

"One at a time," he answered, plodding through the underbrush between end table and lamp, going off toward the deep thicket of the chairs. "See any tigers yet from up there?"

"Yes, I see one," she yelled. "Fifty feet long, Daddy!"

"No, that's much too long, my dear."

"He is, he is! I see him."

"Dada says it's too long," Balu told her severely.

"Now I see a leopard and two lions, and a rhinoceros," Sunanda reported.

"Well, in that case," Gopal said, setting her down, "you've seen more than your share already, young lady."

[236]

"Now me, now me," Balu yelled, tugging at his trousers.

"All right, up you go! Hold tight!"

Balu was less passive a customer. He tugged at his father's hair as though it were made of rope. He pulled at his ears, indicating which direction he wanted Gopal to turn. He shouted at the top of his high-pitched lungs, "Shikar, shikar!" When Gopal finally put him down, Balu cried and pounded the floor with his feet.

"I'll walk out with you," Kamala said.

"Us, too!" Sunanda insisted.

"No, you had better remain here," he said. "We can't risk leaving those tigers and lions free to eat all the sweets, now, can we? Sunanda, I'm appointing you official camp guardian, and Balu, you're her first officer assistant."

"I am higher!" Balu shouted.

"You are not, crazy," she told him. "I'm in charge!"

"Give us a hug goodbye," he said, "and no fighting, you hear?"

"Daddy, can I eat some chiwara?" Sunanda asked after kissing him.

"You do as your mother tells you," he said. "Always remember that, you demoness."

"Why do you call me a demoness, Daddy?"

"That's too long a question for now. Come here, Balu. Remember you're the man in this family, and I expect you to take good care of these ladies when I'm not around, understand?"

"Will you give me one more elephant ride, Dada?"

"Not today, son. Goodbye now," he said, sending him off with a gentle pat on his rear.

She was fighting back tears, he saw, when they got outside.

"Say, what's all this about, Kamala?"

"It is dangerous," she said. "I know it is, Gopal. You never say that to them unless—unless you're afraid you might not— Oh, God!" She was sobbing as she leaned against him with all the softness of her young woman's body.

He held her arms firmly a moment, then eased her away.

"I'll be back tonight, Kamala, I promise you I will."

"I'm such a coward, Gopal. Forgive me."

"I'm the one should ask forgiveness," he said, "for putting you through this every day of our life together. It hasn't been much fun for you, I know—"

"Shhh! You couldn't possibly know or you wouldn't say anything so foolish, my precious jewel. No one *arranged* our marriage, Gopal,

[237]

have you forgotten that? I chose you myself. I would have done it again every day of the last ten years. Please be careful."

"Kamala," he said, "you were worth sacrificing a dowry for."

"That is the nicest thing you ever said to me."

"And if—" but the look of apprehension in her eyes made him change the conditional construction to a positive one. "When I finish this particular job," he said, "you and I will have to go off somewhere for a holiday. What would you think of Dilwara, tell me?"

"That would be nice," she said.

"All right," he told her, "then that is where we will go."

She remained standing inside the gate until his car was no longer in sight.

15

It had not been easy explaining to her why he could not marry. Once he told her of the oath he had taken in joining the Society, Natu expected she would understand. He imagined she would cry some more. That was inevitably a woman's reaction, and he could have left such tears easily enough, having explained himself. Only, she did not cry. Instead, as she heard him out, her eyes became drier, and when he finished she laughed. At first he thought her hysterical, but seeing she was not, he was perplexed and angry.

"Because you're so funny," she explained. "Why do you suppose I'm laughing?"

Now he was the one who failed to understand.

"Oh, for God's sake, Natu, can't you see how incredibly ridiculous you are—all of you, grown men playing this child's game of secret society? You're like fraternity boys at college, can't you see that? It was different as long as the British were here, I'll admit! You were a patriot then, everyone who fought for our freedom was, and I loved you all the more for it—but *now?* What are you fighting for now, Natu? Whom are you hiding from now? This is your own country, Natu, yours and mine—it belongs to no foreign power anymore!"

"It is run by Muslim-lovers and traitors!"

"That's nonsensical—it's ludicrous! You can't possibly be—serious, Natu. I refuse to believe it—I—I simply can't—"

She sounded English. She was fair enough to have been an English lady. "I do not wish to discuss it with you," he whispered.

"Why not? Am I too stupid because I'm a woman?"

"No." He stood again, and started toward the door.

"Well, why then? What are you running from, Natu? Are you afraid? Is that why? Are you so much of a coward—?"

"I warn you!" he said turning, glowering.

"Yes, go on—what? What warning did you wish to give me, my noble Brahman hero?" She walked close to him, smiling, haughty, defiant, all the things the worst of the English memsahibs had always been. "Well, why don't you say it, Natu? Were you going to strike me, is that what you meant? Or were you planning to use that pistol? And I was foolish enough to think you believed the pen mightier than the sword!"

"Will you shut up!"

"No! No, I never will, Natu, not out of fear! I'm not afraid of you, you see, not in the least! I really don't think you have courage enough to dare hit me—"

He slapped her harder than he'd intended. It made her stagger and fall back, though surprisingly again she did not cry. She laughed, this time hysterically. It was unnerving, infuriating.

"I tell you, shut up!"

"What's wrong, Natu? Are you afraid someone will hear me? Is that why you're trembling? Oh, how brave you are, my darling, how terribly brave! You are courageous enough to hit a woman! Would you have dared if Magin was here, Natu? He is much stronger than I am, you know! He might have hit back—he might—if he cared enough—" Now the tears came, and they were more disconcerting than the laughter.

"Rani—don't—"

"If you touch me I'll scream! I swear it! I warn you, I will, and they'll all come!"

But he was not frightened by that. He bent beside her, gently lifting her in the cradle of his arms, carrying her to the sofa where he carefully put her down.

"What would you have done if I screamed?" she whispered, at last in awe of him.

"Please try to understand," he said. "I am doing what I think best for all of us."

"Not for you and me, Natu."

"For us too," he said.

"But it cannot be, not if you leave me. Nothing you do will matter if you leave me. You are all I live for—even the little I have of you now—"

"If you love me, Rani—"

"*If?* Then do you still doubt it? Natu, how can I ever prove myself to you? What must I do to prove my love?"

"Nothing."

"But I want to. I must. Don't you see it is necessary for me?"

"I believe you," he said, his face so close to hers that he could see nothing else, no other thing in the world around them.

"And do you believe how much?" she asked.

"Yes, I believe that too."

"But how can you leave me then?"

"It is my dharma."

"And mine is loving you," she said.

"I do not ask you to abandon yours, Rani."

"Don't you?" She gnawed at her lip and turned her face sharply toward the back of the sofa so that he would not see the tears again. She did not want his pity.

"Maybe tomorrow you will understand," he said.

"I will?"

"Perhaps. You see, in little more than one hour—"

"Yes?"

Had he actually been ready to say it? The realization made him sit upright, breaking the spell of her fragrance, of her hypnotic immediate presence, of the mystic unity which sometimes destroyed the last barrier between them, bridged the final gulf of their individual selves making him forget that she was not his comrade in the Society at all, not Vishnu Apte or Guruji, that some things could never be revealed to her.

"That in little more than one hour—?" she asked, clinging to his shoulders, bringing her face close to his again, bringing her breasts full against his arm and chest. "What will you do, Natu, tell me?"

"I will vindicate our motherland's honor," he said.

"But how?"

"That I cannot tell you."

"Who are you planning to assassinate, Natu?"

"I have said too much already."

"You have said nothing. But there are no secrets between us—Natu? Oh, my God!" Terrified, she jumped away, covering her mouth with her fingertips.

"What are you thinking, Rani?"

"Oh, but no—that would be—Natu, no! Not *him,* Natu, not *him*—please!"

"What are you talking about?" he asked.

She was too dumbfounded to speak. She stared at him now in much the same way as she had when he lifted her, but it was not awe, it was not terror, either; it was worse, stark disbelief, more nearly total shock.

"Rani—"

"No, don't touch me again! Not if—Natu, he is a saint. He is the most pure and gentle spirit—" She had recoiled into herself at one end of the sofa, and as she spoke the tears rolled swiftly down her cheeks, yet she whispered the words without trembling.

"I do not know what you are talking about," he said, rising. He had to leave very quickly now, for he did know, and he could see that she knew, that she had guessed, as she might very well, considering how much publicity the bomb scare had received during the past ten days. He had to leave her room quickly, for he could not kill her.

"God will never forgive you for it," she cried. It was the last thing he heard her say before slamming the door.

Cursing his stupidity he hurried back across the hotel grounds, past the pool and onto the rear verandah where the bamboo shades were mostly lowered to shield the windows of the first-floor residents from the disturbing glare of the sun. Even the sun could be controlled on this island of comfort and joy. Everything was taken care of here. For sixty rupees a week all the world was blissful and lovely! Natu hated them for it, all of them who could afford such luxuries, including her. What does she know of suffering, he thought. What can she ever know of it? What difference does anyone's misery make to her? She could well afford to pity him, to idolize him, the way all the Christian women did!

He walked more slowly across the lobby, though he realized, even as he approached the desk, that the clerk there might already have received her call, or might at this very instant be talking with her, while she screamed hysterically, "Stop him! You must stop him!"

But no one did, not the clerk, nor the bearers, nor the assistant manager who nodded gravely, nor the doorman, who smiled unctuously. He went past them all. He walked down the front steps. He got into his waiting rickshaw.

"Gupta Temple," he ordered.

Then the rickshaw started. He leaned back and breathed easier as they jerked away from the lush flowers inside the high gate of the Palmyra Palms, and turned with a puttering blast of the motor onto the main drag beyond. She was out of his system now. He could forget her entirely.

He saw the road. He heard the motor. He felt the vibrations of the open-sided vehicle. Swaying precariously the rickshaw took its corners on two wheels, making noise enough over the straightaways to have been going eighty instead of a tame thirty kilometers per hour. How strange, yet somehow fitting, it seemed to be riding to his last assignment just the way he had to his first. Only that was in Poona—a long time ago. But it did not seem like a long time. It seemed more like yesterday. No, it seemed like right now. . . .

As they bounced up the center of Lakshmi Road, the driver kept squeezing at the rubber handle of his rickshaw's horn, till the blare of that tin instrument formed a rhythmic counterpoint to the motor's sickly rattle. It was hardly a warning for Poona man or beast to take seriously. Instead of yielding at once, the cyclists in front of his rickshaw tried to pedal faster, as he too had often done. He watched them strain, bent double over their racers' rigid frames, muscle-bulging legs pumping furiously, heads turned momentarily to cast a look of terror and anger at the tormenting monster behind them. Then, finally having spent themselves in so hopeless a burst of defiance, with the rickshaw's horn blowing air at the small of their backs, they swerved aside, cursing the scooter that roared past them like a speed-boat cutting between two sailing gigs, blowing up waves of dirt and exhaust fumes in its wake. So many varied vehicles, animals, and pedestrians competed for the limited area of transportation through town provided by Poona's main road that it looked more like the fun center of a carnival than a city street in the late afternoon of an ordinary day. At each major intersection whistle-blowing, arm-waving police were ensconced safely behind their concrete booths, but no

[243]

one paid much attention to their gesticulations. You went when you could. You stopped when you had to. Horns blew, brakes screeched, tempers boiled. Only the buffalo seemed entirely *dégagé,* whisking their tails with bland indifference to the tumult around them.

Natu lit a fresh cigarette from the stub of his last, distressed to realize that for all his preparation and training, despite the months of patient indoctrination by Guruji and expert instruction at Mankar's gymnasium by Katuk, he got more tense and nervous the closer he came to Kashinath Trimbak's press. He kept rubbing sweat from his palms onto the cloth of his dhoti. It was his first assignment, the first real test of his courage. The short iron pipe felt like a bar of ice against his stomach. He lit another cigarette before he had half finished the one he held, then seeing it was not used up, he continued smoking the old one and flipped the new smoke onto the road. Too late he recognized his mistake, and looked back to see a cyclist braving death by stopping short to retrieve the precious item just discarded. Nothing dropped along Lakshmi Road remained to gather much dust. Even the excrement of its animal passengers was nimbly scooped up by women and children who followed the herds for that purpose, and busied themselves converting feces into fuel cakes. What no one else wanted, the goats consumed.

Calm down, Naturam, he told himself, ashamed to be so nervous about so simple a job, staring at the colorful cloths flapping from the store fronts he passed, distractedly reading the shop names on the old shingle slabs and painted boards: Bharat Apothecary, First-Class Tailors, All-Purpose Accessories, Corn-Blowing, and Palm-Reading. The two- and three-story balconied buildings leaned somewhat perilously over the traffic below. A potbellied householder emerged onto his top-floor balcony, and expectorated monumentally without bothering to look down. He rubbed his sleeve across his mouth and returned to his privacy.

"Stop here!" Natu shouted, tapping his knuckles against the glass shield behind the driver.

The narrow sidewalk was far less crowded than the street. The slanting rays of the setting sun left it entirely in shadow, but it was not yet dark enough for anyone to turn on his lights. The Reformer Press occupied a large corner building. A round clock, symbol of the Press's modernity, hung suspended from the brick front. Every day for the past week Natu had observed this building from the handwriting analyst's second-floor window across the street. He had not long to wait before Kashinath Trimbak would emerge to walk home

[244]

for his tea. The liberal editor was a crusader for punctuality. One of his editorial series, called "What Is Wrong with Our Old Ways," was a tirade against the sins of tardiness. The rest were equally stupid, but generally more vicious. He denounced the caste system as archaic and reactionary. He denounced early marriage as immoral and unhealthy. He denounced religious education as intellectually crippling and outmoded. He denounced religion itself as superstitious nonsense. Yet he was not content to make a mockery of sacred custom and time-honored faith. Though a Brahman himself, he was not satisfied to write words that could only foam the blood of any gentleman from his own community, and would please no one but the missionaries and the foreign masters. He was determined to prove himself a political as well as a socio-religious traitor, by turning finally in his series to a protracted appraisal of what he called "The Reactionary Revolutionaries—Our Nationalist Movement's Right Wing!" He had started his series with an editorial on Dhondo Kanetkar.

Natu examined mangoes displayed as a golden-orange pyramid on a peddler's cart along the curb. He tested a number of fruits for weight and ripeness, then saw Kashinath briskly emerging, and purchased the mango he held, though it was smaller and less ripe than several of the others. He waited for his prey to turn the corner before starting after him. Somehow he had not realized that Kashinath was so tall and sturdily built. From the handwriting analyst's window he appeared much less formidable. Natu had never really been close to him before; in fact that was his major qualification, it seemed, for this assignment. Anyone Kashinath might recognize would certainly never do.

He crossed the side street and followed half a block or so behind. Katuk had insisted that the best time to strike would be as quickly as possible, as soon as they got off to the narrow alleys where the house fronts were all walls to insure privacy, before Kashinath reached his own home, which was less than a fifteen-minute walk from his office. The longer he waited, said Katuk, the more danger there was of Kashinath discovering he was being followed. According to Katuk the fact that it was still light would make it easier. "Everyone fears the dark," Katuk told him, "so we must strike while it is light, you see." Natu thought he had seen when they discussed it. He visualized himself moving up swiftly and silently, extracting the pipe concealed beneath his shirt, gripping it firmly in his right hand, raising his arm as he started to run, and bringing the pipe down hard behind and just above the liberal editor's right ear. Kashinath Trimbak would collapse, and he would continue running till he came to the river, into which he would toss the pipe. Then he would go on to the restaurant and meet his classmates and remain with them for the rest of the evening till he went to bed. He saw it all clearly and was proud to report to Guruji, "I feel that I am now ready for this assignment." He had said it only yesterday.

"Kashinathji, wait for me!" someone shouted from behind Natu, and before he could turn aside, the editor had stopped and looked around to see who was calling him.

He saw me, Natu thought, convinced of it, as he bent hastily, but too late, to pick at his toes as though a pebble had caught between them. The pipe ends jabbed at his groin and diaphragm. He did not dare to look up, for he felt that his facial expression alone revealed the full measure of his guilt. Though it did not really matter any longer whether or not he looked up, for he was positive that Kashinath Trimbak had looked full at him, and had a clear image of his face fixed firmly in mind. Even from across the street he was convinced that the fleeting glimpse had been enough.

Now he knows me, Natu thought, so I am no longer qualified. He seriously considered returning to explain that to Guruji. Shamed at the prospect, he looked up to find Kashinath and his friend walking on, arm in arm, engrossed in animated conversation. But how could he possibly complete his assignment with both of them there? The other was puny enough, yet even if he could not thwart the attack or dare run after Natu, he would surely get a good enough look at his face to identify him to the police.

Everyone passing along his side of the street watched him suspiciously. He realized how foolish he must have looked just bent over there, for no purpose, so he started to walk again. He wondered why any Brahman would be so stupid or vicious to behave as Kashinath Trimbak had done. How did a man like that face himself at night? How did he face his own wife and children, knowing he was a traitor to his people and their faith? He wondered how much the English paid him to write the way he did, for everyone knew that the English paid such people, yet Natu could not imagine any sum of money large enough to induce him to do such things or utter such words, even with his fingers crossed all the time.

At Daruwalla's bridge Kashinath and his friend parted. "Keep up the good work," the other shouted, to which the editor answered, "We will try!" It was all Natu heard, but it was enough to prove the wisdom and correctness of Guruji's assertion that so long as Kashinath Trimbak continued to write as he did without falling victim to some blow of divine wrath, he would encourage others to follow him. People would begin to think there was no karmic justice in the universe, no balance book of rewards and retribution.

Still he hung back. He kept his distance and when he stopped made sure to do so near a tree or by an alley into which he could step. At one such stop he prayed to Ganesh for success, offering his mango as puja, setting it down before the banyan tree which he took to be the symbol of God. Then he resolved to move, but the instant he did so a carriage came clattering along the canal, with a white woman seated in the back. She was as fair and elegant as a goddess. He considered her a good omen, yet waiting for her to pass delayed him, and when he looked again Kashinath was gone.

The sun had fallen behind the clouds just over the western hills now. The first purple haze of dusk filtered through the dust-laden atmosphere of the streets. He could hear the buffalo bells as the cows returned from the fields for their evening milking. Somehow it was the saddest time of day, the loneliest.

It is the hour of magic and of madness, he thought, but he could not remember where he had read it, or whether he had read it at all. He wanted to cry, for no reason. He wanted to run back to the Lakshmi Restaurant and smell the curries that would be cooking there now, and see the talis covered with rice and curds, and the earthen mugs steaming with their strong tea. He wished he had a ten-rupee note so that he could order every single thing on the grease-stained card which the waiters brought round from table to table, since they hand-printed only one menu. He wished he could afford to buy a tin of English cigarettes, a full round tin of Players No. 3. He felt that if he could afford to he would sit down and smoke every one of them, and then he would go to the whores' alley behind Vithal Temple, where the prostitutes sat outside painted like the images of Rukmani inside.

Across the bridge he caught sight of Kashinath again, and he suddenly wondered what would happen if he swung the pipe and missed? Suppose the editor carried a gun, or a knife, or a piece of pipe himself? Or suppose I hit him, Natu thought, and instead of falling down he just turns around and stares at me and laughs? The thought paralyzed him. He watched the gap widen between himself and the man he was sent to stalk. He wished it would widen more swiftly, for without thinking it he had decided to give Kashinath Trimbak a chance to escape. He had decided to test the will of Ganesh, to see whether or

[247]

not the God favored this liberal loudmouth, to see whether or not divine intervention would save even a man who mocked all divinity.

Or am I just a coward, he wondered, for now his body was cold with the sweat exuding from every pore, and his arms felt so weak with fear that he suspected if he gripped the pipe he would not have strength enough in both of them to lift its meager weight. Boldness was one thing, courage another, Guruji had said, and for the first time Natu knew what he meant. Thought was one thing, action another. Wish was one thing, fulfillment another. I cannot do it, he admitted to himself. I am too weak to do it.

Then the pain of that realization started him running, lifted his legs and propelled his body as though it were a leaf caught by the wind that roared out of the mountain gorges and swept down with night to fill the Poona plain with its lugubrious song, its invisible power, sweeping as Shivaji's light cavalry had done out of the hills and rocky nests built by God for the eagle and the panther but conquered by man driven from his home's comfort by fear, haunted by fear till desperation gave him power, pushed by fear till the prospect of life without meaning made him abandon all natural reticence, embraced by fear till its chill numbed both heart and mind, till all rational restraint was frozen and forgotten, all anxiety silenced.

I am too weak, too frightened, too cowardly, he thought, blind to everything before him but the solidly upright back of the man he had never once spoken to, the man whose existence was for Naturam Godse little more substantial than a name and a fragile series of repugnant ideas, and a voice that had firmly stated, "We will try!"

He removed the pipe as he ran. He struck it against his thigh as he ran, surprised at how solid it felt. He struck himself again, as though he were a sluggish bullock loathe to stand up and drag at the plough to which he'd been harnessed, for which purpose he had been born and fed and watered and washed. The next blow he struck landed squarely where Katuk had long instructed him to place it.

He wore no slippers, and like a leaf he had come up behind Kashinath Trimbak, as softly as a leaf wafted by the wind. The impact of his blow brought Natu to a halt, taking all the momentum of his body and transferring it into the energy consumed by that solid smack, which brought down the tall figure as though it were a ripe mango plucked from its long stem, dangling from a low branch. He dropped without a sound, without uttering a cry, without looking around, and he lay without moving, his face pressed to the side street's dirt, his mouth gaping, his eyes closed.

Natu stared down at him in disbelief, suspecting that he would open his eyes and smile and say, "I am only fooling!" But then a ribbon of crimson trickled out of Kashinath Trimbak's nostril, and seeing it Natu had to bite his finger very hard to keep himself from calling out, "Help!" Help, someone has knocked this man down, he wanted to yell, but then he saw several women approaching from the far end of the alley and the panic of consciousness surged over his trembling sweat-soaked frame, chasing him now, buffeting him, pushing his leaden legs, which kept trying to trip as he ran away, gasping for air as he ran. . . .

The rickshaw had stopped. Natu stared out the open side, but saw no temple. Then he noticed a police officer approaching his vehicle and the blood froze in his heart. Instantly his hand moved under his shirt. His fingers locked around the handle of his gun. The policeman's red turban covered his forehead. Natu marked a point below the turban's stiff edge where he would aim his bullet between the heavy brows of the wide-open eyes. It would be easier there than at the heart, since the thick leather strap of this man's holster crossed the left side of his chest over the neat khaki uniform. One shot, and then he would have to run for it. Perhaps he could lose himself in the growing crowd.

"Sorry," the policeman said, bending politely to look in at Natu, touching his fingers to the golden tassel that hung suspended from his turban. "I have been ordered not to let vehicles go beyond this corner, Sahib."

"Oh, I see," Natu said, taking his hand away from his stomach and smiling. "Very well, I shall walk to the temple."

"Accha, Sahib," the officer replied, saluting again and turning away.

Getting down from the rickshaw, Natu handed his driver a ten-rupee note. He did not bother waiting for change.

16

Shortly after four, P.K. returned from the reception at Government House to find Shyama Prahlad waiting in his outer office.

"I come as a mendicant," the saffron-robed M.P. explained, "to beg a few annas of your time." The idea of seeking this interview had occurred to Shyama just after leaving Maharaja Nulkar's suite. His good fortune there prompted him now to gamble on.

P.K. extended his arm, and personally escorted his party's foremost political rival into the inner sanctum. He inquired with the greatest solicitude after Prahlad's health, guided him to a comfortable seat, and even offered to ring for tea, though as P.K. expected, the drink was politely refused. Instead of repeating the offer as custom dictated he should, P.K. leaned back in his swivel chair and waited.

"Yes, let us dispense with formalities, my dear P.K.," Shyama began, somewhat irked at having been cheated out of his tea. "We have known each other long enough to afford the luxury of perfect frankness."

"Of course, Prahlad, of course."

"I call it a luxury, my dear P.K., since I fear that in this corrupt age of darkness in which God has seen fit to cast our lives there is altogether too much guile and deception. We live in an age of falsehood, P.K., and it weakens us, it debilitates us, but worst of all it disunifies us. Just now when all devout Hindus should stand as one man to help defend our mother we are torn apart. You and I, my dear P.K., at opposite sides of our Assembly—where is the logic of it? Where is the reason for it, tell me? Suspicions, fears, doubts, these are the black curses that plague our era. We have lost the harmony, the simple unity of our Golden Age, and I say we shall pay dearly—"

"Well, well, Prahlad, have you come to tell me you are ready to join my party? You are most welcome, of course!"

Shyama curled the ends of his long beard and smiled coyly.

"Believe me, P.K., were it truly *your* party I would have joined long ago."

"Oh, come, come, just what is that supposed to mean, Prahlad? As general secretary and a member for the past thirty years, I surely have as much right as anyone to speak of the Congress as my party!"

"As much right no doubt, but what of the inner truth of your statement, my dear P.K.? Is the spirit of the Congress as genuinely Hindu in character as you would wish it—?"

"We are a national party," the old Brahman interrupted. "Our membership has never been restricted to any one faith—no more than the composition of our nation itself, Prahlad!"

"But is it not this very fiction, my dear—?"

"Fiction? Why do you call it a fiction?" P.K. inquired, rising from his desk and pacing to the windows. "Forty million of our citizens are Muslims, five million Sikhs, millions more Parsis, Christians, Jews —facts, Prahlad, over fifty million of them. Facts your party chooses to ignore. Mine doesn't."

"Not ignore," Shyama replied softly. "It is merely that we view these minorities realistically—as *minorities*. Most of us, after all, my dear P.K., are Hindus—why deny it? We are the most religious-minded nation on earth—why should we pretend otherwise? You remind me of the fifty million outside our faith, but you say nothing of the three hundred million who still worship our gods and live by the eternal truths of our dharma. They are the backbone, the muscle, the soul of our nation, those three hundred million—not the traitorous forty million who lurk with bated breath in our midst waiting and praying for their Islamic brothers to cross our borders so that they can rise up and plunge the dagger into our spines! You know it as well as I do, my dear P.K., why close your eyes? Simply because others in your party like to delude themselves, is that reason enough for a man of your wisdom and piety to do the same?"

"Don't flatter me, Prahlad. I make no claims to wisdom or piety —none at all! I am a simple man. I cannot recite the Vedas hour after hour as you do. What little I know I have learned the hard way —my guru was experience—"

"A worthy taskmaster, my dear P.K., I know of none better," Shyama injected. "Nor, if I may be permitted to say so, do I know of any of his pupils who have learned as well as yourself."

"That is not for me to judge," P.K. protested modestly. "What I mean to say, Prahlad, is that in politics it is not always a simple question of wisdom or piety—even if I concede for the sake of argument that what you say is all true—only for the sake of argument, mind you!—I would still insist that our government must treat Hindu and Muslim impartially! Once we let religious prejudice formulate national policy we open the floodgates of communal rioting—"

"They have been open wide for more than a year already, my dear P.K.!"

"The legacy from our former rulers, Prahlad. Our government must see to it they are closed and remain closed!"

"By sacrificing the wishes of the majority to those of a disloyal minority?"

"By upholding the rule of law, Prahlad!"

"Whose law, may I ask?"

"Oh, come now—"

"British law, is it not, my dear P.K.? We have ousted the British, yet we hug their laws to our bosoms, ashamed of our own sacred heritage—"

"I am ashamed of nothing, Prahlad!"

"Not you personally, I agree," Shyama insisted. "But the very party you call your own is filled with Hindus who have discarded the sacred mantle of their faith for the supposedly fashionable garb of Western secularism, which is little more than Christianity in legal clothing—"

"What is it you wish to propose, Prahlad?"

P.K. had returned to his desk, but instead of sitting behind it, stood drumming the polished top with his stubby fingertips. No matter how much he agreed with Prahlad it would not do to listen patiently to such tirades against his party comrades.

"What I wish to propose, my dear P.K., is that you and I found a new party—a National Hindu party."

"That's preposterous," P.K. responded instantly. "You can't be serious, Prahlad! Come, come, I have always respected your political judgment—don't disillusion me!"

"But I am always serious, my dear P.K. It pains me to see that you find the prospect of a political alliance between us so thoroughly unattractive."

"Nonsense! There's nothing I would welcome more, Prahlad, and you know it! Join the Congress today and you shall sit on the cabinet tomorrow, I assure you! You know it as well as I do! Well, what do you say now? What's wrong? Is my proposal any more preposterous than yours? You'll admit it's more practical at least!"

"Not necessarily," Shyama replied. "Certainly not if the government which our present cabinet represents were to lose the confidence of the people in—uh, let us say, the foreseeable future?"

"Perhaps in twenty years, Prahlad," P.K. injected. "No sooner than that, I assure you!"

"Imagine," Shyama mused. "It just proves how differently different people can view the same circumstances. I should have said twenty days would be a more likely limit—"

The secretary had entered without knocking, paced silently across the long room, and set a small folded piece of paper on the desk before P.K.'s fingers. He hastily glanced at the note, put it aside, and said, "Let them wait."

"But I must be keeping you from more important business," Shyama apologized, rising as though ready to leave.

"What makes you say twenty days, Prahlad?"

"Let us discuss this some other time when you are less rushed, my dear P.K."

"Sit down, I am in no rush. Come, come, you have ventured an estimate—let me hear your reasons for it."

"But surely they are all familiar to you," Shyama said, with a shrug. "It is a time of transition. People are restless. They have sacrificed much, they have waited long for freedom. And now that it is won—well . . ." he paused, and smiled cynically.

"Yes, yes—well?"

"Well, nothing, my dear P.K.—that is the trouble, you see. Nothing

[253]

has really changed, they say. The British have gone. Not the Viceroy, of course, but most of the others—"

"The Viceroy will go in a few months!"

"Of course, my dear P.K. You and I understand the reasons for such delays, but ordinary people, you see, are ignorant of the complexities of administration. They are impatient. They are worried too, especially when they hear their prime minister talk more about the imagined evil dangers of caste, than about the real destruction caused by Muslim fanatics. It confuses them, you see, since most of our people came to believe that the freedom they fought for was freedom to worship as their ancestors did and to follow the sacred rituals of our Hindu religion, which the white Christians tried to destroy—"

"No one in this government is trying to destroy the Hindu religion, Prahlad!"

"Perhaps not, yet ordinary people think otherwise, and there are so many ordinary people—"

"Never mind the ordinary people," P.K. insisted. "Tell me what you think."

"My humble opinion is of little importance."

"Yes, yes, of course, Prahlad. Come, let us dispense with false modesty! You said you wished to speak frankly—or have you changed your mind?"

Shyama locked his fingers together, and stared meditatively at the deeply lined palms of his hands. The life lines were unusually long and firm. His saffron robes alone, if not his popularity and public position, cloaked him with special immunity, kept him inviolate, he knew.

"Very well, my dear P.K., since you press me I will confess that I am not altogether convinced that some of our so-called Hindu leaders have not in fact abandoned their faith—not only the meat-eaters and wine-drinkers, my dear P.K., I am less concerned about such minor lapses than others—our Vedic forebears, after all, ate meat and relished their strong drinks. But when a person who calls himself a Hindu reads the *Koran* from an altar consecrated to Vishnu—"

"Mahatmaji holds no post in our government!"

"That is like saying Brahma is nowhere manifest in our universe," Shyama replied, smiling. "Still, as The-One-without-Attributes He directs it."

"You underestimate our independence, Prahlad."

"Not yours, my dear P.K., or I would not be here. Consider seri-

[254]

ously what I have proposed to you. Remember, Forethought and Readywit—these two prospered; What-Will-Be-Will-Be perished."

"I have not read those animal fables since I was a child, Prahlad."

"There is much wisdom in childhood stories, my dear P.K."

The bull-necked old man moved ominously closer to his gaunt, prophetic-looking visitor. Curiosity gnawed at him now, like a gnat which had somehow worked its way into the convolutions of his brain. It was something about Prahlad's expression when he said the word "perished."

"Why twenty days, Prahlad?"

"Purely an arbitrary number," Shyama replied casually. "I might have said forty or a hundred, even a thousand—"

"Is there something special you expect to happen very shortly? Is that the reason, Prahlad?"

"Something special? Not that I know of, my dear P.K."

"Come, come, Prahlad, why are you so nervous?"

"I can see it is no use to prolong our conversation—"

"Why can't you look at me, Prahlad? What is it?"

"I have said all I wish to say," Shyama told him, clasping his hands behind his back so that P.K. could not see them trembling. "If you wish to discuss my proposition further, you know how to reach me."

Stepping aside, P.K. let him walk unhindered toward the door, but as the bony ascetic's hand touched the golden knob, P.K. called out, "Is it something scheduled for this evening?"

Shyama did not answer. He did not even turn around, but the question stiffened him, bracing his back like a knife wedged between his shoulder blades, freezing his hand upon the knob so that for a moment it did not move. Only a moment of silence, then opening the door swiftly, Shyama Prahlad was gone.

P.K. kept staring at the door in a Yoga-like trance till his secretary filled the space Prahlad had occupied a few seconds earlier. Ramu started to speak but cut himself short to ask, "Is something wrong, sir?"

"Phone Gupta House immediately," he ordered. "Tell Gupta not to let Mahatmaji out of the house until I get there—" He said it hardly above a whisper, his voice too in a trancelike state. "I will be down in a minute—have my car waiting."

"Yessir!"

Distractedly, moving as though in a dream, P.K. returned to his desk, yet when he reached it did nothing but stand leaning against the edge. He had not fully believed Gopal Das. He had considered the bomb a naïve attempt at intimidation, the futile protest of some deranged individual. Now he no longer doubted it was much more than that. He sensed it, no, he was certain of it, less from anything Prahlad had said than from his frozen refusal to say anything.

While the full implications of this new awareness flowed in upon him, P.K. stood immobile, barely breathing, as though a step or a deep breath would be too much of a distraction, disturbing the single-pointedness of his concentration, causing him to neglect something, or to act unwisely. He felt like the least favored son of a wealthy family, who had suddenly learned that a perfectly healthy and vigorous father was about to die, leaving no will.

Mahatmaji, there is something I have to tell you, but first let me ask if you will not reconsider your position about dissolving all parties, P.K. thought, rejecting that approach as soon as he heard it formulated. But what would he say? Mahatmaji, I forbid you to leave. . . . Why should I? He will only hate me more than he already does, and if he fasts unto death then it will be my fault. Why should I force him to live? Mahatmaji, I have come to warn you again!

Yes, that would be enough, and if despite such warning he was still so stubborn as to go— It will never weigh upon my conscience, P.K. thought with relief. And if—

Well, if I am the last to speak with him—then it is I who inherit the legacy of his final words—"Whatever happens to me, Shankaracharyarao, I am confident that with leaders like yourself our sacred nation will survive"—P.K. felt a tingling surge of pride as he thought of several such stirring phrases, which might after all be said—or at least implied.

He was drawn from his trance by the sound of his intercom buzzer. He snapped the switch and Ramu's voice filtered through, reporting that he had completed the phone call and that the car was waiting at the rear exit.

Gopal Das saw the top of the Bentley only after its horn sounded to clear a path through the human barricade, backed up behind the wooden police horses that closed off the road adjacent to the garden. The sun's burnished shield shone like a divine decoration on the polished hardtop of the slowly moving vehicle. From his place near the platform, immersed as he was in a sea of human faces and foamlike waves of cloth, Gopal could see no more than the top, yet he was certain the instant he heard its horn that the car was P.K.'s.

What has brought him back, Gopal wondered. He watched nervously as the car inched toward the garden driveway, then strained to see it turn up the approach to the house. Unless it were particularly urgent he knew very well P.K. would never have returned of his own volition—but why?

Gopal had long since completed his rounds to check the net Bose had woven. There was nothing left for him to do but wait, in effect divested of his rank, stripped of his authority, voluntarily surrendering both, reducing himself to a cipher of equality with every face and form pressed in around him. It had seemed the wisest post when he thought about it in his office, yet now he felt so totally useless, so thoroughly isolated, that he could not help wondering if it wouldn't be far more sensible for him to enter the house. Especially since P.K. had gone in. Something must have happened, something he should be informed of. Possibly something critical! Curiosity mushroomed in his mind, till he could no longer remain standing where he was. Looking around he suddenly decided that he had placed himself in the most helpless, the most distant, the most ridiculous spot in the entire garden. It seemed incredibly obvious to him all at once that any attack made upon Bapu would be made as soon after he emerged from the house as possible! Feeling as impatient, as restless, as he did, Gopal could well imagine how his adversary felt. The man would never wait for Bapu to reach the platform! Why hadn't he realized it before now? He had forgotten the first rule of good criminal investigation—empathy. He had neglected to step mentally into the assassin's slippers, to enter his feverish heart and brain, but now he felt it so strongly that he could no longer hesitate. He began shoving his way through the crowd, moving as fast as he could toward the house.

He will wait, Gopal thought, only long enough to be certain that Bapu cannot run back to the shelter of the building, should he miss with the first bullet, but *then*—it was terrifyingly clear now! He saw it as though in a vision, as a premonition, a preview; he saw precisely how it would happen. He saw Bapu descending the porch steps, and crumpling under the bullet's impact!

It was so real to him that seeing it made Gopal stop. It made him shudder uncontrollably, and all but gasp aloud, "God, no!" Forbid it, dear God, he thought, but he knew better than to rely on prayers alone. Though fully conscious of how dangerous it was to change any plan at the last minute, he extricated himself from the clustering crowd and dashed around the building to the front porch. There was too much at stake for him to worry any longer about preserving his anonymity.

17

Inconspicuously, effortlessly, Natu merged with the mainstream of visitors moving into the garden. He was no more noticed than the germ of a fatal disease upon its entry into the blood. His coloring, size, and shape deviated so little from the norm that like a fish which had joined its own school he lost his identity by finding so many reflections of his image all around.

He felt calm now, supremely confident, completely assured. All day he had vaguely imagined that he would turn a corner or open a door to find them waiting. He had visualized them hovering somewhere ahead with drawn guns, grinning, beckoning to him to enter their traps. But now he no longer worried. Neither fear nor fatigue plagued him now. He felt the way he did when in climbing the Fortress of the Lion he passed the last sharp bend. Though the grade became steeper he no longer gasped for breath since the gate was in sight. At last he could see the rear porch of Gupta House.

He is just beyond that door, Natu thought, standing inside the garden shrub, sorely tempted to rush the house and be done with it. Two minutes, five at most, and it would all be over! His breath came swiftly. He wanted to. He told himself, Now I must do it! Yet something restrained him, held him immobile, like a horse at the post unable to break, like an actor who had waited so long for his moment on stage that now the house lights were down he completely forgot his lines. He tried to comfort himself by thinking, it is safer to wait for him to emerge, it is better to wait in the gardener's hut as we planned. He tried to convince himself it was prudence, caution, shrewdness. He sensed it was something far different.

"What are you running from, Natu? Are you afraid? Is that why?" she had asked.

Someone brushed against him. Frantically he jumped aside. His body was like a compressed spring held by a hair-honed trigger. The person who touched him walked on without turning. Yet what if someone else had noticed his strange reaction? He realized that remaining this way in the open was only to invite recognition, yet he could not bring himself to dash toward the house. He turned instead in the direction of the platform and moved as quickly as possible through the milling crowd to the small hut just beyond. He opened the door without knocking, shutting it firmly as he stepped inside.

A cloud of smoke hung across the upper portion of the low room. The pungent odor of burning dung pierced Natu's nostrils, its smoke smarted his eyes. Only the well-to-do could afford to burn charcoal. Nor was there a chimney in this cramped single-room home, yet it was more elegant than most, for a small glassless window provided light as well as air, permitting the occupants to survive while their door was closed. The door itself was a mark of luxury that proved this gardener's status was higher than that of most villagers throughout the land. For a moment Natu could distinguish no faces, only shadowy forms seated on the floor before the earthen hearth.

"Uhre!" Apte said, jumping to his feet and rushing over to embrace his comrade. "At last you have come! You are safe!"

"But of course," Natu said, annoyed by this needless display of anxiety. "Why shouldn't I be, Cousin? The crowd has held me up, that is why I am late!"

"Yes, yes, of course! Nat——"

"*Cousin,*" Natu interrupted sternly, disturbed to find Apte so befuddled that he could not exercise sufficient caution even about the use of their names. "Do not let me take you from your tea. I see that our good gardener has provided you with hospitality!"

"My woman has prepared a cup for you too, maharaj," the gardener reported, gathering his dhoti from his spindly legs as he rose slowly to his feet. After a lifetime of weeding he could not quite stand erect, and so remained bowed over as though in servile greeting.

"You are a generous host," Natu said, taking his place before the smoldering dung on which the brass water vessel was resting.

"I am sorry I can offer you no more," the gardener said.

"No, no," Natu told him, waving aside the apology with his hand. "You give us shade from the sun, peace from the shoving crowd, and afternoon refreshment as well. What more should we ask, eh? Cousin, have you paid this good man?"

"You are learned gentlemen, maharaj, I trust you—pay later!"

Nor was it an insincere offer of credit, Natu knew, for what could enrich a poor man more than the knowledge that he was the creditor of someone far richer than himself?

"No, but we are mere visitors here," Natu explained, holding out his last ten-rupee note. "We may not have time to pay you tomorrow."

"Do you insist, maharaj?"

"Yes, yes—take it."

"But how can I make change for so large a bill, maharaj?"

"Never mind the change."

"Oh, but what are you saying, maharaj? Five rupees will be more than sufficient!"

"It is all right," Natu explained, sipping the sour tea that the mute woman set so humbly before him.

But the gardener was insistent. He had made a deal and would stick to it. "I will send my woman to Mr. Gupta's house to ask one of the servants there for change!"

"No, you mustn't!" Apte shouted in alarm. He had actually touched the gardener's arm to prevent him from raising it and handing the money to his wife.

"What my cousin means," Natu explained hastily, for he saw the look of bewilderment spread over the gardener's face, "is that Mr. Gupta may then be told that you are renting out space in his cottage, and it might upset him, you see."

"I see," their host said. His mind was not very sharp, yet he was bright enough to recognize the potential danger to his position on Mr. Gupta's household staff which such news might create.

"Why don't you keep the ten rupees," Natu suggested, "and then the next time we come here we will not pay you at all for your hospitality?"

"Ah, I see," the gardener said, nodding gravely, no doubt adding it up in his mind. "Of course, *that* is possible."

"Good—then it is settled," Natu said.

"No, but look here, maharaj—*you* keep the money, until the next time, and then you will give it to me. That way is better!" He smiled broadly, having once again proved himself capable of greater generosity and trust than people so much more affluent.

Natu sensed that this discussion could easily continue into the night, for the gardener was obviously a man starved for company and conversation, and ten rupees after all was a sum worthy of a vast expenditure in time. He saw it was a quarter to five.

"You are a man of honor," Natu said, "and you do not want to cheat us, but we too have our pride, you understand, so we cannot take back the money. Why don't you give it to your wife, and let her hold it? That way neither of us will feel indebted!"

It worked. The poor woman, who had been terrified by her husband's stupidity, hastily hid the note in the ample folds of her faded sari. Having discharged his debt, Natu felt free to ignore his host. He rose and walked to the window. The garden was filling rapidly. Many of the pilgrims sat and did their spinning with hand whorls while they waited. There were groups of young men standing in circles and talking. Entire families had come together, and several children ran loose, playing hide and seek. . . . "All of you grown men, playing this child's game," she had said. Why could he never forget what she told him?

"Natu, I am afraid," Vishnu Apte whispered, coming to his side at the window. "What will they do to us, Natu?"

"Who?"

"All of them out there." Apte gnawed at his fingernails, but there was nothing left to chew off. He had to strip away callous flesh, and spit out the pieces.

"That is their concern, Vishnuji, not ours," Natu told him, noting the panic in his friend's voice, trying to sound as calmly self-assured as he could.

"Natu, I have read sometimes that a mob goes wild and will tear —they will tear a person limb from limb, or trample on him until—"

"Quiet!"

"But what if they do—?"

"Are you a woman to tremble so?"

"I cannot stand pain, Natu. I have never been able to stand physical pain, as far back as I can remember! Sometimes my father would beat me, and it was awful, it was like—like—"

"Like love, Vishnuji?"

"What?" Apte's tearful eyes blinked uncomprehendingly.

"Was the pain you felt like being in love?" Natu asked, draping one arm around his friend's neck.

"What do you mean, Natu?"

"Haven't you ever loved a woman, Vishnuji?"

"Of course—my mother."

"Not that way."

"I have slept many times with women, Natu. I have always told you about them."

"No, not that way."

"But how do you mean?"

He wanted to tell it all to someone, to explain every single quality about her, every mannerism, every mood, every sudden change of temper and unexpected smile. He wanted to tell exactly about her eyes, about her lips, but he knew she was like the editorial he would never write. She was inside him always. She made him taller somehow. She made him stronger. She made each dull moment exciting. Each languid hour could be filled with passion merely by invoking her image in memory. Each disappointment became insignificant beside the simple prospect of seeing her again—tomorrow, next week, next month—he did not mind the waiting as long as the promise of finding her there also waiting hovered before him. Yet how could he explain that? How could he convey that to the ear of Vishnu Apte, or anyone else in fact, and expect him to do anything but laugh or look dumb? It was the same sort of thing he had learned at his desk, whenever he really tried to write what he felt.

"Tell me, Natu, how do you mean?"

"I was only fooling, Vishnuji—women are all the same."

"My mother was different, Natu."

"What are you crying for, Vishnuji? Stop it."

"I—I can't—Natu, I can't—"

He could not contain the tears any longer. Nervously, Natu glanced around, but the gardener and his wife were huddled together in the corner of the room, apparently so preoccupied with their plans for spending the ten rupees that they did not seem to notice at all.

"Will you pull yourself together, you idiot?"

"It—it's no use, Natu. I cannot do it."

"Are you insane?"

"Believe me, I have tried. You know how hard I have tried, Natu—"

"Pull yourself together, Apte!" He had drawn his gun, and placed the mouth of it forcefully against his comrade's belly, at the same moment bracing Apte's back with his arm, so that he could not jerk away from the pistol.

"Natu?"

"I say pull yourself together!"

He watched the moisture ooze from Apte's brow and fear-contorted cheeks like sap squeezed from a stalk of sugar cane as it rolled through the press. He had seen fear many times, but never so naked as this, never so all-consuming as the fear which transformed his friend's youthful face before his eyes into a terrified mask of old age, helpless, trembling, hovering on the threshold of death yet refusing to accept its imperative call.

"Do it, Natu," he whispered, his arms numb at his sides, offering no resistance whatsoever. "Kill me now—it will be easier like this— with you."

"Bah! I see that I should!" Natu snapped, securing the gun once more under his money belt, biting into the knuckle of his fist and turning sharply to stare again out the window. It was the second time today he had been unable to fire, not simply from the legitimate apprehension that shooting would give him away and ruin everything, but out of sentiment. Sentiment, which had no place in his life, certainly not with regard to his work in the Society, which could only interfere with duty; sentiment, more than any other consideration, had prevented him first from shooting her, and now it had saved Apte! Will it stop me again, he wondered, gnawing at the flesh over his knuckle till he had drawn blood. The slippery taste made him spit through the window bars.

"Please do not hate me, Natu."

"You will not escape, Apte." He could not look at his friend.

"I know."

"And I assure you Katuk and Shankar *will* tear you limb from limb if that is what has made a woman of you!"

"But you will not hate me, Natu?"

"Why do you continue questioning me like an idiot? What concern is it of mine if you become a sniveling—? I have no time to console you! Leave me alone. Run if you like—see how far you will get!"

"You are the one true friend I have known all my life, Natu—besides my mother," Vishnu said, refusing to move away.

"I have no friends," Natu said.

"You have saved my life more than once, Natu. You are my friend, whether I am yours or not."

"Oh, shut up!"

"Natu, together—you and me—"

"So that is what you are thinking, eh?" He did face him now, though from the tears and the swelling around his eyes he could not help wondering if it was not a "her" he stared at. "You actually think I would join you? You think because I would not waste a bullet on your Muslim-loving flesh—"

"Natu, that is not true!"

"Then what is true, Apte?"

"So many people call him a saint, Natu, and I have been thinking—I have been thinking, what if they are right and we are wrong?"

He was ready to spit into Apte's eyes. Now he swallowed the saliva, turned suddenly, and walked out of the hut. *God will never forgive you,* she had cried.

It was two minutes before five.

18

"But my dear Shankaracharyarao, what you fail to see is that truth and nonviolence alone could resolve any dispute, if we merely practiced them," Bapu explained ingenuously.

"I ask you for once in your life, Mahatmaji, to be realistic," P.K. retorted, determined this time not to lose his temper, and impressed with himself for remaining so calm.

"What you call realism, I am afraid, is no more than laziness—"

"Excuse me, Mahatmaji, but I think I have worked as hard—"

"Please do not be offended, my friend. I am not speaking of physical laziness. Your robust vigor is well known to me. Your capacity for labor needs no testimonials—"

Modestly, P.K. inclined his head so that he would miss none of the softly whispered words of praise.

"—but for that matter," Bapu continued, "the ox who drags at a plough from dawn to dusk is more vigorous still! It is moral energy which really counts, you see, and when I speak of your laziness, my dear Shankaracharyarao, it is *moral* laziness I mean."

P.K. scowled and straightened up. He glanced anxiously at the doorway to Bapu's room, where the old man's granddaughter stood waiting to accompany him across the garden. Several paces beyond her, Gupta and Das were waiting with lowered heads. If they had heard this reprimand, at least none of them gave any sign of having done so, yet there was always the risk that he would say something even more insulting in a louder voice. Such words had a way of reaching the long ears of the press. P.K. wrung his hands nervously, probing for some inspiration which could drag forth a stirring tribute from this frustratingly unpredictable human being. He had hoped to extract a word or two signifying approval of a more militant policy in Kashmir. That inspiration had come to him in the car on his way over. The tack he had decided upon was that a little bit of force now, just a slight amount more, a few drops of blood shed today and tomorrow, would avert a major war in the near future, saving countless lives. If only he could greet the Chief with Bapu's approval of such a plan, nothing could prevent a complete and permanent victory, a swift and simple resolution to the most urgent problem confronting the nation. The highest patriotism, the noblest religious faith inspired him. No base or selfish motive even crossed his conscience, and for this he was rewarded by being compared with an ox!

"Mahatmaji, I have always taken you as my model guide in public life—why do you ridicule me so?"

"Truth is not ridicule, my friend—that is your confusion. If hearing the truth you feel pain, then at least you still have the capacity to purify yourself so that nothing you say or do will be out of harmony with nonviolent truth. I will pray this evening that God may help you to find a way."

"Wait!"

"Yes?"

"Tell me, is there nothing I have done which meets with your approval?"

"Who am I to pass judgment on you or anyone?"

"But you have done so adversely countless times!"

"Unintentionally perhaps—"

"Then you did not mean what you said about politics corrupting us—about dissolving the Party?"

"Of course I meant it, Shankaracharyarao."

"Yet that is passing judgment, can't you see!"

"Not at all. I merely said what was truth by the light, no doubt a faint light, within me."

"A *faint* light! So you admit you may be wrong?"

Bapu lowered his head without answering. He had wrapped his long gray shawl over his shoulders some moments ago in preparation for going outside. But for the shawl his torso was bare, as were his legs. He extracted his large watch from the folds of his loincloth and squinted to read its message.

"I am afraid I am late," he whispered.

P.K. hesitated. He had not intended waiting so long before delivering the warning which had really impelled him to come back in the first place. He had meant to say it at once in fact, immediately, and so forcefully that its impact would have absolutely dissuaded the Mahatma from leaving the house under any circumstances. He still meant to say it, even with the bitter taste of so many insulting remarks so fresh upon his mind. He meant to, he wanted to, he positively intended to—but he could not. The words were all formulated in his head. They were all arranged in his mouth. They hovered on his tongue, but when he opened his mouth nothing happened, none of them emerged. Then to his own surprise, P.K. yielded, he stepped aside, clearing the passage to the door. As Bapu left the small room, P.K. bowed his head forward till his brow touched the tips of his upraised fingers. He made no further effort to detain him.

Gopal had heard none of their conversation clearly, but from the expression on P.K.'s face he guessed that it was some fresh news confirming his own worst conviction that had brought the old party leader back here. He knew that P.K. had sources of information in some ways more extensive than his own, but he also knew that if he stopped to interrogate P.K. at this point, he would miss Bapu. For as the stooped balding figure entered the enclosed porch, his granddaughter went to him, and he placed one hand upon her shoulder, using her, as he often put it, as "my walking stick." Another granddaughter stood at the porch door, ready to open it.

"Bapu, wait," Gopal said, stepping in front of him.

"What is it, child?"

"I beg of you—don't go out there!"

"But we have discussed this already," he said, not angrily, though with just a trace of annoyance in his tone.

"Yes, I know, but—" He hesitated only long enough to moisten his lips, deciding that in this particular case the lesser evil was lying. "When we spoke to you earlier we were positive another attempt would be made on your life this evening; now we have learned that the moment you descend from the porch they will shoot!"

"Oh, my God," Gupta muttered, asking P.K., "Then this is why you have returned?" But P.K. did not answer. Nor could he long meet the brimful, probing eyes of his host. Shame forced him to turn away from them all. The soul-chilling torment of shame spread its paralysis from his dumb-struck mouth to the outermost extremities of his hulking frame. He could not speak, move, or think. He stood there, face averted, while Gopal Das uttered the words he had meant to.

"Please let me pass, child," Bapu said to Gopal. "I still find it somewhat tiring to stand." It was almost two weeks since he had ended his fast, but his bodily vigor had not yet returned. Though it was not just that, he knew, which debilitated him. Many times in his life he had felt strongest in the midst of a fast, precisely when to all outward appearances the last morsel of nourishment and energy had been drained from his limbs, when the doctors in their practical wisdom had virtually abandoned hope for his recovery, at those very moments of utter helplessness, of total weakness and physical frailty, because they were as well the moments of greatest self-purification, he had experienced exhilaration, power, and ecstasy unlike any other he had known. Such moments had given him a glimpse of the pure force of man's naked soul, and of the miracle of God's grace. He understood then how the meek would inherit the earth, how the seemingly weakest possessed the most strength, how humility could be power, and death deliverance. He understood then how nonviolence would one day conquer over violence, though that day might still be a thousand years away, for it would not come until all mankind recognized that the apparent paradoxes of Scripture were not paradox at all, but Truth in its blinding brilliance, in its hardly believable simplicity. Yet now he felt weary.

"Bapu, did you not hear what I just said?" Gopal asked, amazed, for to him the terrifying impact of the vision he had felt obliged to pass on as fact was so awful that he did not understand how the target himself could possibly remain unaffected by fear, how he would not at least show some signs of anxiety.

"Certainly I heard."

"And still you wish to go out?"

"Of course."

"But why? Bapu, why? Forgive me for detaining you this way,

[268]

but I must beg you to explain this more fully to me or I will lose my sanity entirely, I am certain of that, if nothing else!" Gopal looked to the others for help, but none of them seemed capable of doing a single thing, or saying a word to dissuade him. He felt now that he was going mad, that he alone was the lunatic surely, for the others remained so calm. Only Gupta was crying, yet what good did tears do? "Please, Bapu, help me to understand it! I tell you there is no doubt, there is not the slightest reason to doubt, that seconds after you walk from that porch beyond this very door, someone, perhaps several people, will aim their guns at you and fire! How can you persist in refusing to call off the meeting now, or at least granting me permission to walk out ahead of you?"

"But what you fail to understand, child," Bapu said, gently, "is that this old body of mine is nothing precious. It is no ornament worthy of silk decoration—you see how inelegantly I keep it covered. You know how simply I feed it—"

"Please, Bapu, do not denigrate yourself. You are the most precious person alive," Gopal insisted, determined not to succumb as meekly now as he had earlier in the afternoon.

"That is kind of you to say—"

"I would not say it if I did not mean it."

"Yes, I am sure you are sincere, my child. It is sincerity that makes you bold—"

"Forgive me."

"No, that was not meant in reprimand, but tell me, if you can, what makes me so precious, child?"

"Everything you stand for," Gopal said. "Everything you live for, and inspire others to do."

"But what are some of those things?"

"Everyone knows, Bapu, they are truth, nonviolence, freedom, equality, ethical purity—the list is practically endless!"

"Yes, it is a familiar list," he whispered. Possibly too familiar, he thought. Perhaps that was why his life had proved so spectacular a failure. He had placed so much faith in words that they had become mantras, sacred utterances, that everyone spoke, but no one seemed to believe or truly understand. God knew he had said them often enough, had labored to the limit of his meager powers to explain what he said and wrote; every day of his mature life he had worked at it with voice and pen, till his voice all but lost its volume, till the pages he had covered with writing became a burden to many libraries. Yet to what avail? Nonviolence was his credo, but in the last few

[269]

months he had walked over soil saturated with blood. His pilgrimage through Noakhali District, hailed all around as so singular a success, had only served to bring home to him the utter failure of his life's effort, the ultimate futility of relying upon verbal communication as a means of salvation. He had made "Himalayan blunders" before, but none so enormous as this trust in words, in the words of the world. They did no work, his words, they accomplished nothing. They spun no thread. They wove no cloth. They ground no corn.

"Don't you see," Bapu explained, as if he had been thinking aloud while he stood silent with his head hung forward, "I have said it all so many times, till now as you yourself admit—everyone knows."

"Yet we need you to help us understand, Bapu."

"I cannot live forever, child." He no longer hoped even for the 125 years he had thought vouchsafed to him once. It now seemed too exhausting a prospect.

"Bapu—surely you don't want to die?" Gopal asked weakly.

"*Want* to?" He smiled enigmatically as he repeated the phrase. Somehow it had all been perverted, everything he had meant to accomplish, everything he had labored for, everything he had dreamed of and longed to see come true. Less than a fortnight after the signed pledge by leaders of all the religious communities in the nation had lured him back from the doorstep of eternity, from the brink of a paradisiacal bliss and repose to which six days of fasting had brought him, and already reports of fresh violence poured in upon him from every corner of the country. Reports of the corruption, the venality of officials, even in high places, had never ceased. Instead of peace, brotherhood, and happiness, independence had brought conflict, hatred, fear, and grasping. Had anyone ever listened to what he said? Truly listened? Somewhere along the line of transmission from his lips to another's brain, from his pen to another's eyes, the meaning of his words had been twisted. By some fiendish transmutation the love he advocated turned into hate, the humility he preached became pride, and his selflessness inspired the selfish. What was the use of his lingering any longer? His heart was burdened with sorrow. His soul hungered for release. Why had they dragged him back? Why did they cling to him still?

Gopal waited for him to say, "Of course not, of course I do not want to die—nobody *wants* to die!" But he did not say it. He said nothing more. Till at last Gopal Das thought he understood, and though he could not keep back the burning sensation from his eyes, he stepped aside. For he would not use force against this man, not even to save his life.

On the porch, Bapu paused before descending to join the crowd. It was restless, he saw, impatient, anxious for him to begin the prayers, perhaps anxious for them to be over as well. The past few evenings he had detected a growing element of restlessness among those who gathered here. There was more noise than there used to be. Several times in the last week he had been obliged to stop praying in order to wait for silence. It was as though more people came out of curiosity than from a sense of devotion. He had become something of a curio to certain people, he knew, a relic of a bygone era which had to be seen to be believed, an object of cultural interest like an old temple or a ruin. Perhaps he had simply become short-tempered because of his infirmity, his age. His spirit had begun to sag like the flesh of his neck.

Descending the broad steps toward the path, Bapu sang to himself the poem of his dear friend Tagore, the Gurudev, whose golden words had so often consoled him in moments of darkness or doubt.

"If no one responds to your call, walk alone, walk alone. . . ."

19

The shock of realizing what Natu was about to do had been so overwhelming to Rani that for fully ten minutes after he left her room she was unable to act. She felt literally too weak to move, too numb to think. She simply stared at the spot where he had stood before opening the door, and actually expected that because she willed it so strongly he would somehow reappear there and say, "Don't be foolish, my dear, I am not capable of such a thing."

Yet she knew he was. She had known it from the moment their eyes first met. She had seen something inside them no other eyes ever showed her, a terrifyingly passionate loneliness so calmly intense yet wildly reckless that it often made her tremble merely thinking of it. She feared him because of that, but it made her love him as well, not because it was there but because she hoped that her love could remove

[272]

it from his eyes, by the mystic power of love's surgery. She wanted to cure him of that loneliness, save him from it before it destroyed him, before it consumed his spirit entirely with its alternating fire and frost. She thought that what he needed was someone to love him as she herself was capable of loving. He was at long last a challenge, not just to one fraction of her being, not simply to a minute particle of her talent, her energy, her capacity for love, which was all that Magin demanded, but to her entire soul, mind, and body. He was insulting, infuriating, unpredictable, often irrational, but that made him only more of a challenge, for somewhere beneath it all she sensed he was truly worth the effort of taming. Until he had walked from her room today she had doggedly believed herself capable of doing just that. She told herself she *had* to do it—if for no better reason than because her life without him was unused somehow, wasted.

Rani's senses returned only slowly, as though to a patient emerging from anesthesia, and even then there was a dreamlike quality to her thoughts. She thought, "I must *do* something. . . . I must prevent him. . . . I know, after all, and so I must—act." But *how?* The idea of calling the police seemed so total a betrayal that even now, even after all he had done and proved himself capable of, she could not bring herself to that. Her insides would not let her, the still warm consciousness of him in her womb would not permit her to dispense with him as a common criminal, a public menace to be dealt with by an impersonal force. He was hers after all; despite the finality of his rejection, he belonged to her. He was her only child. He was her father as well, her brother, her lover. . . . God help me, she thought, I still love him.

Then she knew that there was only one way. Leaving her room she ran across the garden and out through the lobby, ignoring the puzzled stares of the hotel personnel, dashing down the front steps before the doorman had time to salute or raise his taxi whistle to his startled mouth, opening the rear door herself as she jumped into a waiting taxi.

"Take me to the place where the Mahatma speaks—you must know where it is! Please, hurry—please, it's terribly urgent!" she told the puzzled driver.

"Gupta House, Memsahib?"

"Yes, that's it—Gupta House! Do hurry, won't you! Please hurry!"

"Yes, yes," the driver said, nervously turning the ignition on, and pumping the starter, which of course failed to catch at first try.

"Oh, please, do hurry, won't you!"

"I am *trying,* Memsahib!" The poor fellow had been half-asleep. All day without a fare, and then suddenly this madwoman appears!

The evening rush had begun, cyclists returning in droves from their day's work at the office buildings which sheltered armies of clerks, who moved the papers of state from one desk to another in their endless round; rickshaws funneling onto the main roads from nameless alleys and side streets, drawn by human horses whose bare soles were as tough as the asphalt they raced over but whose lungs had never been meant to drag the weight of a family miles without rest; bulging buses, cars, and taxis, the ubiquitous bullock carts, all appeared now as though by design to hinder her progress, as if they had been demoniacally put there to prevent her from reaching him in time. Not that she even knew how much time was left.

"Can't you go any faster?" she asked the driver.

"Look for yourself, Memsahib, my car has no wings!"

"Well, don't yell at me!" she yelled. Why were all Sikhs so incredibly belligerent?

"Take another taxi if you prefer, Memsahib!" he shouted, stepping on the brake. "I will charge you nothing!" Out of seven brothers he alone had been fool enough to drive a taxi—the rest joined the military, where no woman ordered them around.

"No, no, go on," she insisted. "Just do the best you can." Distractedly brushing the hair from her temple, Rani settled back, and gazed out the side window instead of the front. It was the most you could ask of anyone, really—to do his best. Yet she always asked it of herself, but it never had been enough, never quite enough. Only this time it must be, she thought—just this one time! If she could only reach him before it was too late she would make her own body a shield—or a target if he preferred.

Waiting for him to emerge into the open, Naturam felt himself losing control. He had felt it in the gardener's hut with Apte. He had felt it in Rani's room as well. But as the hands of his watch told him that five o'clock came and was gone, he felt panic of a different kind, he felt more than fear—he felt hope. Hope of release from his obligation. Hope of divine intervention that might liberate him. Hope of escape. It was the one thought he had managed to obliterate from his mind all day. For the past three days in fact, ever since he had drawn the broken matchstick, he had consciously erased that most insidious and debilitating of ideas from his brain, aware of its power, aware of how thoroughly susceptible to its alluring wiles he had been in the past. As long as he remained convinced that the destruction of this enemy demanded the sacrifice of his life in its present form, and positively no less, he was confident of his ability to carry out his mission. He was enough of a soldier for that. He could stare at certain death without running away, not for any price perhaps, but the life he agreed to take for his own was a fair exchange. That realization was enough to overcome his fear. It had been enough to harness his impatience, to stifle all thoughts of tomorrow. It had kept hope under control the only way hope could be controlled, by denying its existence.

But as the minutes crept past five, as time advanced and nothing happened, as the questioning murmur spread through the crowd while the porch remained empty, Hope sprang from the vault of darkness in which he'd imprisoned it, and burst upon the retina of his brain with all the dazzling brilliance of the golden-scarlet now exploding across the sky. For it had suddenly occurred to Natu that perhaps he had died naturally. As the minutes moved on and he who never was late still failed to appear, the possibility assumed all the attributes of reality in his hope-suffused skull, till he almost shouted joyously, "He is dead! God has killed him at last! God has punished him!"

He actually cried now for joy. A tremor of joy rolled with quake-like intensity through his body. He wanted to jump, to dance, to scream at the top of his lungpower—*God has saved me! Now I can live! I have been released!* He wanted to run from the garden without even waiting for confirmation of what he suspected. He felt he could run the entire distance to Rani's room without tiring. He wanted to embrace her, to hold her, to tell her that a miracle had intervened, and now they were free to remain together always. He would ask Guruji to let him leave the Society, and after all he had been through Guruji would grant his request. He would give them his blessing, and they could go off together—to Bombay, to Juhu, to Trimbak—anywhere really. What difference did that make so long as they were together?

The pain hovered behind his eyes, a cold, contracting numbness like a fist of metal clenched around his brain, jabbing needles of ice against the pupils of his eyes, forcing him to press the lids shut. That only broke the needles, it did not remove them. Then they spread to his stomach, sharp against his gut, till he could feel his intestines writhing, coiling and uncoiling from the alternating stabs. He felt he was going to be sick.

"Do you feel faint, babu?" the man beside him asked.

"No—nothing," Natu replied curtly, instinctively easing away from his interrogator, shouldering ahead toward the cleared carpet of green that ran from the porch to the platform. But why was he moving this way instead of in the other direction? Why was he drawing nearer to the front row of those who lined the path? Was he not free to leave now?

He *is* dead, he must be dead, Natu thought, shoving between an elderly lady and a heavy Sikh so that he could see the porch clearly from the front row. But the porch was no longer empty. Hope had deceived him.

Yet such was its power now that he had unleashed his hope, that Natu persisted in believing the old man would fall of a heart attack, or be stricken by a thunderbolt from heaven, or swallowed into a gaping fissure of the earth, that something would happen to destroy him miraculously before he could cover the fifty paces between them. For that was the only way he could escape, and now he wanted more than anything to escape. He wanted it more than revenge, more than glory, more than the satisfaction even of knowing he had done his duty.

Let me be, he prayed. Let me continue to be—just one more year. Even one month! How had it come to this for him? Why must it be me, God, he wondered. Out of so many hundreds of millions, how had it fallen to him alone, this peculiar honor? Desperately Natu's tormented brain groped with this question, realizing to his amazement that it had not occurred to him before, yet it seemed so significant he could not ignore it now. Why *me*, God? Somehow he sensed the English were to blame.

Why couldn't the sons-of-bitches leave us alone, he wondered. Why did they have to sail halfway around the world to torment and torture others? What was it made them leave their own homes and fields, their wives and mothers, to risk death on the dark waters, to come to a land they claimed to hate for its miserable climate and hostile people? What disease of the soul drove them? What sickness of discontent lured them, what insatiable greed? Had any Hindu ever invited them? Or any Muslim for that matter? It was their cursed policy of divide and rule that started all the rioting in the first place! Those Bible-bearing bastards, with their altruism and their white-man's-burden cross! They started it all, the merchants and the missionaries, talking reform the way a whore talked of chastity, confusing everyone with their greatest-good-for-the-greatest-number calculus smoke screen that let them steal all they wanted, and made women dissatisfied with the way their husbands treated them—Christ and Jeremy Bentham, Twin Saviors of the Blacks! He had written an editorial called that once.

The sun dipped to the level of the tallest trees. A chill wind rustled the leaves that ringed the garden. Natu extracted the pistol from his waist, keeping it covered within both palms, pressing his outstretched fingers very tightly over it so that his hands were in the closed lotus shape of reverential greeting. The Bereta felt like a piece of cold marble or jade, a sacred amulet to be touched and fingered as a soothing balm, nothing more. But why didn't he die? Why did he keep walking closer?

Lord Shiva, why have You chosen me? You are so much more mighty than I, You with Your neck blackened by the poison You swallowed without dying, You with Your thousand arms, why have You left him to me? Natu bit through his tongue, yet that pain did not force him to cry or run away, though every fiber of his soul longed to run, and every heartbeat rumbled in his ears like the roar of the panthers who roamed restless all night atop Singhagar. He had heard them more than once when he went up there determined to die, after the Army had rejected him, and his father refused to welcome him home. He would climb to the top of the Fortress of the Lion, and walk to the wind-swept edge of that flat barren platform in the sky, and stand there for hours staring down at the shadowy plain far below, hearing the panthers' roar, and waiting, sometimes praying, that they would help force him to jump. Now he felt that he stood there again, only this time the roaring he heard was his heart.

Natu stepped forward. He could see every wrinkle in the old man's face, every tired crease of flesh. But as he moved, the face approaching him changed. Instead of the Muslim-loving devil, he saw his own father before him on the path. He blinked his eyes. Yes, it was his father, no one else! It was impossible! He had shouldered one corner of his father's bier the full distance from their home to the cremation grounds, and he had stood staring at the protruding death mask of his father's face, which alone could be seen above the flowers that so colorfully covered the rest of him, while the torch was put to the sandalwood pyre. He stared at that face as the tongues of flame seared its flesh, till the smoke that blackened it rose in choking billows to suffocate him, and only when his brother dragged at his arm did he back away, but by then there was practically nothing left of the face, not the nose or the lips—

Dada, he cried out, though his lips did not move. Do you not recognize me, Dada? I am your son, Natu!

[277]

"Naturam has left us," the old man whispered.

No, but I have come back now, Dada!

"Naturam has made his pilgrimage to Mother Ganga. He will not return perhaps. He may remain in Benares to do God's work!"

Why must you keep saying that, Dada? Everyone knows I am home! Why must you continue making fools of us both? People say you have lost your mind!

"Naturam has gone because I told him to," the old man replied. "My Naturam has always obeyed his father."

Dada, will you look at me? *I* am your Naturam—

"No, Naturam has gone—"

Stop acting as though I am dead, or I swear to God—

"He has left some time ago—"

I swear I will kill you, Dada! I swear it, do you hear me, as surely as you have tried to kill me!

"Let me pass," his father said. "I do not know you."

But I am Naturam Vinayak Godse! I am Naturam Vin— He had to say it over and over again, and each time he said it louder, till he thought it was thunder out of heaven that echoed his name for all mankind to hear, for all creation to come, for all eternity to remember. Only someone stone-deaf could not have heard him!

Bapu had removed his hands from his granddaughters' shoulders slightly more than halfway along the path toward the platform. They had stepped aside then to let him go on. The last few paces he always managed alone. So long as he had strength enough to walk, he would take no crutches to the altar of God. Now that he prayed in public, he tried at least in this symbolic manner to adhere to the ancient custom of his faith by which each individual approached the sanctum sanctorum alone. Even so he brought with him so many burdens, so many problems and difficulties, so many questions unanswered. Daily the volume of his correspondence grew larger, his number of visitors increased. At the stage in life when he should have been shedding the last of his worldly obligations, breaking the last of his mortal bonds, the reverse was happening. For weeks he had hoped to be permitted to return to his ashram in Wardha, to the peaceful simplicity of the village community he loved most, where in microcosm he and his disciples had created the ideal society of his dreams, a commonweal of love, a brotherhood of day laborers devoid of distinctions of caste or class, of race or religion, or nationality, a family of friends none of whom coveted the possessions, or powers, or privileges of anyone else, for craving they understood brought suffering

[278]

and was born of ignorance. What was needed would be given, as freely as a mother gave milk from her breast to her infant, as bountifully as the soil fed its faithful tiller. The sophisticated called him a utopian, he knew. The economists made fun of him, for they memorized all the formulas he had never taken the time to learn—all but the formula of love, which nourished the babe in arms till it could manage to nourish itself.

He longed to get away from the subtleties and sickness of urban life, to escape from its passions and its noises, its filth and frivolity, its extremes of wealth and privation, but most of all, its violence and falsehood, all products of mankind, of the so-called civilization which human avarice and greed, impatience and ignorance had fashioned out of what was once a garden of peace where each labored for the uplift of all, and where the gods had walked hand in hand with their creations over lanes sun-strewn and sweet—

"You are late," he heard, but Bapu recognized neither the voice, nor the face of the young man who had emerged from the crowd to salute him so reverentially.

"I am sorry," he began, for he never meant to disappoint anyone who waited.

Then he saw the gun, and felt the first bullet's impact even before hearing its angry noise. "Hé, Ram!" he cried, calling God's name.

Gopal Das had tugged open the zipper of his case the instant he saw that figure emerge from the crowd. There had been no time gap between the warning signal his eyes flashed to his brain and the swift response of his hands. Yet the gun he relied on was useless, for the back of the saint whose life he would gladly have given his own to preserve now stood between himself and the assassin. Even in death Bapu had served as a shield against violence. Gopal dashed forward as the second shot rang out, followed by the third. After that the fanatic dropped his pistol and stood, head bowed, weeping as a child might have done. Gopal pointed his gun at him, but did not pull the trigger, for Bapu had slumped against his feet, and Munda and Bose took hold of the madman's arms.

Stooping reverentially, Gopal lifted the gentle saint. He carried him back without aid to the building. No one tried to block his path. They had all backed away dumbstruck, and only as he stepped onto the porch did he hear the first wail of anguish, so plaintive, so tortured, so pitiful in its infant-like uncomprehending sorrow that he could not fight back his own tears any longer. The sun had not set on the garden, but darkness was everywhere.

[279]

20

Swiftly they came, silently, mournfully. Singly and in droves they came, the ragged and the rich, the aged and the young, Hindu and Muslim alike, the healthy and the lame. Those who could not walk were carried, supported by others, or they hobbled there on crutches, alone. Somehow all of them managed to find the way. Somehow all of them heard, as though heaven itself had carried the report, as though it were written on dusk's fading face—

Our little father, Bapu, is dead.

From every corner of the city they came, leaving dinners untouched, leaving doors unlocked, leaving possessions unguarded, leaving the petty problems and anxieties of their own petty lives behind them, forgetting themselves entirely, forgetting jealousy and fear, forgetting hatred and falsehood, elevated, united, if but for this moment, by the enormity of their loss, the immensity of their shame.

Like pilgrims on a pilgrimage they came, emerging so it seemed from the ground itself, from the very soil of the nation he had bequeathed to them, filling each path that converged upon Gupta House with their numberless numbers, the rumble of their naked steps as lugubrious as any dirge ever chanted, as eloquent in its wordless, rhythmless song as any prayer that had ever been sung.

He had attained his liberation. He had become immortal, imperishable, one with God. No one feared for his salvation, for the destiny of his spotless soul. It was for themselves they mourned, for the loss of the best of their fellows, the wisest of their gurus, the gentlest father any nation had ever been privileged to call her own. It was the sin of their negligence that made them mourn, the burden of their guilt, the crime of their unworthiness. For no one felt entirely absolved.

We failed to offer him the atmosphere he needed for life, their drawn faces and haunted eyes seemed to say, and so we helped destroy him—we helped drive him away. The most militant among them looked meek, and the most timid appeared unafraid. No police force could have held them back, but no policeman tried, for it was not an army of the angry which came, it was not a mob bent on revenge or retaliation. Unarmed, like children, like infants in their innocence, they came to pray, not to do battle; they came to hang their heads low within seeing distance of the building where he lay; they came to cry for themselves, and their brothers, to beg his forgiveness.

Rani reached the garden just as the first shot rent its hallowed air. Her best had never been enough. The sound of each bullet had torn through her like a ragged knife seared with flames, and clutching her stomach with both hands she had crumpled to the ground, for she knew before hearing the whispered word of shock what had happened. Then as the crowd moved away, as if from fear of pollution by the mere shadow of an untouchable, or in terror at the passing of a leper, she saw him taken away. For an instant she thought he saw her as well, but there was no glimmer of recognition in his eyes, no trace of anger, or joy, or sadness, or triumph, no life at all in fact, only the glazed dullness of death, the awful emptiness of insanity's blank stare. He was not the Natu she had known.

You have murdered him too, she thought, and something burst then, like a light bulb exploding in her brain, tearing through the optic nerves of her eyes, leaving her to sink into a sea of total blackness from its stroke.

The shroud of night enveloped them all. A cold veil of mourning stretched over the sky, till one by one the stars emerged, no more than pinpoints of light, feebly blinking their luminous messages of hope across all the vast emptiness of cosmic space and time, radiating through all that imponderable void their tranquil promises of survival, of rebirth, of life's ultimate imperishability, like flames which consume the flesh, but are born out of its destruction. Then a girl in that silent crowd started singing Tagore's "Morning Song of India," and slowly, tentatively at first, others took up the chant.

Soon many voices were carrying that anthem with its vow of unity, and its stirring prophecy of Victory—"Jaya jaya jaya jaya he!"

ABOUT THE AUTHOR

STANLEY WOLPERT received his doctorate in South Asian studies from the University of Pennsylvania, and has taught Indian history for the past three years at U.C.L.A. He has twice visited India, arriving there first in 1948 on the day after Mahatma Gandhi was assassinated, and returning in 1957 for almost a year as a Ford Fellow. An authority on Indian nationalism, he is the author of *Tilak and Gokhale: Revolution and Reform in the Making of Modern India,* a scholarly analysis, which is being published by the University of California Press.

Prior to his professional career, he worked as a licensed marine engineer and traveled extensively in South America, Europe, and Asia between 1947 and 1951. For the last seventeen years, however, whatever else he has done or been, Mr. Wolpert has considered himself a novelist. His first novel, *Aboard the Flying Swan,* published in 1954, is the story of life on a merchantman during one voyage between New York and Rio.

Mr. Wolpert was born in Brooklyn in 1927; he is married, and lives in Los Angeles with his wife Dorothy and their son, Daniel.